Henriette

SHE-MAJESTY GENERALISSIMA

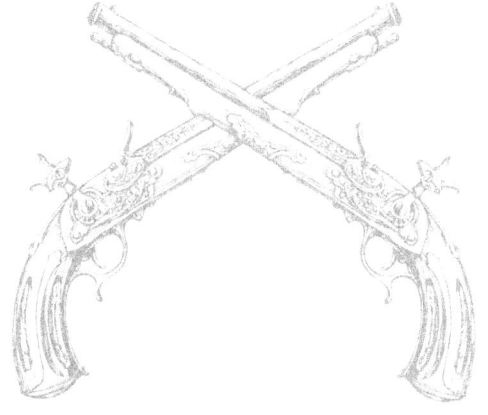

Copyright © 2021 by Chris Pickard

All rights reserved. No part of this book may be reproduced or used in any manner without written permission of the copyright owner except for the use of quotations in a book review.

Dedicated to
my uncle, Charles Grayson

Historical notes

This is a fictional account and as such makes assumptions about historical characters – their motives, actions and words.

That said, all but the most minor characters in this story were real people and all salient events took place.
Where we have records, such as letters between Henriette and Charles, some of these words have been imported into speech.

To make reading easier, seventeenth century language has been avoided. Money has been adjusted for inflation.

The prologue

The elderly lady wears a black linen dress with narrow white lace collar and a black scarf loosely thrown over the back of her head; neat curls of grey hair frame her face. She leans back in a tall wicker chair with her feet dangling off the ground, protected from the sun by a generous-sized, royal blue gazebo. A second figure sits beside her on an upright and uncomfortable looking wooden chair borrowed from the dining room. She is late middle-aged with a round face, pronounced double chin and slightly chubby cheeks. In front, on a small rectangular table she peruses the tools of her trade – two dozen sheets of parchment secured by a glass weight against a gentle southerly breeze, a large white porcelain mug with small streaks of black running down the outside in which a bunch of quills compete for space and a terracotta pot filled with ink. The terrace offers the two ladies a spectacular view of the River Seine winding lazily through a wooded valley below. Behind them, a grand chateau with a pleasing number of turrets and spires watches over the late afternoon activity.

The lady in black clutches a piece of paper close to her face and reads aloud in a slow monotone:

'The sun sinks slowly below the sagging roofline of an ancient barn, casting a swathe of golden light across a sloping meadow full of daisies, knapweed and clover.' She pauses and stares at the sun disappearing behind the treeline across the valley. 'Very appropriate.' She nods her approval and resumes. 'The sun's rays pick out the white rooftops of a vast canvas encampment. There is no breath of wind; small pennants embroidered in rich colours – gold, burgundy, and royal blue – hang limp from a host of tents. Thin plumes of smoke rise vertically from a hundred campfires, each surrounded by a huddle of soldiers roasting meat on the tips of swords and daggers. In the middle of the field is a circle of larger tents with a bonfire blazing in the open space in the centre.'

She glances at her companion. 'I fancy it will be difficult to transfer this scene to a stage without burning the theatre down. Mama used to fuss about the number of candles we used; I think if we had installed a camp fire she would have had a heart attack.' Her eyes return to the page of black ink beautifully etched in neat script: 'Gentlemen and ladies rub shoulders with soldiers, actors,

Henriette

poets and priests, an eclectic and bewildering mix of travellers. There is only one person who could possibly persuade all these diverse characters to gather together in a farmer's field.' The wrinkled face with large brown eyes and protruding yellowing teeth pauses, looks up and smiles at her companion. 'That's me.'

The scribe cleans her quill with a well-blotted damp cloth and frowns. 'I thought it was the narrator speaking.'

'The words will be delivered by a narrator; I was referring to the person who assembled everyone in the field.' Waving the paper in her gnarled hand, she makes no effort to hide her irritation. 'I am weary of this project. The first volume of memoirs made me look ridiculous, and things only go from bad to worse in this instalment; why would anyone want to bother visiting a theatre on a cold, wet winter's night to witness this sorry tale unfold?'

'I think your story is inspirational.'

'Depressing more like.' She shrugs. 'Everyone leaves me in the end.'

It saddens Madame de Motteville to see her friend, once the epitome of energy and optimism, so downhearted. 'I am here,' she says, placing a reassuring hand on the old lady's hunched shoulder. 'And Minette; she never left you.'

She slowly nods her head and makes an effort to straighten her crooked back. 'Beautiful, sweet Minette; she will make a brief appearance at the end of Act Four.' The good cheer hovers and then subsides; her body crumples. She pauses to adjust her headscarf before continuing. 'Where were we? That's right, in the middle of a field, as Harry would say.'

'Are we not racing ahead a little?' asks Madame cautiously. 'You left your audience at the end of the first story with a heart-wrenching parting from King Charles at Dover.'

'I abandoned my dear heart in a good cause.' She looks out across the valley as the sun disappears. She pulls her shawl closer to her shoulders. 'Holland was depressing and drab; we will skip that episode.'

On occasions such as this, Françoise de Motteville regrets agreeing to assist with her friend's memoirs. She certainly never anticipated that her companion would wish to transform the tale into a theatrical extravaganza.

'We should include some reference to your adventures in Gravenhage.'

She-Majesty Generalissima

'Why does everyone call it an adventure?' mutters the lady in the garden chair.

'You became a shopkeeper,' Madame pauses, 'and an arms dealer. I remember reading your letters; Queen Anne and I used to be in awe of the challenges you overcame.'

'I am tired. If I spend hours detailing all the actions and the scenery, it will give me terrible toothache.'

'Why don't we concentrate on the script and leave dear Monsieur Poquelin to organise the theatrical directions?'

The old lady closes her eyes. There is a long pause and Madame de Motteville wonders if her friend has fallen asleep.

Suddenly the eyes open; they still sparkle on occasions. She struggles to stand up, steadying herself with a stick.

'Perhaps you are right about Gravenhage. My task in Holland was an unusual calling for a princess.' She begins to walk slowly along the terrace and speaks without turning round. 'Besides, Monsieur Poquelin can have a nap during the opening scene. We only need a plain stage with a handful of tables.'

'And the crown jewels,' adds Madame with a smile.

Act I of Five Acts

Act I, Scene 1 ~ New Palace, Gravenhage

'Put that table over there,' she shouts. 'No, not like that – we are trying to create a U shape, not a T.' Henriette struggles to be understood in either French or English so she resorts to drawing a u-shape in the air with her finger. Eventually she strides over and moves the trellis table into the preferred position herself.

Her Dame of Honour, Susan, Countess of Denbeigh, follows in her wake, worrying about anything and everything. 'You really should not be lifting tables in your present condition, your majesty.'

Henriette pauses with her slender hands clutching the table and frowns. 'I am not pregnant – at least I pray that I'm not.'

'You have been unwell,' says Susan. 'The headaches and paralyses.'

'I am still alive.' Henriette grins as she moves the table into position. 'Besides, activity has always been the best cure when I'm feeling under the weather.'

Her new senior valet, Mr Groenefeld, on loan to Henriette from the Prince of Orange, acts as translator for servants who do not speak English. He walks up to the Queen, tugging at his grey beard, which is fuller than the fashion. 'Is the furniture in the correct position? If so, I shall arrange the white tablecloths.'

Henriette adjusts a couple of tables and expresses satisfaction. As Mr Groenefeld wanders off to organise the next stage of the project, Susan shakes her head: 'My goodness, I really don't know.'

Henriette glances at her companion. 'What is troubling you, Susan?'

'They don't bow or curtsy, no one calls you by your correct title, your majesty. It is most insolent.'

'I think it's because they have a republican monarch in Holland.' Henriette lowers her voice. 'Don't tell Charles about their casual ways or he will suffer a heart attack.'

Susan slumps upon the nearest wooden chair, an uncomfortable piece of furniture which would have been consigned to the servants' quarters in England.

She-Majesty Generalissima

'Bad manners all round us, your majesty, having to sell precious possessions like a street hawker, everyone speaking in a strange tongue – I find the whole situation deeply depressing.'

Henriette helps a Dutch servant spread the white cloth across the table. She turns back and glares at Susan.

'Who said you could sit in the presence of Henriette Marie, Queen of the Three Kingdoms?'

The Countess of Denbeigh, who in her sixtieth year is the senior member of the royal party, jumps up.

Henriette raises her eyes to the ceiling. 'I was joking, Susan.' The Queen flattens the creases in the cloth and stands back to admire her handiwork. 'See, even a rickety old table can look smart with a nice starched cloth over the top.' Henriette pulls up a small bench and sits down. She pats the vacant half, inviting the Countess to join her. 'I apologise for being flippant. You know I find humour is a good way to get through a difficult day, not to mention year.'

Susan sits down. The Countess is tall and skinny and the Queen is petite and almost as slim – there is plenty of room on the bench.

Henriette continues: 'I agree we are treated in an unconventional manner, but I comfort myself that they behave this way to all royalty, including their own Prince of Orange. It is nothing personal. I would rather be treated commonly here than specially at home where they want to execute me.'

'Oh your majesty, I cannot think of such terrible things.'

'I am just reminding you why we are here and what we are doing,' says Henriette gently. 'The King is facing our enemies alone and is in need of weapons and soldiers. I cannot go back while parliament threatens to impeach me for treason, even though the charges are false. Look what they did to poor Thomas Wentworth. The courts acquit him, parliament ignores the verdict and he is beheaded. These are the evil people we are dealing with.' Henriette stands up and vigorously brushes the folds in her dress. 'And that is why we are going to smile sweetly, ignore the lack of decorum and raise as much bloody money as we can.'

Susan never likes to hear the Queen swear, but she agrees with the sentiment. The Countess lifts herself out of the chair slowly and stands unsteadily.

'I don't know about my ailments,' says Henriette lending an arm, 'you have not been eating or sleeping properly for weeks.'

Henriette

The Queen shouts across the large audience chamber to the Duchess of Richmond. 'Mall, I want you to take over from Susan; she needs to rest.'

'Nonsense, I don't need a rest,' replies Susan.

'It's a royal command,' says Henriette in a grave tone.

Susan is never quite sure when her mistress is being serious. 'Well I will have to go Dutch and ignore your royal majesty.'

Henriette laughs. 'That sounds more like my dear friend.'

Mall Stuart arrives clutching a small, wooden box overflowing with straw. The Queen's senior lady of the bedchamber was brought up within the royal family after the assassination of her father, the Duke of Buckingham. Once a feisty teenager in the mould of Henriette, Mall now manages the Queen's much-reduced household. She places the box on the table.

'What have you there?'

Mall pulls out an object wrapped in soft cloth. She carefully peals the layers to reveal a stunning array of bright rubies.

'The great collar.' Henriette looks at Susan. 'Where is the valuation list that Sir Edward Nicholas drew up?'

Susan produces two sheets of paper and starts looking down the descriptions. 'Oh my word, three hundred thousand pounds.'

Henriette takes the collar in her hands and holds it up to the light of the large window. 'That's why it is called great.' Her eyes sparkle as brightly as the precious stones.

As the three ladies begin to display the precious gems across the tables, two elderly palace guards shuffle into position at the main doors. Henriette points to the decrepit pair: 'I sincerely hope no one is planning to steal our jewels.'

Four young girls in the corner of the room play a variation of hopscotch using the patterns in the wood block flooring. Much laughter and giggling accompany their efforts. They abandon their game and run across to examine the shiny gemstones, a mixture of Henriette and Charles's personal possessions and crown jewels that the Queen and her supporters smuggled out of the royal palaces.

The youngest girl picks up a necklace and places it against her body.

Henriette speaks sternly to the child. 'Mary, I would prefer you not to handle the sale items.'

She-Majesty Generalissima

The Queen's eldest daughter, only ten-years-old and married to the heir to the Dutch throne, drops her lip. She is a carbon copy of her mother. 'Can I not have some jewels for my coronation, mam?'

'No one is getting coronated just now,' says Henriette. 'Don't wish your father-in-law into his grave, poor man. And when you do become Queen you will wear the Dutch crown jewels.' She speaks to Susan under her breath so her daughter cannot hear. 'Assuming a republican queen is permitted such luxuries.'

The other three girls watch Henriette as she carefully lays out a flat cluster pendant with nine large stones and three pendant pearls.

'I shall include that in my next portrait painting,' says the oldest girl. Louise is the twenty-year-old daughter of King Charles's sister, also an exile in Gravenhage. Louise is an accomplished artist, which impresses her aunt greatly.

'It is beautiful, your majesty,' says her sixteen-year-old sister. The teenager is rapidly becoming Henriette's favourite niece, partly because her name is Henriette Marie.

The third sister, Sophie, closer to Mary in age, stares intently at a gold collar. 'That is the most lovely piece of jewellery I have ever seen.'

It is part of Henriette's personal collection and the Queen is flattered by the compliment. 'That is kind of you, dear. I would happily lend it to such a pretty young girl if it were not for the fact that I must try and sell it.'

The young Henriette Marie looks around the room. 'Why are you selling these wonderful jewels?'

'Some horrid people are trying to stop me and your Uncle Charles from ruling the Three Kingdoms which belong to us.'

Louise sighs. 'We were exiled from Bohemia.'

'Yes,' says Henriette, 'Evil persons in our country are trying to do something similar. We intend to fight with a mighty army and I am selling jewels to raise money.'

'Mother thinks Uncle Charles should make peace with his enemies,' says Louise. 'Mama claims that taking up arms in Bohemia was a mistake and that's how we lost our crown.'

'Well each situation is different,' says the Queen tactfully. 'Your mother is giving advice based on her unfortunate experience, but your uncle and I believe we have a good chance of overcoming our foe.'

Henriette

Mr Groenefeld signals that the tables are laid out and that it is eleven o'clock, the agreed time for the public sale to commence. The Queen, her ladies and the children gather around the outer edge of the tables ready for the sale to begin. Mr Groenefeld hovers close to Henriette in case he needs to translate. As it turns out, his services are not required as the diamond and gold dealers of Gravenhage are experienced international traders and speak French and English.

'I wish Harry Jermyn or Edward Sackville were here,' whispers Henriette.

Mall Stewart nervously surveys the spread of precious stones. 'I have never been a shop keeper before.' The twenty-year-old daughter of the first Duke of Buckingham is a member of the senior aristocracy through her marriage to the Duke of Richmond. She is rapidly becoming one of the Queen's closest confidantes, sharing a love of poetry and theatre. Mall wears her hair in a similar style to the Queen with brunette curls cascading down the sides of her face. Some people mistake her for Henriette's baby sister. Since losing all her wardrobe in a shipwreck on the journey from England, Mall has been borrowing royal dresses, hastily altered by the Queen's seamstress, Madame Ventelet.

'Running a market stall is not regarded as essential training for a duchess.' Henriette groans. 'Or a queen.'

The tall double doors open and a handful of men enter. Henriette was expecting a larger crowd. As she surveys the elderly, portly gentlemen in dowdy colours and old-fashioned breeches and waistcoats, it confirms her view that Dutch men, her new son-in-law Prince William aside, are rather small and ugly. Henriette has a tendency to judge people from first appearances although she can be persuaded to change her mind, in particular if they share her interest in the arts or possess a sharp wit.

The Queen is shaken out of her thoughts by a loud voice. 'Have you got any smaller pieces of jewellery?'

Henriette turns to face a man who shares her modest height. Squat with bushy whiskers and beard, he stares into her face from uncomfortably close range. She has to consciously avoid recoiling from the strong odour of fish on his breath.

'These are the jewels we are selling.' Henriette bursts into a broad, false smile. 'Are they not amazing?'

'Too expensive,' snaps the man.

'What is their provenance?' asks his companion. This dealer is taller, thinner and clean shaven but Henriette thinks he has a sour face.

'They belong to the King and myself,' says Henriette politely. 'Otherwise I would not be selling them, would I?'

'But do you have the permission of your government?' The man puts a well-used handkerchief to his nose and makes a strange trumpeting noise that Henriette imagines an elephant might make when sneezing. 'One must have provenance,' says the dealer wafting his soiled handkerchief in her direction.

Trust me to pick an avid republican, thinks the Queen. She continues to smile sweetly. 'The King and I represent the government of England.'

Susan is amazed at her mistress's constraint; she is only too aware of Henriette's capacity to explode.

'Do you have written authorisation?' he persists. 'I am not likely to spend the kind of money you are asking to discover that the item is taken off me by some order of your parliament.'

'I can obtain written authority,' says Henriette, wondering exactly how she might. Perhaps Charles could send a signed letter. 'Would that ease your mind?'

The man does not reply. He studies the items on the table and shrugs. 'I don't think there is a dealer in Gravenhage who can afford these precious pieces.'

Mall realises that the Queen is struggling to remain composed. The Duchess intervenes. 'So where do you suggest we offer these items for sale, sir?'

She receives another shrug of the shoulders. 'Amsterdam, in the Jewish quarter, maybe, or Antwerp.'

Henriette moves down the table to greet two gentlemen who show interest in a ruby necklace that belonged to her late mother-in-law. 'Can I help you?'

One of the dealers grips an eyepiece between his cheek and his eyebrow; he holds up the necklace to the light. After several minutes he places the jewels down and offers half the valuation. The Queen has never been introduced to the concept of bartering and politely declines the offer. The man does not appear concerned and walks away without a backward glance.

The barrel man, as Henriette has dubbed the first Dutchman, catches up with her. He leans over and examines the same necklace as if he is short sighted. He straightens up and speaks as he starts walking away. 'Too expensive.'

The Queen puts her hands on her hips, always a dangerous sign. Mall creeps up behind and whispers. 'I know it's tempting, your majesty, but you did say we had to smile and grit our teeth.'

Henriette turns round and gives Mall a mischievous grin, for once allowing a glimpse of her protruding teeth. 'I was only going to say what a fetching waistcoat he is wearing. I bet it's cheap.'

Act I, Scene 2 ~ Scheveningen

Elizabeth stares at her forlorn guest. 'How did the jewellery sale go?' King Charles's sister has invited Henriette for afternoon cake at her country retreat on the coast. 'Can I top you up?'

Queen Henriette's colloquial English is limited and she does not make the connection between the question and her empty cup of hot chocolate. She mumbles through a mouthful of exceedingly tasty carrot cake. 'We did not sell anything.' Henriette is deflated after her first foray into market trading and would prefer not be socialising with her husband's rather bossy elder sister.

'Oh dear, that won't do,' says Elizabeth studying her sister-in-law. Henriette is only four feet and eleven inches. Her arms are slender and her hands quite long and thin. Large brown eyes dominate her face, eyes that can fix you with a sparkle or a glare depending on the mood. The Queen's famed and intricate curls have been reduced in number and complexity since her voluntary exile in Holland. Only one of her hairdressers accompanied her on the sea voyage. The long brown hair is gathered in a bunch at the back. Her skin is white and soft; she reminds Elizabeth of a delicate porcelain doll. But she knows that Henriette is not to be underestimated. Despite the demure and slightly fragile appearance, Henriette's famed temper and sharp wit precede her. Today there is little evidence of the fiery princess who courtiers cross at their peril. Elizabeth knows that her brother the King is not immune to a Henriette tirade, although their marriage is renowned across Europe for its affection and loyalty.

Henriette stares back at her husband's elder sister; she is not in the mood for a lecture. 'The gold and diamond dealers in Graven-hage advise that we need to be selling in more wealthy markets.

We were told to try Amsterdam and Antwerp.'

'That may be the case,' says Elizabeth, pausing to consider the problem. She is only too familiar with fighting to keep her family from poverty. In her day she was as feisty as Henriette. 'Speak to Prince William, he has agents working in both cities.'

Henriette was wondering how to retail jewellery in distant foreign towns. She decides her sister-in-law may prove useful after all. 'That sounds a sensible suggestion,' she replies gracefully.

'I had to sell most of my jewellery when I was first exiled to Gravenhage. We also melted down our gold plates to make coins.'

'We did that at Dover before I sailed.' Henriette watches her hostess pour a second cup of chocolate. Elizabeth is elegant, tall and poised, confirming Charles's claim that his sister was renowned for her beauty. 'What happened to your family in Bohemia?'

'A disaster is what happened,' says Elizabeth. 'It turned sour very quickly; one minute we were living a happy life in Heidelberg, the next we were on the run without a penny to our names.'

'That sounds familiar,' says Henriette ruefully. 'My life has slithered away; I still have nightmares that I am drowning.' She reflects on two disastrous years. 'Charles and I ruled the Three Kingdoms enjoying peace and prosperity – no wars, no obnoxious parliaments and a boom in trade. Suddenly, we face rebellions in Scotland and Ireland, vicious enemies in England attacking our friends and counsellors, the death of poor little Anne and finally the threat of my impeachment and execution.'

Elizabeth does not appear to be listening. She sighs. 'If only we had stayed in Heidelberg.'

'I thought you ruled Bohemia?' Henriette's grasp of English history is sketchy, but her knowledge of central Europe is non-existent.

'We were rulers of the Palatine on the Rhine; Heidelberg was the capital city. We lived in a beautiful castle.' Elizabeth contemplates her idyllic home. 'We had the gardens completely redesigned by a clever English architect, a fellow called Inigo Jones.'

'Mr Jones,' exclaims Henriette. 'Is there no limit to his influence?'

'Mama recommended him. He assisted her with royal masques and the renovations to Denmark House.'

Henriette is lost in thought as she conjures up visions of her long and illustrious partnership with Mr Jones – the creamy white House of Delights at Greenwich with its magical spiral staircase, elaborate stage sets for extravagant royal masques and the exquisite gold chapel screen at Somerset House.

Elizabeth is also daydreaming. 'I adored our home in Heidelberg.'

'So why did you leave the Palatine?'

'The people of neighbouring Bohemia invited Frederick to be their monarch. They were concerned that a Catholic would ascend to the throne and Freddy and I were Protestants. We took up residence in Prague in the autumn and were welcomed by everyone. Unfortunately by the early spring the Catholic armies of the Hapsburg Empire mobilised against us.'

'Could you not call for assistance?' asks Henriette.

'Our Protestant friends melted away.' Elizabeth chokes. After a pause she recovers her composure. 'Even papa would not come to our aid.'

'King James would not send an army from England?'

'We never received any help from my father, or from my brother.'

'I think it was too late when Charles became King.' Henriette remembers that her husband regularly received pleas of help from his sister. Charles always told Henriette that sending English troops into the middle of Germany would be suicidal while ever the Spanish dominated the region.

Elizabeth gives a half-hearted laugh. 'They called us the Winter King and Queen.'

'Why was that?'

'Because we survived a single winter; after that we fled here to Gravenhage. Poor Freddy died a few years later.'

Henriette tries to think of a subject that will raise her sister-in-law's spirits. 'You have brave sons; perhaps one day they will seize back your kingdom?'

'Maybe,' says Elizabeth, 'but like you, we are finding it difficult to persuade other countries to assist us.'

'Prince Rupert and Prince Maurice tell me that they are keen to sail to England and join their uncle's army.'

'I have tried to dissuade them,' says Elizabeth sharply. 'I sympathise with Charles, but we have enough troubles of our own.'

'You do not support your brother's argument with the English parliament?'

She-Majesty Generalissima

'I should have thought my unfortunate experience would teach Charles that it is wiser to talk than to fight.'

'The leader of parliament, John Pym, used to say that.' Henriette cries out in frustration. 'I tried to parley with him. The next thing, he murders our closest adviser and drives the rest of our court into exile. Then he comes after me.'

'I have very few counsellors; I cannot afford their wages.'

The morose Queen of Bohemia is not providing the tonic that Henriette needs after an exhausting and fruitless day at a jewellery sale. She feels sorry for Elizabeth but Henriette has an important mission to complete.

'I have lost most of my staff, including my letter writer.' Henriette puts the mug down firmly on the shiny brass trolley. 'I had better get back and start drafting my correspondence to Charles. Apparently I need written permits from the King to sell our jewellery.' She puts her arm to her forehead in dramatic pose. 'We are forced to correspond in cypher; it is maddeningly slow and always gives me a horrible headache.'

Madame de Motteville puts her pen down and rubs her wrist.

'You have written for too long, Françoise. If you are not careful you will be afflicted with dreadful head pains, just as I was when corresponding with Charles. I told you we should have skipped the tedious Dutch scenes.'

'Well we have started now, your majesty, so I suggest we plough on.'

'I remember that letter I wrote to my dear heart from Gravenhage.' Henriette grins. 'I had lost my scribe, Mr Jermyn, who was doubtless living the high life in exile in Paris. I recall beginning by asking Charles if he recognised my small hand.' Henriette chuckles to herself.

Madame de Motteville looks blank.

'You know how large my writing is, Françoise; it was a joke.' Henriette shakes her head. 'I trust Charles saw the humour in it.' She relapses into gloom. 'These memoirs are much more difficult without my dear heart. You will have to prompt me, Françoise, and suggest the next actions.'

'Shall we write about Mary?'

Henriette's eyes sparkle. 'I love to include my children in the story.' The Queen looks around the narrow wooden veranda of her beloved Chaillot. 'Mary adored this place when she visited Paris. Do you remember that wonderful summer – for a few months, I almost forgot the heavy burden of grief.'

'We are racing ahead, your majesty.'

Henriette nods slowly. 'You are right; first we should introduce my newly wed daughter and her handsome husband. I will ask Mr Jones to recreate the Hofvijer lake on stage; he always likes a challenge.'

Madame de Motteville pauses with her pen and stares at Henriette. 'Inigo Jones is dead, your majesty.'

Henriette nods slowly as she watches the barges moving up and down the Seine. 'These memoirs are very confusing; I am flitting from the present to the past and back again. At least, we are not trying to emulate Margaret Lucas, writing about the future; that would drive me to distraction. We must introduce Margaret later in our story.'

Madame tries to steer Henriette back to the task in hand. 'The Hofvijer Pool can be a challenge for Monsieur Poquelin's theatre company instead of Mr Jones.'

'Yes, Françoise; he will be interested in this next scene. Poquelin was very taken with Mary when she visited Paris you know. Mind you, most men were besotted with my headstrong daughter. It was the same with Minette, and as for Charles and James with their string of mistresses.' Henriette sighs. 'I thought my dear heart and I provided a good example of a strong, faithful marriage, but all my children turned out to be sex maniacs.'

Act I, Scene 3 ~ The Hofvijer Pool, Gravenhage

'You say "ik spreek geen nederlands", mam.'

'What on earth does that mean?' Henriette walks hand in hand down Staedt Straat with her daughter Mary. Her son-in-law accompanies them along with the Queen's dwarf, little Jeffrey, and four of Henriette's lap dogs.

'It means: "I don't speak Dutch",' says Mary.

She-Majesty Generalissima

'But if I say it in fluent Dutch they are going to think I can understand the language and they will start to rattle at me six to a dozen and I shall have no idea what they are talking about. I used to have exactly the same problem in England.'

Henriette has escaped New Palace after another exhausting day of jewellery negotiations to take advantage of the April sunshine. She has received a letter from Charles authorising the sale of crown jewels and has persuaded Mary's new father-in-law to underwrite loans.

She stares at the grand houses with their steep-sided high roofs; the buildings remind her of northern France. In all directions, in between the buildings, she glimpses the countryside.

'Gravenhage is tiny compared with London,' says Henriette.

Her son-in-law replies. 'It began life as a hunting retreat, your majesty, for our royal family.'

'It seems very compact for a capital city, William.'

Mary smiles to herself. She has made her mother promise faithfully not to address her son-in-law as "Master Orange".

'The Dutch states couldn't agree who would host the capital,' explains her son-in-law. 'So they chose the small village of Gravenhage as a safe compromise.'

'I love the Binnenhof Palace and this lake,' says Henriette.

'The Hofvijer Pool.' William is unsure if it is appropriate to correct his mother-in-law. He has been warned that she is a dragon, although up to now she has appeared nothing but sweetness and light.

Henriette turns round to find her dwarf struggling some way behind with the dogs. 'Do keep up Jeffrey.'

Little Jeffrey is only twenty inches tall, but in perfect proportions, and has been a companion of Henriette's since he arrived as an unconventional seventeenth birthday present. Jeffrey serves a role as court jester; he is also proud of his conjuring tricks, even though most of them go wrong. In time, this proves more entertaining than the illusions that succeed and the Queen has a sneaking suspicion that the magical catastrophes are deliberate.

'You don't need to worry about understanding Dutch,' says William. 'Everyone at court speaks French and many also converse in English.' William speaks fluent French, even if the accent is slightly unfamiliar.

Henriette

'I want to speak Dutch,' says Princess Mary firmly. 'It will show that I am interested in the country that I am adopting.'

Henriette agrees. 'I should have learned English much earlier.' She puts an arm around Mary's shoulder. 'At least you will not be dogged by religious complaints. I was constantly criticised, despite the fact that nearly all my advisers were Anglican.'

'I am a good Catholic,' shouts a small voice from behind.

'Yes Jeffrey, I am thankful for small mercies.' The Queen grins at her own joke.

'Very witty, your majesty,' shouts Jeffrey as the dogs drag him past the Queen and nearly dump him in the lake. 'You could always deputise as the Court Fool.'

'Thank you Jeffrey for that thoughtful suggestion.' Henriette shakes her head. 'Coming to Holland and trying to sell the Crown Jewels qualifies me as a fool, don't you think?' She peers at the tall, narrow pinnacles of the Binnenhof Palace. Her eyesight has never been very sharp. 'What are those enormous birds?'

'They are storks, your majesty,' says William, 'the official symbol of Gravenhage. The fishermen use them to sort through the remnants of the catch.'

'You employ birds in the fish factories?' She strides on leaving the others behind, muttering to herself under her breath. 'That sounds like one of Steenie's tall stories.'

Mary catches up with her mother. 'How are the jewellery sales going, mam?'

Henriette's eyes light up. 'A gentleman called Mr Webster in Amsterdam has advanced one million gilders on rubies and pendant pearls and the Burgomaster of Rotterdam has loaned half a million gilders.' Henriette stops to consider the recent successes. 'I convinced one of the bigger dealers in Gravenhage who did not attend our table-top bazaar to part with one million gilders for items from my personal collection.'

'That's wonderful,' says Mary. 'How much have you raised?'

'I rely on Susan to keep the ledger, but I think we are not far off two million English pounds. The grand collar has been offered to the King of Denmark; that would take us well over.'

Mary smiles. 'Not bad for someone who was never apprenticed in trade.'

Henriette marches off again, speaking as she strides out. 'Now I need to discover where to buy arms and ammunition.'

Act I, Scene 4 ~ New Palace, Gravenhage

Mr Groenefeld performs a modest bow. 'There is a deputation to see you in the Audience Chamber.' The ardent republican cannot bring himself to add the epithet, "your majesty", and he certainly does not intend to start walking backwards out of the room at his age, but he has decided a small bow is a suitable sign of respect. After two months working closely with the Queen of the Three Kingdoms he openly admits his admiration for her indomitable spirit. As he says to anyone prepared to listen at the Bierkelder Staedt, while supping ale: 'Whatever you think about royalty, that lady is tenacious, and she has a sharp wit.'

'More dealers?' Henriette cannot conceal her lack of enthusiasm. 'I had better ask the guard to bring out some of the lesser priced items.'

'I don't think they look like they could afford the gems, ma'am.'

The Queen studies Mr Groenefeld. His facial expression never changes and it is difficult to read him. However, she has begun to develop a grudging respect for the man. Out of earshot, Henriette calls him 'the grand Groenefeld.'

'In fact as deputations go,' he adds, 'a wilder bunch of scoundrels I dare say I have never seen.'

Henriette glares at her adopted chamberlain. 'What exactly are they doing here? Do I have to grant them an audience?'

'I think it probably would be wise,' says Mr Groenefeld.

Sometimes his oblique replies remind Henriette of her husband. The Queen sighs and looks at Susan and Mall.

'Well if Mr Groenefeld advises so, we had better make our way to the Audience Chamber.'

The double doors open and Henriette sweeps in, determined to make the audience a brief one. She takes three paces into the room and abruptly stops. It takes several seconds for her stern face to break into a smile and for those wide-open eyes to sparkle. A few feet in front of her, in an orderly row, stand four of her exiled courtiers – Harry Jermyn, William Davenant, Francis Windebank and Lord Digby. They have been living in Paris. Never in her life has a group of familiar faces meant so much.

As the men bow, Henriette recovers sufficiently to avoid revealing her immense relief. Although a great dramatist when it suits her, the Queen rarely likes to play the damsel in distress. Hands on hips, she frowns. 'Do any of you lot know where I can buy two thousand muskets, fifty cannon and a pile of gunpowder?'

'That was a watershed moment,' says the old woman as she descends carefully down the stairs to the convent chapel. Madame de Motteville attempts to assist, but the offer is rejected in a vigorous flailing of the arm. 'I am only fifty-eight years old; I am not completely decrepit. The Duchess of Vendome is in her seventies and she manages stairs on her own.'

Madame accepts the rebuke. 'They are such steep, narrow steps.'

'The Duchess suggested we replace them with a sweeping marble staircase.' Henriette raises her eyes. 'Imagine what the nuns would have said – they objected to the tapestries and carpets I commissioned. They were all taken away; most of them are in Minette's grand palace now.'

'You were saying, about a watershed,' prompts Madame de Motteville.

Henriette reaches the bottom step and pauses to recover. 'I am pathetic, running short of breath going down the stairs. I shall probably have a heart attack going back up– at least it will save me finishing these wretched memoirs.'

Madame shakes her head. 'We are reaching an exciting scene: your new career as an international arms dealer.'

Henriette ignores her companion. She starts walking slowly towards the chapel door. 'I clearly remember the morning after my friends arrived; we visited a Dutch fishing village on the coast, a place similar to good old Burlington, which will feature in these memoirs shortly. I saw something that day that taught me the importance of having loyal friends working as a team, rather than arguing among themselves. It is a lesson I remember to this day.'

Act I, Scene 5 ~ Scheveningen

The five riders canter across the broad sandy beach at Scheveningen avoiding the fishing boats stranded like beached whales. Close to the pier, the last vessel in the fleet is being dragged out of the water on two ropes. Henriette stops her horse and watches in fascination as over thirty women and young boys from the village haul the heavy boat out of the water.

'Women's work,' exclaims William Davenant with a grin as he comes to a halt beside the Henriette's horse. The Queen's soldier poet has long, mousey brown hair and bright blue eyes, but his face is dominated these days by a deformed nose resulting from a bout of syphilis. He has also put on weight in exile and is no longer quite the dashing chevalier that the Queen remembers.

Henriette does not return his smile. 'I think it is very instructive.'

Lord Digby and Harry Jermyn catch up and bring their horses to a halt.

Henriette points to the communal activity. 'The village depends on fishing, so everyone rolls up their sleeves.' As the Duchess of Richmond's horse canters up, Henriette points towards the heavy boat creeping up the gentle sandy incline. 'Look, Mall, the whole community lends a hand.'

'A bit like your exiled royal court working together,' says Mall.

Harry Jermyn recalls another comparison in the latest letter from England. 'Like the King taking young Prince James with him to Hull to assist in breaking the siege.'

Henriette winces. 'That's not a good example, Harry. Three hundred troops and a pile of artillery might have been more effective than deploying my nine-year-old son.' Henriette shakes her head in frustration. 'I must have written three times to Charles urging the storming of Hull. Now the garrison is reinforced and the enemy munitions shipped down to London. If I had got my hands on the warden of the port, I would have chucked him over the battlements.'

Jermyn does not doubt for a moment that the Queen would have tried.

'What happened?' asks Mall.

Henriette lets out a cry. 'Well of course they invited poor young James into the city, and then slammed the gates shut on the King. Charles had no right jeopardising our son's safety. The rascals might have held James hostage. What on earth was Charles thinking of?' The Queen steers her horse away from the boats and slowly walks her coloured cob towards the sand dunes. 'Every time I think of our failure to seize Hull, it gives me toothache.'

Henriette

Lord Digby is first to catch up with the Queen. His wavy ginger locks blow in all directions as the wind sweeps off the German Sea. Ever since he switched sides and threw his hat in with the King, the young cavalier with a reputation for direct action has been a favourite with the Queen. Not everyone agrees with Henriette; his critics regard him as over optimistic and rash.

'Your nephew Prince Rupert wants to join the King in England,' says Digby. 'If the Prince of Orange provides a boat, William Davenant and I would like to go too, your majesty.'

'An excellent idea, the sooner some decisive military men surround my dear husband the better. I told him frankly in my last letter that neither God nor men of honour will abandon him, provided he does not abandon himself.'

The Queen kicks her horse and trots up to the crest. She holds on to her hat as gusts of wind bend the course marram grass on the ridge of the sand dune. The undulation is the equivalent of a mountain peak in this country, in front is a pancake flat landscape pockmarked with windmills, canals and tiny irrigation ditches; it reminds Henriette of the countryside around Newmarket.

The male members of the party descend from the dunes and compete to jump the narrow water channels criss-crossing the flat landscape. The Queen and the Duchess ride side-saddle and walk their horses sedately between the ditches.

'It was always my biggest concern,' mutters Henriette.

'What was that, your majesty?' Mall often struggles to keep up with the Queen's butterfly mind.

'If I came to Holland to gather support for our cause, I worried that Charles would hesitate. When the Scots rebelled against the new prayer book, delay and indecision contributed to our downfall.'

'I think the King likes to weigh up the pros and cons,' says Mall diplomatically.

'I think the King listens to the last piece of advice he receives.' Henriette groans. 'I write to him daily to urge him to stand steadfast. If Charles does a dishonourable deal with the puritans I shall retreat to a convent. I have told him so.'

Mall and the Queen walk their horses slowly down the side of the field. The absence of forests and hills lend an unusual depth to the landscape. Gravenhage's small cluster of buildings and towers is the only discernible feature in the distance. The equally expansive skies fascinate Henriette; each day produces a different display of dramatic cloud formations. Mall and Henriette catch up with the male contingent at a narrow bridge. Mall steers her horse alongside William Davenant and quizzes him about a poem he is writing. The barren scenery has inspired the Queen's soldier poet to pen new verses.

Henriette canters down the track to talk with her most trusted adviser, Harry Jermyn. An early recruit to her court circle, his reputation for gambling and womanising are frowned upon by Henriette, but his sense of humour and fierce loyalty endear him to the Queen. Like Davenant, wild living has chipped away at his good looks, although he still boasts a thick head of light, curly brown hair. Unusually, he has no beard, just a thin, pale moustache. Henriette notices that exile in Paris has not improved his girth.

The Queen rarely wastes time with small talk: 'How do we turn gold coins into soldiers and weapons, Harry?'

Jermyn is used to the Queen's impatience. 'Francis is investigating the local market, your majesty.' He reins his horse back to a walking pace. 'If you want to do business with Dutch arms dealers, Secretary Windebank is your man.'

'And how do we recruit men?' Henriette is relentless.

Jermyn looks over his shoulder. 'Lord Digby and William Davenant have contacts from their days as officers serving in the European wars. They will find you experienced soldiers. Digby has brought a list of contacts from George Goring and the Marquis of Hamilton. They also fought as mercenaries alongside Dutch troops for many years.'

The Queen is pleased. 'We are like the fishing village – working together to help our King.'

'That is why I am confident of victory, your majesty.' Jermyn brings his horse to a halt. 'We are united, whereas are enemies are divided.'

Henriette smiles. 'And we are cheerful whereas they are grumpy.'

The party heads back to Gravenhage skirting the edges of vast arable fields growing wheat and barley. When the riders reach the palace stable yard, Henriette goes in search of her Secretary of State, impatient as ever to progress her mission. She discovers that Francis Windebank has disappeared into town. He is one step ahead of his mistress and has already commenced negotiations with shadowy merchants who ply their trade in the drinking houses close to the docks.

Act I, Scene 6 ~ New Palace, Gravenhage

The Queen catches up with Francis Windebank in his study late in the evening. His prodigious work rate reminds Henriette of his successor, Sir Edward Nicholas, who remained behind in England to support the King. Windebank stands up and offers the Queen his chair.

'How did your negotiations fare?' Henriette is glad to sit down. She is recovering her strength after months of ill health.

'I have completed an order for two hundred muskets and pistols, six cannon and a hundred barrels of powder. It is early days, but I think the European wars have created quite a stockpile of weapons.'

'This is encouraging news, Francis.'

'Our next challenge is transporting the arms to England without bumping into the parliamentary navy.'

'Our navy,' says Henriette sharply. 'The Puritan Pirate stole the ships from us.'

'Quite so,' says Windebank. 'They patrol off the coast of Holland and in the waters close to Newcastle.'

'We will have to charter fast vessels and experienced captains and endeavour to outwit them,' says Henriette. 'Prince Rupert and Lord Digby and scores of officers need to be transported to the north along with the weapons.'

'I am hopeful that we can recruit experienced Dutch crews who know the German Sea.'

Henriette considers the problem. 'The English Parliament will not want to upset the Dutch by sinking their ships. We need to sail up the Dutch coast as if we are heading for local ports and choose our moment when the wind direction is favourable to strike across the German Sea.'

'The biggest danger, your majesty, is when our boats approach the English coast, especially if winds are against a landing.'

Henriette frowns. 'I shall ask Father Philip to pray for advantageous currents and breezes.'

'That will be most helpful, your majesty.' Secretary Windebank no longer disguises his sympathy for the Roman Catholic faith. 'May I be permitted to join your prayers?'

'You are most welcome, Francis.' Henriette smiles. 'How are your sons?'

She-Majesty Generalissima

'Christopher continues to work in our embassy in Madrid; Thomas and young Francis have joined the King's army at York.'

'That is welcome news, although like me you must worry about your children in such troubled times.'

'I could not stop them if I wanted to, and I do not. I am proud that they are fighting for their King.'

Henriette lifts herself out of the chair and rubs her side. 'I am all aches and pains after the horse ride this morning. I need to regain my strength.' She laughs. 'Sometimes things have to be broken, Francis, before they can be put back together. That includes me.'

Henriette walks towards the door where Harry Jermyn is standing guard. 'Come on, Harry, help me encrypt a letter to the King. For once, we have some good news, our first shipment of weapons to aid the cause.' Her hand rests on the ornate gold doorknob. 'Assuming, of course, my husband hasn't changed his mind and taken my son James down to Westminster for a friendly chat with the enemy.' She opens the door and speaks as she leaves the room. 'In which case I shall retire to Paris and live in a convent.'

Harry Jermyn follows his mistress into the study. Henriette immediately begins to dictate a letter. As with most things, her limited patience is severely tested; she paces up and down the room, occasionally peering out of the window as her trusty scribe does his best to keep up.

'What on earth is Rupert doing?'

Jermyn finishes the uncoded version of the letter. He stands up and joins the Queen at the window. 'Probably exercising that dog of his; they seem to be practically married.'

Henriette stares at Jermyn. 'We have faced similar accusations, Harry.'

'I shall go and encrypt the letter, your majesty.'

'How do we smuggle it to the King?'

'Francis will put it on board the Dutch merchant vessel taking Prince Rupert to Newcastle.'

Henriette nods. 'While you are applying the cypher, I shall go and have a word with my nephew.'

Minutes later, Henriette is sitting beside Prince Rupert in New Palace gardens. The latticed wooden arbour is smothered in pink and white roses. The sweltering August afternoon with its complete lack of breeze has postponed his ship's departure. The Queen is thankful for a faint spray of water droplets from the central fountain a few feet away. She surveys the flowerbeds.

'This reminds me of the layout of the terrace garden at Somerset House – minus the river, of course.' She stands up and studies the meandering layout and narrow paths. 'It could do with a spruce up from Mr Jones.'

Her nephew strokes his white poodle. Despite being a large hunting breed, the animal is harassed by the Queen's half dozen spaniels.

'Ignore them,' says Henriette. 'They will sort out the pecking order.' Henriette scoops up the noisiest offender. 'Mitte, there is plenty of garden for you all.' She clings on to the yapping miscreant. The others lose interest and return to exploring the interesting smells in the shrubbery. Even standing up, Henriette barely reaches eye level with her nephew sitting down. The six foot four inch giant with his long flowing brown hair and heavy features is the talk of the ladies of Gravenhage. He is only twenty-three years old, but he has been fighting other people's wars for nine seasons.

'I love the outdoors,' says Henriette breathing in the fresh air. 'I used to enjoy escaping the rabbit warren of White Hall Palace for a stroll in Saint James's Park.'

'I also crave wide open spaces,' says Rupert. 'Probably because of my confinement in a German prison for two years.'

'White Hall felt like a prison, but at least I could escape.'

'Captivity was greatly improved for me when I fell in love with the gaoler's daughter.'

Henriette glances at her nephew. His reputation with women is almost as legendary as his exploits as a daring cavalry commander.

'I cannot wait to reach Newcastle,' says Rupert. 'Once I have the cavalry organised at York, I can march on London and restore Uncle Charles's throne.'

Henriette frowns. 'That will be a short campaign; my husband only raised his standard at Nottingham last week.'

'It's a question of exploiting the advantage of cavalry,' says Rupert in a brash tone. 'We have learned in the European Wars that success depends on charging the enemy without pausing to discharge weapons. I am sure we will break the parliamentary ranks and disrupt their traditional formations.' He smiles. 'I will be back in Gravenhage for Christmas.'

Henriette generally warms to dashing chevaliers; she has a long list of favourites – George Goring, William Davenant, Harry Jermyn, Lord Digby and until their fallout Henry Rich. But Rupert's youth and excessive optimism concern the Queen.

'We made the mistake of underestimating the Scottish rebels. It would be unwise to repeat the error with Mr Pym's army.'

'He is a lawyer and a politician,' says Rupert with a sneer.

'Yes,' says Henriette slowly, 'but parliament has experienced soldiers to call upon like the Earls of Essex and Manchester.'

'Leave it to me, auntie, I will scatter your enemies.'

Henriette has never taken to the title of aunt; on balance she will be happy to see the back of her nephew. She consoles herself that Prince Rupert will be accompanying a major arms shipment. She wheedled a large loan from the Prince of Orange and is sending one thousand saddles for Rupert's cavalry corps, five hundred carbines, two hundred muskets and yet more powder. As she put it in the encrypted letter to her husband, enough gunpowder to blow up parliament.

'Steady, Boy.' Rupert holds on to the poodle's collar. His inseparable companion is the Prince's saving grace in Henriette's eyes.

'I can see you are fond of dogs.'

'And monkeys.'

'My monkeys had to stay behind at Somerset House. Your mother has an impressive collection of apes.'

'Mama prefers monkeys to children,' says Rupert.

'Surely not.'

'I was nearly left behind when we retreated from Bavaria. I was three years old and one of the servants found me in the nursery and threw me into my parents' coach as it was moving off.'

'Well I must thank your devoted retainer; without his intervention my husband would be missing his military saviour.'

'That's true.' The Queen's sarcasm is lost on young Prince Rupert. 'Are you planning to join Uncle Charles?'

'The idea is that once William Cavendish has control of the north of England, it will be safe for me to return.' She stares at her nephew. 'I would happily sail with you tomorrow; I never let fear dictate my actions. The concern is being captured and our enemies using me as a bargaining counter against the King.'

'It's ironic that your life is following such a similar course to that of my parents, forced into exile here in Gravenhage.'

'I find irony is generally depressing.' The Queen puts Mitte on the ground and the lap dog scuttles off. 'I have no intention of staying here a minute longer than necessary.' She stands up and surveys the garden bathed in sunshine. It brings back memories of the day at Hampton Court when news of the Scottish rebellion disturbed their family idyll. She smiles at Prince Rupert. 'After all, dear nephew, you are going to solve all our problems with a sweeping cavalry charge.'

'Quite right, auntie.' There is not a flicker of a smile on the young man's face. 'Leave it to me and my brother Maurice; we will rout the enemy and rendezvous with you in London.'

Act I, Scene 7 ~ New Palace, Gravenhage

The old man sits behind a large desk piled high with papers and books. He removes his spectacles and rubs his eyes.

'Two ships made it through the blockade but the third had to put in at Yarmouth and was captured by parliament. It is a severe blow.

'How much have we lost, Francis?'

Secretary Windebank consults his large ledger without his glasses, peering closely at the neat row of figures. The Queen is suffering migraines and blurred vision so is no help. 'Two hundred and fifty sets of horse armour and about a thousand muskets.'

Henriette groans. 'Imagine how many hard won jewellery sales that represents. All because the wind changed direction at the wrong moment; I shall speak to Father Philip.'

You can never be sure when the Queen is joking, but when it comes to her religious affairs she rarely does. Her confessor is her longest serving adviser and someone who Henriette consults daily.

'There have been some notable successes too.' Francis Windebank lifts his nose out of the book. 'One of our ships last week was outnumbered three to one in the mouth of the Humber Estuary and the captain managed to outwit his pursuers and beach the vessel up a small creek beside an old ferry wharf. All the cargo was unloaded and taken safely to York.'

'And the boat?'

'They floated off on the high tide and returned to Gravenhage unscathed.'

She-Majesty Generalissima

Henriette offers a brief smile of encouragement but then her shoulders droop. 'I am desperate for news from the King. I have not heard for five weeks and it is driving me mad.'

'It is very frustrating, your majesty.' Windebank is aware that the Queen's impatience is severely testing her courtiers. 'There are many obstacles in the way of our correspondence.'

'The last message talked about marching north to York,' says Henriette. 'Now I hear nothing but rumours about battles lost, the death of the King and even reports that Prince Charles has been captured and taken to the Tower of London.'

'I would not listen to such talk,' says Windebank. 'Harbours always generate a great deal of wild gossip. After all, who is going to contradict the report of a sailor off a ship that has travelled across the seas? It is fanciful stuff.'

'But Mall says that one man actually swears he saw the King's body at Nottingham, lying bloodied in a ditch.'

'And how did a Dutch sailor travel inland to witness such a sight, may I ask?' The old man slams the ledger shut. 'We will hear soon enough.'

Francis Windebank is a tower of strength for the exiled Queen. He has worked tirelessly through the summer and autumn converting jewellery sales into arms and furnishing boats to transport the weapons to northern England. He meticulously records every shipment and its fate. The sixty-year-old loyal servant has informed the Queen that he will not travel with her to England when the time comes. This is probably his last great contribution to the cause.

As it turns out, Francis Windebank's prediction proves accurate. It is Michaelmas Day and the nights begin to draw in at New Palace. Princess Mary has moved in with her husband's household and Lord Digby and William Davenant have joined Rupert and Maurice in England. Harry Jermyn is at the Danish court in Copenhagen trying to sell more crown jewels. Henriette's inner circle is reduced to Windebank, who works in his office all day, Susan, Mall and little Jeffrey.

A Dutch ship from England drops anchor off the coast at Scheveningen in the early afternoon, bringing with it a most welcome guest. Mr Groenefeld delivers the good tidings to Henriette in his usual deadpan manner.

Henriette

'Your majesty,' a prefix recently added by her republican valet, 'I wish to inform you that the Duke of Richmond requests an audience.'

'The Duke of Richmond,' shrieks Henriette. 'Here, in Gravenhage?'

'To be accurate, here in New Palace,' says Mr Groenefeld without a glimmer of a smile.

'Oh my God,' cries Henriette putting her hands to her face. 'Advise the Duchess of Richmond that her husband has arrived from England.' Before Mr Groenefeld can submit his mini-bow or say another word, the Queen runs out of the room.

'James Stewart,' shouts Henriette. Her voice echoes in the vast high-ceilinged audience chamber. 'You don't know how pleased I am to see you.'

As the Duke bows, the Queen rushes up to him. She stops short and stares with those penetrating brown eyes. Although he is smiling, it suddenly occurs to Henriette that a personal envoy might be the harbinger of bad news. Her voice wavers.

'You do not bring me cruel tidings?'

The Duke is taken aback. 'Definitely not, your majesty; may I say I am also pleased to see you.' He looks towards the doorway as Mall appears.

'Go to her,' says Henriette softly. 'We don't bother with protocol out here. Go and greet your wife.'

James runs across the room and hugs Mall. He picks her up and whirls her round once, twice, three times. They laugh, kiss and hug each other.

Henriette watches the happy couple. She is pleased for them, but it underlines her separation from Charles. She yearns to be with her gallant husband. Eventually Mall whispers in James's ear and he puts her down. She brushes her dress and walks across to the Queen, curtsying.

'Don't mind me,' says Henriette with a smile. 'I would do exactly the same, my dear.'

'It is such a surprise.' Mall turns to her husband. 'We had no clue you were coming.'

'Nor did I until six days ago,' says James grinning. 'The King is tired of letters and cyphers – his exact words were: "My Lord, please get yourself to Holland; I want to know how the Queen fares".'

'We have been waiting weeks for news,' says Henriette. 'I think letters must have gone astray. And then we received reports that the King had been killed in a great battle and Prince Charles captured.'

'Rubbish, all lies,' says James. 'The King is well and at York, as are both princes. Prince Charles is desperate to join the army but your husband says you will not permit young Charles to fight.'

'Not at his age,' says Henriette. 'Prince Rupert was fourteen when he first went into battle and that is young enough. I am having enough stress worrying about the King. If I thought Prince Charles was at risk too, I think I would suffer a heart attack.'

'There have been no battles?' asks Mall.

'Just a few minor skirmishes,' says James. 'The Earl of Essex commands the parliamentary army and is advancing north. Our forces are growing daily, and of course Prince Rupert and the Dutch contingent has arrived.'

'Oh that's all right then,' says Henriette, gesticulating with her arms. 'We can go home, my nephew is going to win the war singlehanded.'

The Duke laughs. 'Yes, he is a little gung-ho.'

'A little?' Henriette pulls a face. 'I may have been a trifle precocious at twenty-two, but he is so forward he is in danger of leaving his troops behind.'

'How are Henry and Elizabeth?' asks Mall. The two youngest royal children have been stranded at Hampton Court Palace for six months.

'They have been moved to St James's and are fine,' says the Duke. 'Parliament has put guards on the palace and their staff and tutors come and go unhindered.'

'I would rather they had not used soldiers,' says Henriette. 'It makes the children sound like prisoners.'

The Duke tries to reassure the Queen. 'It was debated in both Houses and the children are considered non-combatants due the protection of the State. They are quite safe. As you know, Lady Roxburghe returned to Dover last month and she has resumed her role as Governess.'

'That's good to hear,' says Mall. 'I must let Princess Mary know; she has been fretting about the little ones. She will be pleased that parliament allowed Lady Roxburghe to look after them.'

'Where is everyone?' asks James, looking at the empty room. 'Prince Rupert reports you have a flourishing court here at Gravenhage.'

'Mr Jermyn is in Copenhagen,' says Henriette, 'trying to persuade the King of Denmark to buy the great collar. If anyone can sell that thing, Harry will.'

'I cannot understand why such a valuable jewel cannot be traded,' says James.

'Precisely because it is worth so much and people are worried that it will be taken off them by the English parliament.' Henriette looks over her shoulder as Susan and Francis Windebank appear in the doorway. 'Look who has arrived from England.'

After greetings and many questions, Henriette steers the party into her withdrawing room, part of a modest suite of apartments that she has made her Dutch home. Windebank lists the amount of money raised and the number of boats sent to England, pointing out that at least three consignments did not reach their destination of Newcastle.

'We are short of arms,' says James, 'but without the Dutch supplies we would be in a perilous state.'

'We should be able to despatch a couple more boatloads soon,' says Windebank. 'If Harry can offload the great collar then we will equip half a dozen more.'

Henriette puts her hand on the Duke of Richmond's arm. 'Is it safe for us to return to England? I am desperate to join Charles.'

'The test will come when our army meets the Earl of Essex's force; a decisive win for the King will leave the road to London open. Then you can safely land at Newcastle and follow us south.'

'Is an encounter likely?' asks Susan.

'I think it is inevitable in the next few weeks,' says James. 'I am to stay here three days and then return to Newcastle. Our army needs every officer.'

Mall is reminded of the danger and that the reunion is a brief respite. 'I cannot bear to be separated again, please let me come with you.'

'You must stay with the Queen,' says James. 'We will be together before long.'

Henriette turns to Mall. 'Take James away to your rooms. We are being selfish making him answer all these questions. There will be time before he returns to England for us to talk.'

Mall hesitates and the Queen nods as if to confirm her command. Mall takes James by the hand.

As they turn, the Duke of Richmond reaches into his pocket. 'I nearly forgot, your majesty, I have a letter from Paris.'

'From my brother?'

'No, it is from a Madame de Motteville.'

'Ah, Françoise has tracked me down, bless her.' Henriette takes the letter. 'Madame de Motteville and I correspond; she was the only one of my maids of honour who did not travel to England when I married Charles. I don't know how I shall send a reply to Paris.'

'We can employ the services of the French ambassador here in Gravenhage,' says Windebank.

Mall gently tugs at her husband's arm; he bows to the Queen and they leave the room. Windebank picks up a news sheet that the Duke brought with him from England.

'What is that, Francis?' asks Henriette.

'It is a scurrilous parliamentary paper, your majesty.'

'Read it to me,' says the Queen. 'I need to know what lies they are spreading.'

Windebank lets out a cry. 'The insolent beggars.'

'What is it?' Henriette tries to read over his shoulder.

'Listen to this,' he says, reading from the propaganda leaflet. 'The supply of arms from Gravenhage to the Royalist army must cease. Anyone assisting in the sale of crown jewels or the transport of weapons is an enemy of parliament. Representations will be made in the firmest possible manner to the Stadholder of Holland pointing out that his Protestant republic is aiding and abetting…' Windebank's voice trails away.

'Go on, Francis,' urges Henriette.

Windebank pauses.

'Read on, we are all agog,' says the Queen.

Windebank reluctantly continues. '…is aiding and abetting the Popish brat.'

Susan gives her mistress a worried glance. She half expects an explosion from Henriette. Instead the Queen laughs.

'I like that. We must have seriously upset them. That is most reassuring; it makes our efforts in exile worthwhile.' She takes Susan by the arm. 'Shall we organise a nice supper for the Duke

of Richmond? Perhaps little Jeffrey can devise some entertainment.'
Henriette grins. 'The Popish brat is starving.'

> The autumn colours creep into the garden at Colombes; Henriette sits in her favourite arbour watching her grand daughter gathering fallen leaves.
>
> She smiles at her companion while trying carefully to conceal yellowing teeth. 'That is your first mention in our story, Françoise.'
>
> 'I find it strange to think of someone playing my part.'
>
> 'You do not make an appearance just yet; we will leave your stage debut for the final act I think.'
>
> 'At Saint Germain en Laye?'
>
> Little Anne holds out precious red and yellow leaves as an offering. Henriette smiles at the toddler. 'Thank you my dear; we can make a very pretty display with these.' She turns to Madame. 'The circle is completed at Saint Germain, but not the story. I remember Minette going on about circles and I prayed for them.'
>
> Madame de Motteville frowns; she wonders if Henriette is a little delirious; she has suffered several blackouts in recent weeks.
>
> 'Never mind about circles.' Henriette waves her arms excitedly. 'We have sold the crown jewels and bought piles of gunpowder.' The glint returns to her eye. 'We have a dramatic voyage to recount. I remember the words of comfort I provided Susan at the height of that terrible storm when the waves were crashing over the deck and the timbers were making those dreadful cracking sounds?' Henriette looks pleased with herself. 'I informed my Dame of Honour that everything would be fine – she could be comforted by the fact that an English Queen has never drowned at sea.'

Act I, Scene 8 ~ Off the coast of Scheveningen

> The narrow door is loose on its hinges and scrapes over an uneven wooden floor; a firm shoulder is needed to force a way through. Once inside, it is clear that the room occupies the tip of the ship's bow. To each side there are curved planks of oak that

meet at the apex of the vessel. The only furnishing is a wide bench nailed to the floor with two holes carved out of the seat and corresponding gaps in the floor beneath. Henriette stands beside the bench and looks down the nearest opening. A long way below, she can make out the gentle ripples of the sea.

'If rough weather,' says the captain in fragmented English, 'close hatches and go below.' He gestures and the Queen and her ladies dutifully follow him back to the cabins and down a steep set of steps to the depths of the vessel. He points to the gravel and sand that make up the ballast. 'There.'

Henriette turns to Susan and Mall. 'Well that covers the toilet facilities,' she says briskly.

Susan looks up the steep flight of steps. 'What if the weather is very rough?'

The Captain pulls a face. 'Strap yourself in bunk and no move.'

'I think he is advising,' says Henriette slowly, 'that in inclement weather we use our bed for sleeping and toileting.'

'Oh my God,' says Mall. 'It's a bit basic compared with the Lion.'

'That was a luxury vessel for passengers,' says Henriette. 'Charles made sure we travelled in comfort from Dover. Now we must make do with a merchant ship. I am confident that we will cope.' She turns to Mall. 'Make sure we have a supply of cloth sacks in our cabin with a lining of sand at the bottom.'

'Gross,' says Mall. Henriette is not fully conversant with the latest English teenage slang but she can work out the meaning from the Duchess of Richmond's expression.

Susan stands on the mound of ballast with a mournful expression on her face. 'Harry says that you are unlucky at sea.'

'Don't be ridiculous; when has a Queen of England ever been lost in a shipwreck?'

Mall is tempted to suggest there can always be a first time but she restrains herself.

The Queen takes hold of the Countess's arm. 'We will ask Father Philip to pray for a calm crossing; he is coming with us so he has a vested interest.'

The three ladies, escorted by Harry Jermyn, return to shore in a large rowing boat.

'I am reminded of Boulogne harbour,' says Henriette as the bow of the vessel crunches into the sand of Scheveningen beach.

Jermyn pulls a face as he surveys the broad swathe of sand and low level apology for sandhills.

'It doesn't look much like the French harbour to me.'

The Queen raises her eyes skyward, as she often does when one of her companions fails to keep up with her thoughts.

'You have to use your imagination. I was not making a comparison with the landscape; I was recalling the experience of a teenager standing beside the sea for the first time.' Jermyn continues to look blank. 'The noise of the boat colliding with the grainy sand and the lapping of the waves on the water's edge.'

Harry avoids further discussion by jumping into the surf. He steadies the boat and offers a helping hand to Henriette. The Queen hitches up her dress and climbs out of the boat. She puts two feet firmly on the coarse sand before glancing back at the fleet of eleven vessels two hundred yards offshore.

'What a splendid sight; I must remember to write to Madame de Motteville tonight before we set sail. I never anticipated such an impressive fleet.'

'You can thank Francis Windebank for some last minute bartering,' says Harry.

'And your efforts at the court of Denmark, Harry.'

'Every boat is crammed with armour and ammunition.' Jermyn nods to a boat moored further away from the others. 'And that unfortunate crew is transporting a hold packed with barrels of gunpowder.'

Henriette rubs her hands with glee. 'Wait until I tell Sir Kenelm.' She looks around the deserted beach and shouts at the top of her voice. 'Enough powder to blow up the House of Commoners.'

Susan is less impressed. 'There are no English ships lying in wait I hope.'

Harry Jermyn lifts her on to the beach. 'No enemy ships have been reported. Part of the parliamentary fleet is believed to be undergoing repairs in Yarmouth harbour. Other ships have been sighted off the coast of Northumbria.'

'I would remind you that they are the King's ships temporarily pinched by the puritan pirate,' says Henriette.

'Precisely, your majesty,' says Jermyn, 'so for the time being they should be avoided.'

'We sail come what may,' says Henriette grimly. 'Who knows where the enemy will be by the time we reach the English coast?'

She turns and struggles up the soft sand to the waiting carriage. 'Everything is packed, we wait for the wind.'

Act I, Scene 9 ~ The German Sea

Patience is not the Queen's greatest asset. Little Jeffrey does his best to entertain while Father Philip indulges in intensive prayers. Frustrating hours in the claustrophobic apartments of New Palace are punctuated for Her Majesty's court by walks in the gardens and town. Every so often, Henriette optimistically holds up a handkerchief to ascertain the strength and direction of the wind, on each occasion to be disappointed. It is not until a mild morning early in February that the royal party receives the signal to embark at Scheveningen.

Standing on the headland above the beach, the Queen has several goodbyes to make. She begins with her loyal Secretary of State who has masterminded the purchase of weapons in Holland.

'Well Francis, your work is done.'

The old man struggles to bow, gripping his walking stick tightly.

'Will you return to Paris?'

'At first, your majesty, and then we are planning a trip to Madrid to visit my son.'

Henriette takes a deep breath of sea air. 'With God's will and a strong army we shall overcome our enemies.'

'I am certain that you will,' says Windebank. 'I shall wait in Paris and hopefully receive the call before too long to return home.' He smiles. 'Much as I like the city of your birth, I would prefer to end my days in England.'

The Queen kisses her loyal lieutenant on both cheeks. 'I shall pass on your request to my nephew; Prince Rupert has a cunning plan to seize London before I land in England.'

Windebank laughs. 'Beware the impatient young, they tend to miss the detail.'

Henriette knows that Francis Windebank is a master of detail. Years before, he served her diligently when Charles was absent fighting the Scots. Again, in Holland he has demonstrated his organisational genius. She points towards the fleet of ships anchored off shore. 'All the armaments in those holds are thanks to you. The King and I owe you a debt of gratitude.'

Henriette

'Use the weapons wisely.' Windebank gently kisses her hand. 'That is my only request.'

Henriette moves down the rather bedraggled and windswept line. The leaving ceremony is impromptu like most things in Holland.

Queen Elizabeth curtsies. 'Give my brother all my love. I trust you go to England as an angel of peace. Remember our desperate experience and if you have the chance, mediate with your enemies.'

Henriette thinks to herself it is unlikely that Pym and his colleagues will countenance peace, but she holds her counsel and turns instead to Elizabeth's three daughters.

Henriette kisses her nieces: the eldest, Louise, the gifted painter; her namesake Henriette, ever cheerful; and young Sophie, who is now a firm friend of her own daughter. Despite the jewellery sales and her own desperate shortage of money, the Queen has kept back three small bracelets, which she presents to the girls. There are hugs and smiles all round.

The Queen turns to her son-in-law and the smile vanishes. 'Look after my beautiful daughter.'

Prince William bows. 'I will take care of Mary as long as I have breath in my body.'

He has received a long letter from Henriette, dictated by the Queen to Francis Windebank. It contains a lot of advice about being tolerant to a young wife who does not know the language or the customs of her new country.

Finally, Henriette stands before her daughter. 'Well little Mary, the time has come to say goodbye to your mother.'

Mary bursts into tears and Henriette wraps her delicate arms around her shoulders. After embracing, Henriette stands back and stares into Mary's eyes. The two look so alike.

'I know you will be a good wife, mother and Queen. After all you are the grand daughter of King Henri the Great of France and King James of the Three Kingdoms. I am sure that your children will go on to become mighty kings and queens of Europe.' She grips her daughter one more time. 'Most important of all, enjoy your life.' The young girl buries herself in her mother's arms and eventually her husband has to gently prise her away.

The leaving committee waves from the top of the sand dunes as the rowing boats head towards the ships. Francis Windebank has a tear in his eye; he doubts he will ever see his beloved Queen again.

She-Majesty Generalissima

Princess Mary is inconsolable in the arms of her husband. The surprise addition to the delegation, standing slightly apart, is Mr Groenefeld who raises his hat and waves vigorously. Henriette is not quite sure whether he is wishing her bon voyage or good riddance.

The ship opens up its sails and drifts silently away from the shore. The Queen stands on the deck beside Susan and Mall who wave enthusiastically at the shore party. Henriette looks into the distance and ignores her companions. Susan pauses and stares at her mistress.

'You are not waving, your majesty.'

'I am observing a strange phenomenon, Susan.'

The Countess of Denbeigh peers towards the shoreline and frowns. 'Is it not understandable that your daughter is waving you goodbye?'

Henriette sighs. 'I am not talking about the people. Have you not noticed the peculiar illusion created by the flat landscape?' The Queen points towards the receding coastline. 'The sea is flat, the coast is flat; there appears to be no division between the two. One can almost imagine the boats gliding effortlessly off the water and on to land.'

Susan and Mall stop waving at the figures, now tiny on the beach, and stare vacantly at the shoreline.

Henriette loses interest and retreats below deck, followed swiftly by her ladies. Safely in their cabin, Henriette, Susan and Mall inspect the tiny high-sided bunk beds. The Queen is less than five feet tall and the accommodation is adequate for her, but Mall complains that she cannot stretch her legs. Harry Jermyn, Father Philip and little Jeffrey occupy a second cabin normally reserved for the crew. The sailors settle for hammocks on the lower deck.

The following morning the Queen consults with the commander of the fleet on the main deck. Captain Van Noorden is a short man, although a few inches taller than the Queen, with an unkempt beard and straggly hair that fails to hide his rapidly balding head. His ruddy complexion and blotchy skin can be put down to sea weathering or excess alcohol or possibly a combination of the two. Most of the time, indoors and out, he wears a cap that bears a close relation to the Dutch navy uniform. It annoys Susan that he refuses to remove it in the presence of Henriette, although the Queen has long ceased caring about the lack of royal protocol.

'We do not appear to be making much progress,' says Henriette.

'We move at speed of slowest ship – this vessel, your majesty. The wind is light but favourable; we make ten miles an hour.'

'I shall pray for stronger winds.'

The Captain looks up at the blue sky dotted with large cumulus clouds. 'I doubt that will be needed.' The Queen frowns and is about to speak, but the captain continues. 'I am not happy with cloud formations. We may have rough weather.'

Act I, Scene 10 ~ Gravenhage

A fleet of rowing boats surge out to greet the becalmed ship, which floats on a glass-like, bright blue sea.

The welcoming party is reduced to open mouthed shock at the sight of the passengers limping with the aid of sailors on to the deck. They look like a bedraggled bunch of vagabonds, bearing no resemblance to the smart and refined party that boarded eleven days before. As they are rowed to shore, a distraught Princess Mary accompanied by her concerned husband and parents rush into the shallows to assist the seafarers back on to dry land. The passengers are too weak and off balance to walk unaided.

'Oh Mam, we have been so worried. The ships have been returning in ones and twos with reports of a terrible storm.' Tears stream down Mary's cheeks. 'I thought all hope was lost.'

'I must confess,' says Henriette, wiping her forehead with a handkerchief, 'I steeled myself against an attack from enemy ships, or possibly pirates, but did not anticipate the elements would be our nemesis.'

'It began with a strong northerly wind that the Captain forewarned us about,' says Susan. Despite the calmer weather, she remains as white as a sheet. 'Our entire party was seasick; usually I am the only one to succumb.'

Mall brushes unkempt, straggly curls away from her face. 'The stench from the latrine on the ballast wafted directly upwards through the timbers to our cabin.'

'Thank you, dear, I don't think Mary wants chapter and verse.' Henriette stares at the gentle waves lapping the beach. 'Absolutely typical, we turn back and the storm vanishes.'

She-Majesty Generalissima

'Mam, your clothes are soaking wet.'

Henriette continues the account of their disastrous voyage: 'By the fourth day, the gale had turned into an almighty storm and the crew strapped us into our bunks. The waves came crashing over the bow and water poured through gaps in the planks. After two days lying in our beds, you can imagine the state we were in. The boat heaved almost vertical over the waves before crashing down with a creaking of timbers that sounded as if the boat was splitting in two.'

'You lost four vessels,' says William as he helps his mother-in-law on to dry land.

'No, three vessels reached Newcastle,' says Harry Jermyn, who takes Henriette's other arm. 'They managed to slip past while the enemy ships sheltered in Great Yarmouth. The remaining ship...' Jermyn shrugs. 'We never saw it again.'

'I thought we were going to die,' says Mall.

Henriette tries to steady herself on the beach; it is a strange sensation to feel solid earth beneath her feet. 'I had to listen to Susan and Mall making confessions at the top of their voices, which I would prefer not to have heard.'

'The Queen was marvellous,' says Susan as she is helped to shore by Mary's father-in-law. 'She remained calm in the face of disaster.'

'I must admit it was the most uncomfortable week in my life,' says Henriette, 'strapped to a filthy bed in a dark and noisy room that settled on every angle except horizontal.'

Two coaches transport the exhausted seafarers back to the care of Mr Groenefeld and New Palace where it is agreed that the journey will have to wait for the spring. This is before the queen is consulted. When Harry Jermyn breaks the news, he receives a predictable response.

'My dear Harry, I am not making my husband wait two months for these precious reinforcements. We will spend five days recovering and then we shall take the next favourable wind.'

Susan is horrified. 'But the astrological signs are most disadvantageous, your majesty.'

Henriette tilts her head, looking her Dame of Honour up and down. 'What do you suggest I tell the King?' She gesticulates with her arms. 'I am sorry, dear heart, that you lost the battle due to a shortage of weapons and gunpowder, but unfortunately we could not sail because the Countess of Denbeigh believed the stars were in the wrong place.'

Ten days later, the reluctant party take the short journey back to Scheveningen beach where nine vessels await. Susan and Mall have a horrible feeling of déja vu, not to say sinking sensations in their tummies, even before the ships are under way. Henriette is impatient to board. The same leaving committee wave from the sand dunes, excepting Mr Groenefeld. Henriette wonders if he has lost interest in his strange English visitors. She is never to discover that he was struck down by a fever on the morning of embarkation and by the time the Queen reaches England the stern republican has passed away. His wife is pregnant and when their daughter is born, knowing how much her husband learned to respect the "foreign majesty", she gives the girl a middle name – Henriette. The little girl grows up in the service of Henriette's niece, Princess Sophie, who marries the Elector of Hanover. Mr Groenefeld's daughter becomes nursemaid to their eldest son, George. The German toddler, via several twists of fate, will one day be crowned King of Great Britain and Ireland.

The Queen stands on the deck alongside Harry Jermyn. This time the water is relatively calm and none of her courtiers have to be strapped to their beds. Despite the gentler passage, after a few days the stench from the ballast is overpowering; Henriette is happy to spend long hours up on deck.

'Have you missed England, Harry?'

Jermyn gives the question some thought. 'I miss the England that I remember, your majesty.'

'Which means?' asks Henriette.

'I remember with fondness the time before parliament was called, when life was settled and everyone knew their place; the days when the Three Kingdoms were at peace with themselves – and enjoyed great prosperity.'

'I recall it was a time of gambling and duels for you,' says Henriette with a grin, 'not to mention getting Mall's sister pregnant.'

'I was young,' says Harry.

'And now you are old?' Henriette sighs. 'With all my aches and rashes, I feel ancient.'

'No, you are the radiant and swashbuckling heroine,' says Jermyn gallantly. 'Like the Queen of the Amazon Warriors – the part you played in the last royal masque.'

She-Majesty Generalissima

'The last masque,' says Henriette despondently. Her unique mix of theatre and dance has enthralled the English court these past twenty years. 'Quite possibly my last.'

Harry Jermyn is not daunted by the Queen's pessimism. 'Now you have the chance to act out the role on a real life stage.'

'I always felt that my life was rather like performing in a masque.' Henriette smiles ruefully. 'Except someone keeps interfering with the script.'

'Now you can control the story. You will conquer your enemies with your sword, and those that resist will fall under the spell of your beauty.' His earnest tone suggests he is not joking.

'Harry, be careful. I assured my husband that parliament's grubby accusation that we were having an affair was untrue. If Mr Pymple hears you speaking like that he might revive the libel.' The Queen tries to picture her nemesis. 'Mind you, if the thought of such scandalous infidelity caused a massive heart attack, that would be a very satisfactory ending to the play.'

'Does everyone die of a heart attack in your world?'

'I wish my enemies would.' Henriette lowers her voice. 'But don't tell Father Philip I said that.'

'I don't want them to have heart attacks,' says Jermyn harshly. 'I want to capture them and string them up on Tower Hill. I shall remind them of what they did to Thomas Wentworth before having them drawn and quartered.'

'If our enemies capture you back in England, Harry, they will most certainly charge you with treason.'

'I understand the risk. The only preference I would have is for an axe to end my days.'

'I shall speak to the King. You need a title and then you can request a beheading.'

Jermyn bows. 'Very thoughtful, your majesty; I can think of worse reasons for granting a baronetcy.'

Henriette looks across the deck to where little Jeffrey is performing a magic trick. He appears to have been tied up in ropes by the sailors and is struggling to break free. The Queen is about to intervene when the bindings drop to the floor and Jeffrey runs around the deck with his arms in the air screaming 'that's magic, that's real magic.' Henriette rather thinks Jeffrey has surprised himself as well as his audience and she hopes he does not try and repeat the illusion. Susan and Mall are on the far side of the ship. Susan has her head over the side.

Captain Van Noorden strolls across from the whip staff, the geared tiller that steers the boat. 'I send two of our faster boats ahead. They are small and light and with oarsmen as well as sail. They patrol English coast as we approach.'

'Where exactly are we?' asks Henriette.

'Parallel with Lincolnshire coast but distance out. Enemy boats come from Yarmouth and Hull. We don't want to bump into them.' He looks up at the sails. 'But wind shifts and we may have no choice but to steer to coast.'

For the second time the Captain's forecast is accurate and overnight the wind changes. The fleet is forced to navigate to the northwest and by morning the coast is in view.

'Look Susan,' shouts Henriette, pointing wildly over the side. 'England.'

Her Dame of Honour is deathly pale but attempts a weak smile.

'I told you we would return within the year,' says the Queen triumphantly. She strides to the steps leading down to the cabins and shouts into the gloom: 'Harry, Mall, land ahoy.'

By the time they reach the deck, accompanied by little Jeffrey and Father Philip, the Queen is in earnest discussions with Captain van Noorden.

She turns to Harry. 'We cannot reach Newcastle on the prevailing wind, but the Captain knows of a fishing village with a tiny harbour just up the coast, a place called Burlington.'

'Burlington?' Jermyn has never heard it. 'Well if it's the only place we can make land, it will have to suffice. Presumably there is no risk of a parliamentary reception at a remote fishing village. We will track inland to York as soon as we have informed the Earl of Newcastle of our safe landing. He can send a military escort.'

'I am not waiting for William Cavendish to send soldiers,' says Henriette impatiently.

'Remember what the King instructed in his last letter,' says Jermyn sternly. 'I take military decisions until we reach York.'

Henriette cries out in frustration. 'What's the point of being Her Majesty if I cannot command my courtiers? I thought you said I was the Amazon Queen.'

'Any monarch takes advice from military experts,' says Susan, attempting the unenviable role of peacemaker. 'If Harry suggests we wait for an escort of troops then we should heed his warning.'

The Queen abandons the conversation and walks back to the landward side of the ship. She leans over the wooden barrier.

'England,' she says wistfully to herself. 'I never thought I would miss you so much.' She looks up at the square rigging rising into the grey sky, the sails now filling with fresh wind. She shouts at the top of her voice. 'Watch out, Mr Pymple, the Popish Brat is back, and I have brought a pile of gunpowder. Let's see what you have to say when we stick a barrel under your backside and light the fuse.'

Susan purses her lips in disapproval, Father Philip pretends not to hear, Mall and Harry laugh. Little Jeffrey jumps up and down shouting, 'three cheers for the Popish brat.'

Captain van Noorden shakes his head – it is true, the English are stark raving mad.

Henriette is given a royal welcome in the tiny fishing village of Burlington, fifteen miles south of the larger settlement of Scarborough. A row of thatched cottages hug the harbour front; a handful of farm buildings and labourer huts are scattered along the inland cart track. Unlike Scheveningen, the Yorkshire hamlet boasts a stone harbour, although the Queen's Dutch ships have to anchor out in the bay to avoid being grounded at low tide. The local population are honoured to be hosting their Queen and two cottages on the waterfront are cleared out for her retinue. All the fishing vessels and every rowboat are brought into service to unload the ships. It is slow work transferring guns, artillery, gunpowder and ammunition to shore. Two of the seven ships are emptied by nightfall. The barrels of gunpowder are carefully lifted on to the quay; some are stored in the nearby rope works and others are left by the harbour covered with two layers of tarpaulin.

Harry Jermyn despatches a rider on the forty-mile trek to York to inform the Earl of Newcastle that the Queen has landed short of her destination. As luck would have it, the change of wind has halved her overland journey to York.

Rather like her camping days at Wellingborough, Henriette's enthusiasm for country living makes her surprisingly at ease in the modest surroundings. The Queen chats with women of the village and takes an interest in their children. When she explains that she has not seen her children for a year, apart from Princess Mary, there is much sympathy and some anger at her treatment by parliament. Her English is sufficient these days to get by although she struggles with the strange local accent. There appears to be no 'h' in their alphabet and they use the word 'right' a lot of the time for no apparent reason. Henriette continues to smile graciously and accepts the makeshift bouquets of flowers presented by the daughters of Burlington. She and her companions tuck into a meal at the harbour inn, a delicious spread of freshly caught fish and potato pies. It is an altogether warmer reception than she was expecting and it is comforting to be surrounded by beaming smiles rather than the serious expressions that she became accustomed to in Gravenhage.

Eventually, Henriette, Susan, Mall and two maids of honour retire to a whitewashed stone cottage on the harbour front. It is restful lying in bed without the room heaving up and down. The Queen snuggles under the blankets and prepares to spend a peaceful first night back on English soil.

Act I, Scene 11 ~ Burlington

Henriette dreams. The boat heaves upwards and crashes into the waves, wood splinters and oil lamps shatter, people cry in the dark, the bed shakes. Her eyes open wide; she is awake but on dry land in a fisherman's cottage. Suddenly she is aware that the noise and panic has followed her out of the nightmare – a thunderous crash is followed by a tremor that passes through the building rattling furniture and knocking the candle off her bedside table. Susan screams.

The Queen sits bolt upright; Mall clutches her arm.

'Get up, your majesty, we are under fire.'

Henriette is half asleep and cannot understand what Mall is talking about. Then she hears a whooshing sound and another loud crack as a cannon ball crashes into a nearby cottage. People outside shout above the tumult. Finally, the Queen is galvanised into action and leaps out of bed and runs to the window.

At first it is inky black outside, but the half moon keeps appearing from behind drifting clouds and her eyes adjust. It is a strange sight for the middle of the night – villagers running to and fro, disappearing in and out of cottage doorways or heading for the harbour, many in their nightclothes.

'How dare they?' exclaims Henriette. She waves her arms in the direction of the sea where tiny flames light up the darkness as cannon fire. She shouts at the top of her voice. 'I am the Queen of England and those are my ships.'

She feels a blanket pushed around her shoulders and a voice in her ear; it is Susan: 'Your majesty, for pity's sake get out of the house and run for the fields.'

'If it turns out the puritan pirate is commanding those ships I shall have him arrested for treason. It's outrageous.'

The Countess of Denbeigh is terrified and cannot believe the Queen can stand there arguing with an unseen, unreachable enemy.

'Please, your majesty, if you stop here we will all be killed.' As if to confirm the prediction, a cannon ball crashes into the adjoining cottage.

Henriette turns back from the window and speaks calmly.

'Collect the dogs; I am not leaving without them.'

Susan, Mall and two maids of honour round up the pets while Henriette grabs a sack containing a handful of unsold jewels she has brought back from Holland. Remaining valuables were left in the safe keeping of her daughter in Gravenhage. The women hurriedly put on cloaks over their nightdresses and clamber down the stairs. There are repeated crashing sounds as cannon balls pepper the cottages and the harbour wall.

Outside, they follow the flow of people making for the York road and the fields beyond. A hundred yards behind the seafront there is a broad ditch, similar to one of the waterways in Holland. People dive for cover, sheltering against the bank and keeping their heads down. The delay in corralling the dogs means the royal party is among the last group of people to reach the street. The menfolk are down by the harbour, bravely rolling barrels of gunpowder to safety. Harry Jermyn spots the Queen and her entourage as he races back to the cottages. Henriette is counting dogs.

'Where's Mitte?' she shouts. Everyone pauses and looks at each other. 'Mitte has been left behind,' says Henriette turning back.

Susan abandons protocol and grabs the Queen's arm. 'It's too late to go back.' As she speaks a cannon ball whistles past their heads so close they can feel the rush of air. It skids along the dry mud on the road and then ricochets into a building, demolishing part of the façade.

Henriette shakes herself free and runs back to the cottage. Mall screams but the Queen ignores her. Another cannon ball smashes through the window just as Henriette reaches the open door. As she enters, splinters of wood fly across her face and splatter against the wall. Henriette looks up the stairs. At the top, barking loudly is Mitte. The Queen has lost her cloak; she dashes bare foot up the narrow stone staircase in her nightshirt. She scoops Mitte up, gives the dog a brief hug and then runs down the stairs into the arms of Harry Jermyn.

She smirks at her dashing chevalier. 'I am not dressed for a royal audience, Harry.'

Jermyn says nothing; he grabs a blanket and covers his mistress and her lap dog. He puts his arm around Henriette and marches her out of the cottage. There is a pause in the bombardment as they scurry to the main road and join the others. The royal party heads for the irrigation ditch where the villagers have taken cover. Susan has brought a cloak and gloves, which she insists the Queen puts on. The parliamentary ships open fire again and cannon balls thud into the opposite embankment.

'There are three enemy ships,' says Jermyn, keeping his head down. 'One of our escort vessels returned in the early evening and reported that the enemy were lying in wait off the coast of Scarborough. The change in wind that brought us twenty miles south was a real stroke of luck as it turns out.'

'Good old Burlington,' says Henriette cheerfully. 'I shall never forget this place.'

Jermyn is unimpressed. 'Don't ever risk your life for a pet dog again.' He shakes his head. 'What would I have said to the King if you had been cut in two by a cannon ball.'

Henriette gives him a cheeky grin. 'You would have reported that the Queen was cut in two by a cannon ball.'

'It's not something to joke about,' says Susan harshly. 'Harry has been given the immense responsibility of delivering you safely to the King.'

Henriette always accepts a rebuke from her senior lady in waiting. 'I am sorry Susan, but I truly would rather have died than leave Mitte in that cottage all alone and terrified.'

'What about me?' squeaks little Jeffrey, 'I was alone and terrified too.'

The ship's guns can be heard firing again and Mall lies on her back staring at stars in the night sky. 'I am still terrified.'

They duck as another cannon ball skims overhead and crashes into the field beyond. A second missile hits a Dutch sailor in the back as he makes for cover. His shattered body lands fifty feet from the royal party. Susan screams.

Henriette is furious; she raises her head above the bank. 'You have no right to use those ships, they belong to the King,' she shouts.

Harry Jermyn abandons any restraint and grabs Henriette and pulls her unceremoniously back into the ditch. 'My apologies, your majesty, but the King commanded me to guard you with my life.'

'Apology accepted, Harry, but I hope you agree we need to get to York as soon as possible before anyone else is killed.' Henriette takes her glove off and it drops into the ditch. She wipes mud from her cheek as she reflects on the Parliamentary naval bombardment. 'I intend one day to stand on deck and proudly survey our glorious navy, and I don't expect there to be a puritan pirate in sight.'

> 'I never forgave Robert Rich for stealing our ships.' The old lady takes little Anne by the hand and walks slowly back towards the house. 'I was angry with his brother, Henry, too, when he came skulking back to Oxford.'
>
> 'Henry proved his loyalty in the end,' says Madame as she struggles to pick up her writing materials and catch up with her mistress.
>
> 'It was a bit late by then.' Henriette nods towards the red pianea. 'I keep forgetting what that lovely flower is called. My memory is not what it used to be.' She laughs. 'I'm a fine one trying to record my memoirs.'
>
> 'That is why it is important that we write an account.'
>
> 'Before I become completely senile, you mean.' Henriette waves away her companion's protests. 'Françoise, we shall have some dinner and refresh our minds. Then, if you are not too tired, we shall write about my time in York.'
>
> 'I expect it was more agreeable than Holland, your majesty.'

'I don't think so,' says Henriette sharply. 'All I wanted to do was set off for Oxford to be reunited with my dear heart, and everyone kept putting objections in the way.'

'It was potentially a very dangerous journey,' says Madame.

'Nonsense. I survived dour Dutchmen, a treacherous sea crossing and the attack on Burlington; I brought arms and men from the continent, not to mention piles of gunpowder; I was ready for the march south.'

'It must have been very frustrating.' Madame conjures the impatient scenes.

Henriette lets out a cry of derision. 'I did not sit back and waste my time being frustrated; we seized a castle. How I would have loved to have witnessed Mr Pymple's face when he discovered that the Popish brat had occupied the largest fortification in the north of England.'

Act I, Scene 12 ~ York Palace

'I hear you had a close encounter with the enemy.'

William Cavendish, Earl of Newcastle, has a glint in his eye as he escorts the Queen and her confessor Father Philip through the dining room and into the withdrawing chamber.

'We were temporarily inconvenienced by some impudent parliamentary ruffians,' says Henriette. 'We endured the worst storm ever to grip the German Sea and were forced to dodge bloodthirsty pirates.'

Harry Jermyn, one step behind his mistress, ponders why she feels the need to embellish a story that already contains quite enough drama to satisfy the most adventurous of listeners. He decides it is her theatrical temperament.

Cavendish requires no encouragement. The dashing cavalier with flowing light brown locks and a love of poetry and masques has always been one of the Queen's most ardent admirers. His cultivation of royal patronage paid off when the King appointed him commander of the northern army. At six feet, he towers over Henriette.

'I understand that the enemy disturbed your first night on dry land.'

'It was doubly annoying because the ships that fired upon us at Burlington belong to the royal navy.

'Unfortunately the fleet has gone over to the enemy.'

'I know,' says the Queen. 'That's the thanks you get when you tolerate puritans like the Earl of Warwick. I warned Charles that Robert Rich could not be trusted.' Henriette shakes her head. 'His brother, Henry, has hardly proved any more reliable.'

Cavendish escorts Henriette into a small room lined with bookcases.

'This was the library.' William Cavendish knows the Queen's priorities. 'We have done our best to create a Catholic chapel.'

Henriette looks around. 'That is thoughtful of you, William. The room will suit us very well.'

Father Philip puts down a large sack that jangles as he places it on the floor. He takes out a silver chalice encrusted with diamonds.

Henriette curtsies in front of the makeshift altar. 'We shall give thanks to God for our safe arrival at York and pray for a speedy onward journey to Oxford.'

The Queen and her small group of followers take up residence adjacent to the Cathedral in York Palace, a private house belonging to Sir Arthur Ingram. He entertained Charles for six months the previous year and is now honoured to oblige the Queen. Ingram made his money from questionable property deals, but is now a respectable member of the Yorkshire gentry. In poor health, he remains at his country estate of Temple Newsam, near Leeds. Sir Arthur has provided a full complement of servants, horses and carriages for Henriette's convenience.

The Queen emerges from her chapel in a calm and positive frame of mind and walks through several austere public chambers to the ornate royal blue and gold reception room. Narrow mullioned windows provide a partial view of the mediaeval cathedral. The Earl of Newcastle and Harry Jermyn arrive, accompanied as ever by the Countess of Denbeigh. Susan refuses to let the Queen hold an audience with men without at least one lady-in-waiting present as chaperone.

Henriette as always is impatient for the latest intelligence. 'What news from the southern army, William?'

'We came out of our first encounter with the enemy at Edgehill slightly the stronger. Our forces advanced towards London where there was panic on the streets.'

'My nephew was right then. He was confident of reaching the capital before Christmas.'

'Unfortunately desperation among the enemy ranks turned into resistance; there was a mass turnout of volunteers to defend the city. Our advance came to a halt in the market gardens and marshes of Turnham Green. Skirmishes did not suit Prince Rupert's fast moving cavalry, so the King was forced to beat a tactical retreat to Oxford where he has set up winter headquarters.'

'I am hoping for a letter from Charles any day. He must have been informed of my landing by now.'

A servant enters the room, bows, and hands a rolled up parchment to Harry Jermyn. After examining the paper, Jermyn turns to the Queen.

'You have a letter, your majesty, but it is from parliament, not the King.'

'Oh joy.' Henriette sits down on an oak chair with intricately carved arms. 'Let me guess, they wish to apologise for shooting at me by mistake in Burlington.' Henriette folds her arms. 'You read it; I can feel the start of one of my horrible headaches.'

Jermyn unrolls the paper and peruses the text: 'To your esteemed and most honoured majesty…'

'Well that's a lie for a start,' interrupts Henriette. 'They want to chop my head off, just like Charles's grandmother, Marie Queen of Scots.'

Jermyn continues: 'Members of your most obedient and loyal parliament humbly invite your majesty to repair at your earliest convenience to London where you will be welcomed and comfortably accommodated as befits your position.'

'Comfortably accommodated in the Tower more like,' says Henriette. 'Let me guess, there is a "but" in the next paragraph.'

Jermyn pulls a face. 'I suppose it could be described as a "but", although your obedient and loyal members of parliament have used a "however".'

'That's the same thing,' says the Queen gleefully. 'I told you; please pop down at your convenience for a chat, however we will then chop your head off.'

Susan flinches. 'I wish your majesty would stop saying that.'

'Go on, Harry,' says the Queen, making no effort to hide her irritation at her Dame of Honour's intervention. 'Tell me about the "however".'

Jermyn resumes: 'However, if your majesty should continue to aid and abet the forces set against your true parliament with the supply of diverse weapons, men or encouragement howsoever…'

'That is John Hampden the lawyer speaking,' shouts Henriette triumphantly. 'Who else would put a term like "howsoever" in general correspondence?' The Queen has been gesticulating with her arms but she folds them again. 'Carry on Harry, read it loudly, quietly or howsoever.'

Jermyn clears his throat. 'Then parliament will regrettably be forced to assume that you are set against its members and the wishes of the people and you shall be treated as Queen Consort as any other citizen who takes up arms against their lawful government.'

'You see,' says Henriette, her voice rising. 'Get down here and let us accommodate you in the Tower whereupon we will devise a clever way to chop your head off without resort to a judge and jury, or else stay away and we will come and get you and still chop your head off.'

'Your majesty,' exclaims Susan.

'All right,' says the Queen harshly, 'decapitate me, execute me, judicially murder me – which do you prefer?'

As is often the case, Henriette works herself into a storm and the jokey delivery turns into an aggressive blast; the last four words are hurled at the Countess of Denbeigh. Susan bows her head to hide the tears in her eyes. The Queen accepts that she has overstepped the mark.

'I'm sorry.' She stands up and walks over to Susan. She puts an arm around her shoulder, although this is difficult, Henriette being eight inches shorter than her Dame of Honour. Henriette speaks gently. 'I need to trivialise this desperate situation or else I shall go mad. But the last thing I want to do is upset my dearest, most loyal and affectionate friend.'

The Queen hugs Susan. Protocol is pretty much out of the window after the travails of Holland, the sea journey and the bombardment at Burlington.

'You are so strong,' mumbles the Countess, 'and you treat these puritans with the contempt they deserve.'

'But I shall stop mentioning necks and sharp bladed instruments,' says Henriette with a smile.

'Thank you, your majesty. That would be appreciated.'

The Earl of Newcastle takes the letter from Jermyn and peruses it.

'The more likely scenario is parliament want you in London so they can deploy you as a negotiating card in peace talks.'

'I suppose being a playing card is better than losing one's...' Henriette stops herself and smiles at the Countess. The Queen picks up a cushion from the window seat and places it on her chair before settling down again. 'Do you have any special reason, William, for thinking they want to capture me alive?'

'My spies at Westminster report that John Pym is telling everyone that soon he will hold an advantage that will persuade the King to sue for peace and accept Parliament's terms. Taking you hostage might be that advantage.'

'So our enemies may try and kidnap the Queen?' asks Jermyn.

'We should be alert to the possibility,' says Cavendish.

'I need to travel to Oxford,' insists Henriette.

'We must clear a passage for you first,' says Cavendish equally firmly. 'Parliament controls large portions of middle England.'

'I am not staying in York twiddling my thumbs indefinitely. We have arms that need transporting to the King.'

'The northern army could do with some of your supplies,' says Cavendish. 'Lord Fairfax is threatening Leeds and the Hothams have spread from Hull into Lincolnshire and Nottinghamshire.'

'Don't mention Hull to me,' says the Queen despondently. 'That was an opportunity lost.'

There is an embarrassed silence that eventually Harry Jermyn fills. 'Perhaps we can split the armaments into a consignment for the northern army and a slightly more manageable baggage train that we take south to Oxford.'

Before the Queen can reply, the Earl of Newcastle's equerry enters and announces that Sir Hugh Cholmeley has arrived unexpectedly from the parliamentary stronghold of Scarborough.

'That's odd,' says Cavendish, 'Sir Hugh declared the castle for parliament.'

'Arrest him,' snaps Henriette. 'Chop his...' She stops herself. 'Put him in prison and send our army to lay siege to Scarborough; without their leader they will soon surrender.'

William Cavendish raises an eyebrow. 'Can we hear what he has to say first, your majesty?'

She-Majesty Generalissima

Henriette sighs. 'All right, William, but if this man is for parliament he should be arrested and thrown in prison.'

'He deserves to be heard.' Cavendish is quite prepared to stand his ground against a Henriette onslaught.

The Queen reluctantly gives way. 'Bring Sir Hugh in; the Earl of Newcastle wants to discuss the state of the weather with him.'

The equerry bows, walks slowly backwards and leaves the room. It occurs to Henriette that this is the first time a servant has behaved in a respectful way since she left Dover Castle a year ago.

Two guards arrive with a tall, middle-aged gentleman of striking appearance – long nose, extravagant moustache and thick, dark hair resting over his shoulders. He walks confidently up to the Queen and bows.

'Your majesty, I have pleasure in handing you the keys to Scarborough Castle.' He reaches in his pocket and produces three large keys on a rusty metal ring.

For once, Henriette is stumped for a reply.

The Earl of Newcastle comes to her rescue. 'Am I to understand, Sir Hugh, that you are surrendering Scarborough Castle?'

'I think the word surrender is not appropriate,' says Sir Hugh stiffly. 'I am handing over the castle, my stewardship, my men and my armaments for any useful purposes of their majesties.'

William Cavendish is puzzled. 'But you fought against us at Edgehill, and assisted Fairfax in the assault of York.'

'I did,' says Sir Hugh. 'I also opposed Ship Money tax and the lack of a parliament for eleven years, as did my good friend Sir John Hotham. Here in Yorkshire we say things how they are.'

'So why the change of heart?' asks Harry Jermyn. He is always suspicious of people who change sides; if they do it once, they can perform the trick twice.

'The Queen's spirited return to Yorkshire fills me with great admiration,' says Sir Hugh nodding towards Henriette. 'I did not approve of the threats made to her majesty before she sailed for Holland and I did not like the contents of the letter agreed in parliament last week.'

'This letter?' asks Jermyn, brandishing the puritan missive.

'I believe that is the correspondence,' says Sir Hugh. 'You may also find that Sir John Hotham and his son share my views.'

'You do me a great honour, sir.' The significance of the occasion is dawning on Henriette. Here is one of the leading noblemen of

Yorkshire calmly repudiating the extremists. It is something the Queen has prayed might happen for the past two years. 'I have long believed that a small but vociferous minority in London do not necessarily represent the views of my husband's subjects across the kingdom. We would be most interested to hear from Sir John and the garrison at Hull. My companions will attest to the fact that I was a trifle vexed by the loss of such a vital port.'

Henriette glances at Jermyn. Even her closest friend is struggling to keep his face straight in the wake of such an understatement.

Sir Hugh hands the bunch of keys to the Earl of Newcastle before turning again to the Queen.

'If I may be allowed to say so, your majesty, you are an inspiration to Englishmen everywhere.'

Henriette cannot resist a smile. 'I would love to see Mr Pym's face when he hears that the popish brat, singlehanded, has taken Scarborough Castle.' She looks at Jermyn and winks. 'Not sure we need to bother replying to his kind invitation, Harry.'

Act I, Scene 13 ~ Scarborough Castle

The castle stands proud on the cliff top, towering over the small fishing village with its bustling harbour. Henriette stares out of a narrow window in the turret room and surveys the reassuringly thick stone ramparts hugging the cliff tops. At the foot of the cliffs, waves ripple gently across a sandy beach, a sharp contrast to the rough water that she experienced on her voyage from Holland.

Sir Hugh points to a vessel low in the water close to the horizon. 'That will be a coal barge from Newcastle heading for London.'

The Queen peers into the blue haze; with her poor eyesight she has no hope of picking out the distant ship.

'Could we perhaps attack their supply line?'

Sir Hugh chuckles. 'Exactly my thought, your majesty.'

'What are they building?' asks Henriette, pointing to a team of stonemasons constructing more fortifications near the southern cliff edge.

'I thought it was wise to reinforce the landward approach,' says Sir Hugh. 'With steep cliffs on the other three sides, it is not difficult to predict the enemy line of attack.'

'This is a mighty castle; I had no idea it was on such a scale.'

'It is one of the great castles of the east coast,' says Sir Hugh, 'and as you pointed out it is strategically placed for us to disrupt trade with London.' He points to a large vessel anchored in the bay. 'That is the ship full of arms that you sent from Holland, captured by parliament.' He bows to Henriette. 'You can have it back.'

'Mr Pym will be terribly upset,' says Henriette gleefully. 'Hopefully he will have a heart attack when he hears the bad news.'

The Queen walks back to the spiral staircase and carefully begins the descent to the second floor. In her long dress the narrow steps have to be negotiated with care. She is near the bottom of the staircase when Harry Jermyn's face appears from below. He stops and retraces his steps backwards. Henriette follows.

'Your majesty, a delegation has arrived from York – the Marquis of Antrim and the Marquis of Montrose.'

'Lords from both our other kingdoms.' Henriette is intrigued. 'Have they arrived on the same day by coincidence or design I wonder?'

'I believe they have common cause. They wish to speak to you about the state of affairs in Scotland.'

'Where is our cousin James Hamilton; we rely on him for intelligence north of the border.'

'The Marquis of Hamilton is on his way from Edinburgh,' says Jermyn.

'Well we cannot wait for him. I must head back to York this afternoon.'

The Queen returns to the spiral staircase and descends to the Great Hall on the floor below. The internal stairs go no further. To ensure the Keep is difficult to storm, the first floor can only be accessed from the ground by a set of steps cut into the outside wall. It is a chilly spring morning and a fire burns in the large hearth. Two men stand in the middle of the sparsely furnished room, both tall, handsome and in their mid-thirties, the same age as the Queen. As they bow, Henriette addresses the man with distinctive red hair.

'Randal MacDonnell, how is your sweet wife?'

'She is well, your majesty.'

The Marquis of Antrim's wife, Katharine Villiers, was one of Henriette's earliest English courtiers, mother to her maid of honour, Mall.

'Have you left Kate in Ireland?'

'She travelled across to Scotland with me and will arrive in York within the week.'

'I shall look forward to hearing all her news from Ireland.' Henriette turns to Randall MacDonnell's fellow traveller. 'Scotland is also in disarray, I fear.'

The Marquis of Montrose stands six feet tall with grey eyes and a charming smile.

'It is true there are many factions, your majesty.'

Henriette is wary of the highlander. 'I am told you led the Scottish rebel army at Newburn and were responsible for taking Newcastle.'

'Yes, your majesty, I found myself with divided loyalties.' Montrose stops short of apologising. 'I opposed Argyll and the Presbyterians, but I could not stand by and watch an English army invade my kingdom.'

Harry Jermyn expects a sharp riposte from his mistress, but for once he misjudges her.

'Are you for the King of Scotland or against?' Henriette gives Montrose one of her penetrating stares.

'I am your husband's most loyal follower.' Montrose bows again. 'I am here to alert your majesty to the danger of the Scottish presbyterians joining forces with the English puritans.'

Henriette frowns and glances at Jermyn. 'I was unaware of this threat, Harry.'

Jermyn shrugs. 'We receive a different account from the Marquis of Hamilton.'

Montrose scoffs. 'You would be wise not to take counsel from Hamilton; he has plans of his own I think.'

'What designs might these be?' asks the Queen.

'There is talk he will switch to the Presbyterian side if matters go badly for the King in England. There are rumours that he will accept the Scottish crown.'

'That is wild talk,' says Jermyn.

Montrose is not deterred. 'Royalist hopes rest with the highland clans.'

She-Majesty Generalissima

Henriette's knowledge of Scotland is sketchy. 'I thought the highlanders were wild and undisciplined men.'

Randal MacDonnell comes to Montrose's defence. 'I am from the clan MacDonald, your majesty. The Presbyterian leader Argyll is a Campbell; you can count on nearly all the other clans uniting against him; there is bad blood going back centuries.' He smiles. 'The Highlanders are fierce fighters, but not barbarians.'

The Queen is unconvinced. 'Is it wise to stir up civil war within Scotland; we already have great upheavals in Ireland and an armed rebellion in England.'

'If you ignore Scotland,' says Montrose, 'you will end up with enemies to the north as well as the south.'

'We can ship ten thousand men across from Ireland,' says Randal. 'When they link up with the highlanders, it is the Scottish rebels who will face a war on two fronts.'

Henriette is intrigued by the idea. 'Can you be sure of winning support in the highlands?'

'I am certain of it, your majesty,' says Montrose. 'Most of the clans are Catholic and they will welcome support from Ireland. People don't want to be governed by one religion or another, they want a government that rules Scotland for all Scots.'

'That is what my father achieved in France,' says Henriette quietly. 'I shall write to the King. After all, my husband is a Scot – he should see the sense in your design.'

> Henriette watches as Madame de Motteville completes her notes.
>
> 'Our French theatre director will be kept busy. Burlington, Scarborough and York – I can picture the backcloths.'
>
> Madame looks up. 'I shall send the latest manuscript to Monsieur Poquelin; he says he is happy to compose the actions from my notes.'
>
> 'You mean from my meandering recollections.' Henriette smiles. 'You will not offend me; years of fighting a vicious enemy have toughened me up.'
>
> 'I cannot think of a Queen of England who faced such adversities and triumphed as you did.'
>
> Henriette frowns. 'I would hardly describe the outcome as a triumph.' She recalls a conversation with her son. 'But we did win.'

'Shall we describe your victorious march south in the next scene?'

'Now you are the impatient one, Françoise. First, we shall introduce two old friends. Instruct Monsieur Poquelin to recreate a bustling, colourful market.'

Act I, Scene 14 ~ York

The ladies weave between crowded market stalls – down the row of hog and pig sellers, past fishmongers and poulterers, stopping briefly at bread and dairy stands. The three women ignore the ale sellers and stroll by timber and faggot stalls before pausing to examine samples from the earthenware counters. They finally arrive at their goal – the aisle of wool and linen traders. Dozens of drapers sell cloth, alongside milliners, tanners, glovers and white-tawyers specialising in fashionable white leather goods.

For Henriette, the past twelve months has been a relentless battle against her enemies. It is the first time in over a year that she has indulged in a relaxing shopping expedition; she cannot decide where to begin. Half a dozen soldiers accompany the Queen who wears a cloak and hood to prevent people recognising her. In truth, few people in York know what the Queen of England looks like.

'It's like old times,' says Henriette as she picks up a roll of burgundy satin. She grins at her two companions. 'The Duchess of Buckingham and her eldest daughter out shopping with me while Susan busies herself in the kitchens organising a grand banquet.'

'What an extraordinary year it has been,' says Katharine.

'But not very amazing, Mall,' says the Queen.

The Duchess of Buckingham glances at her daughter.

'Her majesty is picking me up on my slang,' says Mall.

Henriette puts the cloth down and points a finger at the Duchess. 'Actually, it has been down hill all the way since my visit to your old home in Chelsea a year ago. London seemed to be calming down and Mr Pymple was in retreat. No sooner had we entered our carriage and said our goodbyes, Kate, when a bunch of disagreeable youths with circular heads went on the rampage.'

'Now who is using slang,' says Mall with a cheeky grin.

'Your majesty,' adds Katharine, looking at her daughter disapprovingly.

'We don't stand on ceremony, Kate.' The Queen shocks the Duchess by taking her arm. 'When you have braved storms, insolent Dutch diamond dealers, cannon balls...'

'And pirates,' adds Mall endeavouring to keep a straight face.

'Quite,' says Henriette as she guides the Duchess towards the next stall. 'Rest assured that etiquette goes out of the window when faced with such extreme perils.'

'We have suffered a turbulent year too, your majesty. The Scottish settlers seized our castle at Dunluce. Randall was captured and I fled to relatives in Waterford. Then Randall escaped from prison and took a boat for England. A month ago he arranged for me to sail across to Scotland to join him.'

'Protestant settlers attacked your home?'

'Yes, your majesty; we were living happily with our Protestant neighbours for many years, but the civil war in Ireland has ripped the country in two.'

'Why do we allow small-minded people to use religion to break up nations?' Henriette lets out one of her cries of frustration. 'My father proved that it is possible to unite people of different faiths, and in doing so, make a country stronger.'

Henriette looks across at Mall who is studying hats on a stall beside the market tavern. The Queen spies a man approaching in military uniform. She recognises the face.

'George Goring,' she shouts. 'What are you doing here?'

Despite the large hood concealing her face, the new arrival has no difficulty recognising the source of the exclamation, spoken in French.

'I have joined the army of the north, your majesty.' Goring looks around. 'Do I bow or are you enjoying an anonymous shopping expedition?'

'Definitely no bows.' Henriette steers Goring away from the stall. 'Everyone is paranoid about enemy soldiers kidnapping me.'

'They would be brave souls,' says Goring with a grin. 'I have been on their wanted list ever since I defended Portsmouth for the King.'

The dashing chevalier has always been one of the Queen's favourites. His reddish brown wavy hair and boyish looks sealed the fate of a succession of broken hearts. He cannot disguise a slight limp, the result of a war wound when fighting as a mercenary in the European wars.

Henriette

'You served your King – in the end.' Henriette is wary of Goring. Many people believe he betrayed the army plot at a crucial moment in the fight to save Thomas Wentworth. Goring remains adamant that his error was unintentional, the result of idle talk. An element of doubt lingers in Henriette's mind.

Goring reads her mind. 'I spend every day fighting for the King to convince you that I am a loyal friend.'

Henriette pauses at the edge of the market. 'The past is done, George, what matters is the future.'

'Are you planning to join the King at Oxford?'

'I plan it all the time.' Henriette groans. 'Nothing ever comes of my endeavours; either the rebels are too numerous or there are not enough spare officers to accompany me.'

'Let me lead your army south,' says Goring.

Impetuous bravado was one of the chief reasons George Goring became one of her favourite dashing chevaliers, although his critics claim Goring is better at talking about deeds over a drink than carrying them out. Henriette gesticulates with her arms, her hood slipping down and revealing her face.

'The Earl of Newcastle says he cannot spare men until Leeds and Wakefield are subdued.'

Goring puts his hand on his sword. 'Well then, we better go and capture Leeds.'

Henriette grins. 'You always were as impatient as me. The inertia in our army drives me mad.'

'I keep being told that the Queen is the inspiration behind the King's forces in the north. Parliament certainly believes it is so.'

'It is called the Queen's army, but I have little power over it. I can assure you that if I did, things would go better than they do.'

Wandering back to the Queen's lodgings, the royal party recalls happier times.

'Do you remember, George, when we visited Kate's Chelsea home by boat and raced all the way back to White Hall?'

'I certainly do, your majesty.' Goring grins. 'I remember a certain captain of her ship jumping up and down and screaming at the top of her voice.'

'I seem to recall my exhortations worked; I won.'

'A boat race on the Thames,' exclaims Mall. 'How did you avoid colliding with all the ships?'

'They got out of the way when they saw us coming. Harry of course took bets off everyone.'

As the party turn into High Petergate, they spy Harry Jermyn waiting impatiently outside the entrance to Sir Arthur Ingram's mansion.

'Speak of the devil,' says Henriette.

Jermyn appears preoccupied as he approaches the Queen.

'If I could have a word, your majesty.' He steers Henriette through the hall and into the withdrawing room.

Susan is summoned and Jermyn gently closes the door.

Henriette senses bad news: 'Is it the King?'

Jermyn ignores his mistress; he addresses Susan instead. 'Prince Rupert and your husband, the Earl of Denbeigh, set out to attack Litchfield in order to clear a path for our journey south.' Jermyn lowers his head slightly as he speaks. 'On the way they captured a small town called Birmingham where the parliamentary forces had gathered. I regret to inform you, Madame, that during the assault your husband was mortally wounded.'

Susan stares at Jermyn as if seeking confirmation. She begins to shake. Henriette rushes to the Countess and steers her to a chair.

'I'm all right, your majesty,' mumbles Susan.

'No, you're not.' The Queen looks up. 'Harry, ask the Duchess of Buckingham to join us.' Henriette continues to use the relapsed title for her friend.

'He's dead.' Susan stares straight in front, she does not cry. 'William is dead.'

'It is a great shock.' Henriette struggles to find appropriate words of comfort. 'Damn this wretched rebellion.'

The Countess remains calm on the outside. 'Do the children know? I must write to them.' She frowns. 'Perhaps Basil was in Litchfield fighting against his father.'

'I am sure he wasn't,' says Henriette. 'He will be with Essex's army at Reading.'

Katharine enters the room. She looks paler and more distressed than her sister-in-law. Susan looks up.

'He's dead, Kate, did you know?'

Katharine bursts into tears, hugging Susan. Finally this opens the floodgates; Susan cries and wails.

Henriette retreats to the hall where Harry Jermyn is talking with George Goring. They pause and stare at their mistress.

Henriette

'People portray me as the warrior Queen,' says Henriette quietly, 'but the truth is less romantic. I have no desire to extend this fight a day longer than necessary.' The Queen has tears in her eyes. 'Our enemies have driven us to these extremes.'

Grief envelops the Queen's court and Henriette is glad that Katharine is on hand to offer comfort. Only two weeks after the death of Susan's husband, the Earl of Newcastle experiences tragedy with the sudden and unexpected passing of his wife. He absents himself and returns to his estate at Welbeck. George Goring takes command of the Royalist army near Wakefield and promptly is taken prisoner during a reckless cavalry charge.

The stress begins to take its toll on the Queen. Henriette wakes with a headache, which continues to afflict her through morning prayers and during the elaborate hair styling. It is difficult to think clearly. She does not want breakfast; the thought of food makes her feel sick. The head pain also blurs her vision. She sits at a desk in her temporary study and ponders the dozen letters that need writing. Eventually she gives in and summons Harry Jermyn.

'I must reply to the King of Denmark, and to Charles, and I need to communicate with the Prince of Orange about the marriage proposal.' She pauses with her head in her hand, 'and I want to write to Montrose.'

'Can we deal with the correspondence one at a time,' says Jermyn, 'otherwise I shall have a headache too.'

'I am going to offer the King of Denmark a naval base in the Orkney Islands in return for men and weapons.'

'Has the King been informed?' asks Jermyn.

Henriette waves her arms in the air, as she tends to do when she does not want to answer a question.

'Charles has enough to deal with in Oxford.'

'What marriage proposal did you have in mind for the Prince of Orange?' asks Jermyn, moving the conversation on.

'I think my niece Henriette Marie is a lovely girl,' says the Queen, 'and I am suggesting to the Prince of Orange that she would make a perfect match with young Charles.' Henriette pauses. 'Of course we would expect money and a substantial donation of weapons in return for such a beneficial arrangement.'

'Does Prince Charles know about your plans?'

'Harry, stop interrogating me; you are making my headache worse. If someone would get me down to Oxford I could apprise everyone of my designs.'

Jermyn knows better than to labour the point. He sits at the desk, picks up the quill and dips it in the inkpot.

'Shall we start with a letter to the Marquis of Montrose?'

Henriette composes herself. 'I am not quite sure what to say. I have spoken to James Hamilton and he is sceptical of Montrose's plan to recruit highlanders. The King is also of the view that Irish troops and wild scots will not mix well.'

'I thought Montrose talked a lot of sense,' says Jermyn.

'So did I, but contrary to claims in the London news sheets, I cannot overrule my dear husband.'

Jermyn reaches for a fresh sheet of paper. 'Perhaps we should write to the King instead?'

The Queen takes a deep breath. 'I think that is a good suggestion.' She puts her hands on her lap. 'The first thing we must impart to the King is the sad news of the passing of William's dear wife. Charles was extremely fond of Elizabeth Cavendish. We shall balance this tragic event with a happy story about Kate's arrival in York. It is very important to maintain my dear heart's spirits in these difficult times.'

Harry Jermyn begins to scratch the words on to the parchment, dipping the quill in the ink every couple of words.

'I must also nip these ridiculous negotiations with parliament in the bud.'

'The peace party in Oxford is garnering support.'

'People claim that I am against an accommodation with our enemies; I confess I am against a dishonourable one.' Henriette prods the parchment and begins to dictate. 'I hope you are more constant in your resolution. You have already learned to your cost that want of perseverance in your design has ruined you. I conjure you to die rather than to submit basely.'

Henriette gives a nod of satisfaction. 'We will conclude on a humorous note.' She pauses to collect her thoughts. 'Charles sometimes appreciates my jokes. We will write: I go now and pray for the man of sin that has married the popish brat of France.'

Jermyn pauses with pen mid-air. 'I fear your place by his side is sorely missed. There are persons surrounding the King who at the bottom of their hearts are not well disposed to royalty.'

Henriette groans with frustration. 'Here I am, further delayed, owing to George Goring getting himself captured at Wakefield.'

'Leeds is also holding out against our siege.'

'I will never set out for Oxford at this rate.'

'I could lead your army in George's place,' says Jermyn.

'We will suggest this to William when he returns from Welbeck.' Henriette stands up and walks towards the door. She pauses and nods her head with satisfaction. 'I shall take charge of the baggage train.'

Mall enters the room and curtsies. 'A letter has arrived from Paris, your majesty.'

The Queen addresses Jermyn. 'I shall leave you to speak to William when he returns from the funeral; I am not prepared to accept any more excuses for delaying my journey south.'

Henriette follows Mall into her public reception room. Her apartments are less extensive than at former palaces and to her delight they are less cluttered with courtiers and hangers-on.

'The letter is from your former maid of honour, Françoise de Motteville,' says Mall. 'It was sent to Holland and forwarded here.'

Henriette opens the letter absentmindedly as she strolls into her dressing room. She reads it alone. Harry Jermyn is finishing the cypher when the Queen returns to the study. She holds the opened letter in her hand.

'My brother has passed away,' says Henriette in a flat tone. 'The King of France is dead.'

Jermyn stands up. 'I am so sorry, your majesty.'

Henriette shakes her head. 'It's no good pretending we were close. He became King when I was six months old. I don't even remember him leaving the troupeau.' She sits down on the chair that Jermyn offers. 'Of course he used to visit us at Saint Germain, but he was always the King first, and my brother second.'

'Anne will become Queen Consort?'

'Yes, my little nephew Louis is too young.' Henriette reflects on the change of power. 'I got on well with Anne, so maybe French policy will soften towards us.' Henriette gives a half-hearted laugh. 'That would be ironic if the death of my brother helped our cause. He never lifted a finger to assist me while he was alive.'

'We have also received word from London,' says Jermyn.

'About my brother's death?'

'No, your majesty, about you.'

'What has Mr Pymple decided now?'

'Parliament has impeached you, your majesty, on charges of high treason.'

'Good for them,' she says cheerfully.

There would have been a time when the Queen would have flown into a rage; she is tougher skinned now.

'What are the charges, Harry?'

'Smuggling arms from Holland and inciting the King to turn down offers of peace, your majesty.'

'Well I don't deny any of those accusations,' says Henriette.

'They omitted conspiracy to stick gunpowder under Mr Pym's chair,' says Jermyn with a straight face.

Henriette smiles. 'That reminds me, have you sent the shipment of gunpowder down to Oxford yet?'

'It will set off tomorrow.'

'Perhaps we might follow soon after?'

'The army of the north can only spare half the men we originally anticipated. I think if we trade some of the arms from Holland we might persuade Cavendish to provide an extra troop of cavalry.'

'We have been in York three months and it's driving me mad. My husband is surrounded by people who want to make a dishonourable peace and all I can do is write him letters which I cannot be sure he receives. It is time I marched back on to the stage, Harry.'

Jermyn smiles but does not reply. He is used to his mistress's fondness for theatrical analogies.

Henriette walks across to the window and stares at the cathedral before turning to face her loyal chevalier. She has a smug grin on her face.

'I know why parliament impeached me.'

'They want to scare you?'

'I think they are afraid of me.' She puts her hands on her hips. 'Mr Pym is worried what will happen if I reach Oxford. He realises the Queen of the Three Kingdoms is a force to be reckoned with.'

Harry Jermyn nods absentmindedly. 'He's not wrong.'

Act II

The Prologue

She sits on a wicker chair impatiently tapping her foot on the wooden veranda.

'Have you finished, Françoise?'

Madame de Motteville scribbles furiously with her quill. There are several blots on the paper, an inescapable consequence of racing to keep up with the storyteller. 'I have written down Monsieur Jermyn's comment. Is that the last word in Act One?'

The old lady in black snorts: 'Fancy Harry having the final word; I can tell you that didn't happen very often.'

Madame considers it unlikely that it ever was so, but she keeps her counsel.

Henriette tilts her head. 'Did you get my letter?'

'Which letter, your majesty?'

'The one I sent from Gravenhage; Windebank handed it to the French ambassador before I set sail for England.'

'Yes, your majesty, I kept all your correspondence.'

Henriette looks around the narrow veranda overlooking the back garden. 'When Charles sent my courtiers home, I wanted to go and live in a convent.' She stretches out her arms. 'Now, here I am.'

The door opens – Minette and Harry appear.

'We were talking about you,' says Henriette to her old retainer.

'Nothing adverse I trust, your majesty.' Harry winks at Madame de Motteville.

'Françoise and I are about to launch into the story of my triumphant march across England.'

'She-Majesty Generalissima,' cries Jermyn.

'With you, my dashing chevalier, by my side,' says Henriette with a smile.

Minette frowns at her mother. 'Harry, dashing?'

Henriette shakes her head. 'It was a long time ago.'

Act II, Scene 1 ~ Pontefract

A solitary sentry stands on the battlements staring at a distant dust cloud spiralling into the clear blue sky. It is a hot day in June and the mud on the Great North Road is cracked and dry. It takes a lot of horses and wagons to create that amount of haze. The castle is expecting a visitor, but in these uncertain times it is wise to check which army is approaching. The sentry signals the captain of the watch who despatches two riders. High up on the castle wall the sentry continues to track the large cavalcade approaching at a snail's pace. The vanguard of the army is cavalry, several hundred at a guess, and they reach the bridge over the River Ayre at the same time as the scouts from the castle. The old chapel beside the ferry bridge has been converted into a toll keeper's cottage but the guardian of the crossing is unlikely to collect any payment from these travellers. The leading horses clatter over the bridge, followed by a long procession of heavy carts; the sentry reckons over one hundred and fifty. The bottleneck brings the remainder of the column to a halt. It is hard to make out, but there is a large body of men, pikes glinting in the sun, and at the rear the sentry spies more men on horseback. It takes all afternoon for the carts to cross the river, followed by foot soldiers and six cannon and two mortars towed by heavy horses. It will be dusk before the rear guard reaches the safety of the castle walls.

Henriette insists on riding side-saddle despite the heat and dust. She refuses to use the two comfortable carriages organised by Harry Jermyn. The first coach contains Susan, Mall and occasionally little Jeffrey when he tires of his pony or the pony tires of him. The second coach transports the Queen's hairdresser, cook, pastry chef and two maids of honour. Harry Jermyn is hot and bothered after supervising the river crossing.

'Would you like to travel in the carriage for the last leg of our journey, your majesty?'

'My back is killing me, and my backside is aching,' Henriette grins, 'but otherwise everything is fine.' She is wearing a black cavalier hat with a red plume and a tan-coloured dress. She has long since discarded her woollen cloak. She lifts her hat and wipes her forehead with a handkerchief. Her famous ringlets trail down the side of her face. 'I have never been in the saddle for this long before, but I am not giving up this close to our destination.'

Henriette

A rather overweight gentleman with ruddy cheeks and an extravagant moustache steers his lively black gelding alongside Harry Jermyn's grey mare. Sir Thomas Glemham, governor of York, is accompanying the party as far as Newark. The enemy has earned a reputation for daring and fast-moving raids across Yorkshire and the Earl of Newcastle is taking no chances.

'We have made good progress on the dry road,' says Sir Thomas.

'I am not sure my ladies would agree,' replies Henriette. 'The hard surface is not conducive to comfortable carriage riding.'

'We can go on ahead if you wish, your majesty.'

'I am in charge of the baggage train, Sir Thomas, and I must not neglect my command.' The Queen puts her hat back on and points a finger towards her chest. 'I am the most diligent She-Majesty Generalissima.'

Sir Thomas in his fiftieth year is a veteran of the long running European wars. Like all the soldiers, he is impressed by the Queen's indomitable spirit. He points across the river. 'Pontefract Castle, your majesty; probably the best fortification we possess north of London.'

'Really? I have never heard of it.'

'I am surprised,' says Thomas with a smile, 'with your passion for theatre.'

The Queen has taken a liking to her temporary guide. 'Do they have a stage inside the castle? We could perform a pastoral.'

Harry Jermyn shakes his head; he can picture Susan's protests already.

'I don't think so,' says Thomas. 'He begins to recite: "Pomfret, Pomfret! O thou bloody prison, Fatal and ominous to noble peers! Within the guilty closure of thy walls Richard the second here was hack'd to death".'

'Pomfret?' queries Henriette.

'Pomfret was the Tudor name for Pontefract, your majesty.'

'Is that William Shakespeare?' asks Jermyn.

'Correct, Harry,' says Thomas, 'and by all accounts a dose of poetic license; most people about these parts claim Richard was starved to death.'

'I don't suppose it mattered to poor old King Richard,' says Henriette glumly. 'The outcome was the same.'

'Some reckon he escaped to Scotland and died at Stirling Castle,' says Thomas, 'but I suspect that is a fanciful tale.'

'Like the stories in those dreadful parliamentary news sheets,' says the Queen.

Thomas slows his horse. 'Indeed, your majesty.' The congestion on the bridge forces the rear of the baggage train to halt once more. 'Your ancestors have cause to remember Pontefract Castle. The Bourbon princes in mediaeval times were held prisoner here.'

'My poor relatives,' says the Queen in a mocking tone.

'The Bourbons got their own back when I was imprisoned in France,' says Thomas.

Henriette circles with her horse; both rider and animal are impatient for the column to move forward. 'How did you end up in a French prison?'

'I accompanied the Duke of Buckingham on his ill-fated expedition to relieve Rochelle and was captured by your compatriots. I believe I have your late brother King Louis to thank for sending me home for Christmas.'

'He pardoned all the English prisoners to please me,' says Henriette.

'Well then, I have you to thank for my freedom,' says Thomas doffing his hat. 'Much appreciated.'

The cavalcade begins moving slowly forward. Jermyn gently spurs his horse forward.

'Let's get your majesty across the bridge and we can head up to the castle.'

Henriette smiles. 'I hope they will be a little more welcoming to this Bourbon princess.'

'Never fear, it is a royalist stronghold,' says Thomas.

'Just like Scarborough Castle,' says the Queen.

'We are well placed with these two castles and the fortified city of York,' says Thomas. 'We need to defeat Fairfax in battle and secure Hull and then our army will control the north.'

'Don't mention Hull to me,' says Henriette sharply. 'We lost a trick there. I pray that we have more success against Fairfax.'

'He is a cunning general,' says Thomas. 'Fairfax knows we have more cavalry, so he avoids a set battle in open country.'

'The King wanted William to bring the northern army down to Oxford with me.' Henriette lowers her voice, as she often does when about to say something controversial. 'I told the Earl to ignore him.'

'I think that was sound advice, your majesty. We need a strong bastion in the north in case the Scots decide to march south again.'

'The Marquis of Hamilton assures me that the Scottish presbyterians can be persuaded to keep out of the English conflict.'

Thomas nods. 'I pray Hamilton is right. A war on two fronts would be most troublesome.'

The last of the carts roll across the bridge and Henriette and her party walk their horses towards the crossing. The tall ramparts of the castle glow in the rich evening sunlight. It has been a long march from Tadcaster, the journey dictated by suitable river crossings and the need to avoid enemy strongholds.

Henriette is looking forward to a good night's rest, but first she is honoured with a grand banquet in the great hall. At the end of the meal, Harry Jermyn lays out a map between the plates and cups.

'We will have to take a diversion tomorrow, your majesty.'

'Not another twist and turn,' says Henriette. 'At this rate we will complete a great circle and end up back in York. What's the problem this time?'

'The irrigation work around the River Idle has caused flooding.' Jermyn puts down his tankard. 'I understand that the Dutch engineers hired to reclaim the land underestimated the force of water spilling over from the River Trent.'

'Do you mean to say the dour republicans of Holland are thwarting my advance,' says Henriette indignantly. 'I thought I had left that miserable bunch behind in Gravenhage.'

'The drainage work was ordered by the King,' says Jermyn quietly.

Henriette chews on a piece of chicken. 'I shall speak to Charles when I see him. What was he doing asking the Dutch for help?'

'They have considerable experience of recovering flood plains,' says Jermyn.

'Well clearly insufficient experience to sort out the River Idle.'

'The Dutch assisted with the draining of fenland near Cambridge. Henry Rich was one of the chief investors in that project.'

'Don't disturb my enjoyable soirée by speaking to me about Mr Orange,' says Henriette. 'He is a great disappointment to me.' The Queen leans across to study the map. 'Where are we diverting to?'

Harry Jermyn points to a rough line drawn in charcoal. 'We were planning to march through East Retford, your majesty, but the flooding and the strong puritan support in the area will force us west.'

Henriette struggles to read the tiny print on the map. She has shaken off her headaches but the eyesight remains poor.

'Is that Bolsover?'

'Yes your majesty. We don't pass through the village itself.'

'Why ever not?' asks Henriette. 'I once enjoyed the most wonderful masque at Bolsover Castle. I am sure William will be happy for us to stay the night.'

'The Earl of Newcastle is at York, your majesty.'

'I know that, Harry.' She frowns at her companion as if he is dense. 'I waved goodbye to him three days ago.' She looks back at the map. 'I am sure he won't mind us using his facilities; let's send word ahead.'

'I thought you wanted to avoid diversions, your majesty?'

Henriette tilts her head and stares at her chamberlain. 'Susan and the other ladies keep complaining about having to sleep in tents. Here I am trying to sort out a comfortable night's rest at Bolsover Castle and you raise a multitude of objections.' The Queen sighs. 'No wonder I keep getting headaches when people question my every command. What's the point of being a She-Majesty Generalissima if no one obeys me?'

Jermyn holds up his hands. 'I am quite happy to stop at Bolsover, your majesty.'

'In that case, Harry, send a messenger to warn them my army is on its way.'

Act II, Scene 2 ~ Bolsover

Horses canter along a driveway at the summit of a steep escarpment with spectacular views of the Derbyshire peak district. The carriages are two miles behind while the straggling army column is stretched out like a meandering river in the valley below.

The Queen takes one hand off the reins and, without slowing down, points vaguely in the direction of a new building in shiny light coloured grey stone.

'That was under construction during my last visit,' she shouts to her riding companions: Harry Jermyn, Sir Thomas Glemham and

Charles Cavendish. She glances at the Earl of Newcastle's younger brother. 'I am looking forward to seeing the finished interior.'

Charles Cavendish is leading Henriette's cavalry to Oxford and is on temporary loan from the York army. Like most of the cavalier officers, he is in thrall to the warrior queen.

'I shall be honoured to provide a guided tour, your majesty.'

The horses come to a halt in front of a large gate that in turn is dwarfed by a towering keep, built in the same grey stone, but weathered and darker than the new extension. Henriette looks down the steep hillside to where the advanced cavalry is beginning to pitch tents in the deer park. She turns to Cavendish.

'I would prefer to be sleeping under canvas tonight. However, I have agreed to accept your hospitality in the castle, otherwise I fear Susan and Mall might switch sides and become grumpy puritans. I hope we are not disrupting your staff at Bolsover.'

'Not at all, your majesty, William will be delighted that you stopped here. Bolsover is his favourite home.'

The household at Bolsover Castle is less ecstatic about entertaining the Queen at short notice. The lady of the manor was buried four weeks ago and all able-bodied men are away fighting with the northern army. The senior chamberlain and a clutch of servants rush across from the Earl of Newcastle's main residence at Welbeck to provide the welcoming committee. They are caught off guard by the Queen's unconventional arrival. They expect a fleet of carriages and are wrong footed when Henriette arrives on horseback at a brisk pace with just three riders as escort. The Queen is wearing dark tan doublet and breeches with black riding boots having abandoned the side saddle.

'The contrast with my previous visit to Bolsover is stark,' says Henriette as she is helped off her horse. She turns to Jermyn. 'Last time, the King and I brought a huge royal household. It was the furthest north we had ventured on one of our summer progresses.'

'It must have been quite a sight,' says Jermyn.

'Not as spectacular as our army,' says Henriette peering down the escarpment to the deer park where soldiers are beginning to make camp. 'It was also expensive. William admitted many years afterwards that our four day visit cost him three million pounds.'

'He was well rewarded,' says Jermyn. 'Tutor to the Prince of Wales and now Commander of our Northern Army.'

After refreshments and before the carriages arrive with the Queen's modest entourage, Charles Cavendish escorts Henriette around the new wing of the castle and the Queen takes a close interest in the state-of-the-art kitchens, the lavish new staterooms and a long gallery that takes advantage of the spectacular view. Unlike the last visit, there is no grand banquet or outdoor masque in the shadow of the keep. Nor does anyone record the Queen's visit – in these troubled times it is wise not to leave evidence of preference towards either side.

The weather breaks during their brief stay. A fierce thunderstorm sweeps in from the hills followed by steady rain overnight. The following morning the sun reappears and the Queen takes her companions on a guided tour of the keep, retracing the steps that she and Charles took all those years ago. As she circumnavigates the battlements, Henriette points to a motionless fountain and explains that the inadequate water flow was a constant thorn in Cavendish's side.

After a mid morning breakfast her army moves on. As the Queen and her entourage ride into the valley, Henriette glances back at Bolsover Castle. She imagines for a moment that William and his late wife Elizabeth are waving goodbye from the battlements. She looks again and shakes her head; it is just a trick of the light. Two pennants flutter in the wind.

Act II, Scene 3 ~ Mansfield

'Tomorrow we reach Newark Castle,' announces Henriette. 'And so far not a Roundhead in sight.' The Queen appears disappointed by the lack of opposition.

'Let's keep it that way, your majesty,' says Susan.

Henriette is enjoying a pause in her epic march and has organised a picnic with her closest followers. A table and chairs are set up on Crow Hill, a grassy knoll overlooking the village of Mansfield.

'If I may say so, your majesty, it has been an immense privilege riding by your side,' Sir Thomas Glemham raises his mug of ale. 'Sadly, this is journey's end for me. I am required to return to the army of the north.

'You are leaving the stage,' says Henriette. 'We shall miss you.'

Henriette

Sir Thomas is deeply impressed with the Queen's courage, charm and wit. It is in stark contrast to the picture drawn by the London news sheets or the gossips in the corridors of Westminster. The descriptions of a spoiled, bad tempered woman do not match up with the generous and amusing character that he has come to admire.

Henriette pouts. 'Everyone leaves me in the end.' Sir Thomas is about to apologise, when the Queen smiles and her eyes sparkle. 'I am joking.'

'When you look around,' says Jermyn drily, 'very few people actually leave you.' He nods in the direction of his fellow picnickers. 'The Countess of Denbeigh, the Duchess of Richmond, little Jeffrey, Father Philip...' Jermyn pauses, 'and me.'

Henriette laughs. 'Heaven knows what keeps you by my side.'

'Your majesty's indomitable spirit,' says Susan.

'Your pastry chef's tasty cakes,' shouts Jeffrey.

Mall sighs. 'The wonderful masques.'

'God,' says Father Philip without a trace of a smile.

Henriette stands up and touches the overhanging oak leaves. 'I am like Robin Hood and his merry men, camping in Sherwood Forest.'

'Little Jeffrey,' says Mall, 'instead of Little John.'

'Friar Tuck,' says Little Jeffrey pointing at Father Philip.

'Maid Mallion,' says Henriette, giggling at her own joke.

'Who is the evil Sheriff of Nottingham?' asks Sir Thomas.

'That's easy.' Henriette stretches her arms out. 'Mr Pymple.'

'Let me guess,' says Jermyn. 'We jump out from behind a giant oak tree dressed in green as Sheriff Pymple rides through the forest and he dies of a heart attack.'

Susan shakes her head. 'I do believe the country air has had an adverse effect upon you all; you are talking nonsense.'

'We are using our imagination,' says Mall. 'Like inventing a scene for a comic drama.'

'Playing the fool,' squeaks little Jeffrey. He frowns. 'Or fooling the play?'

'That is rather deep,' says Henriette. 'It sounds like a quote from Ben Jonson.' She strolls back to the picnic table. 'You are right, Mall, we are planning the next scene in the masque. For too long, other people have been directing our story. Now I am back, we shall seize the initiative and take charge of the script.'

'So what happens next?' asks Jermyn.
Henriette smiles. 'The Amazon Queen advances on Newark.'

Act II, Scene 4 ~ Newark

After two comfortable nights at Mansfield Woodhouse Manor, Henriette sets out on the final few miles of the first leg of her epic march. A week after departing York, Henriette reaches the comfort and safety of Newark Castle. The travelling has exhausted other members of her court – Susan has a cold and feels under the weather, Mall is complaining of backache after so much time in the hard sprung coach and little Jeffrey retires to his room with dysentery, possibly the result of too many pastries. The outdoor living has the opposite effect on the Queen. Ever since Wellingborough, she has harboured a passion for camping. Communing with soldiers, courtiers and poets around a campfire is nigh on her idea of perfection. The long period of warm weather helps; it has not rained since Tadcaster. She is also buoyed up by the thought that every mile brings her closer to her sweet husband. Henriette is in frenetic mood and Harry Jermyn struggles to keep up.

'Have we heard from Hotham?' asks Henriette as she strides along the bank of the River Trent with her chief adviser.

'His son appeared keen to switch sides,' says Jermyn, 'but he has been captured by parliamentary forces.'

'I cannot wait indefinitely for a reply,' says the Queen.

'I agree, your majesty. Parliament has a strong force at Nottingham and they have put Newark under siege before. It's not safe to stay here.'

'Sir John Digby is confident that the defences are impregnable,' says Henriette.

'They may be, but you don't want to be holed up here for twelve months surrounded by a besieging army.'

The thought of such a calamity concentrates the Queen's mind. 'You are right, Harry, we need to advance. If Hotham decides to give up Hull then we can send troops from Newark. After all, these past ten days we have recruited several hundred extra men.'

'I think we should leave two thousand foot soldiers, twenty companies of horse and armaments for five hundred more recruits,' says Jermyn. 'That leaves us with three thousand men, thirty companies of horse and dragoons and the artillery for the march to Oxford.'

The Queen sighs. 'Charles will doubtless chastise me; I have left weapons at York, men at Newark; he just doesn't understand there is a war going on in the north.'

'There are too many moderates surrounding the King,' says Jermyn. 'People like Falkland and Hyde favour a peace deal with the puritans.'

The Queen lets out a cry. 'Have the last three years not taught us anything? Our enemies cannot be parleyed with. You concede on one issue and they come back with fourteen more demands.'

'I agree, there can never be peace while this perpetual parliament is in session.'

Henriette clasps her hands. 'The King is lost if he agrees to peace before parliament is dissolved; if he does I am absolutely resolved to go to France; I am not going to let myself fall into the hands of the puritans.' She folds her arms. 'I shall live the rest of my life in a convent.'

Act II, Scene 5 ~ Whatton village

The children from the village gather in a gateway to witness the extraordinary scene unfolding in the adjacent field. They listen to the sound of men shouting commands, dogs barking and the dull thud of wooden pegs being hammered into compacted soil. As far as the eye can see, white tents are being erected – a vast, temporary encampment.

The local villagers have no idea that in the midst of this armed host is the Queen of the Three Kingdoms. The arrival of a fleet of carriages gives no clue. Numerous ladies and a handful of gentlemen disembark. No one bows or curtsies; there is no royalty in sight. What the villagers may have missed is a group of horses clattering down the road at some speed, the riders dressed in colourful doublets and breeches, sporting cavalier hats and swords by their sides. There is no one riding side-saddle but an observant spectator might have spotted that one of the group is definitely a woman. A hundred cavalry follow in her wake.

She-Majesty Generalissima

Henriette slides off her horse by a tent set up in the middle of the largest field. The servant with the mounting block is too late to assist. Harry Jermyn and the other officers dismount and join the Queen. The sun is beginning to descend in a clear blue sky as glorious weather continues to bless the travellers.

'Where are we, Harry?'

'In the middle of a field, your majesty.'

Henriette grins; the nearer she marches to Oxford the happier she becomes. 'Very amusing, Harry; could we be a bit more specific?'

Jermyn bows. 'The village of Whatton, your majesty.'

Henriette surveys the hive of activity – men starting fires and collecting food from the quartermaster; horses being brushed and fed while saddles and tack are wiped down; soldiers cleaning muskets or checking the powder stored in their bandoleers. Some officers lie on blankets beside nearby tents with their boots off recovering from the day's ride. The tents in the centre of the field belong to the Queen's courtiers and the army's senior officers. These are surrounded by a second ring of canvas, home to royal servants and bodyguards. Beyond this perimeter is a sprawling camp for soldiers, baggage train and army followers. Henriette has made it clear she does not expect any women of ill repute to accompany the expedition, but it is sometimes difficult to distinguish wives from paid companions.

'Let's get a camp fire going,' says Henriette. As she speaks, Susan, Mall and little Jeffrey appear from two nearby tents. 'It is a beautiful warm evening,' cries Henriette, 'we shall have a party.'

Susan hobbles towards the Queen. 'My back is aching after the carriage journey; I don't know how you possibly manage to ride in the saddle all day, your majesty, and then jump about suggesting we engage in country dancing.'

'A dance,' says Henriette, clasping her hands. 'What a wonderful idea.'

Susan groans and shakes her head.

Three of the officers join the group. 'One of the men has killed a deer, your majesty; we can have a venison feast.'

'Excellent,' says Henriette. 'The ladies will dance and I shall sing.'

The Countess of Denbeigh glances at Harry Jermyn in horror. 'That is out of the question,' says Susan.

'Why?' Henriette is completely nonplussed by her Dame of Honour's negative attitude.

'Because you are the Queen,' says Susan, 'and we are in the middle of a field surrounded by meaner sorts and local villagers and…'

'Soldiers who march for the King are not mean sorts.' Henriette smiles at her Dame of Honour. 'Besides, I am not the Queen for the time being, I am her She-Majesty Generalissima.'

The sun sinks slowly below the sagging roofline of an ancient barn, casting a swathe of golden light across a sloping meadow full of daisies, knapweed and clover. The sun's rays pick out the white rooftops of a vast canvas encampment. There is no breath of wind; small pennants embroidered in rich colours – gold, burgundy, royal blue and silver – hang limp from a host of tents. Thin plumes of smoke rise vertically from a hundred campfires, each surrounded by a huddle of soldiers roasting meat on the tips of swords and daggers. More substantial fires heat large cauldrons of soup and stew. Makeshift wooden stakes and ropes corral scores of horses in the lea of the farm buildings. The grass verges on the approach to the village are home to half a dozen artillery pieces, their cart-horses tethered alongside.

In the middle of the field is a circle of large tents with a bonfire blazing in the open space in the centre. The sunlight is fading, casting a red glow across the horizon. Gentlemen and ladies rub shoulders with soldiers, actors, poets and priests, an eclectic and bewildering mix of travellers. Only one person can possibly persuade all these diverse characters to gather together in a farmer's field. This inspirational leader does not waste time pouring over campaign maps or worrying about the disposition of the enemy; this general prefers to stand on a hay wain and sing a song.

Charles Cavendish stands a distance from the bonfire in the shadow of a nearby tent. 'She is extraordinary; I have never met anyone quite like her.' He looks around at the transfixed audience, which extends far beyond the magic circle of her immediate entourage. He spots rank and file troopers peering between gaps in the tents to catch a glimpse of their Generalissima. 'Does she always have this effect on people?'

Harry Jermyn nods. 'Pretty much; her spell works on everyone except the grumpy puritans.' He winks at Cavendish. 'Her description of the enemy, not mine.'

The Queen is in raptures. This is one of her majestic court masques writ large. Her ladies dance a sarabande and her poets recite verses, although no one anticipates the Queen clambering with the assistance of several handsome Cavalier officers on to a hay wain to entertain the troops. Henriette has not sung in a pastoral for years, but she is energised once more. Her enemies are in disarray. Rumours abound of plots to kidnap the Queen and incarcerate her in the Tower of London. As usual, when the daughter of Henri the Great finds herself under attack, she digs her heels in. The closer she advances towards danger, the stronger she becomes. She has never sung the Arcadian song La Bergerie with more vigour.

Act II, Scene 6 ~ Stratford-upon-Avon

It takes ten days to reach Stratford. Lunch is invariably a picnic in a field and some nights the royal party sleep in tents. There are opportunities for more palatial stopovers such as the royalist held castle at Ashby-de-la-Zouche or the manor house belonging to the Queen's former chamberlain Edward Sackville at Croxall. Henriette is thoroughly enjoying her military pastoral and compares her antics with Alexander the Great. Even Harry Jermyn, her greatest admirer, thinks this is a little far-fetched. Nothing can dampen her spirits, and her confidence is infectious. After Newark, she adds a further three hundred recruits to her ranks.

Parliament is painfully aware of Henriette's triumphant progress through the Midlands but the Queen's enemies are powerless. Prince Rupert has finally delivered for his aunt and pushed back the Earl of Essex's army with a dashing cavalry charge. An obscure officer in the puritan army, frustrated by the failure to act, urges a daring raid to intercept and kidnap the Queen. There is much discussion in the corridors of Westminster but nothing comes of Colonel Cromwell's audacious plan. The Queen reaches Stratford unopposed.

Henriette stares up at the large timber and brick building with its five prominent gables standing proud on the corner of Chapel Street and Chapel Lane. If the Emperor Alexander is her military hero, there is no doubting that the former resident of this house has become one of the Queen's artistic icons. She used to be sceptical of his talents, but years living in England and learning the language has changed her point of view.

'I hardly dare imagine that he once stood on this very spot,' says Henriette. Susan and Mall stand by her side. Harry Jermyn is elsewhere negotiating quarters for the army officers. 'It is less than thirty years since he passed away.' The words of William Taylor on the stage of the Globe Theatre come back to Henriette. 'If you prick us, do we not bleed?'

'I beg your pardon, your majesty?' Susan is exhausted after weeks of trekking across the countryside. She does not share her mistress's fondness for camping. They have located the house where they are to board and she cannot understand why the Queen is standing misty-eyed on the opposite side of the road speaking gibberish.

'Is that a quotation from Shakespeare?' asks Mall.

'Of course it is,' says Henriette, who in truth knows less about the Bard than she cares to admit. 'It's from King Lear.'

'Very good,' says Susan. 'Now can we knock on the door and announce our arrival?'

Henriette is perplexed by the Countess's lack of enthusiasm. 'Your Generalissima has brought you safely this far, has she not? We have crossed rivers, lived in castles and meadows, and met many good people along the way.'

'Yes your majesty,' says Susan. 'But I am a little old for military campaigns and right now I am ready to collapse.'

The Queen stares at the Countess: 'Well try and walk the last ten yards, or do you want Mall and me to carry you?'

Mall can see that Henriette's teasing is badly timed. 'Susan is fine, your majesty; we are all a little tired. Let's go and see if anyone is in.'

They cross the dry mud track. Mall is about to reach for the iron knocker when the door opens. The woman smiles at her visitors and curtsies in front of Mall.

'Welcome to New Place, your majesty.'

Mall points to the smallest member of the party. 'This is your Queen.'

The lady turns to Henriette and curtsies a second time. 'It is a great honour to make your acquaintance and to accommodate you in Stratford-upon-Avon, your majesty. I hope our humble abode is worthy of your attention.'

Susan peers past the entrance into a dark reception hall. 'Is the lady of the house in residence?'

The young woman laughs. 'I have not introduced myself. I am the lady of the house, my name is Elizabeth Hall.'

Henriette turns to her friends and nods with satisfaction. 'William Shakespeare's granddaughter.'

The three weary travellers enter the small wood panelled hall. In days gone by, the arrival of the Queen during a royal progress would have spelled hundreds of courtiers, mountains of baggage and an army of servants. Now, there are a handful of advisers and staff and a single cart of belongings.

Despite, or perhaps because of, the lack of pomp and circumstance, the Queen spends two happy days in Stratford. The heat wave continues into July and Henriette enjoys a quiet garden retreat shielded from prying eyes by the house itself and two large barns either side. There is a narrow strip of grass where the ladies sit out and the remainder of the space is laid out as an orchard with plenty of shade. Harry Jermyn rides south to plan the final part of the journey. With no sign of the enemy, the middle of England in the height of summer appears a peaceful haven. It is during a hot afternoon when Henriette and her ladies are hosting local dignitaries in the garden at New Place that an unexpected visitor appears. The Queen is in mid-stream, recalling and, as usual, embellishing her adventurous march across England. The new arrival strides into the orchard, followed by a giant poodle, and takes off his extravagant plumed cavalier hat, bowing to the Queen.

'Hello aunt, I am commanded to escort you to the King.'

Act II, Scene 7 ~ Kineton

Thomas the blacksmith fires up the village forge before daybreak. He has repairs to complete on the wrought iron gate from neighbouring Charlecote House – no one delivers late to Mr Lucy – and there are half a dozen horses booked in for trimming and re-shoeing. Once the urgent work is complete, Thomas has a large pile of tangled and twisted metal work in the back yard that needs attending to. The damaged fences, gates, cartwheels and farm tools bear witness to the raid on the village the previous autumn. Thomas vividly remembers the huge parliamentary army squeezing through the village of Kineton and hours later the crescendo of artillery fire from nearby Edgehill. The distant dispute in London was suddenly on their doorstep. Late in the day, the roundhead cavalry routed in disorder down the street followed by Prince Rupert and his cavaliers in hot pursuit. They were flush with victory and out of control, rampaging, looting and intimidating the local population. It was a scandal only partially alleviated by a royal clerk of works who awarded the villagers a small amount of compensation several months later. The irony was that most villagers supported the King. Since the uninvited visit from the cavalier vandals, the people of Kineton want nothing more to do with the great rebellion. Unbeknown to Thomas and his neighbours, they are scheduled to appear in the spotlight one more time.

The Queen's hairdresser and her maid of honour spend two hours creating a masterpiece. Henriette wore her hair in various abbreviated styles during the six week march from York. Most of the ringlets were abandoned for the sake of speed and practicality, but today she is determined to look perfect. She dismays her team by announcing that she wishes to arrive in Kineton at the head of the army on horseback. Henriette finally agrees to compromise on her mode of transport; she will stay in the carriage all day and only mount a horse for the last quarter-mile.

Henriette bids her hostess farewell at New Place, leaving behind some rosary beads as a memento. Mall accompanies the Queen. Susan is absent at her nearby Monks Kirby property mourning her husband, who has been interred in the family mausoleum. It will be a bittersweet family gathering, as she meets her eldest son for the first time since he declared for parliament.

Henriette's initial excitement at the thought of seeing Charles is replaced with apprehension. Will he scold her for the forthright letters about war and peace and her bold manoeuvres in the north; will he think her work in Holland was a success or a failure? She looks in her tiny hand mirror.

'Do I look acceptable?'

'Your majesty, that must be the fourth time you have asked,' says Mall. 'The King will be bowled over when he sets eyes on you.'

Henriette has a sparkle in her eye. 'I don't want him to have a heart attack.'

Mall bursts out laughing. 'Maybe you had better be careful later in the evening, your majesty, when you retire to bed.'

Henriette giggles. 'Thank goodness Susan is not here; she would tell you off for that remark.'

'Poor, dear Susan,' says Mall.

The Queen looks out of the window to hide the tears in her eyes. The enemy onslaught over the past three years has turned her into a harder person. But she can still cry at the thought of a courageous man laying down his life for their cause. It makes Henriette even more determined to conquer her enemies.

By mid afternoon the Queen's army has negotiated the tiny hamlet of Wellesbourne with its busy mill and skirted the estate walls of Charlecote Park, a Parliamentary bastion according to Harry Jermyn. A few minutes later the carriage comes to a halt and Charles Cavendish brings up Ruby, the Queen's favourite mount. She is a chestnut mare pronounced moody and unsuitable by Harry when first encountered in York. This was an immediate challenge to Henriette. At only fifteen hands, the mare quickly took a shine to the Queen. Henriette now regularly lectures Harry about how men mistake "sensitive" for "moody" in both mares and women.

The Queen pats Ruby's neck. Henriette knows the arrival of her horse means the King is close by. The cavalry officers cheer as she uses the steps to climb into the side saddle. Little Jeffrey leaps out of the following coach and hands the Queen a single rose with the thorns carefully trimmed. Henriette smiles and places it in the sash of her Cavalier hat. A gentle tap on the ribs and Ruby moves forward, taking the Queen on the last few hundred yards of her heroic march across England.

The villagers of Kineton tie colourful scarves around trees and place ribbons on the handles of open windows. The unexpected appearance of the King and his courtiers has banished all thoughts of Prince Rupert's destructive raid and there is a festive mood in the air. Thomas abandons his shoeing and stands by the door of the Inn watching Prince Charles and his brother James jousting with blunt swords in the road. No one knows why the King has arrived in the village – perhaps it is a stopover en route to battle. Kineton is too small to have a mayor, so the proprietor of the Inn, the local vicar and the largest landowner, a farmer from just east of Kineton, provide the welcoming committee. The King is in jovial mood and takes advantage of the free ale and food on offer. Charles is just over five feet tall, slim but muscular – years of hunting and tennis have compensated for a sickly childhood. He has a high forehead, prominent eyebrows, small eyes and sports a pointed Spanish-style beard. The sunny weather shows no sign of abating; Charles and his senior courtiers sit on benches outside the Inn in the centre of the village, talking and laughing. Every few minutes a rider is despatched down the Stratford road; locals wonder if the King is expecting more troops to arrive.

The first sign of real activity comes when a posse of riders return with the scouts. Thomas recognises Prince Rupert. He is not to know that his companion is the Queen's chief adviser Harry Jermyn. The Prince is unperturbed to be returning to the village where his cavalry disgraced themselves. The two men dismount, bow to the King and hold a brief conversation. Then they both mount and canter back down the road.

Ten minutes pass and the King and his friends finish eating and stand up. When Charles mounts his white horse, Thomas assumes that he is on his way. Instead he remains on horseback stationary in the middle of the road. He says something to the two princes and they return to their horses. The blacksmith is just wondering why the royal party does not move off when he hears a hunting horn. He looks down the Stratford road and gasps. Approaching in the distance are hundreds of cavalry jostling for space; the whole road appears to flex up and down in the shimmering heat. At the head of the troops is a solitary figure. A woman calmly rides side-saddle up the middle of the highway wearing a burgundy satin dress with a grey cavalier hat at a jaunty angle displaying a red rose tucked into the sash. Her black saddlecloth is embroidered with a single golden fleur-de-lys.

The King shares the blacksmith's vision, except Charles knows exactly who is approaching. His beloved wife, Queen of the Three Kingdoms, is making an entrance fit for one of her extravagant masques. Charles kicks his horse and canters down the dry mud road. He brings his horse to a halt a few feet in front of the Queen, takes off his hat and stares at Henriette. She halts and removes her hat. She shakes her head to free her hair and then bows.

'My lord, I have brought you an army and a caravan of weapons,' she says, her voice wavering slightly. 'Most of all, I have brought your humble servant, the Queen, to obey your every command.'

It is a repeat of their first meeting at Dover all those years ago, and again the King is lost for words. He jumps off his horse and runs forward, holding his arms out to help Henriette to the ground. They embrace and kiss.

Thomas the blacksmith glances at the innkeeper. 'It must be the Queen.' He chuckles. 'At least I hope it is.'

Charles holds Henriette by the arms and examines every inch of his beautiful wife. She is more desirable than ever. 'Your return, Madame, is m-most welcome. I think I would have died if we had been separated another day.'

Henriette presses her cheek to his breast. 'I thought about you every hour of every day; I went to sleep yearning for you and woke up hoping it was just a bad dream. Don't ever let me go again.'

'We will never part.' Charles smiles. 'Have you heard the glad tidings? The Earl of Newcastle has w-won a great victory against the enemy at Adwalton Moor and today messengers arrived to tell me that the parliamentary army in the west has been wiped out at Roundway Down. We will soon be m-masters of this country once more.'

The Queen is overjoyed by the news. 'That is good to hear.' She turns to Prince Rupert standing close by. 'And I am told my nephew saw off the Earl of Essex at Reading.'

'The army you have brought south will permit a strike against Bristol,' says Rupert. 'We will take the port and the whole West Country will be ours.'

Henriette is about to say something when she sees two boys riding towards her from the village. It has only been eighteen months but she has to look twice at the figures dressed in full cavalier regalia. 'Oh my goodness – Charles and James.'

Henriette runs forward; the boys dismount and rush into her open arms. She hugs them both. Prince Charles planned to be manly and aloof but the façade is abandoned as he holds his mother.

'We have missed you terribly, mam,' says Charles. He has dark, curly hair and olive skin inherited from Henriette's mother and her Italian family.

'How is Mary?' asks James. He was always close to his older sister. James boasts wavy auburn hair from the Scottish side of the family.

'She is a Princess of Holland now, and she is learning the language and is feted everywhere she goes.' It is a slight exaggeration since the Dutch are fairly underwhelmed by royalty. 'She sends her love to you both.'

While Henriette is talking with the children, the King has a quick word with Harry Jermyn before walking over to the carriage. Mall steps down and curtsies.

'Your husband awaits m-most impatiently in Oxford. You must blame me for leaving him in charge of the city.'

Mall curtsies again. 'It is a great honour, your majesty. I can wait a few more days,' Mall smiles, 'but only a few.'

The King laughs. 'We head for Woodstock and I dare s-say we can permit your husband to join us there.'

'Can we ride with mam?' asks James.

'We will ride together,' says Charles, 'unless your m-mother prefers to use the coach.'

Henriette grabs the reins of Ruby. 'I ride with my men, is that not right Mr Jermyn?'

'All the way from York, your majesty,' says Jermyn. 'The Queen is our leader and our inspiration.'

Thomas the blacksmith watches as two officers carry the mounting block and help Henriette back on to her horse. Henriette holds up her hat and waves it in the air. The soldiers and villagers cheer.

Act II, Scene 8 ~ Oxford

The church bells ring out, bunting hangs from the windows and crowds line the narrow streets. It has been two years since Henriette heard shouts of 'Long live the Queen' and 'God bless your majesty' and they are comforting sentiments. She has suffered exile, dangerous sea journeys, indifferent Dutch republicans and enemy cannon balls. Even at York she felt like a displaced person with half her soul miles away in Oxford. Now she rides side by side with Charles, her two sons a few paces behind, and laps up the cries and shouts of encouragement from her loyal subjects. In truth it is a divided city with mainly university and court supporters lining St Giles. The townsfolk either secretly sympathise with parliament or simply wish for an end to the conflict so that normal life can be restored in the fields and among the market stalls.

The King and Queen make slow progress towards the city. All the roads in and out of Oxford are congested with foot soldiers and cavalry moving to and fro from outlying garrisons. The outer defensive ring of fortified towns and villages is designed to slow down approaching enemy forces. Part of the defensive ring is the village of Woodstock where Mall is given a week's leave with her husband.

The royal party approach the city walls. Charles steers his horse closer to Henriette. 'You see, they love their Queen.'

'I love them too,' shouts Henriette. 'It is the puritans in parliament who I have an argument with.'

'There is one less puritan to worry about,' says Charles. 'Have you heard? John Hampden was killed at Chalgrove when Rupert halted Essex's advance.'

'I cannot profess to being sorry,' says Henriette. 'However, watching Susan's pain at losing her husband I know that a family somewhere will be grieving for Mr Hampden.'

'He was one of the m-moderate puritans who supported peace talks,' says Charles. 'Lord Falkland and Edward Hyde f-found him amenable to negotiations.'

'Why are we wasting time talking to the enemy?' Henriette lets out a cry of frustration. 'The experience of the last three years should have taught us that they cannot be trusted. You give them one concession and they come back asking for ten more. You beat them in the court room, as we did with Thomas Wentworth, and they find a different way to murder you.'

'The talks have f-fallen through,' says Charles hastily.

'Good,' says Henriette harshly. 'Never allow your army to be disbanded until this perpetual parliament is revoked.'

Charles looks at his wife with a pained expression. 'Is it really good?'

'We must break things, and then we fix them.' Henriette turns and smiles at the crowds. When she looks back at the King, her smile vanishes. 'I conjure you to die rather than to submit basely.'

The King ponders his wife's words. She was always passionate, but he detects a harsher tone in her voice.

'I think we can agree that the kingdom is broken,' says Charles. 'In fact all three kingdoms are in disarray. Perhaps the time has come to talk to our enemies about f-fixing things.'

Henriette frowns at her husband. 'The puritans are not interested in fixing anything, dear heart, except perhaps the date for my execution.'

The King and Queen ride past St John's College and through the narrow gap in the city walls at north gate. They lower their heads to avoid the draping flags and colourful ribbons. The crowds are even thicker down both sides of the street inside the city walls. They press close to the royal couple; Charles has to shout to make his wife hear.

'Let's celebrate your return, Maria, and not think of executions or puritan enemies.'

The Queen pulls a face. 'That's easy for you to say; it's not your flipping head they want to chop off.'

Act III

The Prologue

'That was a glorious summer we spent in Oxford,' says the lady in black wistfully. 'We should not forget the optimism, the military successes and the sense of normality, despite our court being squeezed into an overcrowded city with armies roving the countryside around us.'

Madame de Motteville nods. 'The narrator should remind the audience of the complete disarray of your enemies. There were arguments between members of parliament and the army generals, disputes between commoners and peers, not to mention deep unease among the population of London.'

'We were on the cusp of victory, and I was with my dear heart once more.' Henriette looks around her tiny cabinet at Colombes. 'Many of the items I have collected in this room are from those heady days in Oxford.' She stands up with the help of a small cane and walks across to a lacquered cupboard that contains rows of miniature drawers. She begins to pull out compartments, one by one; she knows where each memory is stored.

'This is the order of service for the Master of Arts ceremony.' She wields a creased parchment curling at one edge before delving into another drawer. 'Here are dried leaves collected by the children on our river journey up the Cherwell.' She kisses the final memento and smiles. 'The programme for As You Like It, sans teeth, sans everything.'

'Shall we resume the narrative?' asks Madame optimistically. She has attended at Colombes three times in the last month to no avail. First it was toothache, then head pains and on the last occasion the household was distracted by a sickness afflicting little Princess Anne from England. Today the child is at Saint Cloud visiting Minette; Henriette appears in a more reflective mood.

'The opening scene will require an extravagant backcloth showing the famous buildings of Oxford in their pale yellow stone. We will need to provide some references for Monsieur Poquelin since he has never visited the city. What a shame Mr Jones is not alive to organise the scenery. And I think the audience need to be taken on a tour.' Henriette's eyes open wide; there is still a sparkle at times. 'I know just the person to be our guide.'

Act III, Scene 1 ~ Oxford

'This young man will show you Oxford,' says Henriette.

Mall curtsies. The serious looking character in shabby grey shirt and creased black breeches bows awkwardly. He does not look like a courtier and he is a little old to be a student; the Duchess of Richmond is far too polite to inquire. Henriette continues her introduction.

'John is the fount of all knowledge when it comes to the university. He is undertaking very important work for our cause.' The Queen lowers her voice. 'He is by far and away the most important person in Oxford.'

Mall is desperate to ask who on earth this unprepossessing young man can be. She is familiar with Henriette hyperbole and perhaps the Queen is being over enthusiastic. Mall frowns.

'More important than the King?'

Henriette pauses; she does not wish to sleight her husband. 'Well,' says the Queen slowly, 'Charles is obviously the most important person, he is King, but this gentleman exerts great influence across the kingdom.'

Mall decides that polite etiquette will have to go out of the window.

'The Queen is much praising of your skills, sir.' She looks the young man up and down. 'Pray tell me in what capacity do you serve their majesties?'

Before he can reply, Henriette intervenes. 'John Birkenhead is a man of letters; he edits our first Royalist news sheet.'

The young man searches in a pocket of his doublet, which is folded over his arm. After a wet week, the warm weather has returned to Oxford. He pulls out a creased and torn edition and offers it to Mall.

She reads the title at the top: 'Mercurius Aulicus.'

Henriette nods. 'You must have heard of parliament's Mercurius Britannicus?'

'I thought you always complained the news sheets in London were full of lies,' says Mall.

'They are, but our Mercurius is accurate,' says Henriette forcefully, 'and witty.'

'It takes a satirical view of our enemies,' says John. 'We also report serious news.'

'Satirical?' Mall has never heard the word.

'Yes, satirical.' Henriette looks at Mall as if she is being dense. The Queen had never encountered the term until a week ago. 'I am a satirist,' says Henriette proudly. 'The Puritan Pirate, Mr Orange, Mr Pymple.'

'Calling people names?'

The Queen is frustrated by her companion's discouraging response. 'Satire is taking pompous people down a peg or two.'

'The Duchess is right,' says John Birkenhead. 'We must avoid sounding cruel, or people feel sorry for the victim of the joke.'

Henriette intervenes again. 'Don't bother with "Duchess", it's far too stuffy.' The Queen waves her hand as if to dismiss the idea. 'Only when the King is around do you need to use titles; Charles is bit of a stickler for etiquette.' The Queen links arms with Mall. 'Come on, Mr Birkenhead, begin your guided tour.'

The young man bows and looks round at their surroundings. 'We are standing in the Large Quad at Merton College, which is four hundred years old.'

Mall stares at an empty quadrangle. 'Where are the students?'

'They chose to leave,' says Birkenhead. 'Merton is the only college that declared for parliament and decamped to London.'

'Are you based at Merton?' asks Mall.

'I am a Fellow of All Saints College.'

The Queen is as impatient as ever and takes over the story. 'John writes Mercurius with the King's chaplain Peter Heylyn.' Henriette nudges Mall. 'You know, he wrote that incredibly famous book Microcosmus.'

Mall frowns. 'I have never heard of it.'

'Really,' exclaims the Queen. Henriette had never come across the book until John Birkenhead lent her a copy. 'It's in the eighth edition of printing.'

'It chronicles all the known world,' says Birkenhead. 'It references a wide range of politics, beliefs, climate and geography.'

'Where was that place you mentioned?' prompts Henriette. 'The one I'd never encountered before.'

'Australia, a map of the new land is included in Peter's book.'

'Mr Heylyn also disapproves of the name "America",' says Henriette. 'You see Americo did not discover the continent.'

'Amerigo.' Birkenhead gently corrects the Queen. 'Amerigo Vespucci.'

'Quite so,' says Henriette. 'Mr Heylyn proposes that America should be renamed after one of the actual explorers who found the place.'

'Peter suggests Columbana or Cabotia,' adds Birkenhead. 'I believe the King is keen on the idea.'

Mall is perplexed by her mistress's sudden passion for geography. She looks around the empty college. 'Where is the King?'

Henriette replies. 'Charles has established his court at Christ Church.' As they walk out of the main entrance of Merton College, the Queen points along Saint John Baptist Street. 'It's just a short stroll down there. The Privy Council is based at Oriel College, round the corner. I do believe there is less walking to do than at White Hall Palace. The Compte was right about that dismal place being a shambles – the puritans are welcome to it.'

'There is even a tennis court next to Oriel,' says Birkenhead.

'Charles is either hunting or playing tennis,' says Henriette. 'I sometimes wonder if the rebellion has come to a halt.'

'Is Prince Rupert at Christ Church?' asks Mall.

'The Prince is lodging at St John's College, just outside the city walls,' replies Birkenhead, 'with his brother Maurice.'

The royal party walk up to High Street, closely followed by the Queen's guards. They are met by a noisy and dusty cattle drive. Cows push past stranded carriages and carts, while men and women jump out of the way of the rampaging beasts.

'There are a lot of people to feed in Oxford,' shouts Birkenhead. Once the cattle pass, the noise and dust subsides and general traffic slowly moves again. The young guide points in the direction of East Gate. 'Magdalen College is beyond the city wall beside the river; the artillery is based in the Grove.'

They carefully cross High Street dodging the streams of traffic. As the royal party wanders up Catte Street, John Birkenhead points to the university colleges on the right. 'I started as an undergraduate at Hart Hall and now I am a lecturer next door at All Souls.'

Mall frowns. 'My husband tells me that All Souls houses the royal arsenal?'

'Yes, and the magazine store is round the corner at New College. There is also an ordnance factory on New Inn Hall Street near the Royal Mint.'

Henriette spreads her arms. 'Oxford is the new capital of England.'

'Minus the puritans,' says Birkenhead.

'Paradise.' Henriette points at a large building on the opposite side of the street. A large courtyard is visible through the archway. 'Mr Bodley had the idea of adding three more sides to his original house to accommodate all the university schools. But the day after they laid the foundation stone he dropped down dead. Imagine never seeing your dreams realised.' Henriette cries out. 'I shall probably expire before we manage to regain control of London.'

'James says we have made great advances,' says Mall, 'and now Prince Rupert has taken Bristol.'

Birkenhead nods with satisfaction. 'It will help having a seagoing port on the west coast supplying our temporary capital here in Oxford.' He starts walking towards the Bodley building. 'We use every spare space in the city. The Law and Logic department is a fodder store, while Music and Astronomy have been taken over by tailors stitching uniforms for the army.'

'Does university life continue?' asks Mall.

'In a fashion,' says Birkenhead. 'There are about a quarter of the usual number of students.'

Mall jumps out of the way of a cart rattling down the street. 'The City is very congested.'

'That's because of the royal court,' says Birkenhead, 'and soldiers and civil servants. There is not a spare room to be found.'

Mall moves out of the way of a second horse and cart as it trundles out of the Bodley courtyard, piled high with army uniforms. 'How are we paying for all this?'

'We melt down gold plates from the colleges to make coins,' says Henriette. She watches a bunch of off-duty solders making way for two heavy artillery pieces. The guns are towed by carthorses and the wooden wheels reinforced with metal brackets rattle on the cobbles as they head towards Magdalen College meadows.

The frenetic military activity heartens the Queen. She puts her hands on her hips and smiles at her young companion.

'We are going to beat the rebels, Mall.'

Act III, Scene 2 ~ Merton College

The King appears in the doorway and speaks softly.

'Good evening, my dear heart.'

Charles is always punctual. Henriette is the reverse and usually the King arrives to find a disorganised crowd of maids and dressers. But that was before his wife's exploits raising arms in Gravenhage, surviving storms in the German Sea and leading an army across England. Hers is now a cutdown, leaner court. Charles is surprised to encounter a solitary maid of honour and the keeper of the fire, who adds more logs before retiring.

The Queen's private apartments at Merton College are compact. This appeals to Henriette who has never been fond of sprawling palaces. The staircase in the corner of the Large Quad leads to a suite that includes rooms reserved for the King. Charles has a withdrawing room and a small chamber with a bathroom on the ground floor. His servants help him into a nightshirt before he walks up to the first floor and the Queen's bedroom. The Queen is enjoying their lovemaking. Perhaps both of them have come to understand the fragility of their lives. Charles is less rushed in bed and often sleeps all night with Henriette, returning to Christ Church at dawn. But the intimacy and passion cannot remove the shadow of the rebellion.

As the fire begins to die down, they snuggle under the covers. Charles holds Henriette tight.

'Prince Rupert's success at Bristol is a m-major breakthrough.'

'Your sister was unhappy about Rupert and Maurice coming to England.'

'Was she?'

'She is quite bossy, your sister.'

'She is my older sister.' Charles can imagine there might have been fireworks.

'I think she blames me for the rebellion.'

'I have never s-sensed such an idea in her letters.'

She-Majesty Generalissima

'Well she disapproves of me being a Catholic, that's obvious. And she thinks I encouraged you to take up arms.'

'Well she is wrong, Maria. Parliament spreads similar mischief.'

'John Birkenhead believes they perpetuate that lie to undermine your authority.' The Queen tilts her head towards the pillow as she stares at Charles. 'You don't think I'm bossy, do you?'

'You are a great strength to me,' says Charles with a smile, 'but that is different. I m-make my own decisions. It sometimes vexes you.'

The Queen has the grace to laugh. 'I apologise if I show my frustration. I am driven mad by some of the bad advice you receive. You can always ignore me.'

'I am n-not sure I would ignore you, dear heart. But I do have to weigh differing opinions and make a decision, which sometimes you disagree with. That is why I am King.'

Henriette giggles. 'And I am your Queen, your Queen Mary.'

Charles frowns.

Henriette is harking back to an old argument, but she does not labour the point. Instead, she kisses him. 'So long as you don't think I am getting old and grumpy.'

'Definitely not.' Charles gently strokes her neck. 'Tell me about your adventures in Holland.'

'It was not an adventure, dear heart. The Dutch are offhand; if you saw their lack of etiquette you would probably have a heart attack.'

'Remind me not to visit Holland.' Charles conjures up a vision of the lax Dutch court. 'Mind you, I can remember a certain French court where royal protocol was a little w-wayward.'

'My informal court was nothing compared to the free and easy Dutch.'

Charles moves on to safer ground. 'Everyone here was impressed by the amount of money you raised.'

'You don't know how humiliating it was, standing behind a table hawking the crown jewels to smelly, overweight Dutch diamond merchants.'

'The arms and m-men you sent were crucial at Edgehill.'

'You can thank dear Francis Windebank; he was the one who negotiated with dubious arms dealers in the docks at Gravenhage and in the back streets of Amsterdam.' Henriette relives her days in Holland. 'And if that was not enough, we then had our hard

Henriette

earned shipments intercepted by the enemy, or lost in horrible storms or hijacked by pirates.'

'I was not told about any pirate attacks.' Charles is fairly sure that Henriette is exaggerating.

Henriette pouts. 'Well I am sure it was so. Imagine, after all these hazardous voyages, I had to embark upon the same journey myself.'

'We heard you were turned back at the first attempt.'

'I thought we were going to sink. We were strapped into our beds for five days and nights – imagine not being able to move, not for anything, not even for the toilet.'

Charles wrinkles his nose. 'I think I would r-rather not imagine that.'

'Precisely, those were the lengths I went to, and depths, including nearly to the bottom of the flipping German Sea.' The Queen leans on her elbow and struggles to sit up. 'And if that were not enough, when I land at Burlington the puritan pirate has the audacity to fire his cannon at us.'

Charles arranges the pillows into a back rest and kisses his wife. 'You are truly an Amazon Queen. Everyone is talking about your escapades; Harry Jermyn describes how you led the army from York and recruited hundreds of volunteers en route. Even Lord Falkland and Edward Hyde are impressed.'

Henriette waves her arms. 'They are peace mongers; what do they know about leading armies.'

'Falkland and Hyde have come across from parliament; they are very useful to me.' Charles hugs Henriette. 'If you attend tomorrow's council meeting you can meet them and judge for yourself.'

Henriette puts her hand to her jaw. 'I can feel terrible toothache starting.'

Charles kisses her slender hand and tries a different tactic. 'Your old chamberlain will be at the meeting.'

Henriette cheers up at the mention of Edward Sackville. 'I am glad he is with you. It seems an age ago when he and Harry used to manage my court.'

'So you will attend tomorrow's meeting? We need to plan the next phase of the war effort.'

'We should march on London.' The Queen stares intently at Charles with her large brown eyes. 'The capital is the key to this fight.'

'Remember what we agreed – I listen to everyone's advice before taking the final decision.'

'But definitely no more talk of peace negotiations.'

Charles stares at the dying embers in the hearth. 'You are right, dear heart, the time for talking is over.'

'Good.' Henriette rests her head on his chest. After half a minute of silence she looks up at Charles. 'So long as you don't allow Falkland or Hyde to change your mind.'

'I think you will remind me if they do.'

Henriette nods her head vigorously. 'I most certainly shall.'

'Perhaps we are spending too much time talking about the rebellion.' Henriette sighs, picks up her mug and sips the drink of tea leaves.

'I suppose it is inevitable,' says Madame de Motteville. 'After all, it dominated your lives.'

'Not entirely; despite the threats that surrounded us, we enjoyed a lively court life that summer in Oxford. It was not all doom and gloom.'

'Harry tells me that Merton College very quickly became the centre of social activity.'

'We had to economise.' Henriette's bottom lip drops. 'Rather like now.' She shakes her head slowly. 'I cannot believe my son has cut my allowance, reducing me to a life of miserable impecuniety.'

Madame knows that Henriette is exaggerating but she has the sense not to dispute the claim. Instead, she attempts to revive her companion's spirits. 'It must have been a challenge to conduct court life in such a crowded city.'

Henriette nods. 'I used to hold afternoon parties with hot chocolate and French patisseries. I pinched the idea from my sister-in-law in Holland. We would entertain courtiers and their wives, senior commanders in the army, poets and artists. It was a more economical way of entertaining than formal dinners and better fitted my compact rooms at Merton.'

'I don't know how you managed to adjust so quickly – one minute, generalissima camping in fields with your soldiers; next, elegant hostess at the royal court.'

'I certainly didn't jump on the furniture and sing an arcadian melody at my tea parties.' Henriette's eyes sparkle for a second and then the shoulders droop. 'You see I am doing it again – the rebellion is never far from our thoughts. Take the afternoon we celebrated the return of one of my dashing chevaliers. He fled into exile after the disastrous Army Plot. I remember we ended up discussing how the civil war was tearing families apart. A sombre subject, don't you think, to accompany hot chocolate and honey cake?'

Act III, Scene 3 ~ Merton College

'How is Paris?' asks Henriette.

'It is a beautiful city, your majesty, and I was made most welcome. Madame de Motteville sends her regards.'

'I write to Françoise regularly.' Henriette thinks back. 'We have been corresponding for eighteen years now.'

'She is a close confidante of the Queen Consort,' says Henry Percy, 'especially since the death of your brother.'

'What is your brother up to, Henry?'

'Algernon is at his London residence, although he was in Oxford a few weeks ago.'

'In Oxford?'

'He was part of the peace commission.'

Henriette narrows her eyes. 'I should have guessed; your brother always was a bit wet.'

'He fought at the battle of Edgehill, opposite me, and he says the sights he saw put him off armed conflict for ever.'

'I am sorry, Henry, but what did your brother expect?'

'I think it is the spectacle of Englishman set upon Englishman that disturbs people,' says Henry. 'Algernon believes it is his duty to find a peaceful settlement.'

'My experience of John Pym is that you reach an agreement and then he shifts his ground and asks for more.' Henriette glares at Henry Percy. 'I am not going to give up the fight and then find he is after my head.'

'Algernon is adamant that the Lords would never have agreed to your execution.'

Henriette lets out a cry. 'If you don't mind, Henry, I would rather not test your brother's theory.' The Queen passes him a plate of strawberries. 'What about your sister?' Henriette gives Henry a plaintiff look. 'She broke my heart.'

'Lucy is all over the place as usual,' says Henry. 'She has the Strand mansion and word is that she is close to John Pym.'

The Queen shakes her head. 'I will never comprehend your sister. She was supposedly an intimate friend of Thomas Wentworth. Our arch enemy John Pym murders poor Thomas, and what does she do?'

'Lucy is a mixed up person.' Henry shrugs. 'I think it is partly her strange upbringing in the Tower of London with papa and then the sadness of not being able to have children.'

'So why go round hurting everyone else?' asks Henriette.

'She wrote to me when I was in Paris asking if you were still angry with her.'

'What did you say?'

'I said I did not know, but I guessed you would never forgive her.'

'You guessed right. It was not the betrayal that hurt, so much as the years and years of friendship; presumably that was a pretence because I was Queen and it suited Lucy.' Henriette pauses to consider her long lost companion. 'I never want to see her again.'

Henry bows his head. 'I think she knows that in her heart, your majesty.'

Henriette picks up a jam tart and smiles sweetly. As her closest advisers know only too well, she can switch moods in an instant. 'Now, Henry, what are you doing in Oxford?'

'I am in charge of storing and supplying weapons and ammunition, your majesty. We are based at St Mary's on New Inn Hall Street.'

'Well make sure you look after all the arms I brought from Holland.'

'I certainly shall, your majesty.'

Henriette puts her hand on his arm. 'I hate seeing families torn in half by this rebellion: the poor Countess of Denbeigh and her sons; you and Algernon facing each other across the battlefield, and your sister supporting God knows which side. The sooner we overcome the rebels, the quicker families can start healing the wounds.'

'I understand, your majesty.'

Henriette finishes her hot chocolate and places it on the table. 'The Earl of Newcastle has subdued the north; Lord Wilmot and Prince Rupert between them have swept through the West Country and secured Bristol; we have victory in our grasp.' She clasps her hands in excitement. 'One more push on London is all we need to end this terrible disturbance.'

Henriette groans. 'No one listened to me.' She is sitting in her cabinet at Colombes, squeezed into a small chair alongside her desk. Madame de Motteville occupies a larger, comfortable chair, quill in hand.

'Harry tells me you held great sway over the King on matters of state.' Françoise looks up as Minette enters the room. 'And you have been consulted today about the secret talks with England.'

'Not by my son,' mutters Henriette pushing a small carved Indian box to one side of her desk. 'He has the irritating habit of walking out of the room while I am speaking. It drives me to distraction.'

'He loves you very much, mam,' says Minette.

Henriette snorts. 'I warned him about Scotland, but he would not listen. It was the same with your father over Gloucester. A pointless campaign against an insignificant town while all the time the real prize was slipping from our grasp.' Henriette coughs.

'You must not exert yourself, mam.'

'It's these ridiculous memoirs.'

'Come and see Philippe's plan for our summer dramatics.'

'We produced plays in Oxford.' Henriette's face lights up. 'I remember when the students performed Shakespeare; it was a perfect summer's evening.' Henriette nudges Madame de Motteville. 'It can be our next scene, Françoise.'

Henriette's loyal companion is used to sudden changes in direction. One moment in the depths of despair, the next a feverish outburst of jumbled memories that Madame is required to compile into some kind of intelligible narrative for Monsieur Poquelin.

'I will need more ink and some extra quills.'

Minette scurries off to find the necessary supplies while Henriette shuffles in her chair and closes her eyes.

'The students were rehearsing As You Like It.' She lets out one of her cries – is it anguish or amusement? She nods knowingly at Madame de Motteville. 'The story of my life encapsulated in one simple speech.'

Act III, Scene 4 ~ Merton College meadow

'What are the students presenting, mam?' asks Prince Charles.
'They are performing a Shakespeare play, As You Like It.'
'Will Mr Shakespeare be watching?' asks James.
'Unlikely,' says Henriette. 'Certainly not from the seats; he has been dead for thirty years.' She looks up at the sky full of feathery cirrus clouds. 'I suppose he might view his masterpiece from heaven.'

Prince Charles mocks his brother. 'What a stupid question – everyone knows Mr Shakespeare is dead.'

'You are thirteen and your brother is only ten,' says Henriette. 'You have had three more years to discover that Shakespeare has passed on.'

Charles has learnt to avoid arguing with his mother; he knows he will never win, but he has discovered the art of changing the subject.

'Now that I am thirteen, can I join Prince Rupert's cavalry, mam?'

Henriette is caught off guard. She pauses before replying. 'No you may not.'

'But, mam, George Villiers is riding with the Prince.'
'George is fifteen, the same age I was when I came to England and married your father.'
'So in two years' time can I join Prince Rupert's cavalry?'
'I sincerely hope we will not be engaged in this rebellion in two years' time.'
'I don't want the war to end before I get a chance to join up.'
'And me,' says James.
'Don't wish your lives away.' The Queen surveys the busy scene. A group of young men sit in a circle on the scythed grass at the edge of Merton College meadow scanning sheets of paper. Close by in the garden, builders erect scaffolding on the lawn, constructing a stage and a bank of seats. In the distance, soldiers stand guard on

the city wall watching the activity. Henriette spies Edward Sackville walking through a gateway into the garden. She waves and shouts.

'Edward, it's good to see my old chamberlain again.'

'Less of the old, if it pleases your majesty.' Sackville bows. 'I regard fifty-three as mature.'

'Mam says I can join Prince Rupert's cavalry when I am fifteen,' cries Charles.

'I did not say anything of the sort; you suggested you might.'

Sackville laughs. 'The King put me in charge of your sons at the Battle of Edgehill, but I was damned if I was going to watch from the side lines.' The Earl watches the workmen hammering away. 'What are they constructing?'

Henriette beams. 'An outdoor theatre, Edward.'

Her former chamberlain shares the Queen's love of the stage and between them they sponsored a huge growth in London theatres. Edward's wife Mary, governess to the two princes, approaches across the meadow.

'I am very excited about the play,' says Henriette. 'The plot is very apposite.'

Sackville speaks good French but he is struggling with the word. 'The storyline is relevant,' explains the Queen.

Mary Sackville nods. 'It tells the story of a King wrongfully pushed out of his capital city.'

'They retreat to Arden Wood, don't they?' Edward begins to recall the storyline.

'I think Mr Shakespeare was referring to Ardennes Wood,' says Henriette. 'He probably got the spelling wrong.'

'That's possible,' says Mary slowly. 'There is an Arden Forest near Stratford, so he may have been copying names from nearer home.'

'You are probably right.' The Queen is not always happy to be contradicted, but she has enormous respect for the Sackvilles. 'The important thing is the King gets his throne back at the end of the play.' Henriette smiles. 'I crave a happy ending.'

'As you like it, your majesty,' says Edward, 'or perhaps all's well that ends well.'

Mary Sackville watches the Countess of Denbeigh supervising the two royal children. They have stepped on to the temporary stage and are pretending to act. The hands to the forehead and the wild gesticulating of the arms are perhaps an unintentional impersonation of someone close by.

'How is Susan, your majesty?'

'She returned from Warwickshire yesterday,' says Henriette. 'I believe she is coming to terms with the loss of her husband. It is doubly hurtful when her sons have taken the opposite side in this conflict.' The Queen sighs. 'I was trying to explain to Henry Percy that the quicker we put down this rebellion the sooner we can return to some kind of normality. When I said things needed to be broken, I was not referring to families, but rather the ridiculous situation where a small minority of Commoners dominate state affairs.'

'This afternoon, we decide the next stage in our campaign,' says Edward Sackville.

Henriette puts her hand to her forehead. 'I can feel a headache coming on; these meetings with Falkland, Hyde and Prince Rupert cause me a lot of stress.'

Sackville knows the feeling is mutual but he is far too diplomatic to say so. 'We are in a position of strength. The West Country is ours and the Earl of Newcastle holds the north of England in a firm grip.'

Henriette nods. 'Exactly my point, Edward, I don't see why we require a debate.' She gesticulates with her arms. 'We must march on London without delay.'

Act III, Scene 5 ~ Merton College chapel

The Queen enters the great chapel at Merton College, accompanied as always by her confessor, Father Philip. Within days of arriving, Henriette appropriated the grand building for her Catholic worship. She spends a large proportion of the day attending prayers, Mass and confession. She is convinced that God delivered her from the great storm at sea and from the cannon balls flying past her head in Burlington. He guided the Queen and her army to Oxford. She is certain that the puritans are heretics and that God, with the urging of her priests, will reward the King, even though he is also a heretic. Not even their enemies challenge his divine right to rule his three kingdoms.

Henriette makes a special point of meeting with her priests before visits to Christ Church. Most of the Capuchins in London were forced abroad by parliament, but at great personal risk, three of their number travelled to Oxford. After the service, she sits in a corner of the chapel with Father Philip.

'Our services help to calm me down before I meet my husband's advisers.'

Her confessor smiles: 'Do the meetings cause you great distress?'

'Most of the King's counsellors favour a dishonourable peace at any price, or the complete opposite, like my nephew, Prince Rupert, who needs attaching to a leash.'

'Peace is a noble aim,' says Father Philip. 'But as you say, not at any price.'

'Especially not at the price of my head.'

'What about the other privy councillors?'

Henriette sighs. 'There is my dashing chevalier, Lord Digby, and of course the ever-loyal Edward Sackville. I am not so sure about Secretary Nicholas, he sits somewhere in the middle. At least he comes down on one side or another after a discussion.' Henriette snorts. 'Unlike my old friend Mr Orange who permanently balances on a fence.'

'A rather uncomfortable place to be.'

'I would love to knock him off it.' Henriette holds up her hand. 'I apologise, Father, that is not very Christian.'

Harry Jermyn enters the chapel. 'It is time for the meeting, your majesty.'

Henriette reluctantly stands up and bows to the crucifix.

'I am completely calm.'

Act III, Scene 6 ~ Christ Church

Henriette decides on the longer route to Christ Church across the meadow, accompanied by Susan and Harry. Dress hems have to be lifted to avoid heavy dew. The morning sun casts long shadows across St Aldate's as the party reaches the college entrance. The university's most spectacular quadrangle is unchanged from the Queen's visit seventeen years before when Charles called a parliament far from plague-ridden London. Henriette was new to her adopted country and its strange ways. She found her husband haughty and shy, while the King's favourite, the Duke of Buckingham, was overbearing. The Queen lodged at Pembroke College and schemed with the Earl of Pembroke against Buckingham, much to the King's annoyance. Things are very different today – the Duke is dead, Pembroke has taken parliament's side and the royal couple are deliriously happy, except perhaps at council meetings.

When the Queen reaches the Dean's lodge, the privy councillors have assembled from Oriel College. Lord Falkland and Edward Hyde bow and stand to one side. Henriette glares at them, only conceding a slight nod of the head to acknowledge their presence. She cannot attend Privy Council meetings but she takes part in the discussions that precede them – what Charles calls his war council. Another guest arrives soon after, complete with oversized poodle.

'Hello, Aunt, are you enjoying your stay in Oxford?'

Henriette's bottom lip drops. 'I would prefer to lodge in London.'

Before the Prince can reply, the King's secretary of state walks in. Edward Nicholas was once pronounced ugly by the Queen with his crooked nose and protruding cheekbones. Henriette often initially judges people by their looks, but his work rate and attention to detail soon swept aside her initial, damning verdict.

'Sir Edward.' Henriette curtsies. 'It's good to see you.'

He was absent from the previous meeting; this is the Queen's first encounter with her old comrade-in-arms since her return to Oxford. Henriette and Edward Nicholas organised the homecoming for her husband from Scotland two years before, forcing John Pym on the back foot for several months. The successful partnership led to Nicholas's elevation to high office.

Sir Edward bows. 'The Countess of Denbeigh was recounting to me the details of your successful mission to Holland.'

Henriette notes that he is the first person not to describe her exile as an adventure.

'I did my best to turn jewels into muskets.'

'I have studied Windebank's ledger,' says Sir Nicholas. 'I must say it makes impressive reading. You raised over three million pounds from the jewels.'

'Francis was a great help to me in Holland.' Henriette is reminded of the fishing community at Scheveningen and points to Harry and Susan. 'Everyone in my small court worked hard for the cause.'

'And you suffered a most terrible sea crossing.'

Henriette shakes her head. 'I thought we were going to die.'

'You told me it was fine and we weren't in danger,' says Susan indignantly.

Henriette ignores her dame of honour and walks over to greet another of her favourites, the young and energetic Lord Digby.

'The taking of Bristol has greatly heartened me.'

'Now we can tackle the enemy head on, your majesty.' Digby lowers his voice. 'It is hard making my voice heard with Falkland and Hyde urging peace talks.'

'I thought the negotiations had broken down,' whispers Henriette.

'They have for the present,' says Digby.

'Well they will stay broken if I have anything to do with it.'

The conversation ceases as the King is announced. Susan retires to the adjacent chamber and closes the door. The King and Queen sit on thrones and their counsellors stand in a semi circle before them.

'We celebrate the submission of Bristol.' Charles nods to Prince Rupert. 'A notable victory, sir.'

Rupert returns a flourishing bow.

'Onward to London,' says Lord Digby enthusiastically.

Lord Falkland raises his hand. 'London is well fortified and well provisioned. We will need our southern and western armies, and quite possibly the Earl of Newcastle's northern force if we are going to penetrate the defences.'

'It also means leaving Gloucester, heavily garrisoned by parliament, in our rear,' says Edward Hyde.

Henriette glares at her two opponents; they are always so negative. She is about to interrupt when Hyde continues.

'I believe before we advance on London, your majesty, we should reduce Gloucester.'

Henriette studies Falkland who is nodding slowly as Hyde speaks. He is only thirty-three, a year younger than the Queen, but he looks pale and careworn. He is quite petite with delicate features and his speech is hesitant. He does not sound as if his heart is in the cause. The Queen knows that Falkland fought in the Dutch wars and took part in the Battle of Edgehill. She does not doubt his courage, but questions his resolution.

Lord Digby interrupts her thoughts. 'Gloucester can be pinned down with a small force, perhaps our army from the West Country. The main target must be London. We can win battles all over the country but while we stay in Oxford and parliament controls the capital we are no further forward.'

'I disagree,' says Sir Edward Hyde.

If Henriette cannot make up her mind about Falkland, she has no doubts about the King's Chancellor of the Exchequer. Edward Hyde has a round, chubby face and prominent nose with thick eyebrows. He is the opposite to his friend Falkland, forceful and aggressive in debate. Edward Hyde reminds Henriette of William Laud. In her eyes, both men are ugly.

Henriette decides to wade in. 'We missed an opportunity to take London last year; surely we are not going to repeat the mistake?' Henriette glances across at her nephew, Rupert, for moral support.

'I am as keen as anyone to seize London,' says Prince Rupert. 'But I agree we should subdue Gloucester first. It would be unwise to leave such a large force undefeated in our rear.'

This is not the reply that Henriette anticipated, but she is not ready to concede.

'What about our South Western army?' Irritation creeps into the Queen's voice. 'If they cannot take the town, at least they could besiege its inhabitants and pin the enemy down.'

'The West Country bands will not take kindly to fighting outside their own counties,' says Falkland cautiously.

This morose answer fires the Queen up. 'Are they the King's soldiers or not?' She gesticulates with her arms. 'I hate to inconvenience them, but I would point out that I have been all over Holland and the north of England and I never complained about being so far from home.' The Queen folds her arms. 'I have never heard anything so ridiculous.'

'The Cornish generally look to protect themselves,' says Sir Nicholas in a quiet but authoritative tone. He admires Henriette, but he is not going to be bulldozed by her. 'It suits them to support the King and defend their own land; I would put it no stronger than that.'

Henriette lets out a cry of frustration. 'What is the world coming to? Self interest rules everybody's lives.'

'I think it probably always has, your majesty,' says Hyde.

'Not me,' says Henriette. 'My King rules my life; I hope that is obvious to you all.'

Hyde restrains from mentioning the Queen's many crusades on behalf of her Catholic faith or her personal court favourites. There is a long pause in the conversation.

'I am fighting for my uncle,' says Prince Rupert. 'No one can accuse me of seeking personal gain from this conflict. But I remain convinced that we need to neutralise the enemy at Gloucester before we launch a strike on London. The capital is not an easy place to storm – look how we became bogged down at Turnham Green last autumn.'

'Well I disagree,' says Henriette, refusing to give in. 'We should seize the opportunity of a summer of military success and assault London. I understand Essex's army is in the capital, so surely as we advance he will come out and challenge us.' The Queen stretches out the palm of her right hand. 'There is your set battle; your chance to crush this rebellion once and for all.' She turns towards the Earl of Dorset. 'What say you, Edward?'

Sackville is not afraid of speaking his mind to the Queen.

'I would urge caution, your majesty. If we advance on London and fail, we could lose Oxford. On the other hand, if we secure Gloucester as swiftly as we took Bristol, we have time this summer to march on London. If we are unable to break through against Essex, we have a secure route back to Oxford and we can try again next year.'

The King listens and says nothing. It irritates Henriette when Charles keeps his cards close to his chest. The decision will be taken in the Privy Council. Without Henriette present, she can see it is going to be in favour of the moderates. She decides to have one last try.

'If we fail to win this war…' All eyes are on the Queen; she never speaks of defeat. 'Our failure will be the result of lost opportunities. We lost an opportunity to take Hull and seize the armoury, we lost an opportunity to reach London last autumn and now we risk losing the opportunity of building on the summer successes.' She pauses and stares at Charles. 'Opportunities should be taken, not squandered.'

The King nods but does not answer her. He surveys his privy councillors.

'I thank you all for your advice; you know I value your opinions. The Privy Council will m-meet tomorrow and a decision will be taken on the next stage of the campaign.'

Charles signals with his hand, the meeting is at an end. The counsellors bow as the King and Queen stand up. People shuffle out of the room, leaving Charles and Henriette on their own. The King prepares for a blast from Henriette, but she has other matters on her mind.

'Harry took a huge risk coming back to England, dear heart, and he ably led the army from York to Oxford.'

Charles smiles. 'I thought you led the army, She-Majesty Generalissima?'

Henriette bites her lip. 'That was a slight exaggeration; I did look after the baggage train.'

'Harry tells me you did a lot more than corral the wagons; you boosted the morale of our troops and recruited v-volunteers along the way.'

'Well anyhow, Harry has no title and if he is captured he will be hung, drawn and quartered, which is not a nice end for such a noble gentleman.'

'Not at all pleasant; what shall we do about it?' The King is teasing his wife.

Henriette wrinkles her nose. 'I don't know, could he be awarded a baronetcy?'

Charles pauses to consider the proposal. 'I should think so.'

Henriette hugs him.

'I will be delighted to raise Mr Jermyn to the nobility.' Charles kisses his wife. 'He protected the m-most precious person in my life; it is the least I can do.'

'And who is going to protect the most precious person in my life?'

'You, of course,' says Charles. 'Remember, we are one.'

Act III, Scene 7 ~ Merton College meadows

There has not been a cloud in the sky, the hottest day of a sweltering summer. A crowd of people savour the end of the sultry afternoon as it merges into a reassuringly warm evening. The sun disappears behind the tower of Merton College chapel. Colours saturate and shadows lengthen around the makeshift outdoor theatre. The audience is packed with courtiers, university dons and army officers. Students sit on the grass wherever they can find space. The chief guests are the King and Queen. Henriette walks up and down the terraced seating welcoming visitors and stopping for brief chats. She is in her element, entertaining the court at a theatrical performance. The poet laureate William Davenant, Henriette's soldier poet, is on the front row sitting next to Edward Sackville and his wife. Prince Charles and his brother James sit between their governess and their mother. Henriette in turn sits to the right of the King. Pride of place on Charles's left is reserved for the Duchess of Richmond. Her husband's title takes precedence over the Countess of Denbeigh, even though Susan is the senior lady at the Queen's court.

The meadow has been closely scythed and the cuttings raked away. The smell of freshly cut grass lingers in the humid evening air. Torches surround the stage and line the terraced aisles; ready to be lit when the light fades. The canvas roofing is dispensed with on both the seating and the stage. The all male cast has rehearsed well and they perform to a high standard. Edward Sackville compliments the students – their performance is worthy of a professional London stage. Henriette is glued to the story, which she thinks is both romantic and uplifting. When it comes to the speech of which she knows the first three lines off by heart, she is on the edge of her seat.

'All the world's a stage, and all the men and women merely players;
They have their exits and their entrances,
And one man in his time plays many parts, his acts being seven ages.'

Henriette feels like she has been through more than seven ages, although the performance is rejuvenating her.

'At first, the infant, mewling and puking in the nurse's arms.'

Henriette thinks back to Saint Germain en Laye and the tender embrace of Mamie.

'Then the whining schoolboy, with his satchel and shining morning face, creeping like a snail unwillingly to school.'

She-Majesty Generalissima

The Queen never went to school as such, but there were tutors and a schoolroom and she remembers hating the experience. She is glad that her children show an interest in reading and writing, and she encourages young Charles's fascination with science.

> 'And then the lover, sighing like a furnace, with a woeful ballad made to his mistress's eyebrow.'

That is easy – the fifteen-year-old Henriette meeting her handsome royal husband.

> 'Then a soldier, full of strange oaths and bearded like the bard, jealous in honour, sudden and quick in quarrel, seeking the bubble reputation even in the cannon's mouth.'

No beard but frequently quick to quarrel, by her own admission, the Queen led an army through England, a task she could never have dreamed of a few years before.

> 'And then the justice, in fair round belly with good capon lined, with eyes severe and beard of formal cut, full of wise saws and modern instances; and so he plays his part.'

Perhaps not overflowing with wisdom, she thinks to herself, but tougher and more prepared for life and able to advise her children about some of the mistakes to avoid.

> 'The sixth age shifts into the lean and slippered pantaloon, with spectacles on nose and pouch on side; his youthful hose, well saved, a world too wide for his shrunk shank, and his big manly voice, turning again toward childish treble, pipes and whistles in his sound.'

Possibly this stage is not far off. According to her cheeky eldest son she is already ancient. Her eyesight is atrocious, especially when suffering one of her headaches and her bronchitis becomes more severe each winter that passes.

> 'Last scene of all, that ends this strange eventful history, is second childishness and mere oblivion, sans teeth, sans eyes, sans taste, sans everything.'

Henriette leans over and whispers in Charles's ear. 'I am rapidly heading towards sans teeth and sans eyes; is this my last scene?'

'I pray that it is not, Maria.' Charles puts his hand in hers. 'You are only thirty-three years of age – in the prime of your life, and as beautiful as ever.'

Henriette gives his hand a gentle squeeze. There is a tear in her eye. Despite five years of extreme turmoil and terror, it is a tear of happiness.

'Some of my best memories involve watching open air drama on warm summer evenings.' Henriette stares into the distance. 'Bolsover, Oxford, Hampton Court, Saint Germain…' She sighs.

'Water, water, grandmamma.' The little girl hangs on to Henriette's black woollen sleeve. 'Turn on the water machine.'

'We are waiting for your Aunt Minette and Uncle Philippe.' Henriette turns to her companion. 'This would make a good setting for outdoor theatre.'

Madame de Motteville looks around. 'We should return to the house, your majesty. I cannot possibly remember everything you are telling me.'

Henriette tilts her head on one side. 'I don't intend to repeat myself.'

'We need to find a younger scribe to record your memoirs,' says Françoise, 'someone with a better memory than me.'

Henriette watches her daughter and son-in-law walk slowly down the steep steps at the side of the extravagant, but empty, cascade.

'Margaret had remarkable recall.'

'Margaret Lucas?'

'Perhaps it is time we introduced Miss Lucas.' Henriette stands up with the help of Madame. 'Mall has sent me some notes; she welcomed Margaret to Oxford. Mall was concerned that her bashfulness might irritate me.'

Princess Anne jumps up and down. 'Turn on the water, Auntie Minette.'

Henriette walks slowly towards the steps. 'Margaret was without doubt the most intelligent woman I ever met. Rarely spoke a word, but that girl was sharp. She became a writer, philosopher and scientist; and what did people end up calling her? Mad Marge.' Henriette snorts. 'Absolutely typical.'

Act III, Scene 8 ~ Merton College

The carriage rattles over Magdalen Bridge. The sole occupant peers up at the Tudor bell tower with its thin ornate spires poking into a grey sky. The coach slows down at the bend in High Street before coming to a halt in front of the East Gate of the city.

'Papers,' shouts the sentry.

The coach driver is a stout gentleman in an ankle length grey coat. He heaves his body out of the seat, climbs down the ladder and extracts a sheet from his inside pocket. It has a few lines of writing and a seal at the bottom. The sentry pauses to examine the document before handing it back. He does not speak, but nods to the driver and stands to one side. A few moments later the tall gates begin to open. The passenger looks out of the window; in front of the carriage an archway reveals a crowded street with people walking in all directions, dodging horses, coaches, livestock and even two large cannon on gun carriages. It is surely impossible to progress down such a congested thoroughfare. The coach driver settles back into his seat and slowly inches forward under the arch and into Oxford. Once inside the city walls, the carriage almost immediately takes a left turn into a quieter and narrower lane and a few moments later comes to a halt.

'Merton College,' shouts the driver. The prompt is not necessary since there is only one remaining passenger – a young lady. A fellow passenger was dropped off at the village of Headington and two other passengers alighted outside the city gate on their way to Magdalen College. She steps down from the carriage with the help of a footman from the college. Her luggage is unlashed and taken off the roof.

The Duchess of Richmond appears at the lodge entrance and greets the new arrival: 'Miss Margaret Lucas?'

The visitor blushes a deep red and curtsies. She does not reply. Mall has been warned by Margaret's mother that her nineteen-year-old daughter is cripplingly shy. It is the first time she has been away from home on her own and the family hope it will be the making of the quiet, introspective girl.

'I hope the journey from London was not too much of an ordeal? I am the Duchess of Richmond.'

Margaret curtsies again but still says nothing.

'Please call me Mall. Do you prefer Margaret, or perhaps your friends use a short-form?'

'I don't have any friends.' She speaks so softly that Mall struggles to hear her. She will have to coach the poor girl; if there is one thing the Queen hates, it is people who mumble. 'My brothers and sisters call me Margaret.'

'Then Margaret it is,' says Mall cheerfully. 'Your luggage will be taken to the lodge and I will arrange for a porter to bring it to your room. Let me show you the way. You can have a rest, freshen up and then I will introduce you to the Queen.'

Margaret curtsies a third time.

'Don't curtsy too much around the Queen, once upon arrival is sufficient. And try and speak up as she has a fear of going deaf.'

For the first time, Margaret smiles. It is a broad smile showing plenty of white teeth and it greatly improves her mousey demeanour. Even her blushing cheeks begin to pale.

'Your mother tells me that you are an avid writer,' says Mall.

'Only in private.' Margaret's cheeks flush deep red again.

'I write poetry.'

'Do you?' Miss Lucas is impressed. 'I have always been told it is not seemly for women to be published.'

'I used to think that, but you will discover that the Queen is a great lover of the arts and she will encourage you.'

'Please don't mention that I write,' says Margaret earnestly.

'I think she knows.' Mall smiles. 'Your mother's letter has beaten you to it.'

This appears to worry Miss Lucas and she regresses into silence. Mall detects a melancholic air about the new arrival. The prospective lady-in-waiting will either be declared a romantic authoress and the Queen will adore her, or else Henriette will find her tiresome.

It is a couple of hours later that Mall calls upon Margaret to escort her to the Queen. It is apparent from the number of cases that accompany the young lady and the fittings now carefully laid out in her room that Miss Lucas is not short of funds.

'What shall I say?' asks Margaret.

Mall stares at her. 'You mean when you meet the Queen?'

Margaret's cheeks go bright red again and she slightly bows her head.

'Well try and say something.' Mall is becoming irritated by the girl's reticence. 'The Queen will not take kindly to silence. Answer her questions and thank her majesty for considering you for a place in her court.'

The two ladies walk carefully down the uneven stone steps and across the quadrangle to the Queen's rooms. This is the oldest part of the college and is overflowing with barrels and chests from the kitchens alongside box loads of new supplies arriving daily. The great rebellion has not restrained Henriette's spending habits. Mall ushers the new arrival through an open doorway and up a narrow flight of stairs. The walls are bare. On the landing there is a reed mat and two wall tapestries, but no clue that they have reached the apartments of the Queen of the Three Kingdoms. Mall tells Margaret to wait at the top of the stairs while the Duchess goes inside the first facing door. After a few minutes, Mall reappears and gives her a reassuring smile: 'The Queen will see you now.'

Poor Margaret blushes deep red before she enters the room. Her head is spinning and she keeps thinking what a bad idea it is to join the royal court. She cannot blame anyone else since she made the suggestion to her mother. While she is having second thoughts, her feet move slowly forward of their own accord and before she knows it a small lady with a piercing stare is standing in her path. Mall curtsies and Margaret finally finds her voice.

'Your majesty.' Margaret performs a deep curtsy.

'Miss Lucas,' says Henriette.

There follows a long pause. Margaret is surprised how small and delicate the Queen looks. All the London news sheets make out that she is an ill-tempered and aggressive character without grace or manners. Margaret somehow imagined a figure towering over her; the paintings of the Queen always make her look tall. At just over five feet, Margaret herself is fairly petite.

Henriette senses the need to move the conversation forward. Mall has warned the Queen that it may be hard going.

'How was your journey?'

'It was bumpy, your majesty.'

'It's the unusually hot summer we are having,' says Henriette. 'The dry roads make for a firm ride. Mall complained about the coach journey from York.'

'The Queen rode on horseback the whole way,' says Mall.

Another silence. Margaret is fiddling with her fingers.

'You did not encounter any roundhead soldiers?' asks Henriette.

'No your majesty.'

Henriette

'Your brother is a fine commander in our cavalry I understand. Do I assume he is an older brother?'

'Charles is ten years my elder, your majesty. I am the youngest of eight.'

'I was the youngest in my family,' says Henriette.

Perhaps they have discovered a common talking point, but Margaret stands motionless and says nothing. Out of the corner of her eye she can see beautiful inlaid furniture and adorning the walls there are fine Italian paintings.

Henriette turns away and walks across to the window looking out over the quadrangle. She speaks without looking back at Margaret. 'I understand you wish to join my court, Miss Lucas?'

Margaret is tongue-tied and wishing she had never thought of the idea. Mall is worried that the Queen will lose patience and decides to intervene. 'Miss Lucas writes, your majesty.'

Henriette's ears prick up and she turns round. 'You write,' she says enthusiastically.

'Only bits and pieces, your majesty; merely women's stuff.'

Henriette tilts her head. 'Women's stuff?'

'I realise no one would wish to publish a lady's writing.'

'Why on earth not?' Henriette is interested. 'I keep telling Mall that she should publish her poems. Tell me about something you are writing.'

Margaret is not expecting the question. She never likes talking about her writing; it is part of her private world. The only thing she can think of is a slightly curious idea she has been planning for some while. 'I am writing about a different world, your majesty.'

'A different world?' Henriette returns to the middle of the room and sits down. 'What do you mean? America or the new Australia?'

'Well it's a world that exists separate to our world both in physical space and time.' Margaret is regretting mentioning the project but she cannot stop now. 'You pass through the North Pole, and there you are. It is a land where the animals can talk.' Margaret is extremely fond of animals and talks to them a lot, more than to humans.

Henriette points to a seat next to her. Margaret looks at Mall.

'Her majesty would like you to sit down, Miss Lucas.'

Margaret walks slowly to the chair and does as commanded.

'I am intrigued by your story,' says Henriette. 'I do not quite understand how you can write about the future when we don't know what will happen in the years to come, or do you have premonitions?'

'No, it is an imaginary world, your majesty.'

'A sort of future fiction; can I read the story?'

'It's in my head,' says Margaret. The red flush in her cheeks has subsided because she is on a topic that engages her.

'Then you must start writing as soon as possible,' insists Henriette. 'We will make sure you have time and a desk and quills and paper, won't we Mall?'

The Duchess of Richmond smiles. The Queen is going to take Miss Lucas under her wing.

'I shall also introduce you to John Birkenhead,' says Henriette.

'The editor of Mercurius Aulicus?' Margaret puts her hands to her cheeks, which are burning again.

'You have heard of him?'

'His news sheet is the talk of London,' says Margaret. 'Everyone is asking: who is this John Birkenhead?'

'He is from All Souls College and he and an associate are writing the first ever royalist newspaper. You must also meet William.'

'William Davenant,' explains Mall.

'The poet laureate?' It dawns on Margaret why her mother encouraged her to join the Queen's circle.

'You missed a wonderful production of As You Like It,' says Henriette. 'But never fear, we are hoping the students will perform several more plays.'

Margaret's head begins to drop again.

'What is the matter, my dear?' asks Henriette.

'I am not good in company,' says Margaret. 'I have morose tendencies which lead me to say very little and I wave my hands about in a panic.'

Henriette's head is on one side again, as if she is studying a strange creature. 'I have morose tendencies which have the opposite effect – I talk very quickly and say ridiculous things.' The Queen gesticulates with her arms. 'And I wave my arms and hands about, which is often commented on, especially by the King.' The Queen puts a hand on Margaret's arm. 'It strikes me, Miss Lucas, that we should suit each other very well. I shall encourage you to say something and you can tell me to shut up.'

Mall laughs, but Margaret stares at the Queen in a state of extreme anxiety. 'I could not possibly tell your majesty to stop talking.'

Henriette smiles. 'My dear, once you have listened to me jabbering complete nonsense for a while you will be more than happy to beg me to desist.' The Queen looks up at Mall. 'Is that not right, Mall?'

'Without a doubt, your majesty,' says the Duchess of Richmond with a cheeky grin.

Act III, Scene 9 ~ Christ Church

The clerk to the Privy Council is out of breath by the time he reaches the top of the staircase in Oriel College. He knocks loudly on Secretary Sir Edward Nicholas's study door.

After some delay the door opens.

'Sir Edward,' wheezes the messenger, 'the Queen is on her way to Christ Church and from all accounts she is not in the best of tempers.'

Nicholas frowns. 'Whatever is the matter?'

'The Earl of Montrose arrived this afternoon at Christ Church. Upon discovering the King has left for Gloucester, he requested an audience with the Queen. Apparently her majesty is indisposed but feels obliged to attend the Earl and make him welcome.'

'Why was I not informed?' Sir Edward raises his eyes to the ceiling. 'We better repair to Christ Church forthwith.'

Fortunately, they arrive at Christ Church before the Queen. They find the Earl of Montrose and his two companions sitting in the ground floor reception room of the Dean's lodgings where the King holds his audiences. Before Sir Edward has an opportunity to speak, Henriette arrives, accompanied by Susan and Mall.

'I must apologise that the King was not here to meet you,' says Henriette, making no effort to conceal her irritation. 'The army is besieging Gloucester and Charles has been persuaded to go in person, which gives us no small dissatisfaction. As usual, last minute advice swayed his decision.'

Edward Nicholas knows the Queen is referring to Prince Rupert who talked the King into riding with the army.

She-Majesty Generalissima

Henriette flings her arms about in frustration. 'You see, the place is empty. We must hope that Essex and his army do not decide to march on Oxford while our forces are busy studying the architecture of the city walls at Gloucester.'

'I must speak to the King,' says Montrose. 'The situation in Scotland is causing my supporters much alarm.'

'We received a letter from James Hamilton explaining that he is talking with the Scottish parliament,' says Henriette. 'What is alarming about that?'

'My intelligence tells a different story, your majesty. Our government is about to sign a pact with the English parliament to bring their army south.'

Henriette pauses to absorb this potentially catastrophic news. She ushers Montrose into the King's reception chamber. Only Sir Edward Nicholas follows them through.

The Queen stares intently at Montrose: 'Go immediately to Gloucester and inform the King. I cannot prevail on his majesty; perhaps he will listen to you.'

'If I can beg a change of horses, your majesty, we shall set off as soon as possible.'

'Edward, arrange fresh horses for the Earl and his friends.' She looks up at the tall highlander. 'I fear we have been listening to the wrong adviser. You must impress upon the King the urgency of the matter. If the Scots join with the English parliament, our control of the north will be in jeopardy.'

Montrose bows and kisses the Queen's hand. He and his officers follow the Secretary of State in the direction of the stables.

Henriette walks into the ante-chamber. 'Susan, we shall arrange a meal for our travellers before they set off.'

The Countess curtsies and makes for the door. She stands aside to let Sir Edward Nicholas back in.

The Queen clutches her mouth. 'I have dreadful toothache.'

'Shall I request the physician to attend, your majesty?'

'They will only give me some foul paste. Come and sit down Edward.'

He sits at the table. 'If Montrose is correct, your majesty, and the Scottish army links with the English puritans, it spells trouble.'

The Queen makes no effort to hide her anger. 'In the midst of all this, Prince Rupert has persuaded Charles to swan over to Gloucester to watch a siege. There cannot be an awful lot to excite one at a siege surely until it is resolved and the town is taken?'

'The latest news this morning suggests that Gloucester is holding out,' says Nicholas. 'I don't think it is going to be as straightforward as Bristol.'

'We should have advanced on London,' mutters the Queen, holding her jaw.

Sir Edward is too much of a diplomat to be drawn. 'History is made up of "what ifs" your majesty.'

'What if Charles had married the Infanta of Spain and I had married the Count de Soissons as mama originally planned?' Henriette groans. 'What if Archbishop Laud had not commissioned a new prayer book? What if John Pym had fallen down some stairs and broken his neck before making his big speech about the King's personal rule? What if I didn't have toothache.' The Queen cries out in frustration. 'I shall visit my chapel with Father Philip, feed the monkeys and take the dogs for a walk in Merton meadow. Then I shall be calm again.'

Sir Edward Nicholas smiles. 'That sounds a much better treatment for toothache, your majesty, than an unpleasant tasting physic.'

Henriette stands up and walks to the door. She turns and glares at the King's Secretary of State. 'Find out what you can about affairs in Scotland. James Hamilton says one thing, and the Earl of Montrose says another and I am increasingly inclined to believe what Montrose tells us.'

Sir Edward bows. 'I shall make discreet enquiries, your majesty.'

'Scotland,' muses Henriette, 'it was the bane of our lives. And to think, Charles was born a Scot. I maintain that irony is a cruel bedfellow.'

Madame de Motteville studies the small scrunched up figure in black sitting on the veranda at Chaillot. She knows it will not do to feel sorry for the once spirited Princess of France. Henriette rarely indulges in self-pity these days. Nevertheless, Françoise shares her companion's sense of disbelief – how can a life fall apart so abruptly and so absolutely? Not once but several times. The first occasion culminating in Henriette and Charles fleeing London, the famous night when the whole family ended up sleeping in one bed. Before Madame can absorb the full implications of the second mounting tragedy, Henriette interrupts.

'Let's cheer the audience up with a happy scene.' A sparkle momentarily flashes into her eyes. 'I don't want people to think our life that summer was universally depressing.'

'Will this be the graduation ceremony?'

'Not yet; I am thinking of the boat trip, when the sun shone and Roundhead armies were far from our thoughts.'

'I thought the enemy was approaching fast.'

'Well we didn't know that.' Henriette raises her eyes skyward. 'Obviously, Françoise, if we had known the main Parliamentary army was a few miles from a totally undefended Oxford, it might have been a somewhat less cheerful scene.' Henriette vigorously sways in her rocking chair, staring out at the barges on the River Seine. 'If we use hindsight in these memoirs, we might as well abandon the project because the audience will commit suicide before we get to the final act.' Henriette glares at her long suffering companion. 'Now can we proceed with some joyous actions?'

Act III, Scene 10 ~ River Cherwell

The flat-bottomed craft drifts slowly away from a dilapidated wooden jetty at Magdalen Bridge and heads up stream against the gentle current.

'Land ahoy,' shouts young James.

Prince Charles shakes his head. 'Well of course there is land, stupid; it's a river.'

'Don't call your brother stupid,' says Mary Sackville. 'I am your governess and I will decide if anyone is wise or foolish. Although we have suspended lessons today for the river journey, let us employ our time usefully. Someone tell me what kind of tree we are passing.

'An oak tree,' says the Prince of Wales.

'Correct. Tell your brother how you identified it so.'

'The shape of the leaf with fingers on each side.' Charles breaks into his usual charming smile. 'And the branches spread out; it is a perfect tree for climbing.'

'And that tree?' asks Mary.

Henriette

Charles pulls a face. 'A willow?'

'No, the one drooping over the water next to it is a willow,' says Mary Sackville. 'It is a beech tree. When we stop for a picnic we shall collect as many different shaped leaves as we can find.'

Henriette watches her children from the comfort of a deck chair. She is in conversation with Susan.

'My sons are growing up so fast; soon they will be old enough to join the army. I have to admit the thought fills me with dread.'

'I pray the rebellion will be over in the next year,' says Susan.

'We just need one decisive victory against their main army, then perhaps we can plan for peace.'

Two men propel the vessel with paddles near the bow, assisted by a navigator with a long pole at the stern pushing against the muddy riverbed and using the staff as a rudder. Henriette has seen paintings of Venice and insists they are travelling in a gondolier, even though the boat is nothing of the sort. It is a narrow barge with a shallow draft that is used to transport goods from Oxford to Banbury on the River Cherwell. The Thames is navigable from London to Oxford, but only light vessels can travel further inland.

It is the Queen's idea to requisition the boat for a summer idyll. Sir Edward Nicholas is horrified and deploys cavalry and soldiers along the riverbank to protect the royal travellers. The destination is a manor house at Hampton Gay and the ladies bring a picnic to eat in the grounds. Susan, Mall, Margaret Lucas and Mary Sackville accompany Henriette, along with the two princes. The editor of Mercurius Aulicus acts as guide.

The Queen stares across at John Birkenhead who is sketching the riverbank. 'Tell us the story of this manor house we are visiting.'

'It is owned by Katharine Fenner, a widow, who my family is well acquainted with. She has relocated to her property in Eynsham as she feels isolated at the manor in such troubled times.'

'Is it empty?' asks Henriette.

'Aside from a handful of servants,' says Birkenhead. 'Katharine is happy for us to use the grounds; she has asked me to check on the interior condition and to make sure the few remaining villagers are in good spirits. Most of the village is dilapidated and empty.'

'Because of the rebellion?' asks Mall.

'No, because of the enclosures,' says Birkenhead. 'Katharine's great grandfather bought the manor house and used his fortune to enclose large sections of arable fields on the estate. He converted the land to pasture.'

'How did he make his money?' asks Susan.

'He was a glove maker,' says Birkenhead. 'Wool was a staple of his trade and he wanted to graze sheep. The villagers relied on the common land for growing wheat, as did the village mill. There were riots and the ringleaders were arrested, taken to London and hung, drawn and quartered.'

'That seems excessive,' says Henriette.

'The villagers did not die in vain,' says Birkenhead. 'A few years later parliament passed a law that required all land in Oxfordshire enclosed since Queen Elizabeth's reign to be returned to arable farming.'

'That was when parliament did sensible things,' says the Queen. 'Why can't we have reasonable parliaments?'

'The village is just up ahead.' Birkenhead avoids answering the Queen's question. 'You can see the top of the manor house and the church tower. We will tie up near the mill.'

The party disembark. Margaret Lucas has said nothing all journey so the Queen takes her arm as they walk up the track towards the gates of the manor house. Margaret is unused to such informality and immediately blushes. The more she tries to avoid red cheeks, the worse they become.

'What do you think of the countryside around Oxford, Miss Lucas?'

'It's beautiful, your majesty.'

'Does it not inspire you to write?'

'Most certainly,' says Margaret.

'William Davenant has written lots of poetry since his stay in Oxford,' says Henriette. 'He was showing me some poems about the battles, and another that celebrates the distinctive Cotswold countryside.'

Margaret continues to walk with the Queen in silence.

'Are you happily settled at court?' asks Henriette.

'Most certainly, your majesty.' In reality, Margaret is torn between the rich royal lifestyle with its literary and artistic opportunities, and the guilty feeling that it is a slight irrelevance at a time of such torment for the kingdom. But she never admits her private thoughts to anyone, least of all the Queen.

Henriette

'I like to maintain an air of normality at court.' It is as if the Queen has read Margaret's thoughts. 'The reason I went to Holland and fought tooth and nail to get back to my husband's side is because I want to defeat the rebels. I will enjoy our river trip, but there is not a moment when I don't think of the siege at Gloucester or my good friend William Cavendish and his army in the north.'

'Yes your majesty.' Margaret cannot think of anything to say. She is taken aback that the Queen feels the need to explain her thoughts to someone so lowly.

Henriette smiles. 'Your brother is with Prince Rupert at Gloucester?'

'Yes, your majesty.'

'Is it not hard to imagine the heat of battle when we are strolling through such peaceful countryside? It is our duty while the menfolk are away fighting to maintain the dignity of court life. When they return, it must be to a calm and welcoming home.'

Prince Charles is listening to his mother. 'Mam, can James and I join our father at Gloucester?'

'Absolutely not,' says Henriette.

'But, mam, how am I going to learn the art of war?' Charles pauses and thinks about the best way to persuade his mother. He has inherited her charm and quick wit. 'You don't want me to be plunged, unprepared, into the heat of battle.'

'Perhaps the Prince of Wales has a point,' says Mall.

'Don't encourage him.' The Queen glares at the Duchess.

Mall shrugs her shoulders. 'Perhaps if they just watch from a safe distance; it is a siege after all, not a battle. Charles and James were present at Edgehill.'

'The Earl of Dorset looked after us,' says Charles.

'Please, mam, can we visit Gloucester?' James tugs at her dress.

Henriette sighs. 'Only as spectators, and you will take your Governess and a troop of soldiers as bodyguards.'

'Brilliant,' shouts Charles. 'Thank you, mam; you are the best mother.'

A servant from the manor house chats with John Birkenhead, opening the gates to allow the royal party inside the grounds. He bows to the Queen as she strolls up the drive and heads towards the lawn. The long grass is in need of a scythe.

'We shall put our chairs and blankets down here,' says Henriette, pointing to a shady patch underneath a large sycamore tree. 'And

Prince Charles will tell us what kind of tree we are seated beneath. As the future King, you need to know about trees as well as battles.'

Charles and James clutch at a branch that is dipping down towards the ground. 'Is it a beech, mam?' asks James.

Henriette does not know. 'Ask your governess; she is the nature expert.' The Queen sighs. 'I shall miss Mary when she takes over as governess of Elizabeth and Henry.'

'What are you expert at, mam?' asks Charles.

Henriette pulls a face and thinks about the question. 'Masques.' She pauses to remember something her mother once said, 'and keeping people cheerful through difficult times.' Again the Queen pauses, before smiling and stretching out her arms, 'and leading armies.'

Act III, Scene 11 ~ Hart Hall

The river journey is only a brief respite from the stultifying atmosphere of an overcrowded and overheated Oxford. Henriette escapes Merton College whenever she can. She points out that carriage journeys are fairly pointless as the streets are congested with courtiers, citizens and soldiers. Edward Nicholas compromises on three bodyguards when the Queen walks within the confines of the city walls. Today she is visiting Hart Hall.

'Has it arrived?' asks Henriette as she crosses the threshold of John Birkenhead's office.

'Hot off the letterpress, your majesty.'

Henriette grabs a copy and sits down on a chair by the fireplace. It is an overcast, muggy August day – the stone hearth is empty and the latticed windows wide open. Mall and Margaret are also presented with the latest edition of Mercurius Aulicus. Henriette loves to visit John Birkenhead on publication day.

'Where is Mr Heylyn?'

'Peter is organising the two carts for London, your majesty.'

'When I was in London,' says Margaret, surprising herself at her boldness, 'the enemy did their best to destroy copies.'

'We use various smokescreens,' says Birkenhead. 'The newspaper is usually smuggled into the capital beneath a delivery of vegetables or wool.'

Henriette

'How do we distribute the news sheet?' asks Mall.

'Copies at twenty shillings are distributed to women, eager to earn money while their husbands are away fighting. They sell the paper to wealthy people for up to three pounds.'

'It frustrates me,' says Henriette, 'that such a high price restricts the readership.'

'It is the same with the parliamentary newspapers,' says Birkenhead. 'Bear in mind, copies are shared or posted on walls for those who can read. If the edition sells out, enterprising London printers reprint the title. Parliamentary supporters have been known to produce fake versions with new content adverse to our cause.'

Mall and Margaret shake their heads at this revelation.

Henriette is absorbed reading the front page. 'Look at the report on the battle of Adwalton Moor.' She is hardly able to contain her excitement. 'We must send copies to the Earl of Newcastle and his army; they will be cheered to see a printed account of their victory.'

Mall finds the article and begins to read aloud: 'The Earl of Newcastle's army swept aside the parliamentary force led by Colonel Fairfax.'

Margaret continues to shake off her shyness, adding: 'The news sheet reports the battle was fought on the last day of June.'

Henriette puts the paper down on her lap. 'Is it not extraordinary to consider that we are reading in print an account of a battle that only took place seven weeks ago. Who would have thought a news sheet could be so up to date?'

'That is the power and speed of the printing press,' says Birkenhead. 'Not only can we report up-to-date events but we can quickly distribute the account to many people.'

Henriette picks the paper up again. 'Mercurius Aulicus is so much more professional than those pamphlets that our enemies distribute in London.'

'We use skilled compositors who make up pages in less than a day,' says Birkenhead. 'I must take you to the printers to see the Aulicus being produced. It is a fascinating art.'

'I would very much like to see that.' Henriette turns to Margaret. 'You are very animated this morning, my dear.'

Margaret almost drops the paper and her cheeks go red. 'It is such an inspirational publication, your majesty. Have you seen the account of Roundhay Down?'

The Queen dives back into the paper. Her English is weak as is her eyesight and the tiny type is a challenge. 'Read it to us, Margaret.'

Miss Lucas clears her voice. 'Prince Maurice rode with his cavalry to Oxford and informed the King that royalist forces were under siege in the unfortified town of Devizes. Lord Wilmot, Lieutenant General of the King's Horse, returned with the Prince to the beleaguered town.'

'Good old Wilmot,' says Henriette. 'He doesn't get captured by the enemy like George Goring or sit on fences in the manner of Henry Rich.' Lord Wilmot is rapidly becoming one of the Queen's favourite chevaliers.

Margaret continues: 'During a daring charge against the parliamentary army on higher ground at Roundway Down the enemy cavalry were routed. The King's cavalry then turned and with the help of men from Devizes killed over a thousand enemy soldiers, capturing six hundred more along with their artillery. The parliamentary army of the West is no more.'

Mall shrieks. 'Look at the title of the article, your majesty.'

Henriette peers at the news sheet. 'Oh my God – An eye witness report of the Battle of Runaway Down.' She gives John Birkenhead a mischievous grin. 'That is unkind.'

'It's satire,' says Birkenhead.

'It's bloody brilliant,' says Henriette.

Margaret's cheeks flush bright red.

The Queen grips the news sheet tightly. 'I believe these victories put us in the ascendancy. I just pray this diversion in Gloucester does not harm our cause.' She lets out a cry of frustration. 'We are besieging the wrong city. I told them…'

A knock on the door interrupts Henriette.

Sir Edward Nicholas's chief clerk appears. 'The Secretary of State sends his compliments, your majesty. Messengers have arrived from Gloucester.'

Act III, Scene 12 ~ Merton College

Henriette stands beside Margaret Lucas in the centre of Merton College quad watching her staff slowly dismantle a sturdy wooden crate.

Henriette

'Where on earth has it come from?' asks the Queen.

'It arrived on a cart from a place called Burlington, your majesty.'

'That is remarkably good timing, Margaret.' Henriette clasps her hands. 'They sent a consignment when I was at York. It was a sort of thank you for visiting their village.'

Margaret walks across and peers into the open crate. 'There are blocks of ice, your majesty.'

'Very probably,' says Henriette as she heads towards the kitchens. 'I must have a word with the chef about our banquet.' She grins at Margaret. 'We have solved the main course for our honoured guests from Gloucester.'

Margaret frowns.

'Fresh fish from the German Sea,' says Henriette, disappearing through a door in the corner of the quad.

Margaret runs to catch up. She finds Henriette with a pair of her trusted French chefs, two of the handful of survivors of the purge of her court seventeen years ago. Despite the food shortages in Oxford, they are discussing an ingenious seven-course banquet. Mall joins Margaret in the doorway.

Henriette looks up. 'We must have entertainment for our guests from Gloucester. Mall, you can recite poems.'

The Duchess of Richmond looks horrified.

'And we shall ask the students to perform a series of tableaux between the courses. They are in the middle of rehearsals for Measure for Measure; we can use extracts from the play'

Little Jeffrey appears between Mall and Margaret. 'I shall perform my latest magic tricks, and I can juggle too.'

Henriette nods her approval. 'Excellent, Jeffrey, but don't try and do both at the same time.'

A servant enters by the side door to the kitchen. 'Your majesty, the guests have arrived.'

Henriette rushes back to the front courtyard in time to greet the evening's special guests, the Duke of Richmond and Henry Percy. Mall has spent most of the afternoon with her husband. The Queen is anxious to hear the latest news from the siege, but the first priority is her family.

'How are Prince Charles and young James?'

'Very well and much intrigued by the siege equipment,' says the Duke.

Henriette glares at Mall's husband. 'I trust, James, that they are not allowed near the frontline. I specifically told Charles they must be kept out of artillery range.'

'They are staying at our headquarters at Matson House, which is out in the countryside sheltered by Robinswood Hill – they are perfectly safe, your majesty. Besides the enemy is not firing on our lines. I think they are running out of ammunition – as we are.'

Henriette folds her arms. 'Don't tell me you have used all that gunpowder I sent from Holland; there were shiploads of the stuff.'

Henry Percy is in charge of munitions: 'I fear the battle at Roundway and the sieges of Bristol and Gloucester have reduced stocks to a low level.'

'Battle of Runaway,' says Henriette with a glint in her eye.

'I beg your pardon, your majesty?'

The Queen signals her companion. Poor Margaret's cheeks are bright red as she dutifully supplies the Duke of Richmond and Henry Percy with copies of Mercurius Aulicus.

The Queen moves closer to the Duke and points at the front page. 'Read the article on the bottom left, or rather read the introductory heading.'

Henry Percy laughs as he sees John Birkenhead's deliberate misspelling. 'I must take some of these news sheets to Gloucester; it will provide good cheer to our troops.'

The Duke shakes his head. 'Unfortunately, the enemy is not running away at Gloucester.'

The Queen eyes Mall's husband with suspicion. 'I thought everything had been arranged and the governor was going to surrender the keys.'

'So did we,' says Percy. 'Unfortunately something or someone made him change his mind and we seem to be in for a long slog.'

'The King vetoed a direct assault,' adds the Duke of Richmond.

'Why ever not?' asks Henriette.

'It was felt that casualties would be too high and might affect future plans for a march on London.'

'You see,' says Henriette, hardly able to contain herself. 'I told you that Gloucester was a pointless diversion. And now we are weeks into a siege, casualties are mounting and we are using up all my gunpowder.' She groans.

'Parliament is equally concerned about the siege at Gloucester,' says Percy. 'There is much disquiet on the streets of London. Lucy has written to me saying she regrets taking the side of parliament.'

'Absolutely typical,' says Henriette. 'Let me guess, your sister has fallen out with John Pym having discovered that he is as devious and lacking in principles as she is. Actually they should be a perfect match.'

Henry Percy recalls the long communication. 'Apparently John Pym is in poor health.'

Henriette cries out. 'I am bereft. Send the Kings' physician Sir Theodore Mayerne post haste. I would recommend three spoons of cyanide, twice daily.'

Before the Queen can elaborate on the subject, the remaining guests arrive in the courtyard. Light rain begins to fall and they retire to the dining hall where Henriette has arranged an impromptu banquet. Festivities continue late into the night and everyone declares the evening a great success. It is like the Queen's court of old. The final guests leave Merton College in the early hours, and Mall slips away to be with her husband at Christ Church.

Dawn breaks early with a summer mist hanging over the meadows; the dew is heavy on the grass and the air is damp. A few miles north of the city there is a hive of activity. Soldiers fill leather pouches on their bandoliers with gunpowder and check supplies of shot and fuses for their pistols. Horses are gathered for an early-morning patrol. In the background, a vast encampment is preparing to stir. Parliament's main army lies undetected less than a day's march from Oxford.

Act III, Scene 13 ~ Christ Church

Mid morning and a rider gallops down the empty Banbury road towards the city. He halts at the north gate on Cornmarket before being ushered into Oxford by a sentry. The man heads for Oriel College, where, minutes later, a servant is despatched to Merton. Henriette summons Susan and her bodyguards before heading down the lane to the side entrance into Christ Church.

'How large a force has gathered, your majesty?' Susan walks quickly to keep up with her mistress.

'The reconnaissance is unsure, but at least ten thousand foot and a train of artillery. It sounds like Essex's army slipped out of London without us noticing. He has a large enough force to storm the city walls I should have thought.'

'Oh my goodness,' says Susan. 'We must evacuate before we are surrounded.'

Henriette cries out in frustration. 'I said our army should have been heading to London, not Gloucester.' She stops in her tracks and turns to her Dame of Honour. 'We are not deserting Oxford.'

Susan knows the Queen is stubborn and brave, which is often reassuring, but just now the Countess of Denbeigh would prefer a more timid mistress. She tries a different tack: 'The King would be devastated if you were captured.'

Henriette resumes walking at a brisk pace. 'I would be quite devastated too. We must defend the city and hold up the enemy so that Prince Rupert can march from Gloucester and sweep them off the field.'

They reach Christ Church and the Queen strides along the side of the quadrangle and into the Dean's apartments. In the conference room she finds Sir Edward Nicholas with Lord Henry Wilmot, lieutenant general of the royalist cavalry. Wilmot is another hard drinking veteran of the Dutch wars.

'Henry Wilmot, I am glad to see you,' says Henriette.

'Your majesty, we have the enemy in our sights.' He bows to the Queen.

'The question is, does Essex have us in his sights,' says Henriette. 'And do we have enough soldiers to hold Oxford?'

'I don't think the enemy are intent on taking the city,' says Wilmot. 'Essex has marched around by Aylesbury to link up with forces from the midlands.'

Henriette is not reassured. 'He may head south to attack us; his army is only ten miles away.'

Wilmot shakes his head. 'I believe he's marching on Gloucester to relieve the siege. There has been an outcry in London about Parliament's failure to act. About five thousand men from the trained bands have been added to his regular troops.'

'Thank goodness he is not planning to attack Oxford,' says Susan.

Henriette

Henriette is unimpressed. 'Have a thought for our army at Gloucester. They will end up stuck between two enemy forces.' She pauses to consider the implications. 'My sons are at the siege.'

'The King and Prince Rupert have been alerted,' says Wilmot. 'I will use the remaining cavalry based at Oxford to harass the enemy advance and hopefully slow them down. Prince Rupert will bring the main cavalry force from Gloucester so we can confront Essex.'

Henriette is deep in thought.

'I am sure you are safe here in Oxford, your majesty, but we will leave extra troops just in case.'

'I am not worried about Oxford,' says Henriette slowly. She stares out of the window at the cattle grazing in the middle of the quadrangle. 'This daring advance by Essex could be an opportunity for us rather than a setback.'

'Quite so, your majesty,' says Wilmot. 'The enemy is a long way from London. If we can force them on to open ground we have a golden opportunity.'

'And when we win,' says Henriette, 'the road to London will be open.'

'Provided we beat their army in the field,' says Edward Nicholas cautiously.

Henriette turns and stares at the King's Secretary of State. 'Pray don't be so negative, Sir Edward. After all, we outnumber Essex do we not?'

'We appear to,' says Wilmot, 'especially with cavalry.'

Henriette becomes animated at the prospect of a victorious encounter. 'I shall accompany your cavalry.'

'Out of the question,' says Sir Edward firmly. 'What would the King say?'

'He won't know,' says Henriette.

'You should stay in Oxford,' says Susan. 'You must be here if the King returns the young princes.'

Lord Wilmot is more persuasive. 'The King will never forgive me if you are taken prisoner, your majesty.' He laughs. 'He would probably chop my head off.'

'That would never do.' Henriette smiles, conceding the argument unusually quickly. 'I shall expect regular reports of your progress. This is the opportunity we have been waiting for – a decisive victory against the enemy's main army will be the turning point in this wretched rebellion.'

Act III, Scene 14 ~ Merton College

The Queen's impatience drives Susan and Mall to distraction. Each day she rushes through hair styling and even tells her confessor not to tarry with prayers. She then demands to know if any messengers have arrived. When she is told there is no news, she sends servants to Oriel and Christ Church to make sure nothing has been overlooked. Henriette then organises a walk with the dogs in the meadow and after about ten minutes changes her mind and returns indoors. She cannot sit still for long, looking out of the window or walking down to the lodge to check for despatches. Susan tries to distract the Queen with plans for the next student drama, but Henriette shows no enthusiasm. Mall suggests a visit to John Birkenhead and the offices of Mercurius Aulicus, but Henriette says there is no point if there is no news to report.

After four days, a message arrives from Lord Wilmot. Mall brings the letter into the Queen's withdrawing chamber, a modest sized room in the college overlooking the Large Quad. A few paintings from St James's Palace have been spirited to Oxford by Edward Sackville. The Queen is studying a Correggio hanging above the fireplace, a gift in happier times from the Vatican. The moment Mall appears, Henriette snatches the letter, rips the seal and unrolls the scroll of paper. She reads through the correspondence.

'Is it good news, your majesty?'

'I am not sure,' says Henriette slowly.

Susan opens the door and announces the arrival of Sir Edward Nicholas and Edward Hyde. The Queen moves swiftly to her reception chamber, another compact college room, to cross-examine her husband's advisers.

Henriette dispenses with small talk. 'What do you make of this communication? Are we not engaging the enemy?'

Sir Edward shakes his head. 'Our cavalry delayed the enemy by about a day, your majesty, but Essex pushed through to Gloucester and lifted the siege.'

'Why did we withdraw?' asks Henriette.

'It was twilight and heavy rain ruled out any musket or artillery action,' says Edward Hyde. 'The King had no choice.'

Henriette slumps in a chair. 'So we besiege Gloucester for about four weeks and the moment Essex arrives we retreat.' She puts a hand to her left temple. 'And to make matters worse I have dreadful head pains.'

'Apparently there is a great deal of discussion about what to do next,' says Hyde. 'The King is sorely disappointed by the failure of the siege.'

'I am sorely disappointed we did not force the issue,' says Henriette. 'I know Lord Wilmot wanted to, and I find it hard to believe Prince Rupert would have passed on such an opportunity.'

'There did appear to be some confusion about enemy intentions,' says Sir Edward. 'After relieving Gloucester, Essex took his parliamentary forces to Tewkesbury, so the King's army headed north to defend Worcester. Then in the night, Essex turned south and made a dash for London.'

'So he fooled us.' Henriette waves the letter in the air. 'Instead of blocking his path to London we were dragged on a wild goose chase.' Henriette slaps the letter down on the table. 'It is most disheartening.'

'Our cavalry far outnumber the enemy,' says Sir Edward. 'There is a chance that Rupert and Wilmot can outpace Essex.'

'And what about young Charles and James?' says Henriette. 'I find it immensely worrying and frustrating having to witness events from a distance.'

Sir Edward Nicholas anticipates the next question. 'The King has requested that you stay in Oxford within the city walls, your majesty. There are parliamentary deserters and skirmishers roving the countryside and it's not safe to travel.'

Henriette's bottom lip drops. 'The King is allowed to travel all over the countryside. My sons could be in danger as we speak, but I am a prisoner in Oxford.'

'Perhaps we could pray for the army's good fortune,' says Susan hopefully.

Henriette remains motionless. Just as Susan is about to suggest a trip to Hart Hall to update John Birkenhead, the Queen finally rouses herself.

'I shall consult Father Philip.' She stands up. 'A retreat from Gloucester and a belated chase across half of England hardly justifies a special Mass, but we might consider offering up prayers.'

'We lost over one thousand men in the siege,' says Edward Hyde quietly. 'Perhaps we should also remember the fallen.'

Henriette glares at Hyde and speaks harshly. 'How many horses did we lose? And how much gunpowder did we waste?'

'I don't know, your majesty,' replies Hyde in a flat tone.

Susan greatly admires her mistress, but she recognises that Henriette is a different person from the young princess who first stepped ashore at Dover. The wit on occasions and energy remain, but years of enemy onslaught have hardened her.

'I shall go and pray for victory.' Henriette stands up and walks out; she does not wait for bows or curtsies.

Act III, Scene 15 ~ Merton College

'Gardens have a calming influence on me, like a good Mass.' The Queen lifts the hem of her dress and walks carefully over the damp flagstones of the kitchen garden at Merton.

Susan looks up at the sky. 'It is beginning to rain again, your majesty.'

'I don't think it is.' Henriette pauses and smiles. 'Let's not argue about the weather. It reminds me of a ridiculous disagreement I had with Charles.' She pauses to reflect. 'It was a long time ago. Those unfortunate days belong to a different masque.'

Susan frowns. 'I am not sure I understand, your majesty.'

'My life is one long drama, Susan. It comprises many contrasting scenes – joy and sorrow, success and failure, war and peace.' She sighs and walks on, surrounded by her lap dogs. Suddenly, high-pitched squeals can be heard in the adjoining courtyard.

Henriette looks up. 'Is that little Jeffrey?'

Before Susan can reply, Prince Charles and his brother emerge through a stone archway and sprint across the lawn. The dogs go wild, James hugs his mother's legs and the Prince of Wales stops short and tries to look grown up and aloof.

'Don't I get a kiss, Charles?' asks his mother.

The thirteen-year-old prince reluctantly leans forward and gives Henriette a kiss on both cheeks.

The Queen smiles: 'I do believe you are taller than me.'

'Papa sends his love,' says Charles awkwardly.

'Who brought you back to Oxford?'

'Harry Jermyn and a regiment of cavalry,' says James.

Prince Charles explains. 'Harry is to collect more ammunition and meet up with Cousin Rupert at Newbury.'

'Where is Newbury?' asks Henriette.

'Harry says it is a small market town thirty miles south of here,' says Charles. 'Cousin Rupert hopes to intercept the enemy somewhere between Newbury and London.'

'Henriette glances at the garden entrance. 'Where is Harry?'

'He is at the Ordnance works,' says Charles. 'He says he will join us as soon as possible.'

James continues to hug Henriette's legs. 'When can we go home, mam?'

The Queen looks down and pushes his auburn hair away from his face. 'Do you mean London?'

'That is our home, isn't it?'

'Yes, my dear, we hope that as soon as we engage the main enemy army and defeat them in battle, then we can go home.' Henriette pauses before adding: 'In triumph.'

'Good,' says James, 'I want to go home and see Elizabeth and Henry.'

Charles is embarrassed by his brother's show of emotion. 'Home is wherever you need to be.' He glances at his mother. 'You used to live in Paris, mam.'

'And more recently in Holland,' says Henriette. 'But I know what your brother is saying. It would be nice to go back to our palaces in London and especially joyous to be reunited with your younger sister and brother.'

'We will, mam,' says Charles cheerfully. 'I promise that you will return to London.'

Henriette smiles at her son's confident prediction. 'Tell me about your adventures at Gloucester.'

'It was amazing,' says James. 'The size of some of the siege guns and the noise they made…'

'We only heard them from a distance,' adds Prince Charles hurriedly. He gives his younger brother a piercing stare worthy of Henriette. 'We were kept away from the frontline, mam.'

'I bet you were,' says Henriette. 'Wait until I see your father; in fact, wait until I see Mr Jermyn.'

'Sir Harry Jermyn,' says Charles grandly.

'Can I continue to call him Harry?' asks James.

'Well you had better ask him,' says Henriette. 'It is a criminal offence to insult a baron.'

James stares up at his mother with his mouth open.

'Mam is joking, you idiot,' says Charles.

Henriette glances at her eldest son, narrowing her eyes. 'Are you sure? Shall we test the matter and consult your tutor?'

Charles wavers. He is fairly sure his mother is pulling his leg, but he can never be certain. He has learned that it is futile to argue. The momentary standoff is interrupted by a shout from across the gardens. Harry Jermyn strides towards the Queen waving his hat.

'I am so glad to see you, Harry,' says Henriette. 'No one will tell me a straight story about the campaign.' She breaks protocol and grabs his arm. 'We shall retire to my rooms.' She looks over her shoulder at her children. 'You two, go and find Susan and she will take you to the kitchens for some well earned treats.'

Minutes later the Queen and her counsellor enter a small room that has been converted into a private dining room. This is where Henriette takes her meals unless she is entertaining. She uses the small oak panelled chamber for private discussions with her closest advisers. Her ladies are instructed to wait in the adjoining room.

Henriette sits at the table and Jermyn wanders across to the row of small, diamond-latticed windows.

'So tell me, Harry, what is our true position?'

After a brief pause, Jermyn turns to face his mistress. 'The King is in a dark mood. It is difficult to rouse him into action.'

'I wish I could be with my dear heart.'

'He claims his reputation will be injured by the failure to take Gloucester.' Jermyn sighs. 'He showed me a roundhead news poster; it is ridiculous, of course.'

'What was ridiculous?'

'A large illustration depicted the King lying on the ground with you standing over him. The caption read …' Jermyn pauses. 'It was an absurd libel.'

Henriette speaks slowly. 'What did the poster say, Harry?'

'A weak monarch ruled by a French papist Queen Consort.'

'He is not weak,' says Henriette quietly. She sits at the table, tears welling up in her eyes. 'They are right, I am a Popish brat, but I do not rule my husband.' She lets out a derisory cry. 'He never listens to my advice.'

Jermyn walks over to the dining table. 'The King considers many differing counsels, including yours, but I have always found he makes up his own mind.'

'Eventually,' says Henriette ruefully. She glances at Jermyn and they both smile. 'Shall I write to Mr Pymple? I shall tell him that I am exceedingly vexed because I keep advising the King to do something and he then does the opposite. I shall plead with Pym to recommend a good book on how to be a bossy wife.'

'There is a serious point here, your majesty. Perhaps Mercurius Aulicus should publish an article emphasising the King's strong character, describing how he rallied supporters across the country to his standard. After all Mr Pym doesn't go near the battlefield, while the King leads his army at Edgehill and Gloucester.'

'I like that idea,' says Henriette. 'We could start drawing our own picture of Mr Pym as the slimy, untrustworthy leader, short on honour and fulsome in cowardice – look how he ignored the trial and bullied parliament into murdering Thomas Wentworth.'

'We should not be afraid to compare John Pym with the King.'

'There is no comparison. When I think of that secret meeting I had with Pym, and all the time he was planning to destroy us.' The Queen manages a passable impression of the honourable member for Tavistock's West Country drawl. 'I prefer to talk, your majesty.' Henriette drops the impersonation and speaks bitterly. 'Oh yes, he does not like violence much, except when he executes honest citizens and starts wicked rebellions.' She sighs. 'I thought we had Essex and his army at our mercy so far from London.'

Jermyn shakes his head. 'We lost two days' march north of Gloucester before we started chasing Essex.'

Henriette cries out. 'That's when Charles can be so annoying. It's not that he is weak, he just has to weigh up so many pros and cons and it takes him ages.'

'I think the word is diligent,' says Jermyn. 'He is careful.'

'He thinks much more than I do, because he is wise,' says Henriette. 'However, there are occasions when it is better to act rather than to think.'

'Several of our commanders urged the King not to move towards Worcester. It is easy to judge with hindsight.'

'Essex outwitted us.' Henriette relapses into gloom. 'Have we any chance of intercepting the enemy?'

'Prince Rupert thinks so. I am here to collect fresh ordnance.'

'When do you set out?'

'The ammunition carts will be loaded by morning; they are working through the night.'

Henriette stands up. 'Essex has marched his men to Gloucester and most of the way back again. Surely they will be exhausted?'

'If we can block his path,' says Jermyn, 'then we still have an opportunity to end this rebellion once and for all.'

'I will summon Father Philip and we will say prayers for our army.' The Queen clenches her fists. 'It is so elusive – one victory in the field against their main force will suffice. We just need a decisive encounter.'

Jermyn bows. 'I must return to New Inn Hall Street and help Henry Percy with supplies.'

Henriette nods absentmindedly. 'One victory, that's all we need.'

A knock on the cabinet door interrupts proceedings. The lady in black is sitting on a high-backed oak chair swinging her feet to and fro. Her companion in a bright blue dress, yellow ribbons and pale grey shawl sits to the desk and dips her quill in the ink pot.

Henriette is in full flow when her chamberlain's face appears around the door.

'How am I possibly meant to progress these memoirs when I keep being interrupted.'

Monsieur Fialin frowns; he is certain that no one has entered his mistress's cabinet for at least an hour.

'Well, what is it?' asks Henriette.

'The carriage has arrived for Madame, your majesty.'

'Is it that time already. We will have to resume our endeavours another day, Françoise. I was about to describe the tensions caused by the imaginary war.'

'Imaginary war?' Madame returns the quill to a collection competing for space in an old ceramic mug.

'We existed in this false bubble of serenity – walking by the river, carrying on with prayers and conducting court life as if nothing was amiss. Except that the King and most of his ministers were missing and armies roved the countryside. Imaginations ran riot and that's when tensions overspilled among my senior staff.' Henriette stands up. Madame de Motteville notices that she is unsteady on her feet.

'I think a break is a good idea, your majesty. Our marathon session today has tired you.'

Henriette snorts. 'I am as fit as a fiddle. Victory was within our grasp; it was not the enemy that concerned me, but the doubters on our own side.'

Act III, Scene 16 ~ Merton College

Raised voices can be heard along the corridor and down the spiral staircase. Henriette enters the dressmaking room to find Susan stony-faced and Mall fighting back tears.

The Queen uses her best authoritative tone. 'What on earth is going on? Can we please sit down and calm ourselves.' The two ladies settle on chairs on opposite sides of the needlework table. Henriette puts her hands on her hips. 'Now if we are composed, perhaps my Dame of Honour would like to explain what topic of conversation led to such an unseemly disturbance in my court.'

Susan rests her hands on her lap. 'We were discussing the war.'

'The rebellion,' says Henriette, correcting Susan. 'There are rebels and there is a King.'

'It was a conversation about the rebellion,' says Susan.

'Any particular aspect?' asks the Queen.

'The current situation, your majesty' says Susan.

'Which is?'

Mall breaks the visible tension by bursting into tears and trying to talk between the sobs: 'The whole situation is too horrible ... Susan's son trying to kill my husband and my husband trying to kill her son ... the world has gone mad ... Lord Falkland is right when he says no one is going to win ... there will only be losers ... everyone is going to die ... Susan has lost her dear husband ... it's ... horrible.'

Susan glances at Henriette. 'I just said, your majesty, that I would not like to think my husband died in vain.'

'But it is pointless,' cries Mall. 'We are going to lose in the end.'

'Wait a minute,' says Henriette holding up her hands. 'I can agree it is horrible, but what is this talk about losing? Our side is fighting for freedom from tyranny. Susan is correct, her husband did not die in vain. He was fighting for his King against outrageous cruelty meted out to loyal servants such as Thomas Wentworth.' Henriette stares at Mall. 'That is worth fighting for, and we can win; in fact we will win, however long it takes.'

Susan nods. 'That makes me feel better, your majesty.' She looks at Mall. 'I am distraught that my son has chosen the enemy camp, but I can only pray that he will see the error of his ways and join the King's army.'

'Anyway, what is this talk about everyone losing?' asks Henriette.

Mall wipes her eyes with a handkerchief. 'James says that Lord Falkland believes we should negotiate peace before there are more casualties. He told my husband that if either side won the war it would be too extreme a solution.'

The Queen frowns. 'That is a strange position for our Secretary of State to take. Perhaps he should resign.'

'He has given up,' says Mall, sniffling into her hankie. 'He charged straight at the enemy during the siege of Gloucester and James believes he wanted to die.' She gives a half-hearted laugh. 'His reckless action was so successful his troops nearly breeched the enemy defences.'

'I cannot understand such defeatist behaviour,' says Henriette. 'And I do not see why it is the cause of such a disturbance between my two most senior ladies at court.'

'I was upset at Mall's suggestion that everyone was laying down their lives for nothing,' says Susan. 'I apologise.'

Mall shakes her head. 'No, I am the one who should say sorry – it was thoughtless of me. You have lost your husband.'

'Well can I suggest you forgive each other,' says the Queen. 'We are all worried sick and it is stressful imagining what may or may not be occurring. Who knows who has lost whom? Maybe the King is dead. In Holland I was told it was so about five times. We must stay strong and wait for news.'

Susan and Mall stand up and without any prompting rush into each other's arms.

'Good,' says Henriette. 'The one thing I cannot cope with is my friends falling out. The rebellion has split families asunder, and it has and will cause great sadness, but I do not accept our fight against the rebels is pointless. With the greatest respect, Lord Falkland is wrong.'

Both ladies curtsy. Henriette nods. 'Now if there is nothing else, I shall go and see Father Philip. If Prince Rupert has managed to catch up with our enemies I need to pray for a successful outcome on the battlefield.'

Madame de Motteville steps down from the coach and rushes up the steps of Chateau Colombes. She is barely through the entrance to the withdrawing room when she addresses Henriette.

'Your majesty, are you all right? I was told you fainted.'

'Fiddlesticks.' Henriette is lying the length of her new upholstered sofa surrounded by cushions and lap dogs. Padded chairs are an innovation and Henriette, always a fashion leader of interior design, is the proud processor of a dozen.

'You did faint,' says Harry Jermyn, standing behind the sofa. 'Monsieur Fialin is adamant you were unconscious for several minutes. This is the sixth occasion in as many months.'

'We must cancel our writing session,' says Madame.

'Absolutely not.' Henriette heaves herself up and brushes down her dress. Lap dogs fly in all directions. 'We are getting to an important part of the story. People were talking openly of defeat, simply because we were not achieving quick results. Their pessimism was in danger of becoming a self-fulfilling prophesy; my job was to cheer everyone up.'

Jermyn nods. 'You were an inspiration to us all.'

'I wasn't inspired,' says Henriette. 'I was angry when I saw how low the military campaign had brought my dear heart. Everyone walked around with glum faces despite the fact we hadn't lost a single battle. It is a strange thing how people can talk themselves into defeat.'

'I think there was a general weariness with the conflict,' says Jermyn. 'The defeatist talk began with Lord Falkland, and his tragic end only made things worse.'

'His death was very sad,' says Henriette quietly, 'but only because it was quite unnecessary. It made a mockery of the sacrifices of others.'

Madame de Motteville hovers beside the sofa. 'Are you sure you are well enough to resume your memoirs?'

'Of course I am. I only looked up at the sun and felt a little lightheaded. Now everyone is fussing – Minette has gone to the kitchens to organise some boiled tea leaves.'

Harry Jermyn raises an eyebrow. 'According to the young maids of honour, her majesty was unconscious for several minutes.'

'I don't think we should proceed today,' says Madame.

'This is ridiculous,' exclaims Henriette. 'It is exactly the kind of negative thinking that beset us in Oxford. Besides, if we don't get a move on, I may be dead before we finish the story.'

'That is a little negative, your majesty,' says Jermyn with a grin.

'Don't be insolent, Harry.' Henriette points to the desk. 'Sit down, Françoise, and I shall conjure the dismal winter of 1643 and my efforts to restore morale. It was bad enough contending with grumpy puritans and dour Dutchmen, but to have to fight gloom and despondency among our own supporters was especially disheartening.'

Minette enters the room followed by a servant carrying a tray. 'Here we are, mam, a refreshing drink of tea leaves to make you feel better.'

Henriette glares at her daughter. 'I have never felt better; I did not faint and I am not about to die.'

Minette looks askance at Harry Jermyn; he shrugs his shoulders. The drink is placed on a small table.

'The leaves of tea will do you good,' says Minette firmly.

Henriette ignores her daughter. She nods towards Madame de Motteville. 'Pick up your quill, Françoise. You will all benefit from a lesson in positive thinking. My dear mama said I inherited the talent from my father.' Henriette snorts. 'I am not the daughter of Henri the Great for nothing.'

Act III, Scene 17 ~ City Gate, Oxford

The south gate at Oxford stands open as a long procession of soldiers limps slowly into the city. The men are tired and bedraggled as they battle a cold northerly wind and lashing rain. Onlookers give a muted welcome to the first troops of cavalry but gradually melt away as mile upon mile of troops and equipment take several hours to pass through. Only a handful of anxious relatives stand close to the gate patiently awaiting news of loved ones. The column regularly halts as returning men, animals and carts block narrow city lanes. The news that accompanies the troops is an army that has not been defeated; it is a tactical retreat. Only after the last carts from the baggage train finally cross the city threshold does the rain cease. Water continues to pour off roofs, flowing down the middle of the street dragging mud and waste in its wake. Soldiers stand about with cold, wet feet; horses patiently wait for sodden blankets and saddles to be removed. The sentries slam the city gates shut, a symbolic end to a bitter season of fighting.

The King returns hours before the army column, surrounded by a posse of mounted guards and courtiers. Meanwhile, Prince Rupert's cavalry harasses the parliamentary army as it struggles back to London. Counting casualties, most people regard the Battle of Newbury as a draw. But on objectives – forcing the enemy into a decisive battle and opening the road to London – the royalists are frustrated. On the other hand, relieving the siege of Gloucester and getting back to London without catastrophic losses leads to rejoicing in the streets of the capitol. Success and failure depend on your point of view.

'I cannot understand the glum faces,' says Henriette with her hands on her hips. There is no doubting her point of view.

'People are disappointed' says Charles mournfully. 'We f-failed to take Gloucester and we f-failed to deliver a mortal blow to Essex's army.'

'I don't think it is helpful to talk about failure, dear heart.' Henriette places a pale hand on her husband's arm. 'Neither side won either encounter. I am glad we managed to intercept Essex and I am told we lost no more men at Newbury than the enemy. I don't understand why we had to retreat.'

'We were short of gunpowder.'

Henriette lets out a cry of frustration. 'After all those barrels I brought over from Holland?'

'We need a constant s-supply,' says Charles.

'I think people are being unduly despondent,' says Henriette. 'Gloucester is only a minor setback.'

'The town has strategic importance,' says the King. 'We are recruiting men in Wales and parliament holds the gateway at the river crossing.'

'We will have to march them further north,' says the Queen. 'And clearly we need more gunpowder if we are going to destroy the parliamentary army.'

The King slumps into his chair, visibly exhausted. 'The losses were dreadful,' he says quietly. 'You cannot imagine listening to the groans and cries of wounded m-men across the battlefield. The latest count is about four thousand dead on our side alone – one in four of our troops.'

'The enemy suffered a similar number of casualties,' says Henriette, perplexed by her husband's morose attitude. 'They struggled to gather an army in the first place. Lord Wilmot says they had to resort to the trained bands. Losing all those men will severely weaken their cause and doubtless foster discontent on the streets of London. We know how fickle the public mood can be.'

Charles stares into the distance; he does not appear to be listening to his wife. The royal couple have retreated to the King's study at Christ Church.

'We lost good m-men: the Earl of Carnarvon, Colonel Morgan,' the King is reluctant to continue. Eventually he looks at Henriette and whispers, 'dear Lord Falkland.'

The Queen shrugs. 'I thought he had given up the fight. Mall tells me he has been walking around Oxford telling everyone that the war is pointless. It caused much upset I can tell you. People like Susan, for instance, who have lost their husband fighting for your cause; they don't want to hear such negative opinions.'

'Falkland was depressed,' says Charles.

'He's not the only one,' says Henriette bitterly. She walks around the desk and stands beside her husband. 'I cannot understand, dear heart, when we have won great victories in the north and the west, taken Bristol, given Essex's army a good hammering and forced him to retreat back to London, how anyone could describe this campaign as anything but a victory for the King's cause. The results of our efforts do not depress me, only the glum faces around court.' She rearranges her dress and kneels beside him, resting her hands on his knees. 'Surely we can build on these successes and finish the job next spring?'

'Many of my commanders are w-worried the longer the war continues the harder it becomes to achieve a decisive victory.'

'It is a rebellion, not a war,' says Henriette patiently, 'and if people talk about defeat enough times they will believe it is so.'

'We are short of funds, have lost a large n-number of men and horses, and deployed most of our gunpowder.'

'So have the enemy,' says Henriette, her voicing beginning to rise. 'They marched all the way to Gloucester and all the way back again, lost thousands of men in the process – don't tell me Essex will be having a party tonight.' Henriette puts on her John Pym accent. 'What ho, my Lord Essex, that was a long way to go for a barrel of West Country cider. And by the way, let's celebrate the fact that you lost a quarter of our army.'

Charles does not smile. 'Falkland was convinced that our cause is lost.'

'No that's wrong,' says Henriette firmly. 'He told the Duchess of Richmond that whichever side won, the outcome would be a misery.' Henriette lifts herself up and starts pacing up and down. 'The only misery was Lord Falkland. How could he suggest that defeating these rebels and stopping their perpetual dictatorship is not a good outcome? Have we forgotten about Thomas Wentworth? And poor Archbishop Laud locked up in the Tower? And the extreme abuses of power, trying to make you into a grotesque kind of republican non-King?' Henriette pauses for breath. 'And their plans to impeach me.' She points her finger. 'They want to execute me, and Falkland had the nerve to suggest that our fight is unworthy.'

'Do not distress yourself, my dear heart.' The King stands up and puts his arms around her. 'I am only telling you what some people are saying.'

The Queen starts to sob. 'I am not interested in "some people" and their defeatist talk. All I want is to restore you to your rightful place on the throne of all three kingdoms.'

'You are my rock,' says Charles.

'No, I am the popish brat,' says Henriette, laughing through her tears. 'You are my rock; and I serve you and do as you command.'

'Then I command you to wipe your tears, put your wonderful cheerful face back on and stamp out any defeatist talk in the city.'

Henriette looks at Charles. 'I was brought up never to accept defeat.'

The King wipes a tear from her cheek and smiles at Henriette. 'I confess there was a time when your strong opinions perplexed me; now, your indomitable spirit is a great comfort to me.'

Act III, Scene 18 ~ University College

Long, sturdy oak tables are manhandled through the open double doors of the first floor dining room and, to the accompaniment of shouts and groans, carried down the broad spiral staircase into storage at the back of the stables. The bench seats are moved to the far end of the great hall and more seating arrives from Merton, Oriel and All Souls. Finally a makeshift stage is constructed in place of the top table. Amid the hammering and sawing, the Queen stands with hands on hips and a broad grin on her face.

Drama is her elixir, it is a diversion and as the King has requested, it enthuses everyone around her. It is autumn in Oxford and Henriette is busy organising a new theatre production employing students from the university. Having decided that Shakespeare has been well exercised through the cycle of outdoor summer performances, Henriette has chosen a Ben Jonson comedy – one of the King's favourite plays, Volpone. The Queen is using University College's dining hall as the venue – partly because it is available and more importantly because it is a convenient stroll from Henriette's rooms at Merton. Today she has her two sons in tow along with the theatre loving Earl of Dorset.

'I enjoy a good Ben Jonson play,' says Edward Sackville.

'He wrote my royal masques in the early days.' Henriette laughs. 'He used to have terrible arguments with Inigo Jones. Ben always said the words were the most important part and of course Mr Jones thought the set was the critical bit. After they had both been shouting, I used to go over and say: the words need to fit the setting and the scenes need to blend with the story, and then they would stare at me, shake their heads and get back to work.'

'I have never seen Volpone, mam,' says Prince Charles.

'No, but your father has, many times; it is one of his favourite comedies.'

'What's the story about?' asks James.

'It portrays greedy people and the lengths they are prepared to go to,' says Henriette.

Henriette

'Do they steal the food?' asks James.

Henriette frowns.

'You said they were greedy.'

'They are not after food; they are greedy because they want to get their hands on Volpone's money.'

'He has a funny name,' says Charles.

'Volpone is Italian for sly fox,' says Edward Sackville.

'My favourite character is Mrs Would-Be,' says Henriette. 'She annoys Volpone by talking too much about ridiculous subjects.' The Queen scoffs. 'Rather like me.'

'Why is Volpone Italian?' asks Prince Charles.

'Because the drama is set in Venice,' says Edward Sackville.

'That makes me think,' says Henriette. 'We must invite the Venetian Ambassador from London; do you imagine he would come?'

'He might,' says Edward. 'He loves the stage and, now the puritans are in charge, all the theatres in London are closed.'

'They are such miserable creatures,' says Henriette. 'What part of theatrical entertainment is dangerous and terrible?'

The two princes wander to the front of the stage and watch a group of students reading through the script.

Henriette whispers to the Earl. 'Shall we take a walk?' They descend the stone staircase and stroll across the quadrangle. 'I miss my chamberlain,' says Henriette.

'You have Harry,' says Edward. 'He was deputy for long enough, I am sure he knows what to do.'

'Like you, he spends a lot of time charging around the countryside leading armies,' says Henriette. 'Besides, Harry is Harry.'

'What does that mean exactly?' asks Sackville with a grin.

'He is keen on the luxuries of life,' says Henriette, 'and the ladies.'

'He is tremendously loyal,' says Edward. 'There is only one lady in his life.'

'Don't you start,' says Henriette. 'I have enough trouble with parliamentary gossip and the London news sheets.'

'I did not mean in that way,' says Sackville. 'Everything he does revolves around your majesty. I can see Harry never marrying and settling down; his duty in life as he sees it is to protect and support you.'

'And what about my old chamberlain,' says Henriette. 'I hear you are not so supportive these days.'

Sackville frowns. 'I have stuck with the King through thick and thin.'

Henriette tucks her arm into his. 'What is this I hear, Edward, about you and the peace party?'

Sackville stops and stares at the Queen. 'You always say you pray for peace.'

'I do,' says Henriette, 'but not at any price and definitely not while this perpetual parliament is in session. They want to chop my head off.'

'Perhaps if we talk to them, we can reach an understanding. I cannot believe they want a long drawn-out conflict.'

'You sound like Lord Falkland,' says Henriette as they resume strolling around the quad.

'Lucius was a troubled man,' says Sackville. 'I did not hold with his view that everything was lost or that a victory for either side would be a disaster.'

'I'm glad to hear it,' says Henriette. 'Is it true that he allowed himself to be killed.'

'That is how it was described to me,' says Sackville. 'He charged at a gap in the hedge where there was a line of musketeers. He had no chance.'

Henriette moves her head slowly from side to side. 'I would never give up like that. It is so sad.'

'It is sad, your majesty. He was a fine gentleman and a great lover of the arts like you and me. In a different time under different circumstances you and he would have been great companions.' Sackville nods his head in the direction of the dining hall. 'He would have adored your production of Volpone.'

'It's not my performance,' says Henriette. 'The students are organising everything; I am just helping to provide the venue and the audience.'

'If only Inigo Jones could design the set,' says Sackville. 'How is he?'

'He is living at Basing House as a guest of the Marquis of Winchester,' says Henriette. 'He celebrated his seventieth birthday in July, bless him.'

'Is he in good health?'

'I believe so,' says Henriette. 'Word is that when the rebellion is over Mr Jones will help the Marquis restore Basing House; it is quite dilapidated after years of neglect.'

'I'm not surprised, it is the largest private mansion in England with the biggest maintenance bill.' Sackville looks across the quadrangle. 'What does your Mr Jones think of parliament seizing the King's palaces?'

'He is as frustrated as I am.' Henriette sighs. 'I dare not think what they have done to Somerset House or Greenwich. I am sure there will be plenty of work for him when we return to London.'

'It will be a while yet.'

'Do you think so, Edward?'

'I know so, your majesty. London is impregnable, the parliamentary army is not defeated in the north or the south, the Scottish rebels may come out in support of our enemies and we have limited options for recruiting more men and little money for horses and armour.'

'I don't want morose talk about my court.'

'I am not being morose, your majesty, simply realistic.'

'You are not allowing for the fact that we continue to expect help from abroad. Ormonde in Ireland thinks he may be able to send a large force and it is possible that Hamilton will persuade the Scottish rebels to rally to their King.'

'I admire your confidence, your majesty. Foreign help has not been forthcoming these last four years; Ireland promises much and delivers little.' He shrugs. 'I am not giving up like Falkland, but I do think we face a massive challenge.'

'Do not talk like this at court,' says Henriette quietly. 'We are in danger of convincing ourselves that the fight is lost when it has barely begun.' She stops and stares into his eyes. 'Please, Edward.'

'I shall do my best, your majesty, but we need to get some help, whether it is from abroad, or Ireland or Scotland. I do not think we can overcome the enemy singlehanded.'

Henriette nods. 'We should get back.' They start walking across the middle of the quadrangle. 'I will redouble my efforts; I am optimistic that France will be more amenable now that my sister-in-law is in charge and that dreadful man Richelieu has gone.'

'Harry was right when he said you are an inspiration to us all.'

'I don't feel in the least bit inspired. I hate living in Oxford; I feel like a prisoner. I want to defeat the rebels and return to London with my children.'

'And the King.'

'Of course.' Henriette smiles. 'And Mr Jones.'

Act III, Scene 19 ~ Oxford

A handcart shakes and rattles over uneven cobblestones. A man clings grimly to the wooden shafts as he tows the two-wheeled wagon; his companion walks ahead wielding a large brass hand bell. Both chew tobacco. As they turn the corner into St Michael's Street, the bell is rung vigorously and the cart comes to a halt. The third house down on the right has a white wooden door on which a black cross is crudely daubed above the brass knocker. A torn piece of parchment is pinned beside the cross with the words "Lord have mercy on us." The door slowly opens and a head appears.

'The master has passed away.'

The man pulling the cart veers across the narrow street, kicking waste and straw out of the way, and carefully lowers the shafts to the ground. His companion puts down his bell and drags a well-worn grey blanket from the back.

'Who is left inside?' asks the bell ringer.

'Our mistress and myself and a maid. I am the master's valet; the other servants are serving in the army.'

'You can come with us to the pest house across Osney Bridge or else stay here for the rest of the quarantine period.' He consults a crumpled sheet of paper from his pocket. 'That will be thirty-four days. Food will be delivered on the morning round.'

There is a brief conference in the hallway between the servant and his mistress. The valet then turns back towards the street. 'We will stay. We are just as likely to be infected at the pest house.'

The bell ringer clutches the blanket. 'Burn plenty of brimstone and smoke tobacco, but remember the windows facing the street must be kept closed.' He and the cart driver tie damp scarves around their faces and enter the house. After a few minutes they come out struggling with a heavy bundle, which they heave into the back of the cart. The first man grabs the shafts at the front of the cart and holds them down to level the load. With a heavy lurch, he resumes his uneven journey over the cobbles, the peel of the bell following in his wake.

The streets of Oxford are deserted. The orders pinned to doors across the city ban the gathering of more than three people in public, except for the purpose of shopping at the market. All stray cats and dogs are destroyed on sight and no dung or rubbish can be left on the streets. Plague has invaded the overcrowded city of Oxford.

'Can we not move somewhere else?' asks Henriette. 'What about Bristol?'

'It is too far from London, dear heart.' Charles is lying in Henriette's bed at Merton College. 'But you and the princes could m-move there.'

'I am not leaving without you,' says Henriette. 'We were apart for a year and it was horrible.'

'The important thing is to stay in college and keep away from the common streets.'

Henriette groans. 'It was bad enough being confined within the city walls; now the College is my prison. I will die of boredom.'

'You will die of something a lot w-worse if you don't stay put.'

Henriette's bottom lip drops. 'I suppose that means we cannot proceed with the play.' She shakes her head. 'I cannot believe our bad luck; we were just a week away from the performance.'

'You must cease the rehearsals,' says the King. 'A gathering such as that would breach the plague order.'

'How am I going to see my children?' Henriette nudges the King. 'Or you?'

'Sir Theodore is of the opinion that if we m-move between the two colleges by the meadows and back entrances then we should be safe. If you bring any metal objects such as scissors or pins with you, they must be s-soaked in vinegar for an hour, both before you set off and when you are ready to return.'

Henriette points to a bucket on the windowsill. 'We have arranged bouquets of sweet smelling herbs that Sir Theodore assures me are a great way of expelling the plague ridden air.' The Queen pulls the bedclothes back and slips off the bed. She pads bare foot across to the table by the fire and picks up a sheet of paper. She lingers by the warmth of the fire and reads out the ingredients. 'Rosemary, lavender, sage and mint,' says Henriette. 'And a second mix has nutmeg added. We have made enough to share with your court.'

'That is kind, Maria. I am sure the staff at Christ Church will be grateful. We are burning brimstone vigorously.'

'You should mix saltpetre and amber with the brimstone for maximum effect,' says Henriette.

'Who suggested that?'

'It was a remedy that Sir Kenelm taught me years ago.' Henriette returns to bed and snuggles under the cover. 'And don't forget onions. Peel them and leave dozens all over the place where they will absorb the impure particles in the air.'

'We have buckets of onions scattered across Christ Church. Sir Theodore is m-more impressed by the properties of tobacco. He says it is a great repellent and Charles and James m-may smoke through pipes quite safely.'

'I would not normally approve,' says Henriette, 'but I suppose in the circumstances we must try everything to keep the plague at bay.'

'Tobacco is harmless,' says the King. 'It makes little James cough, but that is preferable to the sickness.'

'Don't let him chew it, he will end up swallowing the stuff.' Henriette sighs. 'I wish they could be with me at Merton.'

'They can visit.' The King kisses her. 'And I can call at night.'

'I long to be back at Somerset House. It seems an age ago that I could wander in the garden, worship in my beautiful chapel and move about town at will.'

'I understand there is considerable unrest in the capital.'

The news cheers the Queen. 'Who brings this intelligence?'

'Three peers have arrived from London. You will be pleased to hear they have switched sides because they are unhappy w-with the puritans. The Lords voted to send a peace commission and the Commoners rejected the proposal. Apparently m-more members of the Lords are of a mind to follow.'

'That's encouraging,' says Henriette. 'What news do they bring of London?'

'There is much pessimism, a great deal of dissatisfaction with Essex and the army, and a growing demand for peace.'

'Who are the peers who have changed sides?'

'The Earl of Bedford, the Earl of Clare and your old friend the Earl of Holland.'

'Henry Rich,' exclaims the Queen. 'Mr Orange is in Oxford. How dare he?'

'He is most apologetic, dear heart.'

'Apologetic,' cries Henriette. She waves her arms. 'I am sorry I voted for Thomas Wentworth's execution and I apologise for sitting in parliament during the rebellion. Hey ho, let's be friends again.'

'I do not think we need to wipe the slate clean,' says Charles hastily, 'but it has to be good for m-morale to have members of the House of Lords deserting the enemy and coming over to our side.'

'It's not good for my morale,' says Henriette bitterly. 'He has a nerve. What about his brother – he pinched our navy. Is he going to tow it up the Thames and drop it off at Magdalen Bridge; sorry I borrowed your ships without permission, your majesty.' Henriette beats her arms vigorously on the bedcover to flatten out the creases. 'I cannot believe the nerve of Henry Rich.'

'He has asked me if he can resume his duties as Groom of the Stool'

'I hope you told him no,' snaps Henriette. 'If you have taken him back I shall be most put out, in fact I might as well retreat into a convent.'

'That will not be necessary, dearest, I told him the position was taken.'

'I certainly believe it is.' Henriette folds her arms. 'And I hope you told him that I shall not be requiring to see him.'

'He did mention that he hoped to visit you.' Charles gives her a hug. 'We want to encourage m-more peers to follow their example. After all, people like the Earl of Holland switching sides is bad news for the enemy.'

Henriette pouts. 'It certainly is bad news.'

Madame de Motteville is about to quiz Henriette about Henry Rich when Minette comes rushing into the withdrawing room at Chaillot.

'Can we please have a bit of decorum,' exclaims Henriette. 'As you know I have never insisted on strict protocol at my court but this is a house of God.'

Minette curtsies. 'Sorry, Mam; I was desperate to tell you the news.'

Henriette frowns. 'I trust it is uplifting news. My memoirs are proving dismal at present; I am in need of good cheer.'

Minette clasps her hands tightly, a mannerism familiar to Henriette's entourage. 'Louis has arranged the date for our trip to Amiens; a boat will be waiting at Boulogne to take me to England.'

Henriette nods with satisfaction. 'That is good news, indeed. Your brother will meet you at Dover.'

'A secret meeting, mam.'

'I know it's secret,' says Henriette, making no effort to hide her irritation. 'I am not a complete novice when it comes to international diplomacy. In fact, before you interrupted me, I was about to tell Madame about the French ambassador's visit to Oxford. I have lost count of how many ambassadors we entertained over the years, most of them full of their own importance. If only my relatives had been as keen to support us in those dark times as they are today.' Henriette scoffs. 'Let's hope it's not too little, too late.'

Act III, Scene 20 ~ Merton College

Harry Jermyn reorganises the furniture in the great hall at Merton College. The servants remove all the chairs and import a large armchair, which they designate "the throne", and place it in the centre. Compared with the grand presence chambers of Somerset House or White Hall Palace the room is modest, but it serves its purpose. Since the plague broke out, there have been few new arrivals in Oxford. Today's visitor is worthy of a full staff turnout – Harry Jermyn, Susan, Mall, Margaret and little Jeffrey are present along with the two princes summoned from Christ Church, plus Henry Percy and the Duke of Richmond. It is a while since the Queen has entertained an ambassador from her country of birth.

'Compte d'Harcourt, at your service, your majesty.' The middle-aged count is a veteran of the victorious wars with Spain and a favourite of the new chief minister of France, Cardinal Mazarin.

'How is my dear sister-in-law the Queen Regent?' asks Henriette, rising from her throne. 'And my nephew King Louis; I trust he is in good health.'

'They both send their esteemed greetings to you and the King,' says the Compte. He steps forward and kisses the Queen's hand.

'Let me see,' says Henriette, 'young Louis must be five now.'

'Indeed he is, your majesty, and exhibits signs of being a great monarch of France.'

The Queen thinks it might be a little early to tell, but she does not comment. 'How was your journey to Oxford?'

'I was greatly inconvenienced by your parliament,' says the Compte.

'Not our parliament,' says Henriette sourly. 'That's the problem.'

The Compte bows to acknowledge the point. 'They granted me safe passage to visit your court, but as soon as my carriage departed London they stopped and searched it. Soldiers examined my baggage and even checked my person for letters. I complained this was a serious diplomatic breach but I have received no apology.'

'Absolutely typical,' says Henriette. 'I am glad you witnessed their insolent behaviour; you see they have no respect for the Queen Regent of France and her legal representative. Perhaps now you understand a little of what the King and I have had to suffer these past few years.'

'I explained that I would converse with you and the King,' says the Compte. 'Hopefully I can return to parliament with proposals for a peaceful solution to the current parlous state of affairs.'

Henriette frowns. 'We are most desirous of peace, but it's not that simple, your Excellency. You are referring to an illegal perpetual parliament that has threatened this Princess of France with execution.'

'I detect a strong desire for peace in London,' says the Compte. 'I received a deputation from the House of Lords, led by a fine gentleman, the Earl of Northumberland.'

'Algernon?' Henriette tries hard to behave herself. 'Algernon Percy?'

'Yes, your majesty, he sends his salutations.'

'Well that's all right then,' says Henriette, 'we have nothing to worry about if Algernon sends his cordial best wishes. We might as well discharge the army forthwith.'

There is an awkward pause and Harry Jermyn thinks it wise to steer the conversation away from the Earl of Northumberland.

'Three peers of the realm have joined us in Oxford, your Excellency. It is a hopeful sign that the House of Lords is regretting the rebellion against their king.'

'I am sure there is great affection among all peers for the King,' says the Compte, 'and for the Queen,' he adds hastily.

'Let me introduce my two sons.' Henriette is smiling sweetly again, now that Algernon Percy has been disposed of. 'Charles, Prince of Wales,' the young man takes a step forward and bows, 'and James, Duke of York.' James bows and then offers his hand to the ambassador. Everybody smiles as they shake hands – the tall ambassador, nearly six feet in height, and the nine-year-old child.

'What about me?' asks little Jeffrey; 'I used to be introduced.'

Everybody laughs.

'Jeffrey is referring to an occasion,' says Henriette, 'when he was mistaken for the Prince of Wales by the Dutch ambassador.' She puts her hand on the dwarf's shoulder and turns to Prince Charles towering above Jeffrey. 'You will understand that was many years ago when the Prince of Wales was a small boy.'

'He overtook me.' Jeffrey drags the throne forward and climbs on the seat. He is now standing eye to eye with the heir to the throne. 'Oh no, he didn't.'

The Queen senses the ambassador is a trifle haughty, but to his credit the Compte steps forward and bows before shaking the tiny hand of the Queen's dwarf.

'Thank you, your Excellency,' says Jeffrey, who is touched by the gesture. Too often people treat him as a joke, although he has himself to blame for playing the fool. 'You shall have a special performance of my latest magic tricks.'

'We provide entertainment for honoured guests,' says Henriette. 'I bet the stuffy old puritans are not such attentive hosts.' Henriette glances at her dwarf, standing on the throne. 'Perhaps for your next trick, Jeffrey, you can make Mr Pymple vanish; it would be especially helpful if it was one of your illusions that goes badly wrong at the end.'

The joke is lost on the Compte d'Harcourt but the young princes laugh.

Harry Jermyn smiles and relaxes; the potentially awkward royal audience is progressing smoothly.

Henriette

Suddenly, Henriette fixes the ambassador with one of her penetrating glares and speaks in a deliberate tone. 'If so many people in London are desirous of peace, why is it they continue to command armies in the field against their rightful King? I cannot believe Louis and his mother the Queen Regent would tolerate such defiance in France.'

Jermyn holds his breath. He knows his mistress is inviting an argument. She switches mood so fast.

The ambassador bows. 'Perhaps both sides need a peace to be brokered, your majesty. This is why I have travelled to Oxford to speak with you and the King. I believe we have a great opportunity to negotiate an armistice.'

Henriette pulls a face. 'Are you sure my Lord Essex and his trained bands are keen on an armistice? And what about John Pym?'

'I have yet to speak with the people you mention, your majesty.'

'Ah,' says the Queen with a knowing nod of her head. 'You need to have a chat with Mr Pym. He is keen on talking and assures everyone that he abhors violent interventions.'

'That sounds encouraging,' says Monsieur d'Harcourt.

'Oh yes.' Henriette becomes animated which Jermyn recognises as a danger sign. 'He will promise the earth. But don't upset him, or instead, he will despatch you from the aforementioned earth with the assistance of a sharp axe.'

The room relapses into silence. Jermyn desperately tries to rescue the situation.

'I understand your Excellency is a fine tennis player. We have a court close by.'

'I would be delighted to play.' The Compte bows to the Queen. 'If you will permit, your majesty.'

Henriette shrugs. 'Feel free. I dare say the puritans have closed all the courts in London. My husband is never out of the place.' She turns to Jermyn. Somewhere in the back of her mind is a conversation with Mamie about the merits or otherwise of sarcasm, but it does not deter her. 'Let's have a few games of tennis before our esteemed ambassador returns to London to conclude the peace treaty.' The Queen smiles sweetly: 'Fancy us not realising how simple it would be to end the great rebellion.'

Act III, Scene 21 ~ Christ Church

The Queen walks her sons across the meadows to Christ Church College accompanied by Susan and Harry. They are surrounded by a troop of the King's Guard whose job it is to ensure no townsfolk approach. So far, the plague has been kept out of Merton and Christ Church. New arrivals to the city such as the French Ambassador are forced to leave their carriages outside the walls while their belongings and clothes are smothered in brimstone smoke.

'I don't think we are going to make a great deal of progress with our new ambassador,' says Henriette, picking up her dress as she walks briskly through the long grass. 'Unless of course we can persuade John Pym to settle the rebellion over a game of tennis with Charles.'

'The Compte is naive about negotiating a truce,' says Jermyn, 'but we shouldn't close the door.'

'I know, Harry, I am being unhelpfully pessimistic. You can say it, I shall not combust.'

'You are right to be sceptical, your majesty, but equally there is no harm in trying to divide parliament. The more peers who want peace, the harder it becomes for Pym.'

'My French relatives only want to talk,' mutters Henriette. 'Where are their ships?'

'We might ask the ambassador for a modest fleet to transport Irish Catholic troops across to England. He should understand that Pym needs to be put under pressure to negotiate.'

'We will ask,' says Henriette, 'but I can guess the answer.'

Henriette deposits the princes in their apartments at Christ Church and goes in search of the King. She is about to enter the Dean's lodgings when she collides with a gentleman hurrying out.

'Your majesty.' Henry Rich bows extravagantly.

'Hello Henry,' says the Queen casually. 'Have we had second thoughts and decided to switch to the winning side?'

'I am here because I don't think either side is winning.'

Henriette looks around. 'You will be relieved to see we have an extensive fence surrounding the Christ Church quadrangle to keep the cattle at bay.'

Henry Rich looks puzzled.

'A fence for you to sit on until you have ascertained which side is your best bet.'

Henry Rich manages a rueful smile. 'You do me a disservice, your majesty. I am here to assist the peace process.'

'My word, we are swamped with peace missions,' says the Queen looking around at Harry Jermyn and Susan. 'Henry, you need to have a chat with the French Ambassador; he has practically drawn up a treaty, except he has been side tracked into playing a game of tennis with the Duke of Richmond.' Henriette gesticulates with her arms. 'While you are at it, perhaps you could assist with peace talks between France and Spain and maybe have a chat with the Holy Roman Empire and then the rest of Europe will be sorted.'

The Earl of Holland is well used to withstanding a Henriette outburst. He speaks calmly. 'We all want peace, your majesty.'

'Do you, Mr Rich? And what about your brother? To be honest, Henry, I don't believe a word either of you say anymore.'

'Does our past friendship count for nothing?' He is met with stony silence. 'I was your dashing chevalier long before Harry came along, or Henry Percy or Lord Wilmot. Was there not something special about our friendship?'

'No, Henry, there wasn't. You helped a keen but naive teenager settle into a strange land.' The Queen glares at the Earl of Holland. 'That character doesn't exist anymore. Too many people have betrayed me or made promises they cannot keep – I am a different person now.'

'Of course, your majesty, these days you have Harry to provide your every need.'

'Don't be insolent.' Henriette's eyes narrow. 'Are you responsible for the vile rumours that are spread about London? Of all people, you know that I have never dishonoured the King.'

'I have not libelled you. I sit in parliament and speak my mind. Nor have I taken up arms against the King; I am here to help his majesty. Why are you so against me?'

'You voted for Thomas Wentworth's execution.' Henriette has a tear in her eye. 'How could you do that? You know he was innocent.'

'The Earl of Strafford was innocent of the specific charges in the courtroom, but he was guilty of encouraging a pointless war against the Scottish rebels.' Henry Rich swings his arms about, rather in the style of the Queen. 'His actions brought all this upon us.'

She-Majesty Generalissima

'He urged war against Scotland, and I agreed with him.' Henriette's voice grows louder. 'You might contest his judgement, but it is not a good reason to execute him. It was judicial murder.' She hurls the last words at the Earl of Holland.

'Your majesty,' says Susan, 'I think we should retire.'

'I don't,' says Henriette sharply. 'I am not going to tip toe about the place for fear of offending someone who fails to respond to the King's call to arms and only switches sides when it dawns on him that parliament might be losing.'

'All I ask is that you give me a chance to prove my loyalty,' says the Earl.

'How can you possibly do that, Henry?'

The Queen strides into the King's apartments before the Earl of Holland can reply. As she disappears out of view, it occurs to him that she never once used his old nickname: "Mr Orange".

Henriette is relieved to find Charles on his own in his withdrawing room. She abandons her staff in the reception chamber and runs into his arms.

'What is the m-matter, dear heart?'

'I am fed up with pompous ambassadors and horrid plagues and disloyal earls.' Henriette refuses to let go.

'You bumped into the Earl of Holland?'

'He is so arrogant,' says Henriette. 'He actually says he does not think he has done anything wrong. How could he? Henry was part of the cowardly conspiracy that led to Thomas's murder.'

'He said the same to me; he cannot see the error of his w-ways.'

'Let's talk about something more cheerful,' says Henriette. 'Next week we are expecting a visit from the Earl of Ormonde, our n-newly appointed Lord Lieutenant of Ireland.'

'I hope he will bring more helpful news than the French ambassador.'

'I continue to have h-high hopes of our Third Kingdom,' says Charles.

'It is ironic don't you think that our salvation looks like coming from a Catholic rebel army in Ireland.'

'Provided Ormonde can strike a deal with them.'

'I believe he will,' says Henriette sitting down. 'Thomas always spoke highly of Ormonde. After all, he had a good tutor in the wise old Earl of Strafford.'

'We will need French ships to transport the Irish army,' says Charles.

'I shall have another word with the ambassador.' Henriette kisses Charles. 'Better still, you have a game of tennis with him.'

'We shall hold a tournament; Richmond and Prince Rupert will join in. I can also invite Henry Wilmot; he is a keen player.

'That sounds an excellent plan,' says Henriette, standing up and brushing down her dress. 'But don't include that dreadful Mr Orange.'

Act III, Scene 22 ~ Christ Church Great Hall

Henriette signals for her wine goblet to be filled up; as usual she refuses to have her drink watered down. Unfortunately, every time the Queen accepts a top up, so does Mall and she is not used to consuming quantities of undiluted alcohol.

Prince Rupert is in full flow. 'The enemy cavalry stood at the top of the hill and thought they were invincible. I signalled an advance and we charged up the meadow. They turned and fled, which only encouraged us to gallop harder. It is easy cutting down an enemy from behind.' Rupert swings his arm from side to side as if he is slicing through the enemy with his sword.

Mall is agog as she leans forward and picks up a piece of chicken. 'I don't know how you fight on horseback and steer the beast at the same time.'

Rupert smiles. 'Left hand on the reins, right hand wielding the sword; and if you are in a real tight spot, left hand holds a pistol or a dagger and reins in the teeth.'

Henriette knows Rupert is exaggerating but Mall is completely in awe. 'That must be incredibly difficult.' Mall puts down the chicken leg without taking a bite.

'Not if you are a seasoned soldier like me,' says Rupert with a swagger.

'I am surprised you have any teeth left to eat the banquet,' adds Henriette drily.

Mall stares at Rupert's mouth and the Prince grins at her, displaying remarkably white teeth for his age. Mall collapses in giggles. Henriette fails to see what is so funny.

'Then I charged on through the enemy and before I knew it I was on my own.' Mall listens open-mouthed. 'I turned to find three mounted dragoons charging at me.'

'Oh my God.' Mall puts her hands to her face. She has to be careful not to touch her cheeks with her greasy fingers. 'What did you do?'

Henriette interrupts. 'The sword and the pistol probably sorted two of them out. Let me guess, you head butted the other one.' She lifts her glass and speaks under her breath. 'Given the size of your head it should have been a fatal blow.'

Rupert ignores the Queen. 'I turned and charged straight at them. I could see the whites of their eyes.'

Mall looks as if she is going to faint. 'But there were three of them.'

'Speed and confidence,' declares the Prince. 'You have to remember when there are three enemy soldiers; each waits for the other to do something. I drove my sword so hard into the first one that he was dragged off his mount backwards and I struggled to free my sword. The second man wheeled round and I slashed him across the chest and the third one galloped off.'

'Oh you are so brave.' Mall dips her hands in a water bowl.

Rupert shrugs nonchalantly. 'It's all part of a day's work for a soldier in the King's army.'

Henriette tries not to be sick on her plate. 'What was happening on the rest of the battlefield?' She has been told by Harry Jermyn that the Prince has a tendency to charge for miles and return to the fray after the main action is over.

'Our centre was holding up quite well,' says Rupert, glossing over the detail. 'I brought my cavalry round and mopped up various pockets of artillery and attacked the baggage train.'

Henriette picks up a chicken leg. 'It's a shame we couldn't press our advantage.'

'Ran short of gunpowder,' says Rupert, 'although I was all for having another go at them. We did harass their column as it retreated to London.'

Mall downs her remaining wine in one gulp. 'I don't know where we would be without you.'

In London rather than Oxford, wonders Henriette unkindly. Before Prince Rupert can elaborate on his plans for the campaign ahead, the signal comes for the end of the banquet. The men and women retire to separate rooms while the tables are cleared away. An hour later, everyone gathers to watch the King and Queen commence the dancing with a minuet. The great hall at Christ Church is a reasonable substitute for the Banqueting Hall at White Hall Palace and the nine-course meal is almost as elaborate as the good old days, despite food shortages. Musicians play in the ornate wooden gallery and little Jeffrey performs magic tricks. The Queen drafts in students, who perform a cut-down masque, a series of tableaux paying homage to the Three Kingdoms. It is an appropriate entertainment for the chief guest – the Earl of Ormonde, Lord Lieutenant of Ireland. The plague has not returned for several weeks as the onset of winter proves a more effective cure than brimstone or tobacco. All military activity is suspended as the rain turns highways into waterways and snuffs out the fuses of muskets and cannon.

'Where is Mall's husband?' asks Henriette as she holds the King's hand and moves gracefully down the full length of the dance floor.

'The Duke of Richmond is in Bristol,' says Charles. 'He is organising some additional defences in case parliament try and recapture the city in the spring.'

Henriette and Charles sit down after the first two dances. The Queen notices that Mall is partnering Prince Rupert. She is unsteady on her feet and keeps laughing each time she misses a step.

'I think Mall has had enough to drink,' says Henriette.

'I am sure Prince Rupert will look after her,' says Charles.

'That is my worry.'

Edward Hyde approaches the King, bows and whispers in his ear; Charles makes his excuse and wanders across to talk to Sir Edward Nicholas and Lord Digby.

'May I sit this dance out with your majesty?' The Earl of Ormonde bows to Henriette.

'Come and sit down, James,' says Henriette. 'Tell me about Ireland.'

Ormonde settles on an ornately carved oak chair and rest his hands on the arms, shaped as the paws of a lion. 'Have you got all night?'

Henriette laughs. 'I hear snippets from my good friends Randal MacDonnell and his wife Kate.'

Protestant Ormonde is wary of Catholic Randal, but he gives nothing away.

'I know Katharine well,' says the Earl. 'I was at Portsmouth when that coward plunged a dagger into the Duke of Buckingham.'

'I did not realise you were a witness,' says Henriette. 'I don't think poor Kate ever recovered from the death of Steenie.'

'I was by his side.' Ormonde thinks back. 'It was the Duke of Buckingham who persuaded me to join him on the expedition to La Rochelle. I was only nineteen, thought I could conquer the world.'

'You conquered Ireland instead.'

'Thomas Wentworth tamed Ireland, I was only his deputy.'

'I will never forgive the puritans for what they did to Thomas,' says Henriette. 'Francis Windebank describes it as judicial murder.'

'He is right. No one has ever managed to achieve what Thomas did in Ireland; they rewarded him with a witch hunt and an execution.'

'Charles tells me you have brought the Irish rebellion to a successful conclusion.'

'I have stopped the rebel fighting, but the trouble with Ireland is you please one faction and then another group feel slighted. So it goes on.' Ormonde shakes his head. 'And on.'

'Three out of every four Irishmen is Catholic; that is hardly a faction.'

'It depends on your point of view in Ireland, your majesty.'

'A bit like here in England,' says Henriette. 'We have royalists and puritans.'

'I wish it was that simple in Ireland.' Mall dances past and nearly falls over, caught just in time by Prince Rupert. Ormonde smiles. 'The Duchess of Richmond appears a little unstable on her feet.'

'She is embarrassing.' Henriette watches as Mall is steadied by Prince Rupert, followed by much giggling.

'We have four distinct groups in Ireland,' explains Ormonde. 'The Anglo Irish Protestants live in the Dublin area known as the Pale while Scottish Protestants occupy parts of the north. They spend their time buying up land and creating vast plantations.'

'This presumably annoys the Catholics who have lived off the land for centuries.'

'Correct,' says Ormonde. 'The Catholics live beyond the Pale and as you say make up the bulk of the population. Their rebellion is directed against the Protestant settlements.'

'And the fourth group?' asks Henriette.

'The Scottish army,' says Ormonde. 'They invaded north-east Ireland to protect the Presbyterian Scots.'

'That is quite a mixture.'

'I think we have brokered a deal with the Catholic rebels and hopefully I can release four thousand soldiers for your campaign in the New Year.'

'That is good news.' Henriette picks up an almond confite. 'Now I must get hold of some ships.' She stands up. 'Excuse me, James, but I must catch the French Ambassador before he returns to London.' Henriette glances at the Earl of Ormonde. 'You don't happen to play tennis, do you?'

Act III, Scene 23 ~ Merton

The Queen vigorously stirs the earthenware mug with a spoon before handing it to her senior lady in waiting.

'Drink that,' she says sternly.

'I have a terrible headache,' says Mall, 'and I feel sick.'

'Drink up,' says the Queen briskly. 'I have mixed a remedy that my mother invented – raw egg, nutmeg, goat's milk and lemon.'

Mall looks as if she is about to wretch.

'Sometimes it is better to be sick,' says Henriette cheerfully. 'It removes the impurities from your stomach.' She holds the mug close to Mall's face.

Eventually the Duchess gives in and drinks the posset.

Henriette stares at her intently. 'Be careful, madam, not to disturb your marriage as well as your tummy. James Stuart is a fine husband.'

Mall frowns. 'I drank too much wine, your majesty, that's all.'

The Queen nods. 'Then there is nothing to worry about. It is acceptable for you to look ridiculous, but not to make your husband look ridiculous.'

'I don't know what anyone has said, but my marriage is fine.'

'Good.' Henriette takes the empty cup from Mall. 'Next time, I suggest you dilute your wine liberally with water.'

'But you drink wine without mixtures.'

Henriette raises an eyebrow. 'I am a princess of France – we learn to drink wine from an early age. I was taught dancing, singing, riding and how to drink wine.' The Queen walks to the door. 'Unfortunately they omitted to teach me how to sell jewellery, or buy arms or lead armies. Now if you are feeling better, I shall go and walk the dogs and think about how to write my begging letter to the Queen Regent of France.'

Henriette takes her pack of dogs for a stroll in the Merton College gardens accompanied by Sir Edward Nicholas. The fear of plague is receding but sickness continues to hover over the compact and overcrowded city. Dysentery, influenza and pneumonia are rife and there have been reports of smallpox.

'You have added a bench by the mulberry tree, your majesty.'

'Very observant, Edward.' Henriette looks up at the grey clouds. 'Unfortunately winter is not the time for sitting about.' One of her lap dogs fouls under the tree and the Queen signals a servant carrying a shovel and sack. 'The Duke of Buckingham used to call him the Keeper of the Royal Dog Stools.'

Sir Edward laughs. 'That must be where young George Villiers gets his sense of humour from.'

'It is a shame that the Villiers boys have been sent to Florence; I don't think Steenie would have approved of his sons disappearing in the middle of a fight.'

'It was Algernon Percy who financed their studies in Italy,' says Sir Edward.

'It was an excuse to remove them from the conflict.'

'Quite possibly; it is unfortunate because Prince Rupert reckons the young Duke of Buckingham has the makings of a great cavalry commander.'

Henriette smiles. 'Steenie would have been so proud. It is harsh to lose children, as I have found, but it must be equally sad to die young and never see any of your children grow up.' The Queen picks up Mitte who is squabbling with one of the other dogs. 'Mary Hamilton was another one who missed out on her family.'

'Her husband remains hopeful of reaching an agreement with the rebels in Edinburgh,' says Sir Edward. 'But I have to say my own enquiries do not support Hamilton's optimism. There are rumours that John Pym has been active in meetings with the rebels.'

Henriette puts Mitte down beneath the mulberry tree. She turns and gives her husband's secretary of state one of her penetrating stares. There is rarely a sparkle in her eyes these days.

'That man Pym will not stop until he has destroyed us.'

Henriette prods the manuscript. 'Have we made the point about Scotland?'

'Several times, I think,' says Madame de Motteville. 'You explained that Scotland was the key to the rebellion.'

'They started it,' says Henriette with a pout. 'Then they stood on the sidelines and kept us all guessing about which side they would choose.'

'A bit like Lord Stanley at the Battle of Bosworth.'

Henriette frowns. History was never her strong subject, French or English. 'What has Bosworth got to do with it?'

'I was just making a comparison, your majesty.'

'There is no comparison with what we suffered. Our own subjects treating us so rudely.' Henriette sighs. 'The whole sorry mess is depressing me. We shall resume tomorrow, Françoise.'

'We are attending the masked ball at Fontainebleau tomorrow, have you forgotten?'

'Do I have to?'

'You promised Minette; she will be so proud if you make an appearance. So will your nephew.'

'Louis spends his life idling his time away. He has no idea what we went through in England all those years ago.'

'He is very fond of his aunt.'

'But he never lent us any ships, did he?'

Act III, Scene 24 ~ The Tennis Court

'Is young James winning?' asks Henriette as she struggles to keep up with the complicated scoring system.

Before the King can reply, the eleven-year-old Duke of York smashes the ball against the service wall that runs the full ninety foot length of the court landing close to Prince Charles who is waiting to receive. Charles swings his racket and sends the ball flying back to the serving end. Young James scoops the shot, aiming for the door gallery hazard, one of a series of pigeonholes in the service wall. Prince Charles moves forward to intercept the ball and volleys to prevent disaster. James misses the next return and it crashes into the net.

'Game to Charles,' shouts the King.

Henriette has never fully grasped the complexities of scoring despite her father bequeathing a series of tennis courts at each of his palaces. Henri the Great was a keen player as is Henriette's husband.

She consults the scoreboard. 'That's three points apiece.'

The huge indoor tennis hall is conveniently placed on Saint John Baptist Street, halfway between Christ Church and Merton. The indoor court is rectangular with a net in the middle. The players are allowed to bounce the ball off the sides, while the eight cavities in the serving wall add an extra dimension to the game. The viewing gallery is situated just behind the server. Prince Charles moves to the serving end while James stands in the hazard court waiting to receive.

'Has Sir Edward Nicholas spoken to you about the Scottish rebels?' asks Henriette.

The King nods. 'There is a great deal of talk about the Scottish and English parliaments joining f-forces.'

'Hamilton has let us down badly if he permits this to happen.'

'The Duke certainly appears active in his own preservation,' says Charles quietly.

'You must recall him to Oxford. We need to adopt Montrose's plan and use Irish troops raised by Randal to link with the Highland clans.'

'If Montrose could pin the Scottish army down, it would greatly assist our n-northern army.'

'Good shot,' shouts Henriette, as Prince Charles fires the ball into the first gallery. 'I knew Montrose and Randal were talking sense when I met them at Scarborough Castle.' She groans. 'I hope this is not going to be another missed opportunity.'

'We did not w-want to trigger a civil war in Scotland. Hamilton was confident of bringing the rebels across to our side.'

'The Marquis of Hamilton claims to do lots of things.' James reaches a difficult return but the ball hits the top of the net and bounces back. Henriette shouts to her son. 'Bad luck, James.'

'Set point,' says Charles.

'It's a close game. Given the difference in ages, I think James is doing rather well.'

Prince Charles launches a serve and James returns the ball aggressively. One error will cost him the set but he is not afraid to take risks.

Lord Digby enters the viewing gallery and shuffles along the row of narrow seats to where the royal couple are sitting.

'Go on James, give it a go,' shouts Henriette.

'Your majesties,' says Lord Digby, 'a messenger has arrived from London. The Scottish parliament has signed an accord with Westminster; we appear to be at war with both kingdoms.'

Young Charles smashes the ball at James who misses the return completely.

'Game over,' says the King.

Act III, Scene 25 ~ Merton College

It is a brave thing to do, some would say suicidal, but the Earl of Holland refuses to leave Oxford without an audience with the Queen.

'Must I see him?' asks Henriette. 'I have a horrible headache.'

Harry Jermyn shrugs. 'He is very insistent; he says he will sit on the step outside Merton until you grant him access.'

'That sounds like Henry Rich of old.' The Queen puts down the embroidery.

'You never know when we might need friends in London,' says Jermyn. 'Perhaps you ought to speak to him.'

Henriette sighs. 'I will allow him in, but not as a friend. He has made that impossible.'

Jermyn bows and goes to summon Henry Rich.

Henriette looks at Susan. 'If I get worked up, intervene and tell me to calm down.'

The Countess of Denbeigh is not enamoured of the idea. 'You will shout at me, your majesty.'

'Possibly,' says Henriette, 'but it will help. I promise to apologise afterwards.'

Margaret Lucas has been an enthusiastic participant in the embroidery circle and she stands up to leave.

'Please stay, Margaret; I know you hate confrontation and it may help me to control myself. Besides, I want to outnumber him.'

Margaret nods and sits down again.

'Where is Mall?' asks Henriette. 'She is never here when I need her.'

Margaret's cheeks blush. 'I think the Duchess of Richmond is at Christ Church, your majesty.'

'As long as she is not at St John's with my nephew; she is spending too much time with Prince Rupert for my liking.'

'I think they share a common love of horses,' says Susan.

'I trust that is their only common interest.' Before Henriette can expound further on the subject, Jermyn returns and announces the Earl of Holland.

Henry Rich walks in confidently and bows. 'Good morning, your majesty.' It could have been the Earl of old when he chaperoned the teenage princess from France to England to meet her new husband.

'What is so good about it?' Henriette wrinkles her nose. 'I know, you are leaving Oxford.'

Henry Rich is not daunted. 'Thank you for seeing me at such short notice; you are right as always, your majesty, I am heading back to London today.'

Henriette does not smile. 'The air in Oxford is not conducive to the Earl's health?' She gives a brief, forced smile. 'Or is it the company that troubles you?'

'I accept that I have lost your trust and friendship, but before I depart, would you grant me leave to speak from the heart?'

'That could be awkward; I thought you mislaid yours some time ago.'

Silence ensues; there is tension in the air. Then in typical fashion, the Queen suddenly changes mood. 'Come on,' she says briskly, 'it's stopped raining, let's go for a walk in the garden.'

Henriette leads the way, followed by the Earl of Holland, Harry Jermyn, Susan and Margaret. They bump into Mall on the staircase; she appears flustered. Henriette puts on a false smile. 'Perhaps you would care to join us in the garden, Mall, assuming you are not too exhausted after your hectic morning?'

Mall gives Susan an enquiring glance and then nods to the Queen. 'I would love to accompany your majesty.'

Henriette

The party wends its way outside and Henriette is suddenly in fine fettle; the headache appears to have vanished.

'A mulberry tree,' she says to the Earl, pointing towards the main feature of the garden.

Henry Rich looks instead at the city walls that loom on two sides of the outside space. 'I hadn't realised you were so close to the walls.'

'You get used to it,' says Henriette. 'One never knows when a pile of roundheads might pop over.'

The Earl of Holland smiles: 'I miss your wit.'

'I miss my friend,' says Henriette, 'but unfortunately he disappeared long ago.'

Henry Rich refuses to rise to the barb. He judges that the Queen is in a mood for some straight talking, like in the old days.

'I believe in my King,' he pauses, 'and my Queen, and I want to broker a peace that will guarantee their position at the head of our three kingdoms. I think I can achieve that more readily at Westminster as a member of parliament.' He stops by the mulberry and examines its branches before turning back to look at Henriette. 'That does not mean I am disloyal or I am changing sides.'

'I am glad to hear it; I am not sure the puritans can keep up with your flipping and flopping.'

'I am not welcome here in Oxford, and I can do no good at court. I understand that.'

'Will you be welcome in London I wonder?'

'Possibly not, but before this rebellion is out, I am going to prove to you that I am a loyal subject and that I never stopped admiring you.'

The Queen walks past the tree and heads towards the city wall. 'I shall not hold my breath, but if perchance you do prove your loyalty, I hope it will be in a useful way that aids the King.'

Henry Rich watches Henriette walk down the path towards the centre of the formal garden. He takes three tentative steps towards her and speaks softly: 'I don't know if we will ever meet again, your majesty, but I give you my loyal best wishes for the future.'

Henriette turns back and walks up to the Earl of Holland. She offers her gloved hand. He holds it, very gently the Queen thinks, and kisses it.

'I would lay down my life for you, Princess of France.'

She does not reply; her face gives nothing away.

Henry Rich bows and walks slowly backwards. He turns as he reaches a stone archway that connects the garden to the quad.

Henriette finally speaks. 'God be with you, Mr Orange.'

The Earl of Holland pauses and smiles, but does not turn back. He walks into the shadows and disappears.

Act III, Scene 26 ~ University College

'Oh, rid me of this my torture, quickly, there;
My madam, with the everlasting voice:
The bells, in time of pestilence, ne'er made
Like noise, or were in that perpetual motion!
The Cock-pit comes not near it. All my house,
But now, steam'd like a bath with her thick breath.
A lawyer could not have been heard; nor scarce
Another woman, such a hail of words
She has let fall. For hell's sake, rid her hence.'

'I worry that perhaps Lady Would-be is a joke at my expense.' Henriette walks away from the stage where the students are rehearsing once again. 'Ben was cross with me when I asked you to take over the scripting of royal masques.'

'He did not have you in mind, your majesty, unless he had magical powers.' Sir William Davenant smiles. 'Ben wrote Volpone before you were born.'

'That's all right then; I love her character, she never stops talking.'

'People say that Ben Jonson was writing about his wife, who he described on many occasions, quite unfairly, as a shrew.'

The Queen sits down at the far end of the dining hall. 'I am a brat, not a shrew.'

'Ben shared quite a lot in common with Will Shakespeare, they both married young and both spent their lives moaning about their wives.'

Henriette laughs. 'I was fond of Ben.'

'I loved Ben too,' says Davenant. 'I visited his grave in Poet's Corner at Westminster Abbey; I told him I would hopefully join him one day.' He chuckles. 'I was amused by his epitaph – "O rare Ben".'

Henriette

'Well it's true.' Henriette misses the pun.

'It is a clever Jonson-style joke,' says Davenant. 'Orare is Latin for "pray for". I wish I had thought of it first.'

'You are both accomplished with words,' says Henriette. 'I was lucky to have such talented playwrights crafting my royal masques.' Henriette stares at the rehearsals continuing on the stage at the far end of the hall. 'I do miss our theatricals.'

'I remember the last masque we produced when you were the Amazon Queen descending on to the stage with your warriors.'

'I am reprising the role, but this time it's for real.' Henriette tries to shake her right arm. 'But I didn't have ill health to contend with in the masque version; this paralysis is driving me mad.'

'What is ailing you? Edward Sackville told me you were unwell.'

'I think it is an excess of grumpy puritans, or else too long a confinement in this overcrowded, disease-ridden city.'

Davenant glances at the Queen. 'I hope you are not criticising my home town.'

'I didn't know you were born here.'

'My parents owned the Crown Inn, and my father was mayor of Oxford,' says Davenant proudly.

'Well Oxford is nice enough and I have comfortable apartments at Merton College; the problem is not being able to travel outside the city walls. You know me, always restless.' The Queen rubs her side. 'The rash comes and goes; I wish I could do the same.'

'Can the royal physicians not provide ointments to ease the rash?'

'No one knows what's causing it,' says Henriette. 'Mayerne is stuck in London, but he always thinks I make my sicknesses up. He used to be the same about my migraines and toothache. But contrary to his opinion, I am not a hysterical woman; all I want is to feel healthy again.'

'You should seek a second opinion.'

'I have received a third and fourth; no one has a clue.' The Queen stands up. 'Come on, let's stop worrying about rebellions and sickness; we have a play to watch. The students are excited; it is not every day they practice in front of the Poet Laureate.'

After the rehearsals, the Queen takes a sedan chair from University College around the corner to Christ Church. The King has left orders that she is not to walk anywhere outside of Merton until the doctors have resolved her ailments. It is a well-intentioned precaution but it only makes Henriette feel more hemmed in. The royal couple meet in the great hall; the same venue where the House of Lords presided in Henriette's first year in England.

'I wish our theatre was as grand as this.' Henriette stares up at the elegant vaulted ceiling. 'Actually it's probably a bit too big.'

'The dining hall at University College is ideal,' says Charles. 'How are the rehearsals going?'

'Very well,' says Henriette. 'It is interesting; you get to know a story much better when you watch the players practising day in, day out. Ben was witty.'

'Like my good wife.'

Henriette shakes her head in disagreement.

'You are too m-modest. John Birkenhead was showing me the latest edition of Aulicus and he told me how much you and Lord Digby are involved with the news sheet. He thinks you have a sharp sense of humour.'

'Just as well, considering what God has thrown at me these last few years. In fact, now I come to think of it, God must have quite a sense of humour. I shall have to suggest to Father Philip that we throw a few satirical jokes into our prayers.'

'That is unlike you, Maria, to be flippant about your devotions.'

Henriette's shoulders droop. 'I am tired and worn down. A good Mass used to revitalise me, but now I find it makes little difference.'

'It is your illness that drags you down,' says Charles.

'And the rebellion and the puritans and the infighting on our own side and this crowded smelly city and the plague and the Scots…' Henriette waves her arms in frustration. 'And everything.'

The King takes a few steps down the centre of the Great Hall and turns to face Henriette.

'How about this for an idea to cheer you up?' It is Charles's turn to spread out his arms. 'Here, in this very chamber, I am going to s-summon a parliament.'

Henriette frowns. 'But there is a parliament in London; we are fighting to try and get rid of it.'

'Exactly so,' says Charles. 'It is an illegal parliament sitting against the w-wishes of their King. I shall call a true parliament here in Oxford; we have a precedent for conducting the business of the Houses from this city.'

'What a cunning design.' Henriette's face lights up. 'I cannot wait to see Mr Pymple's reaction when the House of Commoners here in Oxford impeaches the leader of the rebel Commoners in London.' Henriette performs a quick pirouette and then moves forward and hugs Charles.

'I am glad you approve, dear heart. We will send out summonses before Christmas and open parliament in the New Year.'

'I have an even better idea,' says Henriette excitedly. 'We will invite Mr Pym to our parliament; just as he politely invited me to London. Come along and have a chat, and then we will string you up from the gibbet at Carfax.'

'Our enemies deserve a fair trial; only cowards are cruel.'

'If you insist, dear heart.' Henriette breaks free from Charles and runs the length of the Hall. The King has not seen his wife so energised in months. Henriette turns and shouts at the top of her voice: 'Dear Mr Pym, we would feel bereft if you did not join our parliament; the whole place would be so dull without you, so do pop up to Oxford and say a few words in our smart new chamber. I promise the soldiers will not arrest you until after your incredibly long, boring speech.'

They both laugh. Unbeknown to them, a messenger is setting off from London. There will be no need to issue a royal invitation to the right honourable Member of Parliament for Tavistock.

Henriette forgets her itchy rash and upset tummy; her eyes sparkle.

Charles is reminded how much he loves her. He walks slowly towards his beautiful wife, holds her in his arms and kisses her. He does not stumble over a single word.

'You are so strong, Maria. Just when people think you are laid low by sickness or hounded by puritan bullies, you fight back. My Queen is by my side; I am ready to do battle.'

Henriette grips him tightly. 'We are one, dear heart. Our enemies will never separate us.'

Act III, Scene 27 ~ Merton College

Susan is woken in the middle of the night by a maid of honour who has been sleeping in the Queen's bedroom. 'Please come quickly, my lady, the Queen is most distressed.'

'Wake the Duchess of Richmond.' Susan throws a gown over her shoulders and sets off towards the Queen's apartments. The Countess has no direct link to Henriette's rooms. She has to walk down the stone steps to the quadrangle, clutching a candle in one hand, and back up the adjacent stairwell. Susan can hear Henriette's screams.

'What has happened, your majesty?' Susan rushes across to the bed where Henriette is sitting on the edge, doubled up.

Droplets of perspiration run down the Queen's face. 'Oh my God I have never felt such pain in my stomach, not even when I lost our first born.'

The Countess can see small specks of blood on the sheet. Mall appears at the doorway as Susan puts her arm around Henriette and tries to persuade her to lie down.

'I cannot lie down, it hurts too much.'

Susan looks at Mall. 'Summon the doctors – tell them to come quickly.'

Mall disappears as several other maids of honour enter the room.

'Get me a bowl of warm water,' says Susan, 'and a bed warming pan. Someone stoke up the fire.'

Henriette continues to clutch her stomach and bend over. 'It eases a little when I lean forward.' She shivers.

Susan turns to a maid of honour. 'You better call Father Philip.' Susan takes off her gown and wraps it around the Queen. She sits beside Henriette. 'Is the pain anywhere else?'

'No, it's just in my tummy.' Henriette keeps gripping her stomach and rocking forward and back. 'Maybe it is something I have eaten.'

'We all had the same meal last night,' says Susan.

Henriette pouts. 'The puritans must have crept into the kitchens and poisoned me.'

Susan smiles. It is an encouraging sign if the Queen can joke about her discomfort. A maid arrives with a bowl of warm water and Susan rinses out a cloth and presses it on Henriette's forehead. The fire is blazing and more candles have been lit.

There is a knock on the door and a maid enters and curtsies. 'Father Philip awaits outside, your majesty.'

'I am not dead yet,' says Henriette. She is about to say something else but a stab of pain forces her to double up. She speaks in a hoarse voice. 'Tell him to wait.'

Minutes later, Mall ushers in Doctor Harvey and his assistant. Susan orders everyone out, the Countess remains as chaperone. The doctors begin to examine Henriette. Susan walks across to the fire and throws on more logs. As the Queen pulls up her nightdress, Doctor Harvey is shocked at the sight. The small blotches that had broken out on parts of her torso at his last inspection now cover her entire body and most of her neck and arms. The marks bear some similarities with measles. He has spent many years at the busy Saint Bartholomew's Hospital in London and is one of the most experienced royal physicians but he has never seen such an unusual rash. He carefully examines the Queen's distended stomach; Henriette lets out cries of pain that chill Susan to the bone.

At the Queen's insistence, her husband is not advised until the morning. Susan and Mall stay up all night, long after the doctors leave, and they are asleep in chairs by the fire when Charles creeps into the room. The King tiptoes across the room and sits on the edge of the bed.

He whispers: 'My dear heart, I have only just been told. You should have summoned me hours ago.'

Henriette flings her arms around him. 'I told the doctor not to disturb you unless I was dying.'

Charles hugs her. 'You should have sent a m-message.'

'Have you spoken with Doctor Harvey?' asks Henriette.

'He has gone to Oriel to attend a patient,' says the King.

'Do not distress yourself,' says Henriette, 'there is nothing to be alarmed about.'

'Are you in pain?'

'The tummy ache has passed,' says Henriette. 'Dr Harvey has specified a strict diet for the next few days, but I think all is well.' She smiles at Charles. 'Has no one told you his diagnosis?'

'All I heard was that you had a terrible night and that the doctors were in attendance.'

Henriette kisses him. 'I am pregnant, my sweet.'

'A baby.' Charles is not expecting this news. 'You are with child?'

The Queen nods. 'Are you not pleased?'

'Of course, dear heart, it is wonderful news.'

'I have to confess,' says Henriette, lowering her voice, 'that I am not sure this is a good time to be bringing a child into the world;

but it is God's will and maybe the new prince or princess will bring us good fortune.'

'I am sure that will be the case. You m-must rest, and continue to use the sedan chair. Does Dr Harvey indicate w-when the child is due?'

'He estimates the late Spring,' says Henriette. 'Will you tell Charles and James?'

'Certainly,' says Charles. 'And we must send a message to Elizabeth and Henry at Saint James's Palace.'

'I wish they could join us,' says Henriette. 'On the other hand Oxford with all this sickness is not a safe refuge for the young ones.'

'We will bring the family together when the time is right.'

Henriette has not slept all night; she is exhausted. She lies content in her husband's arms and rapidly falls asleep. Charles looks across the room to Susan and Mall who have collapsed in their chairs by the fire, snoring loudly.

> Henriette stares at her grand daughter. 'Now, Marie Louise, what shall we have for tea?'
>
> The four-year-old with the blonde cascading curls jumps up and down. 'Pea soup,' she cries, 'and strawberries for Afters.'
>
> Henriette shakes her head. 'I don't understand this obsession among the young for vegetables and fresh fruit.'
>
> 'They are all the rage,' says Madame de Motteville, putting down her quill. 'Minette was showing me her vegetable garden; it is very impressive.'
>
> 'She tried to feed me some revolting, slimy green stuff called spinach,' says Henriette, wrinkling her nose. 'I said I preferred a good slab of meat.'
>
> 'Can we have strawberries, grandmamma?'
>
> 'That's another thing, Françoise, this penchant for plain fruit after the meal. What has happened to sugared fruit and confites?' Henriette takes her grand daughter's hand. 'Let's go and see the cook.'
>
> 'Will we be resuming the memoirs this evening, your majesty?'

Henriette looks over her shoulder. 'Most certainly. The next scene is a happy family occasion. I still treasure the programme for the Master of Arts ceremony.'

'You must have been so proud.'

'I was, Françoise, although Elizabeth and Henry were not present.' Henriette smiles at little Marie Louise. 'I clearly remember my dear heart saying that one day our family would be together again when the time was right. That proved to be true and false.'

Madame frowns. 'I don't understand.'

Henriette shrugs. 'We did all come together many years later, but only the survivors.' Henriette walks slowly towards the kitchen with her young charge. 'Only the survivors.'

Act III, Scene 28 ~ St Mary's, Oxford

Henriette rarely enters an Anglican Church. Today, however, she is content to be sitting on the front row of the University Church of St Mary's. She says a quiet Catholic prayer to herself. The building is no longer used for church services; instead it conducts degree ceremonies. Archbishop Laud, in his capacity as Chancellor of Oxford University, disapproved of employing an Anglican church. He was planning the construction of a purpose-built hall adjoining the Divinity School, but his imprisonment in the Tower brought the project to an abrupt halt.

Henriette is not concerned where the ceremony takes place. The important issue is who is taking part. The Queen sits next to her husband. The royal couple are accompanied on the long front bench by their senior courtiers, army officers and the clergy of Oxford. Henriette's confessor, Father Philip, is invited. The Queen requests that John Birkenhead sits beside her to provide a running commentary – the pomp and circumstance in Latin has not changed much since mediaeval times. Every few minutes, Henriette whispers in his ear: 'Who is that man in elaborate robes?' Then a bit later: 'What is he saying?' and at regular intervals: 'Are these the Master of Arts candidates?' It may have been advisable if someone had warned the Queen that, like one of her extravagant masques, the order of conferring degrees with its intricate ceremonial takes several hours.

Henriette is attentive as the maces conveying the authority of the university are carried in solemn procession, followed by the Vice Chancellor, Registrar, Proctors and senior academic leaders. There are long Latin speeches followed by the calling of individual schools of learning. The first degrees are bestowed on Doctors of Divinity; Birkenhead translates portions of Latin for the Queen and explains the purpose of each stage of the ceremony.

'The two Proctors are submitting the candidate's name,' whispers Birkenhead. 'They walk up and down the congregation to obtain the approval of the Masters of Arts graduates.'

'What if the graduates don't approve?' asks Henriette earnestly.

'It's just a formality. They don't actually vote.'

'I see,' says Henriette, now totally confused.

Henriette watches as a young man holds the right hand of his Professor and walks up to the Vice Chancellor. A Proctor presents the undergraduate with a bible and the candidate places his hand on the book. The Proctor begins to recite in Latin.

'He is taking the oath of allegiance to the University.'

The candidate then recites in a clear voice: 'Do fidem'.

Birkenhead whispers, 'I swear.'

The Vice Chancellor takes the bible and touches the man's head, rattling off a long speech in Latin, which Birkenhead does not bother to translate. The young man walks away and disappears out of the Church.

'Is that it?' asks Henriette.

'Not quite,' says Birkenhead. 'He now has to pay his College servant for a new gown and hat and in a moment he will return to receive the congratulations of the congregation.'

Moments later the young man reappears in an ankle length gown with embroidered sleeves and a hat with a central tuft and a wide soft brim flopping over his forehead. After bowing to the vice chancellor he heads for an empty seat.

'Because he has graduated to the highest level of Doctor he joins the congregation,' says Birkenhead. 'When we come to the MAs and BAs they will sit on the empty benches at the back of the church.' As Birkenhead speaks, the whole process is starting again with a second candidate. Seventeenth century Oxford does not believe in batching its graduates.

By the time every student has been presented for the schools of Divinity, Civil Law and Medicine, followed by Doctors of Letters and Science, Henriette is ready for falling asleep. As she whispers to John Birkenhead, 'I am not sure if it's my condition with child or the length of this ceremony, but my backside is aching and I need the toilet.'

'The Master of Arts students are next,' says John Birkenhead.

Henriette looks towards the back of the church and to her delight, at the front of the queue of a dozen young men are the Prince of Wales and the Duke of York. This time, she takes a close interest in the ceremony. Her hands are clasped and there is a tear in her eye as first young Charles and then James are inducted as Masters of Arts at the University. Most students spend sixteen terms over four years to reach this stage, and even sons of nobility are expected to attend for three years, but Charles and James are an exception. It is not entirely honorary. Over the last twelve months they have received college tutor time from leading scholars in Latin, Greek, Science, Divinity, Law and Arts, coordinated by their personal tutor. Prince Charles has inherited his mother's short attention span for learning, but James laps up the teaching, taking a special interest in divinity.

Henriette requires no further commentary from Birkenhead and she slips her arm into her husband's. When the two boys return in their full regalia, everyone applauds spontaneously and Henriette stands up and curtsies before her sons. For a moment she forgets about parliaments, rebellions and aches and pains. The Queen is a happy and proud mother.

There is a grand banquet at Merton College to celebrate the university's two newest and most famous graduates. Henriette sends servants to other colleges to raid their larders to ensure a magnificent feast. She instructs her chefs to create an authentic French-style spread. In the evening, the guests move across to University College where they view a performance of Ben Jonson's Volpone. It is during the first interval, while the audience are treated to more wine and confitures that a messenger arrives from London.

Sir Edward Nicholas takes the King to one side. After a brief conversation, Charles walks across to his wife. Henriette is in conversation with William Davenant.

'I have an urgent communication from London, dear heart.'

Henriette is alerted. 'Not our children, not Elizabeth or Henry?'

'No, the children are safe; it is news from Westminster.' Charles stares at his wife. 'John Pym has passed away; apparently he was suffering from a cancerous growth.'

Henriette's face is impassive. 'Pym is dead.' She speaks quietly. 'I suppose I should jump for joy; my nemesis is vanquished.' She turns away and stares at the stage as it is prepared for the next Act. 'His passing means nothing to me.'

Act III, Scene 29 ~ Woodstock

Two riders canter across the deer park under a clear blue sky. They negotiate rolling hills, meadows, woodland and winding streams. Pockets of frost cling to the grass where the sun cannot penetrate. Both riders are wrapped in coats, scarves, gloves and hats as their horses cut through the icy air. When the couple reach the boundary wall, they stop and look back, laughing and joking, their breath condensing. The narrow stone turrets of the medieval hunting lodge, part palace part castle, rise above the woodland.

'There used to be lions within these w-walls,' says Charles.

'I hope this is not another elephant story,' says Henriette.

'Elephant story?'

'Steenie once assured me that your father kept an elephant at Theobalds Palace.'

'He did; it was a gift from the King of Spain.' Charles stares at the moss-covered stone walls. 'And Henry the First kept lions and leopards here.'

Henriette looks across to a herd of fallow deer. 'I bet that cut down on the poaching.'

'I shall take Charles and James on a New Year's Day hunt tomorrow.'

'I would love to join you but I think three months into my term I should stick to trot and canter.'

'This must be your last horse riding until the baby arrives.'

'I feel better than I did before Christmas.' She breathes in the chilly air. 'It is wonderful to be free of those forbidding city walls looming over the college. I prefer King Henry's boundary round Woodstock Manor.' Henriette frowns at the modest six foot walls. 'I am surprised the lions did not jump out.'

Charles smiles. 'I think they were kept inside a special enclosure.'

'It was a splendid idea to celebrate St Stephen's Day at Woodstock,' says Henriette, 'even if the hunting lodge is a little old fashioned.'

'Back in the thirteenth century, defence took priority over comfort. Henry could never be sure when some m-member of the nobility might try and seize his crown.'

'Not much has changed, except now it is commoners rather than lords who seek to pinch the throne.'

The deer scatter as the royal couple edge around a coppice and descend into a gently sloping valley that cuts though the park. 'This vista is spectacular,' says Henriette. 'If I was building a house here in Woodstock Park, I would put it up there.' She points to a natural plateau in the distance.

'I think you have enough building projects.'

'Somerset House and Greenwich will need renovating by all accounts.' Henriette sighs. 'If I ever see them again.'

'We are plotting our return, Maria. The Privy Council has agreed a two stage approach. First our army of the west will push towards Sussex and Kent and cut the British Sea ports off. Then our Oxford army will approach from the n-north and west.'

Henriette nods her approval. 'Do we have enough men?'

'Lord Hopton and Prince Maurice are recruiting for their Western Army while they winter at Winchester. We will send a detachment from our Oxford army and they should be ready to march on Sussex by March.'

Henriette coaxes her horse into trot. 'This news fills me with great joy; I can finally see an end to the rebellion.'

'The puritans have lost their leader, we are receiving reports from London of great divisions, and there is much criticism of the Earl of Essex. There are rumours that the Eastern Army led by the Earl of Manchester is hell bent on pursuing its own ambitions. We can count on a much weakened enemy this spring.'

Henriette and Charles navigate a narrow path through the woodland covering the southern half of the deer park, their mounted guard following a hundred yards behind. Henriette can hear children's voices. The couple enter a clearing where an elaborate mock tudor summerhouse stands on a small, grassy mound. The young princes have appropriated the wooden hut and are fighting a mock battle.

'What are you doing Charles?' asks Henriette.

'We are fighting the siege of Bristol, mam,' says her eldest son.

'We're winning,' says James.

'And that's before I lead the cavalry charge.' Charles beams. 'I am Prince Rupert.'

Henriette looks puzzled. 'A cavalry charge at a siege?'

James pipes up. 'I am Lord Wilmot.'

'And the enemy?'

A high-pitched voice emanates from the summerhouse.

'Little Jeffrey,' exclaims Henriette. 'An enemy ten inches tall is hardly a fair contest.'

The King laughs. 'You desire my cavaliers to win, dear heart, surely?'

Henriette smiles as she turns her horse away and sets off at a gentle pace towards the hunting lodge.

The King and Queen stay an extra two weeks at Woodstock. A light flurry of snow covers the ground and the nights are freezing, but the days are blessed with blue skies and sunshine. The Queen and William Davenant begin planning a small-scale masque for the students to perform on Shrove Tuesday. They requisition the summerhouse to seek inspiration for their drama. It is during a scripting session one afternoon that the King arrives with Lord Digby.

Susan opens the door and announces the King's arrival. Henriette glances up from the table: 'You are just in time to hear William's prologue, dear heart.'

The King stands motionless in the doorway with Lord Digby behind. Grave faces tell Henriette it is not good news.

'Reports from the north,' says Charles in a flat tone.

'What is occurring?'

Lord Digby bows. 'The Scottish rebels have crossed the border, your majesty.'

'In winter?' Henriette stands up. 'Is it possible to move an army in these conditions?'

Lord Digby shrugs. 'It will be slow progress with muddy roads and full rivers, but it's possible.'

The King enters the room and moves towards the fireplace. 'The Earl of Newcastle reports a couple of cold, dry weeks. The hard, f-frosty surfaces will aid the enemy's progress.'

Henriette

Henriette can feel her stomach muscles tightening. 'Where is the Marquis of Hamilton? He assured us that the Scots would not take up arms against their King.'

'He was wrong about the pact with the puritans, and he is wrong about their m-military intentions,' says Charles. 'I think Hamilton is persuaded that f-future tasks are easy while current problems are best ignored.'

Henriette slumps back in her chair. 'That sounds a complicated way of saying that he betrayed us.'

'I think he has been out manoeuvred,' says Digby diplomatically. 'The word from our spies in London is that John Pym forced through the deal with the Scots, despite puritans misgivings.'

Henriette speaks under her breath. 'Even dead, he is our most deadly foe.'

Digby nods. 'Pym completed the arrangements with Scotland only days before he passed away.'

'We must contact Montrose.' Henriette glances at her husband. 'He was right all along.'

'Sir Edward Nicholas has returned to Oxford to speak with Hyde,' says Charles. 'They will send an urgent message to Montrose and his highlanders.'

'Can we stop the Scottish army?' asks Henriette.

Lord Digby takes a step forward and closes the door to block the chilly draught. 'The Earl of Newcastle's northern forces should delay their progress. Montrose will need time to gather his men and launch an offensive in the rear.'

'We will n-neutralise the north of England,' says Charles. 'Then we can proceed with our plans for London. We still have our army at Winchester and the troops billeted in Oxford. We will surround the capital and force Essex into a decisive encounter. I am confident that once the Scots realise that their newfound allies are in disarray, they will sue for peace and return h-home.'

The Queen sits hunched over the desk. She is not convinced by her husband's optimism. She remembers her time in York and the struggle to stamp the King's authority over far flung towns and cities across the northern counties. That was before any intervention from the Scottish army. Henriette stands up.

'I will write to the Earl of Newcastle and urge his northern army forward. I observed at York that William can on occasions be overly cautious.'

She-Majesty Generalissima

'We return to Oxford today,' says Charles.

Henriette picks up Davenant's notes for the masque. She peruses the top sheet and then chucks the bundle of papers back on the table.

'I fear, William, that our enemies have torn up the script.'

Act IV

The Prologue

The withdrawing room is decorated in colours of nature – green, yellow, brown and ochre. The furniture is the height of fashion featuring comfortable upholstered chairs and a circular table decorated in ash and oak marquetry. This is the room where Minette played the board game Cupid with her brother one Christmas when the snow draped Colombes like a picture postcard. A harpsichord sits in the corner but is never played. It was last employed as an accompaniment to Mary and Jean Baptiste Lully at an intimate soirée attended by the French royal family many years ago.

It is midwinter and the cold wind can be heard penetrating cracks in the shutters. Candles flicker in the draught. A small woman dressed head to toe in black tugs at a blanket around her shoulders.

'The summer and winter of 1643 in Oxford was a metaphor for our troubles,' says Henriette slowly, 'or was it a simile? I can never remember the difference.'

'Well, a metaphor is when…'

'I am too old to learn grammar, Françoise, or any more of those new-fangled English words that Mall and her friends use. All I am saying is that a warm carefree summer gave way to a pestilence in autumn, creeping into our homes like some unseen enemy, and ended in a ferocious cold winter. Cooped up in an overcrowded city, the seasons reflected our declining fortunes.' She sighs. 'New Year brought precious little cheer with a Scottish army invading the north before the spring thaw. I don't think I can carry on with this memoir.'

Madame de Motteville realises that her companion is approaching a heart-breaking moment in the story. Henriette is reluctant to re-visit the scene. There will only be one other day to follow in her life that is more desolate.

'It was a metaphor, your majesty,' says Madame gently.

Henriette shakes her head. 'It was a tragedy.'

Act IV, Scene 1 ~ Oxford

'Tell me about Elizabeth first,' says Henriette eagerly. She sits with her hands clasped as the Earl reports on her eight-year-old daughter.

'She reminds me of you.' Edward Sackville has a twinkle in his eye. 'She loves dressing up and performing pageants, and of course she drafts in her three-year-old brother. When Henry runs amok, Elizabeth becomes exceedingly vexed.'

Henriette speaks without the trace of a smile. 'Just like me, although I never had a younger brother.'

'Henry is talking, but he is quite serious and only says something when it is important, like "more pudding" or "horse ride".'

'He is riding a horse?'

'No, that is his word for the coach,' says Sackville. 'Now winter is coming to an end, they are allowed to ride within the confines of Saint James's Park.'

Henriette's bottom lip drops. 'They are trapped like we are in Oxford.'

Despite the Queen's misgivings, there is room for some chivalry, even in a bitter civil war. Edward Sackville is permitted to cross enemy lines and visit his wife, Mary, newly appointed governess to Elizabeth and Henry at Saint James's Palace. At the end of each visit, the Earl of Dorset reports back to Henriette on the wellbeing of her two younger children and on the state of affairs in London. He has also spirited several art works out of London on his travels. Henriette is chatting with the Earl of Dorset in her withdrawing room looking out over the Large Quad at Merton College. Also present are Harry Jermyn, Susan and a new lady in waiting.

'Elizabeth is learning to play the lute,' says Edward Sackville 'My wife has arranged for a small-scale instrument to be made so that your daughter can reach all the strings.'

'That's a lovely idea,' says Henriette. 'I shall look forward to playing a duet with her one day.'

'Elizabeth is an accomplished dancer but she has not inherited your singing voice.'

'Mary is the singer,' says Henriette. 'Can Lizzie ride?'

'Yes she has a pony and often accompanies the carriage on horseback. While I was there, the Earl of Holland paid a visit and rode out with Elizabeth.'

'That was thoughtful of Mr Orange,' says Henriette. 'It saddens me greatly that Henry Rich supported the attainder against Wentworth.' The Queen stares into the distance, lost in thought. 'It was a turning point when Charles signed Thomas's death warrant.'

'You make it sound like there is no way back,' says Sackville.

'It gets harder, Edward. Have you heard the latest news from the north?'

'No, your majesty, I came straight here.'

'Tell him, Harry.'

Jermyn takes a step forward. 'Messengers arrived today to report that the Scottish rebels are besieging the port of Newcastle.'

'And we know what happened last time,' says Henriette.

'It has taken them a month to advance from the border to Newcastle,' says Sackville.

'But where will they be in another month?' Henriette groans. 'Whether it is this pregnancy or my aches and pains, but I do not feel as optimistic as I did at Christmas.'

'The baby is bound to change your outlook on events,' says Susan. 'You want to bring the child into a safe world.'

'Nowhere is safe for me in England.'

Susan glances at Jermyn. They have never heard the Queen in such a dark mood. She has always insisted that she will stay with Charles in Oxford whatever the outcome.

'We still have our plans for the spring campaign,' says Jermyn. 'Our western army will be ready in a matter of weeks to launch its assault on Sussex and Kent.'

'Oxford gets me down,' says Henriette. 'Even when I take a walk in the garden, the city walls frown at me. And if I go into the streets they are full of people, half of whom are coughing from one sickness or another. It was a different place in the summer.'

'London is dismal too,' says Sackville. 'All the theatres are shut, so are lots of shops, others are open but have empty shelves, no royal court or masques, empty palaces – apart from Saint James's – and the City streets full of soldiers short of pay. Westminster is like a ghost town, other than a handful of members attending parliament.'

'We had a good turnout for the royal parliament at Christ Church.' Henriette perks up at the thought that Londoners are downcast. 'Edward Hyde and the lawyers advised against forming a rival body, so Charles is simply calling it the Oxford sitting of the current parliament. More than half the peers and about a third of the commoners are present. The Lords are based at Christ Church and the Commoners are using the Divinity School.'

'It has had a big impact on the London parliament,' says Sackville.

'We should have set up an alternative power base years ago. It would have weakened the puritans if half the parliament had followed Charles to Oxford in the middle of the debates about perpetual parliaments and Grand Moans.'

'Grand moans?' queries Sackville.

'John Pym's Grand Remonstrance,' explains Jermyn, who knows his mistress's shorthand off by heart.

'Playing "what if" is an elusive past-time,' says Sackville.

Henriette cries out. 'I indulged in that game with Sir Edward Nicholas a while back and we agreed it was unsettling.' The Queen turns to her new lady in waiting. 'Edward, you remember Lady Anne Dalkeith?'

The Earl of Dorset bows to acknowledge the new arrival at court.

'Anne is another recruit from London,' says Henriette.

'I desired to escape the dismal atmosphere in the city,' says Lady Dalkeith.

'Out of the frying pan,' says Susan with a smile. 'You have discovered how congested Oxford has become.'

'There are extra army officers congregating for the spring offensive,' says Jermyn, 'and students returning from Christmas holidays as well as the Christ Church members of parliament with their families, servants and advisers.'

'And now I have added myself to the numbers.' Anne Dalkeith is Susan's half niece, another member of the extended Villiers family. The thirty-three year old brunette with striking good looks has already made an impact on the Oxford court in exile.

Henriette nods. 'I hope you find your rooms here at Merton comfortable?'

'They are very spacious, your majesty.'

'Have you seen the drawer chest that Anne has brought with her?' asks Susan. 'It's the latest accessory in London.'

'Chest of drawers,' says Lady Dalkeith, correcting her aunt.

'I must see this chest of drawers,' says Henriette. 'What is its purpose?'

'It contains a set of drawers that can store almost any item of clothing,' says Lady Dalkeith. 'Each drawer can be pulled out, a bit like a suitcase.'

'I am not understanding,' says the Queen. 'Bring it in.'

'It's far too big to carry from room to room,' says Susan.

'Where do you store it then?' asks Henriette. 'Is it kept in the stable?'

Lady Dalkeith shakes her head. 'It fits in my room but it is too big and heavy to move, especially when it is full of clothes. The version I have brought with me contains four small drawers, but you can get almost any size chest.'

'I must see this,' says Henriette.

After bidding goodbye to Edward Sackville, the ladies decamp to Lady Dalkeith's apartment in the second quadrangle of Merton College. The Queen is seriously impressed by the chest of drawers. Despite her financial straits, she returns to the withdrawing room and tells Jermyn to investigate where she can purchase one.

'I think Anne is going to be a breath of fresh air,' says Henriette. 'Susan is getting very set in her ways and Mall is absent so often, chasing either her husband or Prince Rupert. Margaret is a lovely girl and a talented writer but she never speaks.'

'Is it true about Mall and the Prince?' asks Jermyn.

'I have no idea. Mall denies it but she spends a lot of time away from college. I know on several occasions she has not been at Christ Church with her husband.' Henriette returns to her chair. 'Don't say anything to James; I don't want him upset just before he heads off on a fresh campaign, and besides it may not be true.'

'Look at the lies that are spread about us,' says Jermyn. 'Friendship and loyalty can easily be twisted by people.'

'It does not help matters that you remain single, Harry. It really is time you found a wife.' Henriette starts to think. 'Susan is a widow now.'

'With the greatest respect, the Countess is sixty and I am only thirty-nine,' says Jermyn.

'Plenty of people get married with an age gap as great as that or more.' Henriette pauses to consider alternative candidates. 'What about Margaret?'

'You said yourself, she never speaks.'

'That would be regarded as a benefit by many husbands,' says Henriette with a smirk.

'I am happy as I am, your majesty. Besides, being single means that if I am killed in the coming battles no one will be left a widow.'

Henriette stares at Jermyn. 'Don't get yourself killed.' She reflects on the coming struggle. 'There will be many casualties if we meet the main parliamentary army in the field.'

'This year's campaign will decide the outcome of the rebellion.'

'We will pray for victory,' says Henriette. 'I cannot bear to contemplate defeat.'

Act IV, Scene 2 ~ Magdalen College

The view from inside the sedan chair is restricted, a series of brief snapshots on a lurching journey. Moss-covered stone walls along Saint John Baptist Street remind Henriette of her old nightmare, slithering down the steps to the dark, freezing waters of the Thames. Bustling crowds and noisy livestock forcing their way up and down the High are an encouraging sign of a banished plague. East gate is open for business once more; there is a brief pause as papers are shown to the guards. Finally, a partial view of stonework gleaming in April sunshine at the entrance to Magdalen College and once inside, a shadowy glimpse of the porter's lodge window beside which the chair comes to rest.

Susan and Harry Jermyn help the Queen disembark while Lord Digby waits patiently to greet his guest. As always, and despite the complete lack of any wind, his thick ginger hair is sticking out in a multitude of directions; Henriette is tempted to offer him a comb.

'Would you like the sedan chair to convey you to the gardens, your majesty?'

'No Digby, I feel a lot better this morning and I would like to stroll in the sun. I will hold on to your arm if you will permit.' Despite untidy hair, the young chevalier remains one of the Queen's favourites. They agree on military strategy, usually in opposition to the King and Prince Rupert, and they share an interest in the royalist newsletter, Mercurius Aulicus.

Digby walks slowly arm in arm with the Queen. 'My father is feeling under the weather but would very much like to meet you in the dining hall after the demonstration.'

Henriette

'It will be a pleasure to converse with the Earl of Bristol.' Henriette looks around. 'So where are these guns you want to show me?'

'This way, your majesty.' Digby escorts the Queen and her party through a gate and into the park where the artillery has taken up residence. As the royal party strolls into view, a gun in the distance fires, followed at thirty-second intervals by the rest of the line.

The Queen is delighted at the raucous salute. 'What a splendid sight.'

'This is the new version of the saker that we will be adding to our armoury this year,' explains Digby. 'The brass cannon has been founded by Thomas Pitt to a new specification, the space between the bore and the ball being much reduced.'

Henriette nods. Harry Jermyn can see that the Queen has no idea what Digby is talking about.

'Each gun founder designs in a different manner,' explains Jermyn. 'These latest casts are a more accurate fit for the cannon ball so it shoots further and straighter. Is that correct, Digby?'

'Exactly so.'

'Well that will be a great help to our armies,' says Henriette. 'Have we sent any of these new guns to Lord Hopton at Winchester and to the Earl of Newcastle in York?'

'The first three new sakers have only just arrived,' says Lord Digby. 'After completing the tests we hope to start using them on the battlefield. The first army to be equipped with them will be the Oxford artillery units.'

As the deafening noise of the cannons fades and smoke drifts across the park, Henriette spots Lord Wilmot walking briskly towards them through the haze.

'I did not realise Wilmot was staying at Magdalen,' says the Queen.

'He is not,' says Lord Digby. 'He must have walked from Christ Church. He seems in a hurry.'

Lord Wilmot reaches the group and bows before the Queen. 'Your majesty, I have instructions from the King to escort you back inside the city walls.'

'Whatever for?' Henriette frowns. 'I am enjoying the first decent day of spring and inspecting our new artillery pieces.'

'We have received news from Lord Hopton, your majesty. I regret to inform you that our western army has suffered a grievous defeat and is in retreat.'

Harry Jermyn lets out a cry. 'Our winter preparations are undone.'

'The Earl of Manchester is advancing from East Anglia upon Oxford,' says Wilmot. 'It is possible that Essex will also attack the city.'

'We are in danger of being surrounded,' says Lord Digby. 'We need to regroup and attack the enemy before they reach Oxford.'

Henriette tries to remain calm. 'It is no good speculating when we only have half a story. We shall retire to Christ Church. Lord Digby, please offer your father my apologies but we shall have to postpone our luncheon.'

As they reach the sedan chair, Henriette stares at Harry Jermyn. 'I cannot believe that fortunes can turn so suddenly. Yesterday we were anticipating our decisive attack on London; today we discover Oxford is under threat.'

'You must not be trapped in a siege, your majesty.'

Henriette glares at Jermyn. 'I will not abandon the King.'

The wind rattles the shutters as Monsieur Fialin ushers Harry Jermyn into the withdrawing room. Madame de Motteville and Henriette sit on chairs close to a roaring fire. Occasional gusts of wind sweep down the chimney blowing wisps of smoke into the room.

'I refused to leave my dear heart,' says Henriette, turning to the new arrival. 'I told you so.'

Jermyn frowns at Madame who hastily explains. 'We are recalling the spring of 1644 in Oxford when fortune turned against the King.'

'You ganged up on me.' Henriette's bottom lip drops. 'I was exiled from Charles in Gravenhage for over a year.' She slowly shakes her head. 'Never again.'

'There was only one person who could change your mind.' Harry Jermyn approaches the fire, leaning heavily on his walking stick.

'Who was that?' asks Madame.

Henriette looks into the flames. 'My most trusted counsellor, of course.'

Act IV, Scene 3 ~ Christ Church

'You have to go,' says Charles.

'Don't send me away.' Tears trickle down Henriette's face. 'Remember when you sent my French court back to Paris? Now you want to send me away; it will break my heart.'

Charles wraps his arms around her. 'I don't want you to leave; I just w-worry for your safety, and for the baby.'

'The child will take its chances like the rest of us,' says Henriette harshly. 'No one is going to kill a baby, not even enemy soldiers.'

'It is you I am m-most concerned for,' says Charles. 'They have impeached you for treason. Once they surround Oxford, you cannot get away.' Charles looks into her eyes. 'Just think about it; if they break our defences and drag you back to London.'

'You must kill me before they get the chance,' says Henriette. 'If I cannot live by your side I would rather die.'

'You expect me to drive a sword through you and the unborn baby? I could n-never do that Maria.'

'Harry will do it if you haven't the courage.'

'Don't s-say such a thing. Harry would not do it, and it is not because either of us lacks courage. How could you say something so cruel? I am being torn apart with w-worry for your safety.'

'I am in shreds too,' screams Henriette. 'I was apart for a year in Holland; it was a nightmare, I hated every single day and now you want to send me away again.' She slips off the chair and on to her knees. 'I won't go.'

Her raised voice brings Susan and Mall running from the Queen's dressing room. They open the door to find Henriette slumped on the carpet and Charles kneeling beside her.

'Shall I summon Doctor Harvey?' asks Susan.

'What is a physician going to do,' sobs Henriette. 'Can he stop the enemy at our gates?'

Mall looks bewildered. 'They are here?'

Charles shakes his head. 'There is no sign of the enemy; the Queen is talking hypothetically.'

Henriette tries to speak between the sobs. 'I am hypothetical. I want to stay in Oxford; all I ask is that I am allowed to stand and fight.'

'You are in no condition to stand, your majesty, let alone fight,' says Susan. 'You are certainly not strong enough to survive a long siege.'

'I lose everyone in the end.' The Queen stops crying and her voice is clear and cold. 'Now the final injury, the only person I care about wants me to go away.'

'Only for your safety and wellbeing,' says Susan.

'My wellbeing?' She stares at her Dame of Honour. 'You might as well lock me up in a lunatic asylum. I have no life without the King; there is no point in my existence.'

Charles puts his arm around her. 'You can do so much for the cause away from Oxford. Just like in Holland, you can send me arms and reinforcements and m-maybe even persuade that nephew of yours to lend us French troops and ships.'

Henriette scoffs. 'Some chance of that.'

'You can make more impact, free from the confines of this city.'

'And what about you; will you just sit in Christ Church and wait for the city walls to fall? You will be trapped, too.'

'I shall take the army into the field and defeat the r-rebels. I will not be caught in Oxford. That's the point, Maria, how can I lead an army around the countryside with you beside m-me, expecting a baby and stricken with a great sickness.'

Henriette's lip drops. 'You make me sound like a disaster.'

Charles looks up at Susan and Mall. 'The daughter of Henri the Great, a disaster; I don't think so.'

'Where will I go?' asks Henriette. 'Nowhere is safe.'

'You could go to Bath,' says Mall. 'I hear the waters there are beneficial.'

Henriette shrugs. 'And what do we do when the parliamentary soldiers turn up?'

Mall smiles cheerfully. 'Ask them if they want a bath?'

Henriette looks at Susan and neither can resist a brief smile.

'I will send a detachment of troops to guard you,' says Charles. 'And if we hear any intelligence about enemy movements in the area they can escort you to Bristol or Exeter – we have many safe havens in the south-west.'

'We have now,' says Henriette, wiping her eyes with the sleeve of her dress. 'But look how rapidly things change. One minute we are attacking London, then the disastrous defeat at Cheriton and we are suddenly talking about clinging on to Oxford.'

'It is one setback,' says Charles. 'But we have three armies in the field and more troops to come from Ireland; all is not lost.'

'If I use the comfortable carriage, I can follow you round quite safely.'

'We have to be realistic, dear heart.'

Henriette starts to cry again. 'Please don't send me away; I cannot live without you.'

Act IV, Scene 4 ~ Merton College

'This will probably be my last meal in Oxford,' announces Henriette. 'The King is turning me out of the city.' She stares at her plate of untouched food. 'I have no where to go.'

Courtiers close to the Queen are used to her dramatic moods, but no one can recall such deep despair. Since her return from Holland, she has been the upbeat voice in a court full of foreboding and pessimism. They eat in silence around the dining hall top table. Royal etiquette was abandoned at Merton College long ago. The Queen shares the meal with Harry Jermyn, Father Philip, her senior ladies – Susan, Mall, Margaret and Anne – Doctor Harvey and little Jeffrey. It is a popular place to dine as a rule, although the atmosphere has been less congenial since Christmas when the Queen's bad health began to take its toll. Tonight the mood is sombre.

'The King is only concerned for your health and safety, your majesty,' says Susan.

'He told me I was a disaster.' The Queen's bottom lip drops.

Mall refuses to accept such a blatant twisting of the facts. She risks the Queen's wrath. 'I think you are mistaken, your majesty. You said the King's description suggested that you were a disaster and his majesty strongly denied this was so.'

There is silence. There was a time when there might have been an explosion, but Henriette is too tired and ill to put up a fight.

'I think there is another consideration,' says Harry Jermyn. 'The King is concerned that if you are captured by the enemy, they will use you as a bargaining counter for an unfavourable peace. This was their plan when we first landed in Yorkshire if you recall.'

Henriette remains crouched over her meal as still as a statue. She does not appear to hear Jermyn.

'If you were a prisoner of parliament, the King would agree anything to save you,' says Susan. 'You know he loves you dearly.'

'Everyone leaves in the end,' says Henriette in a flat tone. No one is quite sure how to respond. Harry stares at Mall, Susan looks at the Queen, little Jeffrey tries desperately hard to think of something light-hearted and still no one speaks.

A deep chesty cough from the Queen breaks the silence. 'I shall retire to my bedroom.' She tries to clear her throat. 'I am tired.'

'You should try and eat something, your majesty,' says Susan.

'I shall be sick.' With this, she rises from her chair and everyone stands up. Jermyn watches her walk slowly around the table and towards the door, helped by Anne Dalkeith and Margaret Lucas. She shuffles past him, her shoulders hunched, appearing much older than her thirty-four years.

After she leaves the room, Dr Harvey speaks. 'She is seriously ill.'

Harry Jermyn glances at the doctor. 'How serious?'

'If she does not start to regain some weight and strength, then I don't think she will survive the birth; the child may not live either.'

Jermyn nods at the Countess of Denbeigh. 'You must talk to her, Susan. She will listen to you.'

She shakes her head. 'No, there is only one person who might persuade her.'

'The King?' asks Dr Harvey.

'No, we need to draft in Edward Sackville.'

Jermyn is puzzled by her choice. 'You think the old Earl of Dorset can make her change her mind?'

'She trusts his judgement above all others,' says Susan. 'We have our uses, to entertain her or to be her companion. But when it comes to weighty matters like negotiating her daughter's marriage, or extracting funds from the Lord Treasurer for renovating one of her palaces, who does she turn to?'

Mall nods. 'I will speak with him.'

Act IV, Scene 5 ~ Merton College quad

The Queen wraps the blanket around her legs. She is huddled in a large throne-like chair, sitting in the middle of the garden, close to the mulberry tree. Fur-lined riding boots keep her feet warm.

Standing behind her is a servant patiently holding a parasol to shield Henriette's head from the sun. It is a fresh April afternoon although the shadows of the college buildings creep towards her.

'I like to be outside,' says Henriette. 'My physicians complain that the air still contains dangerous winter impurities.' She points to the city walls. 'However, I am reminded of dear Sir Kenelm's theory that flowers flourish because of what he calls vital air. Beyond that wall is countryside where surely his vital air must collect. So I sit in the garden like a flower and hopefully breathe it in.' She rearranges the blanket. 'It certainly makes me feel better.'

Standing beside the Queen is Edward Sackville. 'I am sure you are right, your majesty. I find the spring air invigorating.'

Henriette looks around. 'Get the Earl a chair.'

'Do not concern yourself, I am happy to stand before my Queen.'

'Nonsense.' Henriette's voice is almost the strong commanding tone of old. She then speaks quietly to the servant. 'Put that umbrella down and go and get a chair.'

Two other servants are on the job and a wooden dining chair arrives for the Earl of Dorset, allowing the parasol holder to remain in place. Sackville positions the chair at an angle to the Queen with the sun to one side. He sits down.

'That's better,' says Henriette. 'I was getting neck ache looking up.'

Her former chamberlain smiles: 'You were never one for protocol; I recall we did most of our business ensconced around a table.'

'We sit together for meals here at Merton,' says Henriette. 'I much prefer it. Unless Charles attends, of course.' She lowers her voice to a whisper. 'He's a bit stuffy you know about observing ceremonials.'

'I believe so.' There is a twinkle in Sackville's eye; it is as if the Queen has forgotten that he led her household for fifteen years.

Henriette appears to guess his thoughts. 'I was only eighteen-years-old when I appointed you.' She laughs, and it makes her cough. 'It was quite an astute choice for a wild young teenager.'

'It was a huge honour, your majesty.'

'And Charles is promoting you to grand chamberlain of the King's court and president of the Privy Council.' The Queen is amused by this idea. 'He used to insist on making my appointments, but now he follows my recommendations. Perhaps he will make little Jeffrey speaker of the House of Commoners.'

'I can think of worse candidates, and much less amusing ones.'

The Queen perks up. 'Jeffrey could attempt one of his magic tricks and make the parliament in Westminster disappear.'

Two more servants appear with a table, a white cloth, two earthenware mugs containing light ale and a plate of miniature French jam tarts.

'I find a little beer in the afternoon improves my temper; I don't know what mama would say.' The Queen picks up a mug. 'I still drink a goblet of wine in the evening.'

'You are very generous, your majesty,' says Sackville, 'and I am pleased to drink to the Queen's improving health.'

Henriette raises her eyebrows. 'I fear it is declining at present, but I still hope that after the baby is delivered I may regain some of my strength.'

'When is the child due?'

'End of May.' Henriette pats her stomach. 'Only another six weeks or so.'

Sackville looks at the Queen; she looks even smaller than usual, engulfed by the large chair. 'A lot may happen, your majesty, in the next six weeks of the campaign.'

'I know what you are going to say.' Henriette stares intently at her old confidante. 'I should leave Oxford.' Henriette looks over her shoulder at the mulberry tree. 'However, I would rather remain here and die with the King.'

'The trouble is the King will not stay and allow himself to be trapped in the city.' Sackville points to the walls. 'Despite that barrier, and even after flooding Christ Church meadows, the city is not designed to withstand a concentrated bombardment.'

Henriette does not reply. She picks up a jam tart and studies it. After taking a small bite she speaks with her mouth full. 'I led an army down from York; I am used to sleeping under canvas.'

'Not in your present state,' says Sackville gently. 'Besides, I think the time for war is rapidly coming to a close; we must address the peace.'

'You never approved of the fight, did you Edward?'

'I made it clear to the King when he raised his standard at Nottingham, I would not desert him, but I did not relish Englishmen killing Englishmen. I have written to the Earl of Essex asking him to consider peace talks; I believe he may be of the same opinion.'

'You would let them take me to the Tower and chop my head off,' says Henriette. 'I suppose you are right, if it stops more battles and casualties.'

'I would never agree peace without a guarantee of both your safety and the King's.'

'Do you think you could trust this Westminster parliament?' Henriette finishes off the tart. She munches in silence for a few moments. 'After what they did to Thomas.'

'If an Act was passed guaranteeing the continuation of the monarchy and an amnesty against all actions prior to the settlement, on both sides, then I would be satisfied.'

'If it does come to peace talks, you are the only person I would trust to represent the King.'

'The other concern is if you are captured,' says Sackville. 'That would change everything. Parliament would then be in a strong position to dictate terms.'

The sun disappears behind a cloud and the Queen pulls her blankets closer. Susan arrives and hovers close by. 'Would you like to go inside, your majesty?'

Henriette looks at the sky. 'Not if the sun comes out again. Leave it a few minutes, Susan.' The Queen turns to Sackville. 'I have four servants to move my throne about; it's a bit like a mini sedan chair.' She begins coughing and Susan moves forward but Henriette waves her away.

'If your former Chamberlain may be allowed to humbly offer some advice,' says Sackville, 'I suggest a temporary move to Bath, your majesty.'

Henriette grimaces. 'Everyone is ganging up on me.'

'We are concerned for your safety.'

'I don't want to leave him.' Henriette's eyes fill up. She lets out a groan of frustration. 'I don't know what is wrong with me, I keep crying. I am getting rather pathetic.'

'No, your majesty.' Sackville is close to tears himself observing his Queen in such a wretched state. 'You are the strongest woman I have ever met, stronger than most men.'

'Your wife is also a formidable lady. How is poor Mary?'

'She is not poor. Like me, she is honoured to serve her King and Queen. And she adores Princess Elizabeth and Prince Henry.'

'You are apart from your wife. That is my fault.'

'It is our duty, not your fault,' says Sackville. 'But yes, we live apart at present because we believe that we best serve our King by so doing.'

Henriette smiles. 'You are too polite to say it, Edward, but what you are telling me is, I should also do my duty by the King. Like you and Mary, I should accept the situation and leave Oxford.'

'For the time being; only until we can all return to London.'

'I hear they have closed the theatres.' Henriette shakes her head. 'The puritans are a boring bunch of sad faces.'

The Earl laughs at the Queen's description. 'Yes, even my beloved Shaftesbury Theatre is locked up and gathering dust.'

'We shall open them again one day.' Henriette's face brightens. For the first time in days her eyes sparkle. 'We shall put on shows the like of which the public has never seen before. We will have singing and dancing, perhaps we will shock them by allowing female players on the stage, like in my royal masques. You and I will sit in the box and applaud and laugh and the puritans can stay away and be miserable.'

'I look forward to that, your majesty.' Sackville has to pause to stop his voice breaking up. 'You will light up London again, I am certain of it.'

Henriette puts her hand on the Earl's arm. 'Tell the King I shall go to Bath to take the waters. When it is safe to return, I shall be back.'

Susan curtsies. 'Shall I make preparations, your majesty?'

Henriette ignores her Dame of Honour. She stares intently at the Earl of Dorset. 'Edward, if I don't survive this child birth…'

Sackville puts his hand up to stop the Queen. He has tears in his eyes. 'Do not say such a thing, your majesty.'

'Listen to me, Edward.' Henriette smiles. 'I want you to know that you were my wisest and truest adviser, and I am confident you will perform the same service for my husband. When Charles dismissed my French court, I screamed the palace down and wanted to enter a convent. I never believed that I would ever find English advisers that I could trust and love.' Henriette nods her head. 'But I was very lucky, with Harry, Susan, Mall … and others. But most of all, I found you – honest, principled, a lover of the arts, and wise. You never left me.' Henriette looks around the garden as the sun appears from out of a cloud. 'Unfortunately, it is my duty to leave you. Just promise not to shout the palace down and enter a convent.'

Sackville wipes a tear from his cheek. 'I promise, your majesty – no screaming and definitely no convents.'

Act IV, Scene 6 ~ Merton College

The carts line up in Saint John Baptist Street. The first is reserved for chapel finery that accompanies Henriette wherever she travels. A second wagon takes a small selection of the Queen's wardrobe and two more carts transport baggage belonging to her entourage. The idea is to journey as light as possible to avoid arousing suspicion along the way. The baggage train will set off with a low key escort. The Queen and her courtiers plan to follow two days later in three coaches guarded by a squad of cavalry. The front quad at Merton is piled high with trunks and chests. It rained earlier in the day and most items are covered in tarpaulins, making it difficult to track where everything is stored. Susan and Harry endeavour to co-ordinate the packing. Henriette retires to her throne chair, which is placed by the window in her bedroom. Mall sits on the bed.

'Well little Miss Villiers,' says the Queen quietly, 'it is nearly time for us to say our goodbyes.'

'This reminds me of my wedding day,' says Mall. 'My first wedding that is; do you remember I called you Ettie?'

'I do; that was Mamie's nickname for me and after she was sent back to France I thought I should never hear it used again. You cheered me up that day.'

'Mother told me off after you left.'

'She should not have done that,' says Henriette. 'People worry too much about etiquette. I would rather be called Ettie than Your Majesty any day.'

Mall looks around the bedroom. 'I am going to stay here at Merton College.'

'And your husband can move across from Christ Church.' Henriette spreads her arms wide. 'You will have plenty of space.'

'Perhaps,' says Mall.

'I hope he does,' says Henriette. 'James is a good man.'

Mall lowers her head. 'I know he is.'

'As long as you don't take him for granted, just remember how lucky you are. I am parting from Charles. Look at poor Edward Sackville and his wife Mary living apart. I would swap all my worldly treasures and my crown to be with the King.'

'You will return,' says Mall.

'Indeed I shall,' says Henriette, 'although whether it will be to Oxford or London, no one can tell.'

'You must send news of the baby. I shall start knitting a bonnet.'

'It is time you had children too.'

'I would like to bring children into a more peaceful world, your majesty.'

Henriette sighs. 'Don't wait too long or you may miss the opportunity.' The Queen picks up a manuscript on the table. 'Can I take this collection of your poems?'

'Of course, your majesty; I would be honoured. They are not very good, but you are welcome to them.'

'You are too modest. You have real talent, like Margaret.'

'She is writing a book,' says Mall. 'That is truly awesome.'

'Is awesome more wonderful than amazing?' asks Henriette with a smile.

Mall laughs. 'Definitely, very amazing.'

'Margaret told me about her book; it's a kind of future fiction. When this rebellion is over she must find a publisher.'

'No one will print a book written by a woman.'

'Why ever not?' Henriette gesticulates with her arms. 'If the printer gets sniffy about the idea, she can tell them her name is John Lucas.'

Mall giggles. 'Do you think it would be possible to fool a publisher?'

'She should send little Jeffrey in with the manuscript. You know how he loves to show off; he would be happy to claim the work as his own.' Henriette holds Mall's loosely bound sheets aloft. 'And we shall see you published too.'

'It would be lovely.' Mall briefly smiles. 'One day perhaps.'

'It will come to pass. Men do not have a monopoly on words or ideas. In fact, in my experience, women often have better ideas.'

Susan peers around the door. 'The sedan chair is ready to take you to Christ Church, your majesty.'

The Queen raises her eyebrows. 'The big send off. I hope no one is going to make a boring speech about how much I will be missed.

Edward Hyde will be glad to see the back of me, as will Prince Rupert.'

'I believe Sir Edward Nicholas has arranged a small luncheon party,' says Susan. 'He did not want to tire you.'

'That is kind,' says Henriette. 'I shall miss Sir Edward.'

'Margaret will accompany you,' says Susan. 'I have a lot of packing to organise here. Dr Harvey and Father Philip will also attend.'

'My doctor and my priest; is that in case I drop dead between here and Christ Church?' Henriette smiles at Susan. 'I know, stop being flippant. We must not mention axes or chopped heads.'

The Countess looks suitably stern. 'Just remember the King is upset about you leaving and he will not want to hear wild predictions of your imminent demise.'

'Yes Madame,' mumbles Henriette. 'I shall do my best to maintain an air of joyous ecstasy.'

Act IV, Scene 7 ~ Christ Church

Despite her misgivings, the Queen enjoys the afternoon. Prince Rupert is campaigning in the north and Edward Hyde is presenting fund raising proposals to the Oxford parliament. Loyal friends surround Henriette and they are truly sad to see her leave. The King remains quiet.

Henriette attempts to raise his spirits. 'I hear my nephew is keeping Chester open for our troops from Ireland. I have written to Anne in Paris and pointed out that we need ships urgently to bring the troops across.' Henriette recalls the advice of her nursemaid Mamie years before. 'I used tact and diplomacy in my letter, dear heart.'

'I propose a toast,' says Sir Edward Nicholas, lifting his flagon of ale. 'To the Queen of the Three Kingdoms.'

Everyone stands and lifts their drinks. 'The Queen of the Three Kingdoms.'

Henriette bows her head. 'I shall miss such a loyal group of friends.'

'A poem, William,' cries Sir Edward.

Davenant has been drinking heavily, but he stands up, bows and addresses the Queen. 'A poem dedicated to ladies in arms.' He recites from memory.

'Let us live, live! for, being dead,
The pretty spots,
Ribbons and knots,
And the fine French dress for the head,
No lady wears upon her
In the cold, cold bed of honour.
Beat down our grottos, and hew down our bowers,
Dig up our arbours, and root up our flowers;
Our gardens are bulwarks and bastions become;
Then hang up our lute, we must sing to the drum.

Our patches and our curls,
So exact in each station,
Our powders and our purls,
Are now out of fashion.
Hence with our needles, and give us your spades;
We, that were ladies, grow coarse as our maids.
Our coaches have driven us to balls at the court,
We now must drive barrows to earth up the fort.'

Henriette claps. 'Bravo, William, you have written an ode to the She-Majesty Generalissima.'

'It is part of a story I am writing,' says Davenant. 'It tells the tale of the siege of Rhodes.'

'Perhaps it could be the Siege of Gloucester,' says Henriette, 'or better still, the taking of Scarborough Castle by a certain female warrior.'

'Don't encourage her, William.' Edward Sackville puts down his beer tankard and nods towards Henriette. 'No taking up arms while you are carrying a prince or princess.'

Henriette smiles. 'I promise to store my spade until I have delivered.'

The Duke of Richmond holds Mall's hand. 'I must thank you, your majesty, for releasing my wife from your court.'

'You may need her in your cavalry regiment.' Henriette holds up her goblet. 'Here's to ladies in arms.' She smiles at the couple. 'You take good care of her, James Stewart.'

'I will, your majesty.'

'What about you, Lord Digby? You are keeping quiet.'

'I shall miss the wise counsel of my Queen.'

'Don't fret,' says Henriette. 'I shall write every day and doubtless interfere in my usual manner.' She grins at Charles. 'Is that not right, your majesty?'

'I pray that you will, Maria. I shall look f-forward to your letters; they will provide some comfort while you are away.'

'We will soon be together again,' says Henriette. 'You know me; I have no patience.'

'To victory,' shouts Lord Digby holding up his goblet. 'And the return of the Queen.'

They stand up. 'The return of the Queen,' is the rousing chorus.

Act IV, Scene 8 ~ Abingdon

Mall Stewart and her husband wrap up warm to stave off the cold morning air. They stand in the entrance to Merton College and watch the cavalcade prepare to move off. Last to arrive, as usual, and looking pale is Henriette. She stops and hugs Mall.

'God speed, Ettie,' whispers Mall.

'I shall miss you Miss Villiers.'

There are tears in Henriette's eyes as she turns and climbs into the carriage. Susan, Margaret and Anne Dalkeith accompany the Queen. In the following coach are little Jeffrey, Father Philip, the Queen's chef and her hairdresser. The final coach contains Dr Harvey and one of his assistants, a valet and two maids of honour. Harry Jermyn is on horseback. The party set off, turning left on to High Street and past Carfax and down to the main entrance to Christ Church College where they pick up their escort, led by the King. The procession travels under the arch of Oxford's south gate. The rising sun picks out Magdalen Tower, the flooded meadows glisten in the foreground. The convoy passes a few scattered houses and heads into the Oxfordshire countryside.

The roads have dried out and they make good progress. The party atmosphere evaporates and reality slowly sinks in. No one speaks in the Queen's carriage. Henriette stares blankly out of the window at the fields, interrupted by occasional tiny hamlets or a crossroads. She is unaware of how far or for how long they have travelled. The rolling green hills and valleys remind Henriette of her first coach journey in England when she travelled with Charles from Dover to Canterbury. All along the route people waved and cheered. This morning, Henriette is racing through countryside, anonymous and unannounced.

The carriages come to a halt outside a coaching inn beside the main street in Abingdon. Henriette draws breath and prepares for the last farewells, the hardest of them all. She descends from the coach as King Charles and her two sons dismount.

'This is as far as we can escort you, dear heart.' It is an obvious statement but all Charles can say without losing control of his voice.

'You will make it back to Oxford much quicker without the carriages,' says Henriette. There is a brief awkward silence before she turns to her children. 'Come here, James, you are not so old that you cannot give your mother a farewell kiss.'

James runs into her arms and clings on desperately. Henriette's eyes begin to fill up. It is no good; she is not going to be able to remain composed.

'Come on, it is only a brief parting, like my journey to Holland.'

'I don't want you to leave, mam,' says James.

'Nor do I,' she whispers. 'But we must be brave.'

Prince Charles stands before her, taller than his mother. 'I am not going to cry,' he says.

'Quite right,' says Henriette briskly. 'You must practice so that one day you shall be a strong King like your father and your grandfathers.'

James lets go of Henriette and the Queen moves forward and gives young Charles a gentle kiss on his cheek.

'But I am allowed to cry.' She stands and looks at her dark, handsome son. 'One day, you will be King.'

She turns away before the tears start to run down her cheeks.

Charles walks over and hugs Henriette. 'I am going to miss you, dear heart, every minute of every day.'

'I don't want to leave,' sobs Henriette. 'Let me stay; I have changed my mind; I want to be with you.'

'We agreed, Maria; you must get better and deliver the baby. When it is safe to return, I shall summon you.'

'Please, sir, I beg you, let me stay.' Henriette's legs give way and she kneels on the dusty street. The Queen wraps her small arms around her husband's legs.

Susan, Margaret and Anne are crying. Prince Charles puts his arm around his younger brother.

The King slowly and gently lifts Henriette up. 'I adore my Queen, but you must go to a safe place. I will stay and fight for our kingdoms. I cannot enter the fray unless I am certain you are safe.'

'I don't want to leave you,' says Henriette. 'We are one.'

'We always shall be. Write to me every day and before long we will be together again.'

'I love you.' Henriette stares at him with her big round eyes. 'I shall always love you.'

Charles steers her towards the carriage. Tears blur the Queen's vision and Harry Jermyn rushes forward to guide her into the coach. She feels as if she is falling through the air. The next thing Henriette remembers is the countryside flashing past the window. Her cheek is pressed against the cold leather seat of the coach.

'Where are we?' she whispers.

Susan has her arm around Henriette to prevent her from falling forward. 'We are ten miles south of Abingdon, your majesty.'

Henriette wipes her eyes. 'He's gone.'

Act IV, Scene 9 ~ Bath

The four ladies wear canvas petticoats and linen caps and walk gingerly down smooth stone steps in their leather slippers into warm green-coloured water. Their garments have strips of lead sewn into the hems to prevent them floating in the bath. As they reach the floor of the pool, a female attendant guides each of the ladies to a stone seat in the water. There is an additional block of stone, like a pillow, on the bench where Henriette sits. Otherwise, the diminutive Queen would disappear beneath the surface.

'The water is so warm,' says Henriette. She spreads her arms out as if she is about to swim. Then she coughs.

She-Majesty Generalissima

'I told you it was not a good idea to enter the water in your condition,' says the Countess. 'I don't know what the King will say if you catch a cold.'

'Doctor Harvey advises that the spa is good for me,' says Henriette. 'Besides I cannot be any worse than when I am not in the water.'

Margaret Lucas shocks the others by speaking without being spoken to, a rare occurrence. 'What a marvellous sensation; how do they heat the water?'

'It's a natural hot spring from the earth,' says Lady Dalkeith. 'Have you never been to Tunbridge or Wellingborough?'

'Never,' says Margaret. 'We went to the seaside once on the Norfolk coast, but of course we did not enter the water.'

'No you wouldn't,' says Henriette. 'I first visited the seaside when I stayed at Boulogne on my journey from Paris to London. My brother Gaston and I took a rowing boat into the harbour.'

'I have never seen the British sea,' says Margaret.

'In France it is called La Manche, or "the sleeve".' Henriette raises her arm out of the water. 'The sea between England and France is shaped like so.'

'I think I shall return to the slip room,' says Susan as she climbs out of the water. 'This bath is a trifle warm.' The Countess of Denbeigh wraps herself in a towel and settles in the sedan chair. It is lined with red baize and specially adapted with short poles for manoeuvrability. To ensure privacy, the ladies are carried to and from the baths and their bedrooms.

Lady Dalkeith nods towards Henriette and whispers. 'It is the hot flushes.'

The Queen pulls a face. 'I think the water is a lovely temperature.' She puts her hand on her bulge. 'I wonder what baby thinks of it?'

'Probably a lot happier than bouncing about in a carriage,' says Margaret.

Henriette speculates if some property of the spring water makes Margaret more talkative.

'I am glad we have this private bath,' says Henriette. 'I would not want to share the water with lots of people.'

'I believe this water is warmer than some of the other baths,' says Anne Dalkeith. 'Our private bath is linked to the Hot Bath.'

'When we visited Wellingborough,' explains Henriette, 'the ladies' bathhouse at the Red Well was reserved for my court.

Everyone lived in tents, just like on our march to Oxford last summer.'

'It must have been quite a sight,' says Anne.

'We went two years in a row,' says Henriette. 'It was during the second visit that we received the terrible news of Steenie's assassination. I had to rush back to London and comfort his family. Poor Mall was only nine years old when she lost her father.'

Anne stands up in the warm bath water. 'The assassination of the Duke of Buckingham is one of those shattering events that everyone can remember where they were and what they were doing when they heard the news.'

'Where were you?' asks Henriette.

'I was with mama in Ireland in a small village called Youghal,' says Anne. 'Father had recently died and we were preparing to return to England. I was only eighteen years old and I vividly remember the coach arriving from Dublin with the terrible news.'

'Steenie was your father's half brother?'

'All the siblings from both marriages treated themselves as equals. Susan was papa's half relation, but he always called her sister.'

'And then you go and marry a Scot,' says Henriette. 'You have connections with all our three kingdoms.'

Margaret stares at the Queen. 'You also married a Scot, your majesty.'

Henriette frowns and tilts her head. 'You are talkative this morning.'

Margaret blushes deep red, thinking she may have offended the Queen. 'I must apologise for being too forward.'

Henriette smiles. 'There is nothing to be sorry about; and you are quite correct, I married a Scot. Unfortunately, his fellow countrymen appear to have foresaken him.'

'Not all of them,' says Anne. 'My husband still holds the Orkneys for the King.'

'Indeed he does,' says Henriette. 'Charles tells me that the Orkneys could prove a useful port for supplying Montrose and his army.' The thought of the military campaign makes the Queen shiver, even though she is immersed in warm bath water. 'I pray that our fortunes will turn soon. We began last year with such high hopes and enjoyed victories in the north and the West Country. Then there was the wasted campaign against Gloucester, the indecisive encounter at Newbury, the invasion of the Scots and finally defeat for our southern army.' Henriette sighs. 'I feel like I am slithering down the stone steps at White Hall and the water is dragging me under again.'

Anne Dalkeith frowns. 'Did you slip on the steps and fall in the river?'

Henriette makes her way slowly through the green water towards the side. She speaks without turning round. 'I have been drowning ever since.'

Madame de Motteville collects the papers together while Minette bravely attempts to persuade her mother to take some honey.

Henriette tries to speak through a coughing fit. 'I am ... perfectly ... all right,' she splutters.

Minette tilts her head to one side as if doubting her mother's sanity. The mannerism would be familiar to Harry Jermyn, Susan or a dozen other confidantes of the Queen.

'I don't think you are, mam.'

'We shall resume another day,' says Madame de Motteville. 'All the talking has exhausted you.'

'I am getting feeble if a brief chat lays me so low.'

'Where have you got to?' asks Minette.

'Bath,' says Henriette with a sly smile. 'We are close to your grand entrance, and not far from Madame's arrival on stage.'

'You left papa, Charles and James in Oxford.'

Henriette slumps back in her chair at the thought of that sorrowful parting. 'Looking back, it is quite extraordinary how I clung on to hope and optimism. My journey down the slippery steps had been relentless, the dark waters of despair were beckoning, and yet I kept on hoping that out fortunes would revive.'

'That's because you have spirit, mam.'

Henriette closes her eyes. 'My spirit was crushed. I did not realise it at the time but I was close to death. The enemy were on our heels, hell bent on dragging me back to London and soon we would be completely surrounded.'

'Did Harry rescue you, or was it the good Doctor Harvey?'

Henriette opens her eyes and smiles at her daughter.
'No, it was you, little one. You dragged me back from the brink.'

Act IV, Scene 10 ~ Bath market square

'Where are we going?' The wind is gusting and Henriette clings to her hood to stop it slipping off her head.

'It's a secret,' says Harry Jermyn as he leads the party out of Abbey Church House and down the street towards the market place. 'If I told you, it would not be a secret anymore.'

Henriette stares at a row of stone lodging houses that provide for city guests. 'They look as if they were built quite recently.'

'After Queen Elizabeth took the waters in Bath there was a big expansion of the town,' says Jermyn. 'The house we are staying in is turn of the century. But the place we are visiting is slightly more contemporary and should be of special interest to you.'

'I wish you would stop spinning riddles and tell me where we are going.'

Susan is walking one step behind. 'You should have taken the sedan, your majesty.'

'Well Harry told me it was a short walk,' complains Henriette. 'If I had known we were hiking around the whole of Bath I would have used the chair.'

'Here we are,' says Jermyn, pausing and pointing at the square in front. 'The market place.'

Henriette looks at the serried rows of Tudor buildings. 'So?'

'Look over there, the modern building above the old market house.'

'How strange,' says Henriette. 'The bottom part is Tudor and the top half is classical.'

'Very observant, your majesty.' Jermyn steers her through the crowded square, dodging coaches and carts. Eventually they stand solemnly in front of the building. 'This is the Guildhall, designed by one of Bath's most famous sons.'

'I like it, the top bit at least.'

'I thought you would,' says Jermyn. 'In fact, I was certain of it.'

'What are you saying, Harry? You are talking in riddles again.'

'This is another Inigo Jones design.'

'Mr Jones was born in Bath,' exclaims Henriette. 'I am sure he never told me that.'

'Perhaps you never asked.'

'Maybe so.' Henriette is deep in thought. 'Do you know, wherever I go I cannot escape the work of Mr Jones; he has left his imprint across the whole kingdom.' She pauses to reflect. 'And in Heidelberg.'

'We gaze on the work of a genius,' says Jermyn.

'It makes me homesick for the Queen's House at Greenwich and the Banqueting Hall.' The Queen lowers her voice. 'But not the rest of White Hall Palace – a dismal, smelly place.'

'It is a shame that Inigo never completed his plans for the new White Hall,' says Jermyn.

'He will have his day,' says Henriette. 'Have faith, Harry. We will return to London and Mr Jones will build a palace fit for Kings and Queens. The name "White Hall" will become famous around the world.'

Act IV, Scene 11 ~ Bath

A cavalry troop rides under the arch of east gate, slowing to a trot as it negotiates the rabbit warren of narrow streets. The soldiers ask directions to Abbey Church House. Minutes later, the Captain dismounts before a wooden door braced with iron. He hammers loudly, standing back as the entrance swings opens. After a brief conversation, the riders are directed down the alley to a stable where they can rest their horses.

Henriette watches the visitors from a narrow, latticed window in her front room.

'Shall we visit the spa again in the morning?' Henriette returns to a bench seat surrounded by her lap dogs. She is discussing plans with Susan and Anne. 'I do think it helped my cough and my aching limbs.'

There is a gentle tap on the door and Harry Jermyn enters, followed by Father Philip. 'My apologies for interrupting, your majesty, but soldiers bring word that Essex and his London army have slipped past Oxford and are heading for Bristol.'

'Are we in his path?' England's geography is not Henriette's strong point.

'Pretty much,' says Jermyn. 'He is certain to send skirmishers to Bath in order to make sure a royalist army is not threatening to ambush his flank.'

Henriette gives a deep sigh. 'Is there no where we can go?' She pauses to consider their plight. 'Can we perhaps return to Oxford?'

'That would be dangerous,' says Jermyn. 'Essex may swing north and with the Earl of Manchester approaching from East Anglia, Oxford would be surrounded.'

'I am a fox being hunted down,' says Henriette glumly.

'I think we should make our way to Exeter,' says Jermyn.

'That is further into the south west,' says Father Philip. 'Might we not become trapped?'

'From Exeter we can catch a boat to France,' says Jermyn.

Henriette glares at her chamberlain. It is the first time anyone has raised the possibility of leaving England.

'I am not deserting the King.'

'My instructions from his majesty are to avoid your capture by the enemy at any cost,' says Jermyn. 'That may require drastic measures such as withdrawing from England temporarily.'

Henriette's bottom lip drops. 'No one mentioned boat trips.'

'France could be the best place to seek support for our cause,' says Father Philip. 'Look what you managed to achieve in Holland.'

Henriette folds her arms. 'I am not abandoning the King.'

'The idea of moving to Exeter is to remove ourselves from the path of Essex's army,' says Jermyn. 'If he attacks Bristol, we can stay in Exeter. It is only if a parliamentary army follows us down the peninsula that we would have to consider other options. Taking a boat across the British Sea is one possibility, and it means we are not trapped. That was the whole point of leaving Oxford.'

'Can we not defend Bath?' asks Henriette.

'The walls are weak,' says Jermyn. 'When parliament surrounded the town two years ago, it fell within days. Exeter is much better fortified; Prince Maurice built additional defences when he occupied the city in the autumn.'

Henriette lets out a cry of frustration. 'Why do we have to keep running? The puritans sit in London and laugh at us.'

'Our spies report great divisions among the enemy,' says Jermyn. 'I very much doubt that they are laughing about anything.'

'Nor am I,' says Henriette. 'We have only been here nine days.'

Susan stands up. 'Shall I supervise the packing of the baggage, your majesty?'

'How far is it to Exeter?' asks Henriette.

'About eighty miles,' says Jermyn. 'The coaches should make the journey in three days, perhaps four if we find the bridges damaged or the roads in poor condition.'

Henriette sits looking miserable. Eventually she lifts herself out of the chair.

'We go to Exeter,' she says, 'but no further. That is where my baby will be born. If I survive, that is where I make my last stand.'

Act IV, Scene 12 ~ Exeter

The screams can be heard throughout Bedford House. Harry Jermyn, Father Philip, little Jeffrey and Sir John Berkeley, governor of Exeter, stand about helpless in a dark oak-panelled room that has hastily been requisitioned as the Queen's withdrawing chamber. Two rooms away, Henriette is writhing in her bed, watched over by Doctor Harvey with Susan and Anne in attendance. A local midwife has been summoned although the ever-faithful Madame Peronne has landed at Portsmouth and is expected any time.

'I cannot bear this pain.' The Queen is doubled up on the bed; Anne struggles to apply a warm cloth to Henriette's forehead.

Susan looks at the midwife. 'Have the contractions begun?'

'No, my lady; there is no sign of the baby.'

'Oh my God,' says Henriette, 'the pain never ceases.'

Doctor Harvey takes Susan to one side and whispers. 'I fear that we will lose them both.'

The Countess has seen enough. She leaves the room and walks through the privy chamber into the withdrawing room. The men stare at her anxiously.

Susan does not hold back: 'Harry, Father Philip, we must do something; the Queen is dying.'

'We should send for Sir Theodore Mayerne,' says Jermyn.

'Will he come all the way from London?' asks Father Philip.

Susan slumps into a chair, exhausted. She has hardly slept for three nights. 'Will parliament let him?'

'I think so,' says Jermyn. 'They have gone to great lengths to protect Elizabeth and Henry; they don't want to be accused of mistreating the King's children. They know that would play badly with people.'

'Then, for heaven's sake, get a message to him,' says Susan. There is an eerie silence from the Queen's bedroom. 'Let us pray it is not too late.'

Lady Anne Dalkeith tries hard to stay awake as she watches over the slumbering Queen. Anne is exhausted and after a while she sits on the bottom of the bed. Henriette wakes a few minutes later to find her lady-in-waiting snoring, lying sideways at her feet. The acute pain has eased, possibly because of the two grains of opium that Doctor Harvey finally persuaded her to take. Henriette resisted the medicine as it might harm the baby, but Harvey replied bluntly that both mother and baby might die if she didn't follow his advice. Henriette is in a dreamy state; it is a strange sensation as if she is floating above the bed and staring down at her own prostrate body and that of her companion. Henriette wriggles her body alongside Anne, pulls the bed cover over both of them and cuddles up close. Then she loses consciousness.

Lady Dalkeith wakes to find Henriette's skinny arm wrapped tight around her stomach. She is not entirely sure what the etiquette of the situation demands, but the last two weeks have been so traumatic that she does not care. She gently pushes Henriette's hair away from her face, at which point the Queen opens her eyes.

'Where am I?'

'You are in bed,' says Lady Dalkeith, 'and I have to confess I was so tired I must have fallen asleep too.'

Henriette smiles. 'Not so much a lady-in-waiting as a lady-in-bed.'

Anne laughs. 'Are you feeling any better?'

'Not entirely,' says Henriette. 'All the muscles that were aching feel tight, but the stabbing pain has gone.'

'That is some comfort.'

'The baby is going to be the wisest of all my children,' says Henriette.

'Why is that?'

'Because he or she has the brains not to want to enter this horrible world.'

'Well if the child is to be super intelligent, you better find a good tutor.'

Henriette stares at Anne. 'Will you be Godmother and governess to my baby?'

'Me,' exclaims Lady Dalkeith. 'I thought you wanted the baby to grow up wise.'

'You would make a wonderful Godmother. Don't repeat this to anyone, but Susan is too old and Margaret is too quiet.'

'I see,' says Anne with a grin, 'so I am the best of a bad lot.'

'I don't mean that.' Henriette's eyes sparkle. 'Your independence of spirit and good humour are qualities that I admire. Please say you will.'

'I am not sure what either of our husbands would say,' says Anne. 'Here we are lying together in bed discussing the royal baby's future household.'

'Charles would probably have a heart attack,' says Henriette. 'He would say something like – I pray, Maria, that you have not taken an unhealthy liking to the Lady Dalkeith.' Henriette is a good mimic and can replicate her husband's mild Scottish accent very accurately. She never mocks his speech impediment.

Anne collapses in giggles. 'Imagine what Susan would say.'

'She would sack you,' says Henriette, 'or at least she would try until I forbade it, then she would say, I really don't know what the world is coming to.' Again Henriette catches the Countess of Denbeigh's accent and intonation perfectly.

'If you ever did need an additional job to being Queen,' says Anne, 'you could always do impersonations.'

'Me and little Jeffrey would make a great act, my jokes and his magic; you see I always loved the stage.' The Queen looks at Anne. The shared humour and lack of barrier between them reminds Henriette of her former friendship with Lucy Hay. It makes the Queen reflect on the past.

'Promise me one thing, Anne.'

'What is that, your majesty?'

'Whatever happens, do not betray my baby. Say what you like about me and Charles, but never, ever let my child down.'

Anne frowns. 'You know I would never do that.'

'I thought I knew my friends, but over the years I have discovered that few people are friends with me, they are companions of the Queen, and that is very different.'

Lady Dalkeith pulls herself up. 'Well let me say, while no one is about, that I am your friend, Henriette Marie, and I shall stand by your baby through thick and thin. If you want me to address the Queen of the Three Kingdoms, then I shall, your majesty.'

Henriette throws her arms around Anne's neck. 'Thank you, your friendship is more important than all the gold in London.'

At this moment, the door opens and Susan appears.

'Your majesty, what ever is the matter?'

Henriette remains clinging to Lady Dalkeith. She turns to look at her Dame of Honour. 'I needed someone to hug.'

'Just as long as we remember who we are,' says Susan, frowning at Anne. 'It is not usual for a lady-in-waiting, Lady Dalkeith, to drape herself across the Queen's bed and indulge in intimate contact.'

'I was just giving Anne a hug to thank her for looking after me,' protests Henriette. 'Come here, Susan, and let me thank you too.'

The Countess shakes her head. 'A short letter of thanks will be quite sufficient, your majesty. Where on earth have you got these strange ideas? The King would be dismayed by your lack of protocol.' She shakes her head. 'I don't know what the world is coming to.'

Henriette and Anne look at each other and burst out laughing.

Act IV, Scene 13 ~ Exeter

He stands over his patient; his face is so close she can smell the fish he ate for lunch. It reminds Henriette of the disagreeable Dutch jewellery merchant in Gravenhage.

'Open wide,' he says, staring down her mouth. He proceeds to hold her arms outstretched and gently guides them over her head and down by her side. He examines her stomach and prods her legs. He turns to Madame Peronne. 'Is the baby in the correct position?'

'Yes, monsieur.'

He turns back to the patient. 'Lean forward and if I may, your majesty, I shall lift your night shift and examine the rash.'

Henriette leans forward without speaking. As she does so, she coughs.

'Can you cough again, please, your majesty.'

After completing the examination, Sir Theodore Mayerne puts his instruments back in his bag. 'We can do nothing but wait for the baby to arrive.'

'It is thirteen days overdue,' says Susan.

'Another twenty-four hours and we may have to intervene,' says Sir Theodore. He gives the Queen a perfunctory bow. 'I need to compare notes with Doctor Harvey and the midwife, if you will excuse me, your majesty.'

Henriette is in too much discomfort to care. She waves him away without speaking. She lies on her side and draws her knees up as far as she can. Madame Peronne sits down on a chair beside the bed.

Sir Theodore retires to the withdrawing chamber where he meets with Harry Jermyn, Father Philip and Susan. He does not call in the doctor or ask for the midwife.

'The Queen is seriously ill,' says Mayerne. 'You should be prepared for the very real possibility that she will not last many more days. I expect that the baby will be stillborn, but in any event the delivery will probably kill the mother.'

Susan puts her hand to her mouth and lets out a short cry. Jermyn guides Susan to a chair while Father Philip bows his head and makes the sign of the cross.

'Should we tell the King?' asks Jermyn.

Mayerne shrugs. 'What good will it do? He is in no position to abandon his army and come down to Exeter.'

'What about the news we received yesterday?' asks Susan. 'We have not told the Queen yet.'

Jermyn feels sick in the stomach; he offers a chair to Mayerne before explaining: 'Essex is marching his army towards Exeter rather than Bristol. He is possibly seeking to re-take the West Country, but he may be targeting the Queen. Spies tell us that kidnapping her majesty is a high priority for our enemies. They see it as the quickest way to end the war.'

Mayerne grimaces. 'They could be right.'

Jermyn studies the doctor and wonders about his loyalty.

'We cannot move the Queen,' says Father Philip. 'We must deliver the baby here in Exeter; only then can we make a decision about where to go.'

'Is there anything you can do to alleviate the Queen's condition?' Jermyn knows that Mayerne is a leading authority on chemical treatments. The royal physician has long campaigned for specialist shops to replace the current practice of dispensing cures from grocery stores.

'I have a couple of solutions that may help,' says Mayerne.

'I doubt she is strong enough to be bled,' says Susan.

'I would disapprove of that remedy,' says Mayerne. 'The idea of balancing the body's fluids is widely discredited these days.'

'Then I suggest you utilise your skill and experience to provide the Queen with enough strength to cope with childbirth,' says Jermyn. 'God knows, she is a strong character inside.'

'I have always thought she has a tendency to dramatics,' says Mayerne, 'although I concede she is not doing so now. She is extremely sick.'

Susan is irritated by the man's arrogance. 'The Queen has an iron will and huge reservoirs of personal strength. Believe me, I have been close to her for nearly twenty years. But she needs your help, doctor.'

Sir Theodore bows. 'Doctor Harvey and I will get to work straight away. In addition to Madame Peronne, I advise two experienced midwives to be present, day and night.'

'I will speak to Sir John Berkeley,' says Jermyn.

Mayerne looks around the room. 'Is this not the home of my friend the Earl of Bedford?'

'Sir John is renting the premises,' explains Jermyn, 'while he fulfils the King's appointment as Governor of Exeter.'

'I saw Bedford in London only a few weeks ago,' says Mayerne.

'He returned from Oxford with the Earl of Holland,' says Jermyn. 'They claim to be working for the King back in London, but in truth I am unsure where their sympathies lie.'

The physician picks up his bag. 'These are troubled times.'

'Do you have a preference for the outcome, sir?'

Sir Theodore shakes his head. 'Doctors must be prepared to cross battle lines. Today I am fighting to save the Queen's life. Last week I was treating one of the parliamentary commanders for depression. It is not for me to take sides.'

'I am heartened to hear that the enemy is depressed,' says Jermyn. 'Who was your patient?'

'That is a confidence.' Mayerne pauses for a moment. 'Well, I dare say it does not matter; he is not a soldier of any great moment – a cavalry officer by the name of Oliver Cromwell.'

'I knew him as a member of parliament,' says Jermyn. 'I am not surprised to hear he is unwell; I always thought his piety was a trifle over-indulgent.'

Sir Theodore heads towards the door. 'As I say, it is not for me to judge my patients. Right now, I must fight to save the Queen.'

Father Philip stands up. 'I shall pray for you, master physician.'

Mayerne shakes his head. 'Don't worry about me, Father, I would suggest you pray for your Queen.'

Act IV, Scene 14 ~ Exeter

The distraught cries emanating from Henriette turn Susan's stomach. These are not the spirited shouts of pain and bad language that accompanied previous births, but horrific shrieks of anguish. At one point Susan manages to find a gap between Mayerne and one of the midwives and grasps Henriette's slender hand. The Queen squeezes so hard that Susan fears that her bones may break.

Henriette is in labour. It is her ninth delivery and the first without the King in residence. Harry Jermyn, Father Philip and little Jeffrey are barred from the Queen's apartments as Susan insists on a traditional lying in. Sir Theodore has an impressive team at his disposal – Madame Peronne, Doctor Harvey and his assistant and two local midwives from the town. It is so crowded that Margaret and Anne wait in the adjacent privy chamber organising fresh towels and hot water while Susan attends in the Queen's bedroom.

Harry Jermyn is all for abandoning protocol and storming into the bedroom. There has been an ominous silence for fifteen minutes, no more cries of pain and no sounds of a newly born child. Father Philip and Sir John have to physically restrain him.

'She is dead,' says Henriette's chamberlain. 'They are both dead. What am I going to tell the King? This is the end of everything.'

Little Jeffrey is at ease when playing the fool or the failed magician, but serious moments are challenging. Even with Jermyn slumped in a chair, Jeffrey only reaches as high as Harry's waist.

'We should kneel and pray,' says Jeffrey quietly, 'that is what the King would want us to do. Is that not right Father Philip?'

'You are quite right, Jeffrey,' says Henriette's confessor. 'We need God's help.'

Henriette

Jermyn is shaken out of his despair. 'Bless you Jeffrey, we will pray.'

Just as Harry Jermyn slips on to his knees, the door opens. It is Margaret Lucas and she is as white as a sheet.

'She's gone,' says Jermyn. 'We have lost her.'

'Her majesty has passed out,' says Margaret. 'She is still breathing.'

'And the baby?' asks Father Philip.

'We have a little princess.' The tears in Margaret's eyes betray her next words. 'Sir Theodore fears the little one is fading.'

'I must see the Queen,' says Jermyn. 'I have a duty to see with my own eyes so I may give a true account to the King.'

Margaret is unsure of the protocol. 'You had better ask the Countess of Denbeigh.'

Jermyn brushes past Margaret and strides across to the bedroom door. He knocks loudly.

'Am I permitted to bear witness for the King?'

Anne appears at the door. 'Shssh, do not make such a noise. You may come in but you say nothing and stand beside me. Do you understand?'

Jermyn nods. Anne opens the door wide and beckons him in. Jeffrey and Father Philip stand outside trying to peer in. Anne firmly closes the door.

The scene that greets Jermyn remains in his memory to his dying day. Despite it being a warm sunny afternoon, the curtains are drawn and a fire is lit. Candles cast a pale light across the bed where Henriette lies motionless. Madame Peronne is gently mopping the Queen's brow. Jermyn can make out blood on the sheets. Mayerne and his colleagues stand in the far corner; it looks as if they have been holding a conference but now they just stare at the bed. The two midwives bend over a cradle. When Jermyn walks a step closer he can see the wrinkled face of a baby wrapped in a blanket making no sound. That is the thing that strikes him – after the agonies and screaming, there is nothing.

After standing motionless for half a minute, it feels longer to Jermyn, a faint sound breaks the spell. He cannot stop himself; he walks forward and watches the little baby's head moving slowly from side to side. She is not crying, it sounds more like a kitten mewing.

Jermyn turns towards the bed and stares at the crumpled body of Henriette. 'Is she alive?'

'She is breathing,' says Mayerne, 'but it is very irregular and her pulse is weak. She needs peace and rest. You can do nothing here.'

Susan whispers to Anne. 'Ask Father Philip to join us.'

Jermyn wants to grab the Queen's hand, go down on one knee and tell her that no woman in the world means anything to him except her. But that is impossible. She is Queen of the Three Kingdoms and he is her humble subject. He stares at Henriette's limp, tiny body on the bed. He feels useless. Susan takes Harry gently by the arm and leads him out of the bedroom.

Act IV, Scene 15 ~ Exeter

Susan closes the door and stares at the sombre faces. 'She is too ill to make her wishes clear. We will have to decide what to do.'

Father Philip, Harry Jermyn, Anne Dalkeith and Margaret Lucas sit down one side of the oak dining table. Sir John Berkeley sits opposite and Susan pulls up a chair beside the Governor.

'I vote for the Fal estuary,' says Harry Jermyn. 'Pendennis Castle is secure and we can use the deep water harbour to gather boats.'

'My brother-in-law and sister live in Arwenack House at the mouth of the estuary,' says Margaret. 'They are loyal supporters of the King. The manor is roomy and comfortable; we would only need to retreat inside Pendennis Castle if the enemy approached. There is a small collection of cottages at Smithwick beside the manor house; all the tenants can be trusted.'

'Can the baby princess be moved?' asks Anne.

'Mayerne believes not,' says Jermyn.

'Then I shall stay here in Exeter with the child.' Anne smiles. 'She is to be my god daughter.'

'Will the Queen permit a separation?' asks Father Philip.

'She has no choice,' says Jermyn. 'I shall take responsibility for the decisions we take.'

'Her majesty will understand if I explain the circumstances,' says Susan. 'She falls in and out of delirium.'

Father Philip shakes his head. 'I think it is too dangerous to move the Queen, never mind the baby.'

'Sir Theodore believes the Queen is likely to die whether we stay in Exeter or not,' says Susan.

'But if we stay, she will almost certainly end up a prisoner of parliament,' says Jermyn. 'I know that is the one thing she fears above all else. If she is captured, she is concerned that the King will make a dishonourable peace to save her life.'

'Can we not defend Exeter against a siege?' asks Father Philip.

'We could not hold out for more than a few days,' says Sir John, 'especially against an army of the size that is approaching.'

'Pendennis Castle is our last chance,' says Jermyn. 'If the Queen was in full possession of her senses she would accept the risk.'

'The main concern has to be enemy patrols scouring the countryside,' says Sir John. 'A large convoy leaving the city would be spotted immediately. There are parliamentary spies everywhere.'

The room relapses into silence, everyone overwhelmed by the impossible dilemma they face. After about half a minute, a wavering voice pipes up from the far end of the table.

'I shall walk with the Queen.'

Everyone stares in amazement at Margaret Lucas. For one thing it sounds a crazy plan. For another, no one ever expects Margaret to speak. She immediately turns bright red.

'The Queen cannot walk a step,' says Father Philip, 'let along ninety miles.'

'We will carry the Queen in a sedan chair,' says Margaret. 'If we are stopped and questioned, I shall tell people that my sister Mary is inside the litter, dying of the plague and we are taking her back to her home at Arwenack.'

'I can provide four strong labourers to carry the chair,' says Sir John.

'What about the rest of us?' asks Susan.

'You can follow separately to avoid arousing suspicion' says Margaret. 'We will arrange to join up a few miles west of Exeter, once we are safely through the enemy cordon.'

Harry Jermyn has never heard Margaret say as many words in a day, let alone in the space of a few minutes.

'It could work,' he says slowly.

'The Queen on her own, unprotected,' says Father Philip. 'It's madness.'

'It may be the only chance of sneaking through enemy lines,' says Jermyn. 'We are not besieged, but parliamentary patrols are circling the city. In a day or two we will be totally cut off and it will be impossible.'

'I think it's worth a try,' says Susan firmly. She surprises herself; she is normally the cautious one. 'Harry is right, an insignificant set of travellers are the only people who might pass undetected. Who will want to look inside the sedan chair if they think the occupant has the plague? Besides, unless they have seen one of Mr Van Dyck's paintings, how will they recognise the Queen?'

The door opens and to everyone's horror, swaying in the entrance is Henriette. She takes a step forward and sinks to her knees.

'Your majesty, what are you doing?' cries Susan as she rushes to help. Harry Jermyn and Father Philip jump up and lift Henriette into a chair.

'We must get you back to bed,' says Susan.

'No thank you,' whispers Henriette. 'It is the paralysis in my legs that is preventing me from standing; I am fine sitting in a chair.'

'Margaret, get a blanket,' says Susan.

Henriette clutches her stomach. 'I don't understand what's happening. I thought after giving birth the pain would ease. My womb feels solid and heavy.' She tries to laugh, but can only wheeze. 'It should be empty.'

The Queen's eyes begin to roll and she looks as if she is about to pass out. Susan and Anne kneel either side of her, holding an arm each.

'I am all right.' Henriette knows she is gravely ill but she hates to admit weakness. 'What have you been discussing? Have you been planning my funeral?'

'Your majesty,' exclaims Susan.

'We have been plotting your escape from the clutches of the enemy,' says Jermyn. As always, he knows it is best to speak plainly with his mistress.

'That sounds a good idea,' whispers Henriette. 'I shall ride on horseback. That way we can put a good distance between the enemy and ourselves. Unfortunately my baby will have to travel in a carriage.'

No one is sure if the Queen is joking or delirious. Father Philip goes down on one knee. 'The enemy is very close and we have formulated a design to fool them.'

Henriette smiles and leans forward. 'I like cunning plans, especially if they outwit Mr Pymple.'

Father Philip wonders if the Queen in her confused state has forgotten that John Pym is dead. 'Margaret will conduct you in a sedan chair to her sister's home beside Pendennis Castle. If you are stopped, she will explain that you have the plague.'

'I probably have,' says Henriette. 'At least it should deter anyone taking a peek.' The Queen pauses for breath. 'Do you think Margaret might need some help lifting the chair?'

Jermyn smiles. She may be desperately ill, but Henriette's wicked sense of humour has not deserted her. 'We will employ four sturdy men to carry the sedan.'

Father Philip gives the Queen's hand a gentle squeeze. 'The baby princess is too weak to travel, your majesty. Lady Dalkeith has offered to stay behind and look after the child until she is strong enough to join you.'

Henriette takes the news calmly. She turns to Anne. 'That is kind.' She smiles. 'My baby is in good hands.'

'We will need to set off tomorrow,' says Jermyn. 'The enemy is approaching fast.'

The Queen sighs. It may be the illness or the medications, but Henriette appears unusually compliant. 'I shall go and pack.'

Susan shakes her head. 'You are going back to bed to rest, your majesty. I will pack.'

'I thought I was the Queen,' says Henriette. 'And the She-Majesty Generalissima. I am meant to give the orders.'

Anne laughs. 'You must take a rest from both jobs, your majesty, until you have your strength back.'

Henriette nods. 'I am nearly better.' The Queen makes an effort to stand up and promptly passes out.

Act IV, Scene 16 ~ Road to Pendennis

It is a few minutes after dawn; billowing cumulus clouds advance over the horizon, invading a pale blue sky. The tall gates on the south side of the city shudder as they slowly open and a sedan chair with black crosses daubed on each side is carried carefully over the cobbled threshold. A lady in a black cloak and hood walks behind the chaise, her gaze firmly fixed on the ground. The small group crosses the packhorse bridge over the River Exe and turns right at the far bank. The population of Exeter has long since spilled out beyond the city walls and for half a mile the small party trudges along narrow streets with houses to either side. The two men leading the sedan follow their instructions and head along the Okehampton road towards the northern edge of Dartmoor. They meet a handful of townsfolk heading into the city to work in the wool warehouses, shops or livestock market. Two men on horseback overtake them but they look more like gentlemen farmers than soldiers. Once in the countryside, a sunken lane with steep banks smothered in wild flowers restricts the view. It is impossible to see more than a few score yards ahead to the next corner. The travellers regularly stop and listen. Every time they halt a small face appears out of the window.

'Are we there yet?'

The lady in the black cloak dutifully replies. 'Just a few more miles, your majesty.'

'I am meant to be your sister, Margaret. Less of the "your majesties".'

No one can see under the hood, but Margaret's cheeks are a deep red. 'I am sorry, your majesty.'

'You've done it again. What's your sister's name?'

'Mary.'

'Well that's ironic because I hate people calling me that; but on this occasion I will be very content for you to address me as Mary.'

Margaret is about to reply when one of the men puts his hand up. 'No talking, please.'

They carefully lower the chair and listen. Distant voices compete with other familiar sounds: the jangling of harnesses and the pounding of hooves, wooden wheels clattering over a rough track and dogs barking.

'It could be a group of farm labourers,' says one man.

'It could be a roundhead patrol,' says the Queen.

The four men pick up the sedan chair without another word and move towards a field gate. Margaret runs in front but struggles with a rope tied to the post. The sound of the approaching group grows louder; there are marching feet and voices. The sedan chair is put down and one of the labourers pulls the rope clear and pushes the gate open.

'I think they are soldiers,' says Henriette.

Henriette

The men lift the sedan chair and move quickly into the field. Margaret throws her cloak back and desperately manhandles the gate until it is closed. She abandons the rope and runs after the others. The thick hawthorn hedge provides good cover and they are soon out of sight of the highway.

Henriette peers out of the window and glances at Margaret. Her lady-in-waiting looks terrified.

'Are we are hidden from the road?' Henriette begins to cough.

One of the men glares at the Queen. His instinct to survive overcomes rank. 'I would advise you muffle the sound with a handkerchief and stay inside the chaise.'

Henriette is not used to being scolded, but she understands their precarious plight. On reflection she realises they should have stuck to their plan and stayed in the lane, telling any soldiers that the occupant of the sedan chair has the plague. If they are found cowering behind a hedge, it will be harder to explain. But it is too late now.

One of the men creeps further along the hedgerow and finds a small gap where he can spy on the road. He runs back to the others with his head down.

'Enemy soldiers,' he whispers.

Henriette can feel her heart beating fast; she is too scared to think about coughing. She can hear marching feet in the lane, followed by what sounds like the rattle and creaking of two or three carts. The Queen hears a man's voice; it can only be a few yards away. How can they possibly not see her?

'We are about a mile from Exeter,' says the voice.

'The papist Queen is surrounded; there is no way she can escape,' says a second voice.

'Forget about her, there will be rich pickings if we take the city.'

Margaret is paralysed. She wants to run across the fields and get as far away from the soldiers as possible. Out of the corner of her eye she sees the Queen leaning out of the window of the sedan chair. Henriette smiles at Margaret. It is such a calm and serene smile; Margaret cannot believe that the Queen possesses such courage. She is a few feet from her enemies and potential catastrophe. In that split second, Margaret understands how special her mistress is. Margaret is less brave and she feels a cold sweat envelop her body as the soldiers march on. How close are they to discovery? Their loyal, volunteer servants are unarmed; the soldiers would seize the Queen and within the week she would be a prisoner in the Tower of London. Still Henriette smiles as if they are resting in Hyde Park under the May blossom without a care in the world. Before Margaret realises it, the patrol has passed. The sound of cartwheels recedes into the distance. Tears run down her cheeks.

The Queen tilts her head and frowns. 'Why are you crying, Margaret?'

'I cannot believe your strength, your majesty. Those soldiers were within earshot. If one of them had leaned on the gate they might have seen us. I thought I was going to faint.'

'Don't do that,' says Henriette quietly. 'If we are confronted, you have got to explain that I am your sister and I am the one with the plague. I am relying on you Margaret.'

'Yes, your majesty.' It dawns on Margaret that it is one thing to plot an escape, but it requires a whole level of extra courage to carry out the design.

Henriette turns to the men. 'How much further before we join the others?'

'It is about five miles to Tedburn Saint Mary, your majesty.'

Henriette nods. 'Well then, we better get a move on. If we are late, Mr Jermyn will become grumpy.' She is about to sit back in the chair when she pauses and looks at the labourer. 'And it's Mary, not your majesty.'

Act IV, Scene 17 ~ Pendennis

Henriette stares up at the sky. It is a blustery summer's day and big cotton wool clouds race in across the water. The view from the castle ramparts is spectacular. On the left are the narrow, deep waters of the River Fal estuary. In front, the white horses of a choppy British Sea stretch to the horizon. The bulky sedan chair that transports the Queen everywhere is parked beside a small set of stone steps. At Henriette's insistence, two soldiers transport her on a small wooden seat to the battlements. She cannot walk, but with a helping hand the Queen can stand for a minute or two.

She leans against the stone parapet and looks out towards France. 'Your young sister is a remarkable lady.'

Mary Lucas nods. 'We were surprised, your majesty, when she asked mother if she could join your court. Margaret is so shy.'

Henriette

'Shy is better than loud. When she speaks, it is meaningful. I know many people who talk a lot and say very little.'

Mary laughs. 'That's me; mother always says that Margaret never converses because I do not desist long enough to give her a chance.'

'You have been kind to me, and your company is most agreeable. Please keep chatting.'

'My sister told me what an inspiration you were on your dangerous journey from Exeter.'

'Beyond Okehampton we did not see an enemy soldier for the rest of the journey.' Henriette sounds disappointed. 'If I had not been so ill I might have enjoyed the country views.'

'I must apologise, your majesty, if I am overtiring you.'

'Nonsense, the breeze is invigorating. I have a friend who has a theory about the benefits of healthy air such as you enjoy here on the coast.' The Queen turns to the guards standing nearby. 'I am perhaps ready to descend from the rampart.' She sits in her chair and the two soldiers carefully carry her down the narrow, uneven steps. They help the Queen back into her more roomy and comfortable chaise.

Mary's husband strolls across from the keep.

'You wanted to meet the prisoner, your majesty,' says Sir Peter. 'We have arranged an audience in the great hall of the keep.'

The sedan transports Henriette across the open ground and through an archway into the guardroom. Built by King Henry, Pendennis Castle is constructed on a finger of jagged rock above Falmouth and, like Scarborough, is difficult to storm. The deep waters of the estuary are also a perfect harbour to protect the few remaining ships that the Royalists command.

The Queen is transferred to the wooden chair for a brief journey to the first floor and across a drawbridge to the tower. Once she reaches the reception hall, she is put down gently beside a small table and chairs.

'Leave me to speak with him alone.'

'Is that wise, your majesty?' asks Sir Peter.

'He will not kill me. It's more likely I will throttle him.'

Mary and her husband usher the soldiers away. One of the guards hovers in the doorway. The Queen looks up at bare walls; she wonders if a few tapestries might cheer the place up. Henriette does not hear the sound of footsteps on the spiral staircase in the corner of the room. As the man reaches the bottom step, he speaks in his distinctive Scottish brogue. 'It is good to see you, your majesty, even if the circumstances are less than ideal.'

Henriette looks up. 'James, we are truly in dire straits.' She glares at the Marquis of Hamilton, once the King's close friend and adviser on Scottish affairs. Her words are more conciliatory. 'How are Anne and Susannah?'

'The children are both in good health and are being looked after by relatives in Scotland.'

'How old are they now?'

'Twelve and eleven,' says Hamilton.

'Mary would have been so proud of them. You will be finding suitable husbands for them next.'

'If anyone will marry the daughters of a disgraced Marquis.'

'You're not in chains.'

'I move freely about the castle,' says Hamilton. 'My apartments are fairly comfortable; I have no complaints.'

'I do, though,' says the Queen harshly. 'You betrayed us.'

Hamilton frowns. 'Never, your majesty; I was tricked by Argyll and the other Scottish covenanters.'

'For someone who was outwitted by his fellow countrymen, you have done nicely out of this Scottish business.'

'I was a fool,' says James, 'I accept that criticism. The rebels offered me every inducement, which I see now was part of their deception.'

'What about the tale I heard that you were ready to accept the Scottish crown?'

'Completely untrue.' Hamilton scoffs. 'That is the last thing I wanted.'

'What do you want, James?'

'To have an opportunity to serve my King; while I sit here a prisoner, the Scottish army is advancing south.'

'We are both prisoners,' says Henriette, 'you, in this castle, and me in Arwenack House. I cannot visit Oxford to be with the King or go to London to see Elizabeth and Henry.' Henriette shrugs. 'I came to this kingdom, embraced England and its people, learned the language – eventually – and now I am not welcome anymore.' The Queen looks around the austere walls of the keep. 'Except in fortresses like this.'

Hamilton stares at Henriette. 'Is this the end, your majesty?'

'No, it is not the end.' The Queen scowls. 'I shall fight for the King until the last breath in my body, which according to Sir Theodore Mayerne may be quite soon.' Henriette snorts. 'What does he know?'

'I beg you, ask the King to allow me to serve him in the fight to come. That's all I ask. After I have done my duty, execute me if you wish. But do not lock me away in some damp, godforsaken dungeon for the rest of my days.'

'I write to Charles every day, or rather Harry helps me. He sorts the cypher, and corrects my spelling.'

'Will you plead with the King?'

'I will not plead,' says Henriette coldly, 'but I will pass on your request.'

'That is all I ask, your majesty.'

'The King is a good man.' Henriette checks herself; she has a tendency recently to choke whenever she talks about Charles. 'It grieves me that so many people in both Kingdoms seek to hurt him. Whether you intended it or not, you wounded him. The Earl of Newcastle is doing his best to undo the damage; if he fails, all is lost.' Henriette signals to the soldier by the door. 'Perhaps you can understand why I find it impossible to forgive the many people who have let Charles down – Lucy, Henry Rich, Algernon Percy, the Earl of Pembroke, to name a few … and you James.'

Two guards arrive.

The Queen speaks softly. 'Take me back to my lodgings.'

They carefully lift the Queen's chair.

As Henriette is carried towards the door, the Marquis of Hamilton bows. The Queen is disappearing out of sight when he shouts, 'God Save the King.'

Act IV, Scene 18 ~ Pendennis

'I cannot cypher that fast,' says Harry Jermyn.

Henriette groans. 'I will have forgotten what I want to say by the time you have written the last bit.'

'I wish you two would stop arguing,' says Susan. 'I am going to talk to our kind hostess about dinner.'

Henriette frowns at the Countess of Denbeigh as she curtsies and leaves the room. 'Susan increasingly reminds me of mama.'

Jermyn laughs. 'You told me once that your mother was the only person you were afraid of.'

'That was in the good old days. Now I am afraid of lots of people – hostile puritans, bloodthirsty roundhead soldiers, Scottish rebels…' the Queen pauses, 'and courtiers who claim to be my friend and then let me down.'

Jermyn scans the sheet of paper in front of him on the desk. 'Did you want to mention the Marquis of Hamilton to the King?'

'I promised I would.' She sighs. 'I fear the safest place for James is locked up here in Pendennis Castle. I don't believe he is a traitor, but he's incompetent. However, I shall pass on his request to Charles.'

'Shall we mention your adventures travelling down from Exeter?'

'I think not. It will only stress Charles to know we sheltered in a ditch with roundhead soldiers marching past within spitting distance. Have we managed to organise any ships, Harry?'

'There are four Dutch boats in the Fal estuary and we are expecting more vessels any day.'

'I cannot pretend that I look forward to another sea journey. It is a great inconvenience that England is an island.'

'It has proved quite convenient for us on a number of occasions,' says Jermyn with a grin.

Margaret Lucas enters the room. 'The sedan chair is ready to take you to the harbour, your majesty.'

Henriette looks at Jermyn. 'Please finish off the letter with my usual assurances to Charles. I do believe he derives strength from receiving my correspondence.' She smiles. 'Except when I am in a grumpy mood and start telling him how to conduct the war.'

'Rebellion,' prompts Jermyn.

Margaret blushes deep red; she cannot believe Harry Jermyn dares to be so insolent to the Queen. She does not comprehend Henriette's relaxed attitude to her closest confidantes.

'Thank you, Harry,' says the Queen. 'You are quite right, it's an illegal rebellion.' She turns to Margaret. 'Now, Miss Lucas, ask the soldiers to carry me in my chair to the chaise. It irritates me to death, but as yet I cannot put one foot in front of another without falling over.'

The complicated travel arrangements are duly completed with a great deal of advice from the Queen along the way. She is transferred to the sedan and carried as gently as possible along the waterfront.

Henriette

The quay is cobbled and uneven with clumps of damp moss; the four men carrying the sedan chair have to watch their footing.

Sir Peter is busy directing affairs. He bows to Henriette and points to a stretch of narrow water on the far side of the estuary.

'That inlet has water deep enough to accommodate the largest ship in the royal navy.'

The Queen leans out of the window. 'It's not the royal navy any more; the Puritan Pirate stole it.'

'The Puritan Pirate?' queries Sir Peter.

The Queen asks the men to put the sedan chair down. 'If they will kindly assist me, I can sit on the wall over there. It is uncomfortably warm in here.'

'It is the hottest day of the year, according to my valet,' says Sir Peter.

The Queen manages to shuffle a few steps with assistance and sits down in the shade. She waves her fan. 'I usually complain of the cold, damp English weather, but today it is too warm.'

'So who is this Puritan Pirate, your majesty?'

'Robert Rich, the Earl of Warwick; he pinched our ships.'

'It was a great pity that Robert chose the opposing side.'

Henriette stares at Sir Peter. 'Pity is not quite the word that comes to mind. A lack of ships has frustrated many of our plans for bringing troops from Ireland or the continent. And moving supplies by land has limited our armies. It was a constant worry when I sailed back from Holland; we had to evade the parliamentary blockade as well as avoid bloodthirsty pirates.'

Margaret Lucas joins the Queen beside the low wall. 'Sir Peter's family used to be pirates and smugglers.'

'Really?' Henriette's eyes widen.

'It was a long time ago, we are respectable now.' says Sir Peter. 'The family has retired from smuggling, apart from organising the King's post to and from the continent.' He smiles. 'Margaret tells me I am called "Peter Post" at the King's court.'

Henriette watches men stacking crates and barrels on the quay. 'Why do we send Royalist letters to the continent via Arwenack House?'

'It is the most southern harbour in Royalist control,' says Sir Peter, 'and Prince Maurice has established a good channel of communication from here to Oxford.'

'Not for much longer if the parliamentary army takes Exeter,' says Margaret.

'I am sure we will despatch an army to challenge Essex,' says Henriette. 'The King will not sit on his hands in Oxford all summer.'

'What about the Scots in the north?' asks Sir Peter.

'I wrote to the Earl of Newcastle before I set off for Bath urging him to hold York.' Henriette shakes her head. 'He took offence and sent a rather curt reply, which is unlike William. All I said was I prayed that the Scots would not advance so far that they might enjoy Yorkshire oat cakes.'

'Perhaps he missed the joke,' says Margaret.

Henriette pulls a face. 'I was trying to cheer him up. I have written back to point out that I only speak plainly to true friends. If William was not so dear to me I should not bother.'

'I worry that we have to defend too many places.' Sir Peter considers the list. 'The North, Oxford, Bristol, the West Country; it leaves us with insufficient men to attack London.'

'Once I get to France I shall make every effort to gather support,' says Henriette. 'I will refuse to take "no" for an answer. There is the Queen Consort in France who is much more sympathetic to our cause than my brother ever was. I still hope to persuade the Pope to assist, and we must transport the forces waiting in Ireland. Prince Rupert went to Chester to keep the port open but now he has been forced to join the Earl of Newcastle at York.'

'That's my point,' says Sir Peter, 'we are stretched in many directions.'

'I shall not give up on the King,' says Henriette. 'The thought of parliament winning and dishing out so-called justice as they did to Thomas Wentworth is not worth contemplating. Our country would enter a dark age.'

'I agree, your majesty. You can be confident that Pendennis Castle will hold out against the rebels.'

'You are a loyal servant of the King; Charles will not forget your steadfast service.'

'Perhaps one day, his majesty may be able to assist with my civic project.'

'What is that, Sir Peter?'

'I want to develop Smithwick into a town here at the mouth of the Fal.'

'I am sure Charles will be pleased to reward such a true supporter. I approve of building projects.' The Queen watches the small boats ferrying supplies out to the ships anchored in the estuary. 'How long will it be before we sail?'

Sir Peter looks up at the clouds in the sky. 'The wind is favourable, your majesty. Once the last Dutch ship arrives in the next day or two, you can be away.'

Henriette does not reply. She watches the flurry of activity on the quayside – carriages, crates, trunks and cases competing for space on the narrow dockside, people moving in every direction, shouting orders, horses tied up, whinnying and snorting, barges queuing up at the harbour wall to transport baggage to the ships. It reminds her of another bustling dockside in another town many years before when she waited for ships to whisk her away from the clutches of the enemy.

'When I was stuck at Dover waiting to sail for Holland, I prayed for a wind to carry me away from my enemies. Now, I dread the moment.' Henriette stares intently at Sir Peter. 'I fear this time I may never return to England, and that thought fills me with despair.'

Act IV, Scene 19 ~ Arwenack House

Henriette prays daily with her confessor for the protection and good fortune of the King and his armies. The household at Arwenack House is staunchly Protestant but Sir Peter has provided a spare bedroom, cleared of furniture, for the Queen and her priest. Father Philip covers a sideboard with a white sheet to create a temporary altar and lays out the key elements of their travelling chapel – gold crucifix, chalice and paten. They kneel before the cross. The Countess of Denbeigh sits on a chair at the back of the room.

'I have a great foreboding, father.'

'God will protect you on the water, your majesty.'

'I am not talking about the sea voyage. I worry that I shall never return to this kingdom; I may never see Charles again.'

'You must remain positive. Once you have recovered from your sickness, I am sure you will view things differently. The King needs you.'

'All I want is to be with Charles. I no longer care about being Queen or possessing grand houses stuffed with expensive furniture and famous paintings. If the King turns his back on his ungrateful subjects and joins me in France, I shall be happy.'

'The King's authority derives from God; he has a divine duty to rule his kingdoms.' Father Philip helps Henriette off her prayer cushion and with Susan's assistance lifts the Queen on to her chair.

Henriette is puzzled. 'Are you saying, Father, that Charles cannot leave England?'

'I am sure he would not wish to,' says Father Philip.

'Then I shall have to rebuild my strength, recruit and equip an army and bring it over to England to be with Charles.'

The door opens and Harry Jermyn appears at the entrance.

'I thought you were organising the packing down by the quay,' says Henriette.

'I was, your majesty, but a messenger has arrived from Oxford.' Jermyn hovers in the doorway.

'Come in, Harry,' says Henriette. 'You missed the prayers.'

Jermyn stares; he does not move or speak.

The Queen narrows her eyes. 'You have bad news, I can tell. Please share whatever message you have received.'

'The army of the north joined forces with Prince Rupert's cavalry and met the enemy on open ground outside York.' Jermyn consults the letter. 'A place called Marston Moor.'

'And the result?' Henriette can guess the answer from the look on Jermyn's face.

'Fairfax and the Scottish rebels drove our army off the field, your majesty. The bulk of our troops were killed or captured and the artillery was taken. The Earl of Newcastle has escaped to the coast; Prince Rupert's whereabouts are unknown. The north of England is in the hands of the enemy.'

The Queen bows her head. 'I am leaving a broken kingdom. I fear for my husband and my children; I cannot desert them at such a perilous time.'

Father Philip speaks softly. 'You promised the King you would stay out of the reach of your enemies. If you try to return to Oxford and are captured, that truly will be the end.'

Henriette cries out. 'If I flee this kingdom, I shall regret it for the rest of my life.'

Act V

The Prologue

'She is too ill to continue dictating her memoirs.' Madame de Motteville ushers Henriette's daughter into the withdrawing room at Colombes.

Minette agrees. 'The story will have to wait. Mam needs to see a doctor and recover her strength.'

'She complains that the doctors want to give her opium; you know her view on that subject.'

'That dates back to when she gave birth to me,' says Minette. 'Mam is convinced that her slow recovery was the result of opium grains administered during her confinement.'

Both women fail to notice Henriette standing in the doorway listening to the conversation.

'What's all this about me not continuing my memoirs?'

Minette swings round. 'Mam, you startled me. I thought you were in bed.'

'You thought wrong,' mutters Henriette. She leans on her stick, draws breath and speaks with more enthusiasm. 'I am perfectly capable of dictating my memoirs. We have reached an exciting bit involving the puritan pirate.'

'You need to rest, mam.'

'If I had taken the advice of doctors and advisers and done nothing for the last twenty-five years, where would we be I wonder.'

Minette shrugs. 'Who is this puritan pirate you keep talking about?'

'I don't keep talking about him; in fact, I try my best to put him to the back of my mind. He was a thorn in your father's side all through the rebellion.' Henriette walks slowly across the room and sits down on the upholstered bench next to her daughter. 'He was Henry Rich's brother, the Earl of Warwick, and before the rebellion he used to pillage Spanish and Portuguese treasure ships, organise slaves at his plantations in the Americas and generally make a nuisance of himself to everyone on the high seas.'

'He sounds quite dashing.'

'He was nothing of the sort,' says Henriette sharply. 'He was arrogant and greedy, and he saw the rebellion as an opportunity to line his own pockets. He pinched our navy, you know.' She nods towards Madame de Motteville. 'Françoise, pick up your quill and I will tell you the story of how the puritan pirate tried to capture my ship.' She scoffs. 'He reckoned without the daughter of Henri the Great. I instructed the captain to scuttle the vessel before Warwick could get his thieving hands on it.'

Act V, Scene 1 ~ The British Sea

The ships weigh anchor and slip out of the Fal estuary. Henriette stands on deck staring up at the walls of Pendennis Castle. She wonders if James Hamilton is watching from the battlements. Sir Peter and his wife Mary wave goodbye from the harbour quay. Margaret stands beside the Queen with tears in her eyes as her sister and homeland recede into the distance.

Henriette glances at the bow of the ship as it points towards open sea. Further along the deck, the Countess of Denbeigh stands with a handkerchief to her face. Henriette hobbles towards her companion, clinging to the wooden rail.

The Countess puts her handkerchief away. Henriette can see that she has been crying.

'What's wrong, Susan?'

'I am sixty years old, your majesty. I am leaving England, my sons, my home, my friends; it is likely that I shall not return.'

'Don't say that.' Henriette places her hand on Susan's arm. 'I have been very grumpy these past few days, but I am resolved to be more positive and work diligently on the King's behalf. Just as in Gravenhage, we will recruit soldiers and arms and then come back to help defeat the rebels once and for all.'

'The Battle of Marston Moor destroyed our northern army,' says Susan. 'I see no prospect of returning any time soon.' Susan smiles wistfully. 'Time is not on my side.'

Henriette

Henriette stares at the disappearing coastline. She is struggling to maintain any façade of cheerfulness.

'I am leaving Charles and my children.' The Queen shrugs, 'As for my homes, they are probably vandalised or destroyed by now.'

Henriette begins to sway. 'I think I need to sit down.'

'Harry,' shouts Susan, 'the Queen.'

Henriette slumps on the deck. Jermyn and Father Philip rush across and gently lift the Queen, carrying her to the steps that lead to the cabins.

'Can we lower her safely down these stairs?' asks Father Philip peering into the darkness.

The Queen regains consciousness and begins mumbling.

The Captain and two of his officers arrive. 'We have a sling which will lower her majesty to the deck below.'

'I am a piece of baggage am I?' mutters Henriette.

'We need to get you into bed,' says Susan.

'I want to wave goodbye to England,' says Henriette. She props herself on Jermyn's arm and looks out to sea. 'Why are those boats drifting so far away from the rest of the fleet?'

The second officer follows the Queen's gaze – three ships hug the coast less than a quarter of a mile away.

'My God,' he shouts, 'they are not our ships.' He runs across to the rail and looks through his glass. 'Enemy vessels approaching.'

'You must go down to the cabins,' says the Captain. 'Their guns could open fire at any moment.'

'They had better not,' says Henriette indignantly. She attempts to walk across the deck and Jermyn restrains her. 'How dare they.' Her illness evaporates as the fiery spirit returns. She shouts as loudly as she can manage. 'I am Queen of the Three Kingdoms.'

The second officer looks through his telescope again. 'It is the flagship of the parliamentary navy; we are under attack from the Earl of Warwick.'

'Robert Rich,' screams the Queen, pointing wildly in the direction of the enemy. 'He's got a nerve. They are not parliamentary ships; those boats belong to the King.'

The Captain whispers to Father Philip: 'For pity's sake, get the Queen below deck.'

Harry Jermyn and Father Philip practically manhandle Henriette towards the steps.

'All right,' she cries, 'I don't need a sling; I am not a sack of potatoes. Just give me an arm to hang on to.'

Jermyn walks down the narrow stairs in front of the Queen and turns to help her carefully negotiate each step. They are clear of the coast and the boat is beginning to rise up and down on the swell. Eventually after a great deal of vexed commentary from Henriette, she arrives safely on the lower deck. They can hear the Captain issuing orders, men running about and extra sails being unfurled as the race of their lives commences.

Susan carefully follows her mistress backwards down the steep steps, not an easy task in a long satin dress with deep cuffs. Once safely below deck, she peers into the dark.

'It's very pokey.'

Henriette is unimpressed with her negative attitude. 'Sir Peter explained that Dutch fluyts are designed to maximise cargo. We are not on a pleasure cruise down the Thames.'

'The Dutch are clever engineers,' says Jermyn. 'Despite the volume of cargo, the narrow hulls cut through the water with little resistance. The boats even have oars to assist when the wind fails.'

Susan remains unconvinced as she opens a door into a tiny cabin. 'There is no space for passengers.'

'Father Philip and I will share this room,' says Jermyn. 'You three ladies are taking over the officers' quarters.' His description is optimistic. They move next door and cram into a modest-sized cabin with four bunk beds.

'It is just as well Little Jeffrey and the servants are sailing in one of the other boats,' says Susan, shaking her head.

'Toilet arrangements are as per our last voyage,' says Jermyn. 'Unfortunately the steps down to the ballast are too steep for your majesty.' He points to a bucket.

'This is outrageous,' says Susan. 'Her majesty cannot...'

Henriette interrupts the countess. 'It will be fine. This is nothing to what are menfolk are suffering back home. Now if Harry and Father Philip will kindly retire, we will do our best to make this compact space as homely and comfortable as we can.' She steadies herself as the boat heaves up and down on the swell. 'And we shall pray the enemy do not overtake us.'

The perils of the previous journey from Gravenhage to Burlington when the boat threatened to split apart as it crashed over twenty foot waves is replaced by a different anxiety. As the boat ploughs gracefully through calm water with occasional gentle creaks from the timbers, they sit on the bunk beds wondering when the attack will commence. Will a cannon ball suddenly rip through the hull; what will happen if the enemy ships overhaul them and men at arms attempt to board?

Susan sits mournfully with a blanket pulled tightly across her shoulders. 'Wherever we go, our tormentors are always one step behind.'

'You cannot blame my bad luck at sea,' mutters Henriette. 'The Puritan Pirate was lying in wait for us.' She tries to get comfortable in the tiny bunk bed. 'I am the smallest person I know, apart from little Jeffrey, so I don't know who these beds are intended for.'

'It's a Dutch ship,' says Susan, 'and we did remark upon the fact that Netherlanders in Gravenhage were unusually short.'

'And round.' Henriette laughs. 'Do you remember that dreadful little man at the jewellery sale?'

'I prefer not to recall that episode in our lives,' says Susan. 'It was disconcerting having to be a shop keeper; I was never trained for a career in trade.'

'It sounds dreadful.' Margaret has not spoken since they left the main deck. Henriette and Susan turn to look at her; Margaret's cheeks blush.

'You should have heard them,' says Henriette, 'pouring over our crown jewels and telling us everything was too expensive. They had their boots on our necks and they knew it.'

There is a knock on the cabin door; Susan climbs out of her bunk and turns the handle. 'Come in, Captain.'

'I apologise for disturbing your majesty.'

'I think it is the Earl of Warwick who is disturbing us,' says Henriette.

'The prevailing wind is in our favour and we are making good progress into the British Sea. Our ships are faster than the heavier enemy vessels.'

'Where are we heading?' asks Margaret.

'The winds should take us to the Brittany coast, although it may be necessary to shelter in the harbour on the Isle of Jersey. We are in the hands of the weather, but so is the enemy.'

'I take it we have no guns to retaliate with,' says Henriette.

'No, your majesty, these are merchant vessels and our only advantage is pace.'

Henriette nods. 'Then I should not detain you, Captain; we will pray with Father Philip for favourable winds. Our deliverance is in the hands of God and your skills as a navigator.'

The calm seas continue into the night. The boat cuts steadily through the water and there is no sound of enemy gunfire to disturb the passengers. They are all tucked up in bed by early evening and Henriette, who is exhausted by the day's antics, falls quickly into a heavy sleep. Just as in the quayside cottage at Burlington, it is Susan who stirs the Queen.

'Wake up, your majesty, we are under attack.'

As Henriette opens her eyes, she can hear the faint sound of cannon fire. 'Have we been hit?'

'I don't think so.'

'I must get dressed and go on deck.'

'That is out of the question, your majesty.'

'It wasn't a question.' Henriette hauls herself up. 'It was a command. Now go and tell Harry and Father Philip that I need help to get up the steps.'

Despite complaints and protests from everyone below deck, Henriette insists on making her way up the steep staircase. Jermyn again attempts to assist, keeping one step behind. The exertion makes Henriette cough and retch. At the top of the steps, she pauses to catch her breath.

'I really am decrepit these days.'

One of the junior officers runs across to the Queen and crouches, clinging on to his hat.

'The Captain sends his compliments, your majesty, but requests for your safety that you return to the cabins.'

'I have only just staggered up the steps,' says Henriette indignantly. 'I am just as likely to get a cannon ball through my bunk bed as I am to be hit up here.'

As the young officer struggles to conjure a counter argument, a missile crashes through the sails near the stern of the vessel. Everyone instinctively ducks at the sound of splintering wood and ripping canvas, except Henriette who peers over the side.

'Was that from Warwick's ship? Was that a cannon ball from the puritan pirate?'

'I have no idea,' shouts Jermyn as he holds on to the Queen. 'We must return below, your majesty.'

'Was that missile from Robert Rich's boat?' repeats Henriette, straining to catch sight of the enemy vessels.

'It is quite impossible to say.' Jermyn is fast losing his patience. 'Can we please return to the cabins.'

The Captain dashes across. 'I must insist, your majesty, that you stay below.'

'Are we damaged?' asks Henriette. The hiss of another cannon ball can be heard passing through the rigging.

'Without wishing to state the obvious,' says the Captain, 'they have closed within range. During the night they picked a better course and gained on us.'

'I cannot be captured,' croaks the Queen. She tries to clear her throat. 'They will take me to the Tower, force a dishonourable peace on the King and execute me.' The talking saps her strength; she pauses to catch breath. Henriette glares at the Captain. 'If they close within boarding range you must light the gunpowder store and sink the ship.'

Father Philip gasps. 'Think what you are saying, your majesty.'

Susan and Margaret are ashen faced.

'I will not be taken prisoner,' shrieks Henriette. 'We either outrun them or I go down with the ship.' She grips Jermyn's arm. 'Take me to my cabin.'

After spending two hours confined in her claustrophobic bunk bed with the relentless but intermittent sound of cannon fire in the distance, Henriette decides that she would prefer to die in the open rather than in the smelly and shadowy bowels of the ship.

'Margaret, will you ask Harry and Father Philip to come across to our cabin please.'

A few minutes later the two men appear in the doorway.

'The Captain tells me we are about a day's sailing from the Channel Islands,' says Harry Jermyn. 'The wind is dropping.'

There is another distant round of gunfire. Henriette speaks: 'I cannot face being stuck in this cabin waiting for a cannon ball to score a direct hit, and certainly not for another twenty-four hours.'

'Will the enemy catch us if the wind has eased?' asks Susan.

'On the contrary,' says Father Philip. 'Our Dutch ships have oars, so we may be able to outpace them. The Captain is hopeful we could soon be out of their range.'

'Please God, let it be true.' Henriette attempts to lift herself out of the bunk but she has no strength in her arms. 'I want to go back up on deck.'

Jermyn shakes his head. 'The Captain's orders are quite specific, your majesty. No one is to go on deck.'

Henriette is irritated by his refusal to help. She continues to struggle to climb over the panel alongside the bed that is designed to keep the crew secure in rough seas. 'Are you refusing a royal command, Harry?'

'The Captain's word is law on a ship at sea,' says Jermyn. 'It is out of my hands.'

'Harry is correct,' says Father Philip. 'We are duty bound to abide by the Captain's orders.'

Henriette gives up trying to haul herself out of the bunk. She leans against the pillows. She is not about to concede the argument.

'Are you saying that if the King was on board, he would have to take second place to the captain of the ship?'

'Theoretically, yes,' says Jermyn.

'But un-theoretically, probably not?' The Queen is not easily deflected.

'The Captain would give way to the King on issues such as where the boat is heading or whether to engage with an enemy, but on purely safety matters relating to passengers and crew, that is the Captain's responsibility.'

Henriette stares at her chamberlain. 'So we are stuck in this horrible dark hold?'

'The Captain is concerned for your safety, your majesty,' says Father Philip. 'How could he face the King and admit that you were permitted on deck in the middle of a bombardment and were killed by a cannon shot?'

Henriette broods. No one speaks. The boat creaks and groans but there is no further sound of gunfire.

'Perhaps we have out-sailed the enemy,' says Margaret hopefully.

'Will you at least go up on deck and find out the latest situation?' asks Henriette.

Jermyn nods. 'Of course I will, your majesty.'

Father Philip says a prayer and the three ladies join in. A few minutes later and with no further sound of cannon fire, Harry Jermyn reappears.

'We are using sail and oars,' says Jermyn. 'It has taken us out of their range, but the enemy are still in pursuit.'

Henriette is calmer. 'In that case, I suggest we take advantage of the lull to try and get some sleep.' She surveys the doleful faces. 'And before anyone says anything, I apologise for instructing the Captain to sink the boat; that was wrong. Harry, please tell the Captain that I rescind that order. However, if the enemy does board the vessel, I shall jump over the side to avoid capture.' Henriette looks at Jermyn. 'I shall expect assistance if necessary, and that is a royal command.'

Susan begins to protest.

Henriette puts her hand up. 'I do not want to discuss the matter further. Let us hope and pray that we can keep out of the Puritan Pirate's clutches.' She pauses to consider her prospects. 'The sight of the Earl of Warwick's smug face would distress me far more than the thought of sinking to the bottom of the sea.'

Act V, Scene 2 ~ The French coast

'French ships ahead,' shouts the watchman from the crow's nest.

Harry Jermyn and Father Philip lift Henriette out of her chair. After a second night of fitful sleep, the Queen has finally persuaded the Captain to allow her on deck. Susan insists on cloaks, hats and scarves to protect against the chill wind. The Dutch fleet is passing the island of Jersey with the three enemy ships in pursuit. There are several tense minutes as the French boats advance but it soon becomes clear that the Earl of Warwick will not risk a confrontation. His boats begin to slowly turn back towards England.

'Thank God,' says Father Philip falling to his knees. 'It is a miracle – the wind, the French fleet, our oarsmen – ten unarmed ships have survived a three day onslaught from the enemy's most powerful battleships.'

'You see,' says Henriette with a nod of her head, 'I am not always unlucky at sea.'

'I would hardly describe it as a lucky crossing,' mutters Susan.

Harry Jermyn, who has been talking to the Captain, returns to the royal party. 'It will be a day's sailing along the coast towards Brest, provided we keep the wind. If he sees a suitable harbour before that, we may drop anchor. They need to complete repairs to the rigging on one of the ships.'

Henriette looks towards a distant grey outline of land. 'Put my chair on this side of the deck.' She sighs as she sits down. 'I have not set eyes on France for nearly twenty years.'

'You will soon be home, your majesty,' says Margaret.

Henriette shakes her head. 'No I have left my home; this is a foreign land.' She manages a smile. 'Mind you, it will be handy to speak the language.'

It takes three days to tack up the coast of France towards Brittany and locate a suitable anchorage. Four rowing boats transport the bedraggled and exhausted travellers to the beach. The small group of men and women gather a few belongings on the shore and prepare to scramble up a steep cliff path. There is a light drizzle falling and it is slippery underfoot. Harry Jermyn is leading the group and he pauses to stare back at the large boats anchored two hundred yards offshore. Four sailors have joined the landing party and they help to carry the sedan chair up the cliff path. Light is beginning to fade as they reach the top of the headland. On the far side, there is a collection of fishermen's huts leading down to the small village of Le Conquet huddled around a harbour. Boats crammed with crab pots moored alongside a stone pier bob slowly up and down on the tide. Jermyn signals to the party and they clamber down the far side of the headland. When they reach the first hut, the chaise is gently put down and a pale face peers out. At the same time, two French fishermen open the door of their cottage to be confronted by the unusual landing party.

'Has your ship been driven on to the rocks?' one of them asks.

'No, our boats are anchored offshore,' says Jermyn in his best French. He notes that the accent of the Bretons is very different from the Parisian dialect of his mistress. 'The vessels are too large to enter your harbour.'

'Where are you from?' asks the second man. It is dusk and he lifts up a lantern to get a better view of Jermyn.

'We have sailed from England in Dutch ships,' says Jermyn. He points to the sedan chair. 'We are escorting the Queen of England.'

Both fishermen frown and walk slowly across to the chaise. The lamp is held up high and they examine the forlorn figure leaning out of the tiny window. They note the gold fleur-de-lys inlaid into the door of the sedan chair and the fine clothes worn by the accompanying ladies and gentlemen. These are no ordinary travellers.

'Do you not recognise me?' She stares at the men. 'I am Queen Henriette Marie.'

It gradually dawns on the men that these forlorn travellers are not playing tricks.

'You are a Princess of France?' asks the first man, half doubting himself.

His companion sinks to his knees and bows his head. 'The daughter of King Henri the Great has returned.'

Tears trickle down Henriette's cheeks.

Act V, Scene 3 ~ Bourbon-l'Archambault

The elegantly dressed ladies converse around large circular tables draped in white starched tablecloths patterned with golden fleur-de-lys. Layered cake stands at the centre of each table offer a feast of mouth-watering patisseries. In the background, just audible above the hum of conversation, a string orchestra serenades the guests with the latest Italian operatic melodies. Waiters dressed in smart blue uniforms with white piping stand attentively beside each table. It is the kind of sophisticated scene that Henriette recalls from her childhood and the comparison with her adopted country is stark. Most important of all, there is no war raging in the countryside; no armies on the move or towns under siege. This is a country that has emerged from decades of European conflict and is enjoying peace.

When the Queen enters the room, the music stops and everyone stands and applauds. Ladies curtsy as Henriette weaves between the tables with the help of Susan and Margaret. Once Henriette has settled at her table, the other ladies sit down and the chatter resumes. It is a level of respect that the Queen of England has almost forgotten exists. The waiter pours spring water into the glasses; the drink is heavy in minerals and quite bitter to taste but is regarded as an excellent cure. The waters of Bourbon-l'Archambault are the most celebrated in France, although the English habit of bathing has not caught on. Deep in the heart of the Massif Central, this is the region where Henriette's family built its power base before her father advanced on Paris and united the country.

Henriette is fascinated by the melodic tunes played by a group of violinists and a harpsichord player.

'What is the music they are playing? I am sure I have never heard anything so unusual.'

The waiter bows. 'I shall ask the director of the musical ensemble.'

Margaret surveys the ladies' drawing room. The tall windows let in large amounts of light and the walls are plastered and painted white. Everything is bright and modern.

'The spa is so different from the cramped rooms at Bath.'

'It makes England look dark and old-fashioned,' says Susan. 'I see what Inigo Jones means when he talks about modern continental styles of architecture.'

'Except there is nothing modern about it,' says Henriette. 'The joke is the designs are based on classical Roman and Greek ideas.'

'I love the large windows,' says Margaret.

'They remind me of the Queen's House at Greenwich,' says Susan.

Henriette's bottom lip drops. 'Please don't remind me of happy times at Greenwich. It breaks my heart to think what the puritans may have done to my house of delights.' The Queen winces as she tastes the spa water. 'They are probably using the reception hall as a sheep pen.'

The waiter returns with the conductor of the small orchestra.

'I understand your majesty was enquiring about the music we are playing?'

'It sounds lively; I am guessing it is not Church music,' says Henriette.

'Certainly not,' says the musical director. 'We are playing melodies from the latest Italian opera Didone by Genovese Cavalli. The story is based on Virgil's Aeneid.'

'Another connection with the Roman era,' says Henriette. 'Mr Jones is not the only person to be influenced by Italy's illustrious past.' She smiles. 'How my mother would have loved to see her country's influence reaching a spa resort in the heart of France.'

'Who is this Mr Jones?' asks the conductor. 'I have not heard of the composer.'

'He is a good friend from England,' says Henriette. 'He does not create tunes; he composes great buildings and public spaces.'

'And spectacular theatrical productions,' says Susan.

'Perhaps he should design the set for this opera,' says the musician. 'It is due to be performed in Paris in the winter season.'

'I doubt that I could persuade him to travel across the British Sea at present,' says Henriette.

'Nor would I recommend that he tried,' says Susan, recalling the scary crossing that they completed two months ago.

Henriette sighs. 'The rebellion is so remote; it is hard to imagine that while we relax in this peaceful oasis there are armies fighting in England. I long for news from the King; I am useless here.'

'You must build your strength,' says Susan, 'then you can play your part again.'

'I promised Charles I would never abandon the cause. The loss of the north was a cruel blow; I hope we fared better in the south.'

'You should worry about yourself first,' says Susan. 'You will be no help to the King if you have a relapse. You know what happened at Tours when we were travelling down and you tried to walk on your own.'

Henriette looks glum. 'I hate being an invalid.' She picks up her cup and swigs the water with her eyes firmly shut. 'Why do cures always taste horrid?'

Act V, Scene 4 ~ Bourbon-l'Archambault

'I shall retire to a convent if the King has lost another battle.' Henriette glances up from the parchment at her companions. She and Susan sit in chairs by the bay window of the Queen's first floor withdrawing room.

Harry Jermyn stands close by. He is even more impatient than the Queen. 'Let me decode the cypher.'

Henriette hands the letter to him. 'Write down the words. If the message brings good news you may read it out aloud to us. If the story is less encouraging, I will read it myself in private.'

Jermyn nods and walks through a doorway to a small study. He sits at a desk, takes a crumpled sheet of paper hidden in the lining of his coat pocket, unfolds the cypher and slowly begins to translate the text.

'It is remarkable to think that small piece of parchment travelled the same tortuous journey as we did,' says the Queen.

'I don't suppose it was chased across the sea by enemy ships,' says Susan.

Henriette ignores her Dame of Honour. 'The speed of modern post is remarkable. Only a week to travel from the heart of England to Pendennis Castle and via Sir Peter's postal service just three days to cross the British Sea. We must thank my sister-in-law for providing a relay of fresh horses to complete the five hundred mile journey across France. Harry says it took a mere ten days. Mall would describe it as amazing.'

'Your sister-in-law has been very helpful,' says Susan.

'It is true she has been generous with funds, but my requests for military assistance have fallen on deaf ears.'

'Maybe she is not in a position to overrule her ministers.'

'She is Regent to young King Louis. This is not England or Scotland; Anne rules the army and, more importantly, controls the country's finances.'

Henriette glances through the doorway to where Harry Jermyn continues with his task. The cypher code consists of a large grid of letters and numbers. Slowly and painstakingly he looks up each character and writes the translated letter on a fresh sheet of paper. It takes over an hour to transcribe the King's message.

Henriette suffers a coughing fit.

'Take some honey, your majesty.' Susan carefully measures a spoonful for the Queen. The Countess of Denbeigh holds a lot of store by the golden elixir of bees. It seems an unlikely cure for a bronchial affliction but it often calms the patient.

'At least my horrible rash is receding,' says Henriette as she recovers her voice. 'I wish I could be rid of the paralysis.'

'Is it troubling you today?' asks Susan.

'It comes and goes, but my left arm and right leg are all pins and needles this morning.' She snorts. 'I may be falling apart, but I am not dead yet. I look forward to returning to England and reminding Sir Theodore Mayerne about his gloomy prediction at Exeter that I would expire within the month. I always thought he was a misery.'

Margaret Lucas arrives with fresh supplies of mineral water.

Henriette points to Jermyn. 'We have a letter from the King. Harry is decoding the cypher.' She folds her arms. 'If it brings bad news I am entering a convent.'

Jermyn strolls through from the study. 'It looks like we will have your company for a while longer, your majesty.'

The Queen stares at him, hardly daring to believe what he is saying. 'I don't need to find a retreat?'

'Definitely not,' says Jermyn, 'unless you want to visit one to arrange a service of thanksgiving.'

Henriette forgets about her ailments and tries to stand up. She sways unsteadily on her feet. Jermyn runs forward and grabs her arm.

'You must be careful, your majesty' says Susan. 'You are not strong enough to walk on your own.'

They steer Henriette back to her chair. As the Queen sits down she smiles. 'Read the letter, Harry. Good news will do me more good than honey or that foul tasting spa water.'

Jermyn returns to the desk and picks up his sheet of translated scribbles. He surveys the expectant faces across the room. 'Shall I read it aloud, your majesty?'

Henriette sighs. 'I am not a mind reader, Harry; of course, read it aloud.'

Jermyn is about to launch into the letter when he is interrupted by a commotion in the street below.

Margaret stares out of the window. The main street of Bourbon-l'Archambault is packed with people, many waving the white Bourbon flag. There is colourful bunting hanging above their heads, the small golden fleur-de-lys sparkling in the sunlight. The coat of arms appears and disappears as the canvas banners flap in the wind. Soldiers attempt to shepherd spectators to the sides.

'Is he here?' Henriette struggles to stand up.

'We should move downstairs to the reception chamber,' says Susan.

'The King's letter will have to wait, Harry. We have a more urgent royal summons.' Henriette walks slowly across the room with Susan and Margaret supporting an arm each and out through the ornate double doors. Jermyn is left holding the King's letter in an empty room.

The Queen descends the grand staircase to the reception chamber on the ground floor where French royalty entertain their guests.

'It was the harbour in Boulogne.' Henriette feels with her foot for the next step as she recalls one of her last happy memories of France as a teenager. 'We set sail in a rowing boat.'

'Is this another of your unfortunate experiences at sea?' asks Susan.

Henriette pauses, turns to her Dame of Honour and frowns. 'Not at all; it was my first visit to the seaside and we had a pleasant time on the water.'

'No storms,' says Susan, 'or enemy ships.'

'Or puritan pirates,' adds Margaret.

'We were rowing around the harbour.' Henriette resumes her slow progress, one step at a time. 'I recall Henry Rich expressing anxiety about us crashing into the English ships that were expected at any time.'

Two smartly dressed footmen greet the three ladies on the bottom step. Armed guards bar the double doors to the left. The downstairs apartments have been deserted throughout the time that Henriette and her party have been in residence. Now they are suddenly a hive of activity with staff scurrying about, while French courtiers newly arrived from Paris stand in small huddles blocking doorways and corridors. All eyes are upon the frail figure of Queen Henriette Marie – a stranger with a familiar face; a foreign sovereign with French blue blood. The English Queen is the talk of Paris, and now she is standing in front of them. Lords and ladies gather in the reception hall bowing and curtsying. There is loud laughter from the adjoining room. Through the half open doors Henriette glimpses a group of men and women heading in her direction. At the front of the procession is a middle-aged man; he looks unfamiliar, but at the same time he is recognisable. The long wavy dark hair, olive skin and cheeky grin are transplanted on to the torso of an over-weight adult. As he enters the hall, his eyes alight on Henriette and he halts. He studies the small woman standing unsteadily in the centre of the room flanked by two taller ladies. All conversation ceases. With Susan and Margaret's support, Henriette shuffles slowly forward. The man's eyes fill up as he reaches out and takes Henriette in his arms, first kissing her on both cheeks and then gently hugging her. Susan has tears in her eyes; Margaret's cheeks are bright red.

'My little sister.'

Henriette clings to him. She has cried every day since arriving in Bourbon and she has more tears to spill. 'I never thought I would see my dear brother again.'

He continues to hug Henriette and then kisses her again on both cheeks. 'Ettie – you have come back to us.'

She stares into his eyes. 'I return a different person from the girl you remember on Boulogne beach.'

He hugs his sister yet again. 'We were told that the English parliament threatened to imprison you; it is a disgrace how they have treated you.'

'I was facing more than jail,' says Henriette. 'But safety is not the reason for travelling to France. My mission is to gather support across Europe for my husband.'

He stands back and studies his sister's serious expression. He holds her firmly by the shoulders. 'You have not changed, Ettie – a steely resolve and always in a hurry.'

'You don't think I came all this way to take the waters; I can do that in England.'

'I am here to escort you to Paris,' he says, 'if you feel you are strong enough to travel.'

'I have been travelling for the best part of two years,' says Henriette. 'I sailed to Holland to raise arms for the King; we suffered the most terrible storms when we returned to the north of England and had to elude enemy ships and pirates; our house in Burlington was destroyed by enemy artillery; I captured Scarborough Castle and led an army down to Oxford and a few months later we were dodging the enemy in the West Country on our way to Pendennis Castle. Finally, we were attacked as we crossed the British Sea.' Henriette smiles. 'You will appreciate that a bumpy carriage ride to Paris is a mild inconvenience by comparison.'

'The British Sea?' He is puzzled.

'La Manche,' says Henriette. 'In England we call it by a different name.'

He realises that his sister has long since switched allegiance to her adopted home. 'Your adventures are the talk of France.'

'I would prefer that my homeland acted rather than talked,' says Henriette forcefully. Despite her pale complexion and stooped shoulders, her brother reckons she possesses just as much fire and spirit as the teenage girl he remembers.

He nods. 'When you return to Paris you will have an opportunity to speak to our sister-in-law – Anne rules France now.'

'I am hoping she will be more helpful than our dear brother Louis ever was, may he rest in peace.' Henriette turns to her companions. 'Let me introduce the Countess of Denbeigh and Miss Lucas; two loyal friends.'

Susan and Margaret curtsy.

Henriette smiles; she can taste the salty tears running down her face. 'This is the Duke of Orleans, my dear brother Gaston.'

Henriette begins to nod off in her chair. Madame de Motteville puts the pen and paper down carefully on the table and stands up.

'Where are you going?' One eye is open.

'I thought you were resting, your majesty.'

'We have a manuscript to finish. Mr Poquelin will be visiting Colombes in the morning to discuss the scenery and the actions.'

'Shall I call for a light supper, your majesty, and then perhaps we can resume your memoirs?'

'That is a good idea, Françoise. My spirits are lifted by the memory of meeting my brother again and receiving the joyous news from Charles. Glad tidings were few and far between in those days.'

'We have not mentioned the content of the King's message yet.'

'Haven't we?' Henriette pauses to recollect the events at the spa all those years ago. 'I spent a quiet evening with my confessor Father Philip. We sat together in my withdrawing room and recited several prayers before reflecting on an extraordinary day.'

Act V, Scene 5 ~ Bourbon-l'Archambault

'I am told that the King's letter brought good news from England,' says Father Philip.

Henriette considers the long communication from her husband.

'So much has happened since we set sail from Pendennis Castle. Imagine, as we were settling into our rooms here at Bourbon, Charles was arriving in Exeter at the head of an army.'

'The King broke the siege,' says Father Philip. 'What about your daughter?'

Henriette clasps her hands, but for once it is with excitement not anguish.

'My youngest daughter was christened at Exeter Cathedral.' She can hardly contain herself. 'Guess the name Charles gave her.'

'I don't think I could possibly guess,' says her confessor.

'Henriette.' Her eyes fill up. 'He named her Henriette. I have cried so many times today I cannot believe I have any tears left.' She wipes her eye with a handkerchief. 'Tears of joy.'

'Henriette,' repeats Father Philip. 'That is the perfect name for a beautiful daughter.'

'Lady Dalkeith is looking after little Henriette,' says the Queen. 'Charles says the baby is very pretty and reminds him of me.' Henriette smiles. 'I think he is being polite.'

Father Philip shakes his head. 'I don't think so. Look at Mary, Elizabeth and little Anne. It is no surprise to hear that baby Henriette is a beauty.'

The Queen tries to picture her children, scattered across England. Only Mary is safe in Holland. 'I must return to England.'

'You know that is not possible at the present time – your health is fragile and England is too dangerous.'

Henriette shrugs. 'After Charles left Exeter he engaged the parliamentary army and inflicted a great defeat upon our enemies. Who knows what is possible.'

'That is wonderful news,' says Father Philip. 'That changes everything.'

'It more than cancels out the loss of our northern army at Marston Moor; we will start next year's campaign with every chance of victory.' Henriette clenches her hands. 'The key now is to recruit more men and weapons and send them across to England. You see why it is vital that I get to Paris.'

'You never stop,' says Father Philip. 'You must regain your strength before you dive into affairs of state.' Her confessor starts to get up and grips his side.

'What is it, Father?'

'Nothing, your majesty; just a pain in my stomach that I cannot shake off.'

'You should consult a physician.'

'It is nothing, your majesty.'

'I know all about aches and pains,' says Henriette. She puts her hands on the sides of the chair and slowly lifts herself up.

'Let me call for assistance, your majesty.'

Henriette ignores her confessor and stands up unsteadily on her feet. 'No, Father, I don't want to wait until my strength returns, and I don't want any assistance.' The Queen takes a step away from the chair and then a second step, her foot dragging slightly on the wooden floor. Father Philip rushes to her side, but Henriette waves him away. She takes three more steps before collapsing into a chair by the door. She turns and grins at her priest.

'That is the first time I have walked unaided in months.' The Queen stretches her arms out to acknowledge her own achievement. 'Charles and Gaston have revitalised me. I have been in retreat since leaving Oxford, feeling sorry for myself, but not any longer.' She cries out. 'Our enemies better watch out, the popish brat is on the warpath once again.'

Act V, Scene 6 ~ Theatre de Marais

It is a magical moment. Henriette sits completely still, an unusual occurrence in itself, and watches in awe as the spectacle slowly unfolds before her eyes. She knows about rich velvet curtains magically revealing an alternative world; she is familiar with mechanical devices and visual illusions; but never before has she encountered a theatrical stage floating behind a giant picture frame. The elaborate arch sculpted with cherubs painted in gold leaf separates the real people sitting in the boxes or standing in the auditorium from the actors on the stage. Henriette imagines she is peeping through a window upon the imaginary lives of the players.

Gaston leans across and breaks the spell. 'Our grand Theatre de Marais impresses my sister? It is hard to imagine that it started life as a tennis court.'

'It is a stunning playhouse.' Henriette is sitting as guest of honour in one of the two boxes closest to the stage. 'I have never seen anything like it.'

'The building was badly damaged by fire last year,' says Gaston. 'It only re-opened a couple of months ago. You are impressed by the new proscenium arch?'

'If that's what it is called,' says Henriette. 'It frames the stage so beautifully.'

Henriette acknowledges theatregoers curtsying as they pass by on their way to their seats. Members of the audience take a detour in order to catch a sight of the English Queen.

Henriette sighs. 'France is far ahead of us with their theatres.'

'We may boast innovation in our stage sets, but we have a lot of catching up to do when it comes to plays.'

'Why is that?' asks Henriette.

'Cardinal Richelieu was a stickler for tradition,' says Gaston. 'He founded the Academie Français to enforce his rules of theatre.'

'Rules?' Henriette frowns. 'Drama is not a game of tennis or cards.'

Gaston stretches the palms of his hands outwards and shrugs, a mannerism familiar to the Queen's entourage. 'The Academie controls the format of all plays performed in France.'

'What are these rules of the theatre?'

'All plays must compose of five acts.' Gaston pauses to consider the complex list of regulations. 'Comic characters must represent meaner classes, while heroes have to be nobles.' He stops to think of more limitations on the creative dramatist. 'Comic and tragic storylines must not be mixed in a single play – which accounts for the previous ban on tonight's play. Comedies must have a happy ending and tragedies must result in death.'

'This play was banned?' Henriette is intrigued.

'Since the death of Richelieu and our dear brother the King, there has been a mild relaxation.' Gaston smiles. 'Hence we are watching Pierre Corneille's tragi-comedy Le Cid for the first time.'

'Goodness knows what Paris would think of Ben Jonson,' says Henriette.

'I don't believe I have seen any of his plays,' says Gaston.

Henriette reflects on the savage satire in Volpone. 'I don't think Paris is quite ready for Mr Jonson,' says the Queen quietly.

Margaret Lucas returns to the empty seat on the other side of the Queen. She has been talking to a young man at the rear of the royal box. Margaret arranges a blanket around Henriette's legs.

'You must not catch cold in your present condition, your majesty.'

'Who was that man you were talking to? Have we found you a suitor?'

Margaret's cheeks turn a deep red. 'Monsieur Poquelin manages the Illustrious Theatre Company with his brother and sister; he is excited about the revival of tonight's play.'

'You could write a play.'

'I couldn't possibly, your majesty.' Margaret's cheeks are on fire.

'You have written poetry and a novel; why not a play?' Henriette shakes her head. 'The only thing holding you back, Margaret, is yourself. I thought I had taught you that there is no such word as "can't".'

The dimming of the candles in the auditorium and the rise of the curtain spares Miss Lucas a lecture from the Queen. Above the stage hang three circular candelabra. As the play begins, Henriette is transported from her seat, through the archway and into the magical world conjured by the Parisian actors. All her pains, worries and money problems recede as she soaks up the virtual world laid out in front of her. She even forgets about Charles for a few hours. The happy memory of planning and performing royal masques comes rushing back as Henriette absorbs the unfolding narrative. If heaven could be built on earth, she thinks to herself, it would be placed inside a theatre.

Act V, Scene 7 ~ Louvre Palace

They peer down the length of the grand gallery, but it is impossible to see the far end. Harry Jermyn stands open-mouthed as he tries to comprehend the scale of the long chamber. Morning sunlight pours through tall windows on to cut-glass chandeliers, projecting rainbow colours against the inside wall. As far as the eye can see there are paintings hanging in the spaces between each window. There is hardly any furniture, just occasional chairs for those who wish to pause and contemplate a particular art work. A narrow, olive green carpet runs the length of the gallery with polished oak wooden floorboards to either side.

'It is a quarter of a mile long,' says Henriette. 'So if you don't mind I will stop this end and wait for you to return.' The Queen has recovered sufficiently to walk fifty yards or so unaided, but that is of little use in the Grande Galerie of the Louvre Palace in Paris.

'It is immense,' says the Countess of Denbeigh. 'I cannot see the end of the room.'

'Papa always liked doing things on a grand scale,' says Henriette. 'It is the longest room in Europe I believe, linking the Louvre and Tuileries Palaces.'

'Now I know where you acquired your love of architectural projects,' says Harry Jermyn with a smile.

'Not just my love of buildings.' The Queen takes a couple of steps forward and taps the wooden floor with her walking stick. 'Below this gallery are hundreds of smaller rooms which are open to artists and craftsmen. They live and work on the ground floor. The tradition began in my father's reign, and the artisans are still there today. This is not just a royal palace.'

'Art and architecture.' Jermyn nods. 'You really are your father's daughter.'

Henriette sits down. 'Go on, both of you, stroll down the gallery and study the paintings along the way.' She laughs. 'You should be back in about an hour.'

As her companions set off on their travels, Henriette carefully props the ivory handled walking stick against the side of the chair and surveys the nearest painting. The half-length portrait of Lisa Giocondo smiles ruefully at the Queen of England. The painting by Leonardo da Vinci was purchased by King Francis and displayed for many years at Fontainebleau Palace. It is one of Henriette's favourite portraits. The subject was the wife of a rich Florentine silk merchant and was known to her mother's family. Henriette's father moved the painting to the Grand Galerie when he began assembling the large number of pictures required to fill its walls.

Harry Jermyn and the Countess of Denbeigh are a hundred yards away when Henriette begins to talk in a low voice to the painting.

'I never thought when I left the Louvre as a teenager, that I would return one day without my husband and children.' Henriette slowly moves her head from side to side. 'My family is scattered in the wind – Charles is goodness knows where with his army, Prince Charles has his own court and I think is somewhere near Bath or Bristol, James is in Oxford, Henry and Elizabeth are prisoners in London and little Henriette is in Exeter. Mary, like me, escaped England.' Henriette pauses to consider her other three children, two who died at birth and Anne who passed away at the age of three. 'I am not feeling sorry for myself,' says the Queen as she wipes away a tear. 'I am crying for my lost children.' Henriette reflects upon the events of the last seven years. 'I am also angry about how our lives have been destroyed by ridiculous arguments over prayer books, altars and bishops.' She gesticulates with her arms as she always does when frustrated. 'If everyone had stuck to the true faith, there would have been no rebellions, no bloodshed and no civil war.' Henriette pouts at the painting. 'It is King Henry's fault, turning his back on Rome because of Anne Boleyn and inventing a new religion to suit himself.'

Henriette does not notice Father Cyprien entering the Galerie. 'What was King Henri's fault?'

'I was not talking about my father,' says Henriette, 'I was berating King Henry of England – the one with all the wives.'

Father Cyprien looks around. Jermyn and Susan are distant dots in an otherwise empty gallery. 'Whom were you talking to?' The Queen continues to suffer relapses, especially fevers, rashes and abscesses and her new confessor, leader of the Capuchin monks, is worried that Henriette may be delirious again.

'I am not going mad.' The Queen points to the spare seat next to her and Father Cyprien sits down. He has prematurely grey hair, a long thin nose and a warm smile. 'I was talking to Lisa Giocondo.' Henriette nods at the painting opposite.

'Ah, the inscrutable lady.' Father Cyprien tilts his head and studies the portrait. 'It is hard to know what she is thinking.'

'She is thinking how ridiculous I am.' Henriette's bottom lip drops. 'She is wondering how anyone could have made such a mess of their life.'

'Father Philip is correct when he says you are too hard on yourself.'

'How is Robert?'

'Not good, your majesty; the doctors say it is a growth in his body.'

'I must go and see him. Father Philip is my longest serving companion. My brother tried to have him sent home in the early days, but I refused.'

'Yes, I know,' says Father Cyprien with a smile. 'Father Philip is proud of the fact that he is the last surviving Oratorian at your court.'

'I do not care whether my priests are Oratorians or Capuchins, in my opinion a Catholic is a Catholic. Unfortunately you cannot say the same thing about Protestants. There are Anglicans, Presbyterians, puritans.' Henriette sighs. 'It's complicated.'

The Queen's new confessor stares down the corridor and watches Harry and Susan strolling back towards them. He holds a scroll in his hand.

'Your majesty, a letter has arrived from England.'

'Is it from Charles?'

'I don't know; the message is in code,' says Father Cyprien.

'It must be from the King,' says Henriette. As she speaks, Harry Jermyn and the Countess of Denbeigh return from their trek down the Grande Galerie. 'You have some cypher work,' says Henriette, the sparkle returning to her eyes. 'Escort me back to my study.'

Jermyn helps Henriette stand up and they walk slowly arm in arm towards the doors that separate the Galerie from the Louvre Palace and the Queen's apartments. After safely depositing Henriette in her room, Jermyn retires with the coded letter to his own chambers on the floor above. It has been agreed that when letters arrive from England he will de-cypher the complete script before reading it to the Queen. This habit has evolved after several stormy sessions during which Henriette's impatience led to Harry Jermyn announcing that it was impossible to de-code and deliver a message simultaneously.

Susan remains with Father Cyprien. He looks up at the portrait of Lisa Giocondo before speaking.

'Queen Henriette is the most remarkable woman I have ever met. In fact, she is the most remarkable person, man or woman, who I have ever known. Long after Pym and Cromwell are forgotten, I hope the name of Henriette Marie will inspire generations to come.'

The Countess of Denbeigh shrugs her shoulders. 'Will that not depend, Father, on who writes the history?'

Act V, Scene 8 ~ Louvre Palace

Margaret Lucas whiles away the time with Henriette as they await the translation of the King's letter. They talk about the previous night's theatre visit. The Queen is still convinced that the young man who accosted Miss Lucas is a potential suitor.

'After all,' says Henriette with a sparkle in her eyes, 'you say he is a theatre producer and writes plays. You would have so much in common.'

Margaret stares at the floor. 'From what I gathered, Mr Poquelin's troupe is in financial difficulty. He was trying to persuade me to arrange an introduction to your majesty.'

'I am penniless,' says Henriette cheerfully. 'He is wasting his time seeking my patronage. Perhaps he should speak to my brother, or better still my sister-in-law?'

'I suggested that you were busy at present with affairs of state in England.' Margaret blushes and continues to look at the floor.

'Good answer.' Henriette grins and gently nudges Margaret. 'Maybe it was just an excuse to engage you in conversation?'

Poor Margaret is ill at ease with any company, but most especially young men. She struggles to withstand the Queen's teasing.

'Don't worry, Margaret, we will find a husband for you. He will need to be artistic, intelligent and amusing.' Henriette considers the paucity of suitable candidates among her limited court in exile. 'Someone will turn up.'

Act V, Scene 9 ~ Faubourg Saint Jacques

Henriette is helped out of the coach after it halts outside the Carmelite convent in the Faubourg Saint Jacques. The English Queen is a regular visitor to the nuns, often staying for several days in quiet contemplation. On this occasion she is visiting their hospice in the adjoining building. Harry Jermyn and two of the Queen's new French servants assist her up the small flight of steps, along a narrow corridor and into a small private room. Once she is comfortably sitting on a chair she orders everyone out.

The room contains a bed underneath a narrow window, a bedside table and a sideboard upon which there is a large bowl, a jug of water and a towel. The pale blue shutters are closed and the room is pleasantly cool. The only light comes from a thick candle beside the bed. There is a painting above the bed depicting the crucifixion.

The body in the bed lets out a cry of pain and Henriette leans across, laying her hand on the patient's shoulder.

'I am here, Father.'

The man turns over to face his visitor. 'Your majesty, help me to stand up in the presence of my Queen.'

'Nonsense, you wouldn't let me stand up when I was ill; now it is your turn to follow doctor's orders.'

Father Philip sinks back on the bed.

'Are you in great pain?'

'Not now,' says Father Philip. 'You make the suffering disappear.'

Henriette smiles. 'I have some excellent news that may help. The glad tidings arrived in the King's latest letter. The Earl of Montrose has defeated the Scottish rebels at Inverlochy and the enemy has been forced to recall troops from England.'

'That is exactly what we hoped would happen in Scotland; that is indeed welcome news.'

Henriette stands up with the help of her walking stick and brandishes it like a sword. 'Montrose and his wild highlanders have opened a second front behind the enemy; my dear husband will be greatly heartened by this development.' The Queen shuffles over to the sideboard and soaks a flannel in water, before carefully hobbling back to the bedside chair.

'You must not exert yourself on my behalf,' says Father Philip.

'Why not? The nuns taught me from the age of three that humility is a virtue that should be practised through life.'

'But you are a Queen and I am just a humble priest.'

'Did no one tell you,' says Henriette earnestly, 'I am the Popish brat who causes civil wars and converts innocent Protestants with a single glance.'

Father Philip smiles. As Henriette limps towards the chair, she stumbles, putting her stick to the ground to stop herself falling. The damp cloth falls on the tiled floor as she lands on the edge of the chair. She is giggling too much to pick up the cloth.

'Be careful, your majesty. Don't concern yourself with me; I am dying, but you need to regain your strength to carry on the fight.'

'Who says you are dying?' Henriette lets out a cry. 'Don't believe everything you read in the news sheets.'

Father Philip pulls his nightshirt up and reveals a huge cancerous growth on the side of his distended belly.

'Not a pretty sight at the best of times,' he says with a smile, 'but there is nothing anyone can do.'

Henriette for once is lost for comforting or witty words. She pulls the bedding up over her patient and gently pats the blanket.

'We shall pray. It used to do me the power of good.'

'You will regain your strength,' says Father Philip.

'I hope so. I dream of one day returning to London and staring at their glum puritan faces. I will put on a magnificent theatrical display, complete with the latest procession arch. It will give them all heart attacks.'

Harry Jermyn has crept into the room as the Queen is talking. 'Proscenium arch, your majesty.'

Henriette turns and scowls at her chamberlain. 'Let's call it a picture frame,' she says forcefully. The Queen gently holds her confessor's hand. 'I cannot believe you have guided me for twenty years.' She shakes her head. 'I wonder how many Masses and prayer sessions we have shared?'

'Too many to count, your majesty.' Father Philip is drowsy.

'You have been my shining light through good times and bad.' Henriette leans closer to her confessor. 'I owe you my sanity.' The Queen pauses. 'Assuming I have not gone mad without noticing.'

Father Philip's eyes are closed, but he smiles. He manages to gently squeeze the Queen's delicate hand.

Henriette speaks softly. 'Let us pray, Father, one more time.'

Act V, Scene 10 ~ Saint Germain en Laye

The old wing of the Louvre Palace occupied by Henriette and her party is dark and old-fashioned; a stark contrast to the light and modern long gallery that her father built. The Queen is grateful to her French hosts for providing shelter and a monthly allowance, but Henriette yearns for the country residences that she enjoyed in England – Hampton Court, Oatlands and most especially Greenwich.

Six-year-old King Louis XIV and his mother Anne, Queen Regent, live across the way in the Palais Royale. Anne is fiercely protective of her son's divine right to be king and tolerates no opposition. When it comes to her destitute sister-in-law, she shows nothing but kindness and respect. It is a cold March morning and Anne collects Henriette from the Louvre Palace for a welcome carriage drive into the countryside surrounding Paris.

'You have been very generous to me,' says Henriette, 'but you will not be offended if I say that I long to return to England.'

'I understand.' Anne pulls the blanket closer to her shoulders. 'But your kingdom is still in a precarious position.'

'I have in England what I do not have here. Without Charles, I cannot be happy; indeed I think I shall never recover my health until I see him again.'

'I cannot solve the problem of your separation,' says Anne, 'but perhaps I can make your stay with us a little more agreeable.'

'You have done more than I could dare ask. Please do not think me ungrateful; but without Charles I am incomplete. We used to say we were one, and it is true.'

Anne smiles. 'You are lucky to share such a strong love. My marriage to your brother was,' she pauses to pick her words, 'less passionate.'

The carriage wheels clatter over the cobbles. Henriette peers out of the coach and glimpses the city walls as they leave Paris behind. The noise of the road is muffled once the coach reaches dirt tracks. The occupants begin to shake about as they bump over ridges and dip into potholes.

'Where are we going?'

'It's a surprise,' says Anne.

Henriette laughs. 'Charles used to say that when he was about to show me a new house.'

'Did he?' Anne shakes her head. 'I am afraid I cannot show you a new house today.'

'Don't worry,' says Henriette. 'The Louvre is fine for our needs.' She is too polite to point out that the medieval palace is dank and depressing.

Anne is surprised that Henriette does not recognise the route. The English Queen must have taken this trip a hundred times, but of course children rarely take notice of their surroundings.

'I have received excellent news from England; my husband reports that our Scottish army has won a great victory over the rebels.'

'Perhaps the tide is turning,' says Anne politely. The reports from her chief minister, Cardinal Mazarin, paint a very different picture.

Henriette sits back in the carriage. 'I know I shall return to England.'

The coach turns a sharp corner and comes to a halt outside enormous iron railings. Guards open the gates and the royal party proceeds slowly up a grand drive. Henriette stares out of the window and realises where she is.

'Oh my God, we are at Saint Germain en Laye.'

'Your childhood home.' Anne smiles. 'And there is someone waiting to welcome you.'

Henriette is the teenager again who left the palace twenty years ago. It is as if the intervening years have dropped away. There is a sparkle in her eyes once more.

'Who is here to greet us?'

Anne does not reply immediately. She waits for the coach to travel up the long tree-lined drive and halt in front of the main entrance.

'She has been one of my maids of honour all the years since you left Paris.'

Henriette stares at the grand stone staircase that she remembers so well. Standing motionless on the top step is a woman who the Queen thinks she recognises. It has been too many years for Henriette to be sure. She hesitates.

Anne nods towards the figure. 'Do you remember now?'

Henriette clasps her hands. 'Madame de Motteville.'

'I want you to have Saint Germain back,' says Anne. 'It will be your country residence until you can return to England.'

The Queen's eyes fill with tears. 'I do not deserve such kindness.'

'I think it is the least you are owed after the terrible hardships you have suffered. Your strength is an inspiration to us all, my dear.'

Madame de Motteville starts walking slowly and carefully down the wide steps, one hand gripping her long dress and one hand resting on the stone balustrade. She pauses on the bottom step.

Henriette leans out of the carriage window. 'Françoise, I cannot believe we are reunited here at Saint Germain.'

'I receive your letters. First you are in London, then Holland, next thing you are writing from York and Oxford.' She smiles. 'I cannot keep up.'

Henriette grins. 'I have quite a story to tell.'

Two servants help Henriette out of the carriage and Madame de Motteville and the French Queen Consort take an arm each, steering Henriette slowly up the palace steps. Childhood memories come rushing back. Moments later, coach wheels crunching on the gravel remind Henriette of how she waved from the steps as her sisters were taken away from the troupeau. She turns to see a carriage draw up.

Madame de Motteville frowns. 'Yet more visitors?'

Henriette lets out a cry as her soldier poet William Davenant steps down from the coach.

'Have you come from England? Do you bring news of more victories?'

Davenant halts on the bottom step. 'Your majesty, I am here to report a mighty encounter with our enemies.' He bows to the three ladies and climbs the staircase until he is on the step below the Queen. 'The King's army met Essex's main force on the field of Naseby. I was there to witness the battle.' Davenant reflects upon the engagement. 'It was a most bloody affair, your majesty. Bodies lay slain across four miles of countryside, and they were piled most thick upon the hill where the King stood.'

'Charles,' cries Henriette. 'What news of the King?'

'He is alive,' says Davenant, 'but no one knows where. Most of our southern army was killed or captured along with artillery and baggage. I lost my horse but managed to escape along the hedgerows towards Leicester. Twice I lay as if dead, covered in blood, as the enemy passed me by.'

Henriette turns to her sister-in-law. 'This is the end. My place is by my dear heart's side. I must return to England.'

'That's impossible,' says Davenant. 'The parliamentary army is roving across England pursuing our few remaining loyal followers and laying siege to a handful of outposts in Royalist hands. Nowhere is safe. Many of our commanders are talking openly of ending the fight – there is a universal weariness of the war.'

Henriette grips Madame de Motteville's arm tightly. 'I should never have left Charles.' She pauses to consider the full extent of the disaster. 'Where is my son? What has happened to the Prince of Wales?'

'He is in hiding in the West Country,' says Davenant. 'His supporters are trying to smuggle him out of the country.'

'The King is alone.' Davenant catches Henriette as Queen Anne and Madame de Motteville struggle to support her. 'I should never have abandoned the cause.' Despite Davenant's best efforts, she slumps on the top step. 'Let me return to England so I can die by his side.' Henriette can barely be heard amid the sobbing: 'We are one, dear heart; no one will ever separate us.'

The epilogue

The bedroom at Colombes Chateau is adorned with beautiful grey silk wall hangings. There is no bed, just a dining table covered by a luxurious pale grey Persian rug. Beside the table stands a solitary chair. The stone lintel high above the fireplace is held up by two carved figures. Either side are paintings of Prince Henry and Princess Mary. Madame de Motteville turns towards the door where a full sized portrait of Prince James in armour stares at her – the artist has captured that penetrating glare.

Through the doorway, Madame watches Harry Jermyn tidying some papers in Henriette's privy chamber. He stands beside the four-poster bed, relocated from the bedroom. Madame tiptoes from a gentle sea of grey and silver to a more strident chamber decorated in crimson and gold. Every piece of furniture has been hand picked by the Queen for its unusual design; each in its own way an avant-garde development during her lifetime: tortoiseshell inlaid wood, Chinese lacquer and intricate paintwork made to resemble marble. Paintings smother the walls – some are famous artists such as Correggio and Titian, others are family portraits of Prince Charles and the Queen's youngest daughter, Henriette.

Jermyn studies the congested walls. 'There are no pictures of the King.'

Madame de Motteville walks across the room, glancing at the amber statuette of the Lady Madonna. She does not answer Jermyn as she wanders through to the small adjoining cabinet, the inner sanctum of Henriette's life. Jermyn joins her, leaning against the doorway and surveying the small tables and shelves crammed with porcelain vases and bowls, far eastern figurines, rare crystals and delicate silver work. Two lacquered cabinets with doors ajar display row upon row of tiny drawers. Jermyn knows each is filled with a precious memory. There is little of monetary value; jewels and gold have long since been pawned or melted down. The walls are again plastered with paintings of different styles and sizes, mostly religious subjects this time with a few family portraits squeezed in between. In this tiny room there must be fifty paintings, one can barely glimpse the cream-coloured wall hangings.

'No pictures of the King again,' says Jermyn.

Madame de Motteville checks the time on the Queen's watch, which hangs from a gold hook in the wall above the desk. She sighs and sits down on the chair, the only seat in the room. She picks up a beautifully bound book.

'The Imitation of Christ,' she says softly. She smiles as she opens the tome at a bookmarked page. 'A chapter a day keeps the doctor away.'

Harry Jermyn walks slowly across to the desk and looks over Madame's shoulder. Françoise has picked up a small, intricately carved Indian box. Jermyn stares at the contents as Madame gently lifts the lid and sorts though several special treasures. She holds up a small locket and opens the clasp.

Harry smiles. 'Ah, I see now.'

Madame returns the silver locket and closes the lid, carefully placing the box on the desk beside a pile of loose sheets of paper.

'This is our manuscript,' says Madame de Motteville. 'The memoirs she has dictated to me these last few years. The re-telling of the tale was about as traumatic as the life she endured.' Madame laughs. 'She described her experiences as a theatrical extravaganza; sometimes she was reluctant to talk about the past, the next day she would be in a desperate hurry to recall her extraordinary life.'

'Patience was never one of her virtues.'

Madame de Motteville picks up the top sheet and peruses her own spidery writing.

'I am required to finish the story.'

Harry Jermyn nods. 'And finish it you shall.'

She-Majesty Generalissima

The story is finished
in

Henriette

ONCE AND FUTURE QUEEN